Praise for *Did Yo...*

'Enjoyable, endearing and k... ...
we'd all like to have as a friend'
Katie Fforde, *A Wedding in Provence*

'A laugh-out-loud book . . . the perfect summer escape'
Lindsey Kelk, *On a Night Like This*

'Hilariously relatable. *Did You Miss Me?* feels like a nostalgic treat'
Sophie Cousens, *This Time Next Year*

'An entertaining page-turner with a brilliantly relatable
heroine. I couldn't stop smiling as I raced through it'
Holly Miller, *The Sight of You*

'I laughed out loud throughout this – no mean
feat! This is a sure-fire summer hit!'
Laura Jane Williams, *The Lucky Escape*

'Full-on funny from the first page, filled with Sophia's trademark
wit and warmth. A great tonic to the year we've all had'
Zoë Folbigg, *The Note*

'Sophia Money-Coutts' writing is sharp and clever,
and *Did You Miss Me?* is no exception. Super
funny, super witty and so warm. I loved it'
Lia Louis, *Eight Perfect Hours*

'A joyful, big-hearted balm of a book from one of my favourite
writers. A funny, life- and love-affirming special book'
Cressida McLaughlin, *The Staycation*

Sophia Money-Coutts is a journalist and author who spent five years studying the British aristocracy while working as Features Director at *Tatler*. Prior to that she worked as a writer and an editor for the *Evening Standard* and the *Daily Mail* in London, and *The National* in Abu Dhabi. She's a columnist for the *Sunday Telegraph* called 'Modern Manners' and often appears on radio and television channels talking about important topics such as Prince Harry's wedding and the etiquette of the threesome. *Did You Miss Me?* is her fourth novel.

Also by
Sophia Money-Coutts

The Plus One
What Happens Now?
The Wish List

Did You Miss Me?

SOPHIA MONEY-COUTTS

ONE PLACE. MANY STORIES

HQ
An imprint of HarperCollins*Publishers* Ltd
1 London Bridge Street
London SE1 9GF

www.harpercollins.co.uk

HarperCollins*Publishers*
1st Floor, Watermarque Building, Ringsend Road
Dublin 4, Ireland

This edition 2022

1

First published in Great Britain by
HQ, an imprint of HarperCollins*Publishers* Ltd 2021

ISBN: 978-0-00-837062-6

MIX
Paper from
responsible sources
FSC™ C007454

This book is produced from independently certified FSC™ paper
to ensure responsible forest management.

For more information visit: www.harpercollins.co.uk/green

This book is set in 11.5/16 pt. Bembo by Type-it AS, Norway

Printed and Bound in the UK using 100% Renewable Electricity at
CPI Group (UK) Ltd, Croydon, CR0 4YY

I don't mean to sound like ABBA, but this is
for anyone who's taken a chance on love

Chapter 1

AT PRECISELY 6.10 A.M., as usual, my alarm went off.

Phone! Where was the phone? My hand groped the bedside table as Gus reached for me under the duvet, mumbling something.

'Huh?'

'TGI Friday,' he clarified as his fingers ran up my stomach.

I fell back on my pillow, alarm silenced, knowing what came next. Sex came next because that's what Gus and I did before work on Friday mornings. Quick, efficient sex where we avoided one another's sour breath by panting into the other's shoulder.

On Saturday mornings we went to the dry cleaners and collected croissants from the French bakery.

On Sunday mornings we bought a *Sunday Times* from the newsagent, ate eggs on sourdough (Gus) and eggs and avocado (me) in the posh coffee shop opposite the French bakery before returning to the dry cleaners to pick up the clothes we'd dropped off the day before.

But on Friday mornings, it was always sex.

'Tees us up nicely for the weekend, Nell,' Gus observed once, rolling off me with a little sigh of contentment, as if our love life was a Spotify playlist.

And right on time this morning, his fingers progressed up my ribcage.

'Good morning, Mr Nipple,' he said, rolling my left nipple between his thumb and his forefinger like a child with a marble.

After half a minute, he moved his hand to my right breast. 'And Mrs Nipple,' he added, before spending another thirty seconds there.

I supposed it was precision timing like this that made Gus such a good cook.

Satisfied that he'd paid due attention to both nipples, he dropped his hand to between my legs and burrowed around there with the same energy I'd seen him deploy on his sock drawer: concentrated and determined.

'It's all right,' I whispered after another minute of frowning at the ceiling, wondering what shirt to roll into my rucksack for the office. I reached for his hand to pull it up again. The white one from Sandro.

It wasn't that I disliked sex with Gus. I enjoyed sex with Gus, especially at the beginning. He'd been the one who'd helped me discover why poets banged on about sex. But, eleven years into a relationship, there was the sort of sex that poets banged on about, and there was sort of sex you had on a Friday morning before work.

This was going to be very much the latter.

'Oh. You sure?'

I nodded.

Unperturbed, Gus heaved himself on top of me and, through

the gloom of our bedroom, waggled his eyebrows. 'Morning, my little *knuddelbär*.'

Knuddelbär was German for 'cuddle bear'. I'd had words with Gus about his peculiar terms of endearment before but he never paid any notice. He liked using them to remind me that he'd read German at Cambridge.

I smiled sleepily back and then he pushed into me with a groan, before dropping his head to my collarbone and muttering: 'Forgot to tell you, the plumber's coming later.'

'What tiiiiime?' I wheezed like an accordion, my voice husky not due to the eroticism of this situation, but because the weight of his torso was compressing my lungs.

A damp square directly under the shower tray had appeared on the kitchen ceiling a few weeks ago and Gus insisted he'd sort it out.

'It's the shower tray, it's definitely leaking,' he'd announced proudly, after half an hour in the bathroom accompanied by a backdrop of crashes as the shower gel and shampoo bottles cascaded to the floor. Gus was the most cultured man I'd ever met: he had strong feelings about Italian films and French wine, and spent his weekdays in a corporate office thrashing out complicated regulatory agreements for tech giants. But he wasn't much of a handyman. Some years earlier, while trying to build an IKEA bookcase that we'd bought to shelve his growing collection of historical biographies, he'd confused a spanner with a hammer.

'He said around seven,' he panted on top of me, between thrusts.

'I might be late, got a new client meeting todayyyyyyy,' I wheezed again, as the air was squeezed out of my chest.

'No… problem… I… can… be… here.'

'Thank you,' I rasped, tracing my nails up and down his back.

His thrusts sped up and he groaned into the pillow under my head. 'Did… you… book… that… restaurant… for… lunch… tomorrow?'

'That place in Chiswick? Mmmhm… ouch, Gus!'

He'd moved his hand to the wall behind us and caught a clump of my hair in his fingers. 'Sorry! You're… an… angel.'

Lunch tomorrow was with Hector and Harriet, two of Gus's Cambridge friends, who'd just had a baby called Homer. When Gus emailed me with the news, I'd sent him a GIF of Homer Simpson but he'd replied solemnly explaining that the name was in homage to the ancient Greek poet. Obviously I knew that; Hector and Harriet would never have even seen an episode of *The Simpsons*. They were the sort of couple who boasted smugly about not owning a TV, as if they sat reading *The Iliad* every night.

'Nearly… there,' Gus panted over my shoulder.

I dropped my fingers to his bottom and pulled him deeper into me. That would help.

'Ooooh,' he puffed, speeding up again, his bottom like a pogo stick, in and out, in and out. 'Nearly there… there, nearly… there, nearly… there.'

I knew what would work: I bent my fingers so my nails dug into his buttocks.

'And I'm THERRRRRRRRRRE,' roared Gus, breathing hotly into my neck. He froze and then collapsed, with his face in the pillow.

I turned my head to glance at the clock. 6.19 a.m. Perfect. I'd be in the office by seven.

***

I always ran into work carrying a rucksack of neatly rolled clothes. From our flat in Clapham, I wound up to Vauxhall roundabout, then along the south side of the river and over Waterloo Bridge.

Here was my favourite view of the city: to my right, the sun rising brightly (on a good day) over St Paul's Cathedral; to my left, the Houses of Parliament. Then it was straight up Kingsway, the wide, four-lane street that buses thundered up and down which obscured a quieter square tucked behind it. My office overlooked this square, a worn patch of green where pigeons pecked at crumbs left underneath benches. It was a distance of five miles exactly, took forty minutes and I ran it every day – summer and winter.

I'd discovered running when I'd started work as a trainee lawyer at Spinks. The hours were crazy and I needed fresh air during the day without being away from my desk for too long. But I didn't have time for the gym, so jogging into work became my solution, almost a form of meditation.

I was embarrassed at first, plodding flat-footed along the pavements, my bag swinging heavily on my back. But then I got better, faster, I bought proper kit and belted my new rucksack around my stomach. I became one of those people who wove through commuters and tourists, on and off the pavement, willing the lights to change up ahead so I didn't have to stop. I joked to colleagues that I was like a dog that needed to be walked first thing. What I didn't disclose was that running meant I arrived at Lincoln's Inn Fields with endorphins surging around my body and I could handle sitting next to Gideon all day.

Gideon Fotheringham was my boss, a sixty-year-old partner at Spinks with a face as ruddy as raw steak from long lunches, and blond hair that was never brushed. He was a pig in a wig who earned just over £2.1m last year. Whenever a new client came in to see us, Gideon joked that he was 'exceptionally good' at divorce because he himself had done it twice. He'd recently remarried a third time, to a woman my age called Ophelia who had a single-digit IQ and spent most of her time deliberating over curtain patterns for their house in the Cotswolds.

Gideon also owned a flat in South Kensington which he supposedly used during the week, although he didn't always sleep there. More than once, when a graduate trainee, I had to race to Tyrwhitt's in the morning to fetch a fresh shirt since he hadn't been home the previous night. I always warned new female trainees not to get in the lift or find themselves alone in the boardroom with him.

But then Spinks and Co was full of Gideons. It was London's oldest, most traditional law firm, situated in a Grade II-listed Georgian townhouse protected by shiny black railings outside, and with thick carpets, mahogany doors and fridges full of small Perrier bottles inside. All the partners were white sixty-something men who'd been to Eton and Oxford; from midday on Fridays, champagne was served to them in the boardroom. Although being old and traditional didn't necessarily make it inefficient in its methods. These men were piranhas in pin-striped suits, going after the biggest corporate and commercial cases they could – and winning most of them.

At law school, places on Spinks' trainee scheme were fought after, the biggest prize for ambitious students. I'd only applied because Gus said I should, and he was proved right when I won a place, much to my astonishment, having assumed they'd mostly go to the posh boys on my course who wore Barbours to their lectures. I was an unworldly student who'd grown up in a cold, damp Northumberland village and never even been to London until I started law school. Landing a contract at Spinks seemed a miracle.

After rotating through different departments as a trainee, I'd chosen to qualify into the family law department, knowing that I wanted to work with actual human beings and the cases that affected their lives rather than on boring tax schemes and corporate fraud claims which took years of court time to unravel. This meant I mostly dealt with rich people's divorces – footballers splitting from pop stars and minor British royals separating from their cousins, that sort of thing.

As I ran along the river, I thought about today's priority: a meeting with a new client. Linzi Lemon was a former model (known as 'Luscious Linzi' when she'd started out on Page 3) who'd recently decided to separate from her celebrity chef husband. Larry had a string of Italian restaurants in shopping centres across the country and appeared on a cooking show every Saturday morning.

Unfortunately, Linzi had recently discovered Larry and a guest from his TV show doing something unmentionable with a courgette in his dressing room, and decided to start divorce proceedings.

The Lemons had been married for ten years and had two children – Lewis, nine, and Liberty, seven. From what I'd already gathered, they owned at least three houses – in Battersea, in Poole and St Ives. I'd also watched a few YouTube clips of Larry's show and wondered how he managed to seduce any woman, let alone with a courgette, given his carrot-coloured skin and the belly as round as a basketball that hung over his apron.

But after several years of family law, it took more than a vegetable sex toy to surprise me.

It's like they say, criminal lawyers see bad people at their best; divorce lawyers see good people at their worst. Although not all our clients were *that* good. One claimed she wanted a divorce because her husband would no longer let their dog sleep on the bed; another that his wife had gone to Korea for a facelift without telling him. A French lady came to us in tears a few months back saying she'd discovered pictures on her husband's phone that revealed he visited a prostitute in Chelsea who indulged his fetish for dressing up like a baby, wearing a nappy and sucking on a giant dummy.

I'd worked at Spinks for nearly a decade, listened to hundreds of clients discuss the reasons for the collapse of their marriage and, as a result, become fairly unshockable.

I enjoyed it, too. I liked helping people out of romantic tangles, helping them find freedom again, to realize an oath they'd made in front of a priest didn't necessarily mean they couldn't change their minds later on. Two years ago, Spinks had promoted me to senior associate which, in turn, had sparked my ambition to become the firm's first female partner by the time I turned thirty-four in August. I was at my desk by seven fifteen every morning and usually got home around eight, but often later. I answered my phone on the weekend and kept it on at night in case a client needed me. When I was away from the office I checked my email approximately every three seconds. When I was in the office, I barely moved from my desk.

It was quiet when I arrived today, the only noise my trainers squeaking across the marble floor of the reception. I took the stairs two at a time up to the third floor, where Gideon and I shared an office.

I say share; Gideon took up most of the space. He wasn't in yet. He never arrived until at least ten. When he did, he'd collapse at his antique desk, which was the size of a dining table and decorated with pictures of his five children and the third Mrs Fotheringham, before spending the day barking orders at me. Behind his desk, hanging on the wall, were sporting photos of Gideon from his school days. It was the same for all the partners at Spinks. While working there, I'd learned that public-school men, no matter what age, needed to have their team photos on public display at all times to prop up their egos.

My own, more modest desk was hidden behind the door, but at least it faced a wide window overlooking the square beneath us, which I often flung open in protest at the noises and smells that wafted from Gideon's desk to mine.

I showered and changed in the bathrooms down the corridor. It was always a suit in this office. Years ago, I'd braved a floral dress but Gideon had asked if I was 'off to a tea party' with a disapproving look, so it was back to muted colours after that. I didn't mind so much. Having inherited my mother's pale colouring, anything too bright washed me out. I'd learned it was easier to blend in with the grey suits at Spinks if you wore one yourself, especially as a woman.

I scraped my curls into a low ponytail, rubbed a layer of tinted moisturizer over my freckles, added a lick of mascara, then folded my damp running clothes into my rucksack and returned to my desk. While tapping at my mouse to kickstart my computer, I reached for my phone to ring downstairs for a cafetière of very strong coffee.

That was another perk of working here – in the basement was a kitchen which produced breakfast, lunch or supper on demand from a new menu that was emailed to all staff every Monday morning. It was presided over by a sixty-something Filipina called Queenie and her niece, Carmelita, who were the most adored people in the office.

Then I sat at my computer, going over the file I'd started compiling on Linzi. Much of my time was spent concentrating on intricate divorce contracts as thick as hardback books, or combing through our clients' multiple bank statements and tax returns. But since our clients were usually high-profile, I also spent a good deal of my day scrolling through the *Daily Mail* website, trying to gather as much information as possible about who we were defending – or who we were up against.

'Good morning, Eleanor,' boomed Gideon, when he swept into the office a few hours later.

'Morning,' I muttered from behind my screen.

'Isn't it a marvellous day? The sun's shining, the sky is blue, the birds are doing whatever the birds do.'

I looked up as he dropped his overcoat on the stand. 'You're in a good mood.'

Gideon flashed his incisors. 'Of course I am. A new client, fresh blood, fresh meat.' He rubbed his hands together and dropped into his seat. 'Could you ring Queenie and get her to send up my usual?'

This meant a cappuccino and a full English which he would eat noisily at his desk while I tried to concentrate. It was like watching a seal use a knife and fork, and he normally dripped egg yolk down his tie, which meant a trainee was dispatched to go and buy a new one.

At such moments, I told myself that when I became a part-ner, I'd move offices and work beside someone else. No longer would I have to listen to the crunching of Gideon's jaw, or see him cup his crotch and rearrange himself every time he stood up. I wasn't sure that he washed his hands after visiting the loo either, so I tried to avoid picking up his phone or using any of his pens.

Please please *please* could I make partner, I prayed, as I called down to the kitchen using my own phone. They were announced at the start of September, which meant that since today was the fifteenth of March, I had just over five months to go. Five and a half months of sitting next to this blond amoeba. I could do that. I'd been doing it for two years, ever since my last promotion. What was another five months?

Carmelita arrived with his breakfast tray twenty minutes later and Gideon grunted his thanks.

'I'll do the talking in this meeting,' he said once she'd left.

'Sure,' I said, without looking away from my computer. This

was the routine with new clients: Gideon welcomed them to Spinks and, as if a dentist probing a sore tooth, asked gently about the circumstances surrounding their separation. My job was to sit quietly and write notes.

For all his (many) faults, Gideon was efficient in these first meetings. He had an authoritative air and conversational patter which meant clients instantly trusted him, and he knew that if he got them to divulge personal information to us, they'd be more likely to instruct Spinks rather than go through the pain and hassle of running through the same details with another firm afterwards.

'The delicate touch today, I fancy,' he continued, as he sawed through a rasher of bacon. 'Get Rosemary to send her up here.'

I frowned. This made me nervous. First meetings were more usually held with new clients in the boardroom in an effort to impress them with the old-school gravitas of Spinks and Co. Its walls were covered in priceless Chinese wallpaper which the townhouse's first owner, Earl Macartney, who led England's first ambassadorial visit to China, carried back with him in 1782. A vast antique table stretched down the middle of the room, oil portraits of past partners gazed down on it, the carpet was as spongy as cotton wool and the whole room was so soundproofed that Gideon liked to joke the prime minister could have held meetings in there.

'And who's to say he hasn't visited us before?' he'd tell a new client, winking.

But occasionally we met clients in our office on the third floor instead, especially more high-profile ones. Or the weepy ones. Women often cried in our meetings and I wished they wouldn't. It wasn't a lack of sympathy; I felt huge sympathy towards anyone who came into our office crying about their marriage, especially women if they'd been badly hurt. We'd all been there. Well, most of us, although my own dose of heartbreak hadn't involved any courgettes. It was years ago, when I'd sobbed for so many days that my entire face swelled red and Mum tried to make me go to the doctor, insisting that I'd developed a new allergy. My swelling was nothing to do with an allergy; I just felt like a lumberjack had taken a swing at my chest. But it was a useful pain in the end, because it spurred me on, encouraging me to help other people going through it, particularly women. It was the spark that drove me towards family law.

So no, the tears of the female clients didn't alarm me because I understood those. It was more Gideon's behaviour towards them. He took advantage of their vulnerability. At the slightest sign of a wobbly lip or a watery eye, he'd shift closer on the sofa and pull an initialled handkerchief from his breast pocket like a magician.

'Here, please, take this,' he'd insist.

Having made this chivalrous move, he'd gone on to sleep with the odd one. 'Part of the service,' he'd boasted once, after the wife of a Goldman Sachs banker forgot to remove me from a cc'd email to us both, and announced that she could 'still taste' Gideon. I had to go for a long walk outside that afternoon.

'In here, really?' I queried across the office.

'Yes, why not?' A small fleck of food – could have been bacon, could have been egg or a tomato pip – flew from Gideon's mouth and landed on the carpet in front of my desk.

'No, no reason. Fine. I'll call down and tell Rosemary now.'

Rosemary was the receptionist who'd worked at Spinks for over forty years, treated the male partners like naughty schoolboys, and was the size of a battleship. Nobody, not even Gideon, messed with Rosemary.

At eleven, Linzi arrived and was shown into our office by a trainee. She had thick blonde highlights, eyelashes as big as butterfly wings and a chin that was already wobbling.

'Mrs Lemon, wonderful to meet you,' said Gideon, leaping up from behind his desk. 'I'm Gideon Fotheringham, senior partner in the family department here at Spinks, and this is my associate, Eleanor Mason. Why don't you come in and have a se—'

He was interrupted by a noise like a whale in childbirth as Linzi burst into tears.

'Oh dear, oh dear, I'm so sorry, Mrs Lemon,' said Gideon, rushing over and circling an arm around her. He guided Linzi towards the cream sofa in front of his desk and flicked at the trainee with his other hand as if she was a mosquito.

As Linzi lowered herself on one end of the sofa, audibly sobbing, he widened his eyes at me and inclined his head towards our door.

'Here, please, take this,' he added, retrieving his handkerchief from his suit and holding it out to her. 'I assure you it's perfectly clean, ha ha!'

Linzi took the handkerchief and smiled at him through watery eyes; Gideon beamed back before sitting on the other end of the sofa; I closed the door.

'I'm so sorry,' she said, before blowing the contents of her nose into Gideon's hankie.

'Not at all, not at all,' he replied smoothly. 'It's a distressing situation.' Then he glared at me and made a scribbling gesture.

I fought the urge to throw my stapler at his head. I knew my allotted role in these meetings, to scribble down what was said so we could start getting a picture of the case, and yet Gideon still bossed me around as if I was a graduate. I sighed while reaching for my notepad from my desk, then sat in the small armchair opposite them.

'Can we get you a coffee, Mrs Lemon?' Gideon was using his seductive voice, the one he deployed on shaky female clients.

Linzi wrinkled her nose across the sofa. 'Don't have any vodka, do you?'

He clapped his hands to his knees and barked with laughter. 'I'm sure that can be arranged.'

'You're all right. Only kidding. And it's Linzi, please, no Mrs. It reminds me of that creep I married.'

'Right, yes, about that,' Gideon said, shifting slightly in his seat, before his voice went up an octave. 'I think what might be helpful is to run through your situation to clarify a few details.'

Linzi sniffed, looking anxiously from him to me. 'I don't know what you've read?'

Gideon flicked his hand in the air. 'Please don't worry about the rubbish the papers print. We want to hear what you've been through, your story.'

'I thought we'd be together for ever,' replied Linzi, before she glanced at her hands and tugged one corner of the handkerchief between her fingers. 'We were childhood sweethearts, see?'

Gideon nodded.

'I s'pose we were pretty young when we got married, both twenty-three. But we were so happy, or I thought. Then came the kids.'

'Two children, correct?'

'Yes,' she replied, 'Lewis and little Liberty. Poor things, they've got no idea about all this, that their dad's a cheating bastard!'

She let out another wail and Gideon shifted closer on the sofa.

'I'm so deeply sorry, Mrs Lem— Linzi. I do understand how difficult this is.'

'It's all right,' she said, blowing her nose again. 'I just never thought he'd hurt me. You can't imagine that when you're in love with them. You never think they'd do anything to hurt you, do you?' She glanced across at me, seeking female solidarity.

'No,' I murmured, 'you don't.'

'So you've been married for ten years, is that right?' pressed Gideon.

'Ten years, yeah. Ten years and he goes and does that! And it's probably not the first time either. It's just the first time that I've caught the lying toad.'

Again, Gideon's voice reached a higher register. 'Yesssss, if you don't mind, can we briefly discuss that? I believe you discovered him with somebody else at his television studio, is that right?'

'In his dressing room, with some girl from the audience. He was…' Linzi dropped her voice to a whisper, 'he was using a… a… a cucumber.'

I crossed out 'courgette' on my notepad and wrote 'cucumber'.

'Most unsanitary. I'm so sorry, Linzi. A terrible incident to witness. I do hope he wasn't intending to cook with the cucumber afterwards?'

Gideon grinned, expecting a laugh, but Linzi and I stayed silent so he cleared his throat and moved on. 'What we should do now is discuss the timeline you might be facing and the settlement you're after, custody arrangements and so forth, if that's agreeable?'

'I mean, how could he do it?' Linzi continued. 'How could someone I love that much, and who I thought loved me, do something so… so… so cruel! How could he do it?'

'I'm so sorry, I do know how this feels,' I offered, deciding to jump in. 'And it's so unfair, and hurtful, especially after all your support of his career. But that's why we're here, to help you move forward from this as painlessly as possible.'

'Yes, thank you, Nell,' Gideon said swiftly, his eyeballs bulging at me in a silent reprimand before he turned back to Linzi. 'Please be assured, you're in excellent hands. I myself am exceptionally good at divorce because I've been through it twice, ha ha! Now, if we could just concentrate on the settlement for a moment, that would be splendid. The sooner we get started, the sooner we can have you out of this situation. Down to business: am I right in saying you jointly own three properties?'

Linzi nodded and I bent my head back to my notepad. Just over five months, I reminded myself. After that, I'd make partner, be able take on my own clients and no longer have to sit mute while being talked over by a man who had roughly the same attitude towards women, and indeed wives, as Henry VIII.

★★★

I didn't get home until nearly eight o'clock that night, having spent most of my afternoon writing up our meeting with Linzi and drafting a letter of instruction for her, while Gideon asked when the letter would be ready every three and a half minutes until I dropped it on his desk for approval. Until she'd signed the letter, we weren't officially representing her.

Finally, letter sent, I'd crammed myself on the Northern line and slunk south, back to our flat in Clapham.

Gus made a face when I called it a flat and insisted that it was a 'maisonette' because we had two floors. Whatever. I'd never heard anyone say, 'Come over to the maisonette for dinner.'

I hadn't loved the idea of living opposite Clapham Common, queuing in Sainsbury's behind Australian twenty-somethings and men whose permanent uniform was rugby shirts. I'd fancied somewhere closer to the river but he'd won that battle ('it's on the Northern line, Nell, great for the City').

And yet even though it was in Clapham, and even five years after buying it, every time I put my key in the door I felt a little spike of pleasure that it was ours. It took up the top two floors of a terraced house: on the first floor was the open-plan kitchen and sitting room, above it was our bedroom, bathroom, and what we referred to as the 'spare room' but was the size of a shoe cupboard. It could, just, fit a single bed but there wasn't room for anything else apart from a wastepaper basket. Gus was always talking about turning this room into his study but it was one of those things – along with mole check-ups and visits to the dental hygienist – that we never got round to.

I found him in his favourite position: crouched in front of the wine rack.

'Hi, my love,' I said, dropping my rucksack on the floor, comforted by the safe, familiar scene after such a day.

Gus swivelled his head and smiled. '*Mein engel* is home! Now, important question, do you feel more like a French Pinot Noir or a very nice Chianti?'

'Neither,' I replied, collapsing on the sofa. 'I feel like a human beanbag who's been sat on all afternoon by a mad dictator.'

'Ah, something stronger, in that case.' Gus stood and came over to the sofa. 'I'm sorry,' he said, leaning to press his lips to my forehead.

'Thank you,' I murmured from my horizontal position, smiling up at him. My kind, supportive boyfriend. I couldn't imagine Gus ever cheating on me. He was too honourable. He not only had strong opinions about recycling bins, but also cyclists who jumped red lights and people who drove in bus lanes even when it was technically allowed. I'd never even heard him swear.

'Plumber's been,' he added, returning to his wine collection. 'Charged £236 to squeeze a tube of toothpaste around the shower tray but says that should do the job. Although we can't use it tonight while it dries. We should have gone into plumbing instead of law. How was your new client, by the by?'

'Not official yet. But I think she will be. Poor woman didn't stop crying while Gideon crept closer and closer; I felt so sorry for her.'

'Because of her proximity to him or her divorce?'

'Both.' I reached my arms above my head and yawned.

'Lucky we're never doing it then. Right, let's give this Californian Zinfandel a whirl. That should do the trick.'

'Mmm,' I murmured, hoping Gus wasn't about to embark on one of his lectures about the perils of marriage.

One of the first things Gus ever told me was that he didn't believe in marriage. The concept of romantic marriage, he explained during our second date, was a relatively new invention in the history of humankind. According to him, it was the Victorians who'd encouraged the idea of marrying for love, (instead of more practical or financial reasons like having children or making a strategic alliance), and this had encouraged society's 'obsession' with finding our soulmate.

'You don't believe in soulmates?' I'd asked in the Holborn pub, my enthusiasm for the bespectacled, fellow law student who asked such intelligent questions in our lectures dimming slightly.

Gus shook his head and went on to say he believed in love and finding someone he could 'build a life' with; he just didn't believe in the saccharine, idealised version of love that was promoted on the front of Valentine's Day cards.

A few more dates in, I realized that Gus's strong attitudes towards marriage (and cheating) had been shaped by his father, a dentist from Basingstoke who'd run off with his dental assistant and left his wife to raise her seven-year-old son alone. He would never treat another half in the same way, Gus vowed, but nor would he marry and 'conform to society's expectations of what a relationship should look like'. And since I was only twenty-two then, and previously stung by love, I was quite taken with the idea of not marrying. Gus made it sound noble, an intellectual decision.

★

We shook hands in that pub and promised we'd never do it, in that jokey, unafraid way you can talk about such topics on early dates.

'Let's have three children!'

'Let's move to the country when we're older!'

'Are you a cat or a dog person?'

'Cat.'

'OK, we'll have both!'

'Let's *not* get married!'

It was a pact that had lasted ever since, a pledge made eleven years ago when we were too young to think properly about marriage, but which Gus still took as seriously as one of his legal contracts.

Four or five years ago, in our late twenties, friends had started going on expensive holidays and posting engagement photos from canoes and on ski slopes. 'The diamond rush,' Gus dubbed it, as we duly started spending more and more weekends on hen parties and stags, then in uncomfortable B&Bs for the weddings themselves. When the newlyweds got back from honeymoon, there'd be yet another dinner where everyone would have to coo over their photos.

At engagement drinks and wedding receptions, these friends would waggle their fingers at us; 'You guys next!' But we always swore it wouldn't be. It was a rational choice that set us apart from the herd, Gus explained, a touch pompously sometimes, when challenged. Actually, he'd often tell me privately, didn't it prove that he and I were stronger than many relationships, because we didn't feel the need to publicly declare our devotion to one another in a church, in front of 150 of our closest friends?

Instead, at Gus's suggestion, I'd drawn up a 'cohabitation agreement' at work, which detailed the legal details of what would happen to our flat and all our possessions if one of us popped it, since we weren't married. And that's nearly as romantic as a wedding, right?

I lay with my eyes closed on the sofa and listened to Gus open the cupboard for his special corkscrew. I'd bought the special corkscrew for his birthday a couple of years ago. It aerated the wine, or something like that, and Gus made a great performance of using it: opening the box as if a treasure chest dragged from the seabed, retrieving the corkscrew, opening the bottle, polishing the corkscrew with its little felt duster afterwards. If I was by myself, I usually just grabbed a screw-top from Sainsbury's.

'Here you go.'

I opened my eyes to see him standing over me, holding a glass.

'Thanks, my love,' I said, smiling gratefully up at him while reaching for it. 'How was your day, anyway? Tell me.'

I lifted my legs so Gus could sit on the sofa, and then lowered them back across his thighs. This, the first sip of wine on a Friday, the seeping of the alcohol into my bloodstream and the comfort of being at home with his hand rubbing my shins, was unquestionably the best part of my week.

He worked in corporate law for an American firm, which meant his hours tended to be even longer than mine and the clients even shoutier. But we both agreed that's what we had to do at this stage in our careers; put the hours in now and, with any luck, we'd both make partner.

Almost as soon as we'd met at law school, Gus had come up with this life plan: we'd become lawyers at good firms, be promoted to partners and be able to afford the kind of life he'd dreamt of while growing up in a Basingstoke cul-de-sac, where he'd been bullied for being a nerd who couldn't name a single Premiership footballer but could cite his twelve favourite Roman generals.

Gus stretched his glass towards mine and we clinked. 'All right. New European contracts with Google making everything wildly complicated but we'll get there in the end. I bought a present for Homer, by the way.'

'Did you, what?'

He put his wine down on the coffee table and leapt up, heading towards a paper bag by the door. I recognized this bag. It was from Frisbee Books, a higgledy-piggledy place in Chelsea where the books were stacked from floor to ceiling, run by a bearded man who looked like Father Christmas. It was Gus's favourite bookshop, where we often went on a Saturday morning and he browsed the history section while I looked for thrillers.

When I was small, around ten, I'd started sneaking into Mum's bedroom to borrow her romance books, her Mills & Boons, which she kept hidden in her bedside table. They had titles like *A Dangerous Kind of Love* and *Castle by the Loch* and were normally about women called Diana or Arabella who were prone to fainting and married men with thick eyebrows and Superman jaws who owned stately houses.

The effect Mum's books had on me was like that science experiment where you drop a Mentos into a bottle of Coca-Cola. My romantic sensibilities exploded into existence and I developed a funny feeling in my stomach for Phillip Schofield and Tim Vincent from *Blue Peter*. They didn't have to be real-life humans, either. Gaston, the cartoon villain from *Beauty and the Beast*, also gave me the funny feeling.

But then I'd been burned and realized that it wasn't wise to base my relationship goals on books in which the duke seduced the housemaid on a chaise longue. Now, thrillers were all I could manage after a long day in the office.

'I'll give you a clue,' said Gus, holding up the bag and flinging one arm in front of him like an actor. 'No man or woman born, brave or coward, can shun his destiny.'

'Huh?'

Gus revealed a hardback copy of *The Iliad*. 'Nell, come on, it's from this.'

'He's three weeks old! I'm not sure he's into ancient Greek poetry yet.'

When other friends had babies, I'd bought them hats that looked like strawberries or cuddly rabbits. A classic hardback seemed extreme, even for Gus.

He shook his head. 'You can never start too early. And anyway, it's not meant for now. It's meant for later on. I've started him a library.'

'A *library*?'

'Mmm, you can do that at Frisbee. I went in and explained that I had a godson and I wanted to build him a collection. So every birthday and Christmas, I gave them his birthday, they send him another classic. This is the first one and I said I'd give it to him myself. But after that, they do all the work, posting it directly to him. Isn't that genius?'

'Yesssss,' I said slowly, remembering birthdays and Christmases when I was small, and hoped for a new nail varnish or a fiver in an envelope.

'What do you fancy for dinner?' went on Gus, lowering the bag. 'I was thinking I might make a cheese soufflé using that cheddar, with a rocket salad.'

'Takeaway?' I ventured. What I really felt like was a pizza but Gus didn't approve of takeaway pizza. He'd once said that takeaway pizza was 'common' and declared that no pizza in London was as good as the pizza you could get in Rome. Nor were we allowed Indian or Chinese since they upset his stomach, but I could occasionally persuade him to get Thai.

Gus frowned at me from the fridge. 'Why don't I make a soufflé? Much nicer. And then there's that new documentary I thought we could watch.'

'Which one?'

'On iPlayer, the one about the communists in Cambodia,' he mumbled into the cheese drawer.

I dropped my head back on the sofa. 'Yup, cool.'

I only woke up fifteen minutes or so later when I heard my phone vibrating in my rucksack. Insistently vibrating. It was either someone calling or sending me 900 messages.

Clawing my fingers across the carpet, I reached for a shoulder strap as Gus hummed along to Radio 3 in the kitchen. Please could it not be Gideon.

It wasn't Gideon; it was my mother. I'd recently taught her how to send voice notes, believing this would break her habit of peppering the family WhatsApp group with bad memes (Dalai Lama quotes, pictures of kittens in teapots, government conspiracy theories and so on. You name it, Mum forwarded it).

Unfortunately, we now got both memes *and* voice notes, and since

Dad and Jack never replied, I felt like I had to acknowledge them instead. Also, Mum hadn't quite mastered the recording of a voice note and sent ten or eleven at a time, each line a new thought.

I lay back on the sofa and hit play on the first voice note.

'Hello, ducks.'

I pressed play on the second one: 'Not sure what you're both up to this weekend.'

The third: 'Your dad and I are having a quiet one at home. Might take the dog to th—'

'I pressed send too early. Might take the dog to the beach, is what I meant to say.'

'But I've got some sad news.'

Ooh, cliffhanger, I thought, just before I hit play on the sixth voice note. Probably, a fox had got one of the chickens. Mum had four chickens, each named after her favourite romantic heroines: Fiona, Jane, Sandra and Violet. I'd given up the Mills & Boons but Mum's fondness remained undimmed.

It wasn't one of the chickens.

'Lord Drummond's died,' Mum went on, 'all quite sudden, and the funeral's next week, Wednesday. Would be nice if at least one of you could come up to suppor—'

There was a muffled noise before her voice piped up again: 'Oh this blasted thing. It's next Wednesday and I do think you should both come. I'll find out the time and let you know but I've got to get dinner on for your dad now. Bye, ducks. Bye.'

Lifting my head, I glanced over the sofa at Gus, standing with his back to me, still humming. He didn't seem to have heard anything.

I flopped back, phone still in my hands.

Lord Drummond was my dad's former boss and unofficial king of Northcliffe, the village where I'd grown up, on a windy, coastal patch of Northumberland. If you drove through Northcliffe, you might easily imagine it was a hamlet where nothing much happened. And this was true, up to a point. There was a patchy green surrounded by the type of squat, grey cottages found in most Northumbrian villages, plus precisely one pub, one shop and a post office.

True, the beach was sensationally pretty, a wildlife haven protected by various conservation orders and home to all sorts of creatures – geese; oystercatchers; otters; small crabs, brown and covered in tiny hairs, that Jack and I used to race against one another; plus the odd hare that you might see leaping through the marram grass. But it also rained 360 days of the year and not much ever happened there (the residents considered it an exciting day if the Spar put the custard tarts on sale).

However, if you continued northwards along the road that cut through the green and cast a glance to your right, you'd spy a vast pair of shiny black gates that looked like the fortress to an ancient citadel. These guarded the drive to Drummond Hall, a vast, Victorian stately home that overlooked the beach, and was owned by the Drummond family. Until he retired the previous year, this was where Dad had worked for nearly forty years, in the stables as Lord Drummond's racing manager. One of my earliest memories was the smell of sweat, horse and hoof oil on his collar when he arrived home every evening to the farmhouse that we rented from the estate.

That Lord Drummond had died was a shock in itself, because Northcliffe was a small place where you couldn't fart in bed without somebody discussing it in the pub, and Dad hadn't mentioned him even being ill. Had he? I made a tight knot with my lips while I thought. Perhaps he had during one of my rare phone calls home and I'd misheard?

But it was a shock that I could already sense giving way to more complicated emotions.

I'd spent much of my childhood running around the gardens and the grounds of the hall since Jack had been best friends with Lord Drummond's son, Arthur. Or Art, as everyone called him. But if I went home for the funeral, out of filial duty, which I probably should since I couldn't imagine my brother bothering, then I'd have to see Art and maybe even speak to him for the first time in fifteen years.

My heart beat harder at the thought, my chest a muddled confusion of pain and anticipation. Mostly pain, I told myself firmly. Really, I'd rather eat my own toenails than face him after so long.

Puffing out my cheeks, I exhaled slowly at the ceiling. If I was going to do this, I'd just have to make sure I was wearing my best suit and an extremely uplifting bra.

Chapter 2

THE TRAIN TO MORPETH took nearly four hours and I spent much of it reading the Lemons' joint bank statements, but I always stopped whatever I was doing for the last half-hour of the journey to stare through the window. This stretch surprised people who'd never travelled here, as if they expected to see factories belching black smoke this far north and were stunned, instead, to be greeted by golden expanses of beach and the silver sea beyond. In the summer, American tourists on their way to the Edinburgh Festival looked up and exclaimed: 'Herb! Honey, quick, get your camera, come and take a picture of the ocean.'

Linzi's case didn't distract me very successfully. While I combed through the statements and their property deeds, I remained aware, every second, that the train was hurrying me towards an awkward reunion with Art.

Every now and then, even though we hadn't seen one another for years, I'd imagined randomly running into him. In this fantasy, I'd look like Nicole Kidman playing a lawyer in a Netflix series: tailored suit, reddish curls pulled together in a loose ponytail, with a few tendrils that had come free around my face, but in a sexy way, not in a dishevelled manner that implied I was an adult who still hadn't mastered her own hair. There I'd be, bouncing along in my heels, looking important and busy.

'Oh my god, Art, hey!' I'd say, stopping in the street and smiling at him. I would not sweat. I would not stammer. We would have a conversation in which I didn't say or do anything embarrassing and, somehow, in the course of this two-minute interaction, I'd manage to impart that I had a terrific life, worked for London's top law firm, had been with Gus for eleven years and, yes, yes, we did own our own place. No children yet, no, but we did have two bedrooms and a corkscrew that aerated the wine when you opened it.

After this, I'd explain that I had to get back to my serious job in my serious office, leaving Art bent over and sobbing on the pavement, devastated that he'd ever let me go.

But as I travelled towards Morpeth, I felt less sure that I could pull off such a confident exchange. My eyes flicked to the emergency alarm at the end of the carriage and I had a dangerous urge to pull it and jump off, to catch the first train back to London. Then I told myself to get a grip. Art had been my childhood friend before anything else and I was simply going to pay my respects to his father.

Actually, he'd been Jack's friend before mine since they were the same age and mucked around together as kids, mostly before Art turned thirteen and was sent away from Northcliffe to boarding school.

That was the moment I'd realized how different we were to him. Or one of the moments. Until then, the social gulf between us and Art hadn't occurred to me. When I was small, when I started tagging along behind the boys, all I knew was that Art's house was bigger than ours. Much bigger. Drummond Hall had 112 rooms, which made for long games of sardines that usually ended with me in tears because I couldn't find either of them. There was also a landscaped garden which we'd never seemed to reach the edges of, a maze (I usually got lost and cried in that, too), a butler called Henry and a chef called Frank, plus Art's nanny, Nanny Gertrude, a tennis court and not one but two large, ornate fishponds spaced as perfectly as crop circles under the French windows at the back of the house.

There were other signs that we were different: they had a nicer car than us – or several cars, since Lord Drummond collected them, kept in a huge garage behind the stable block. Art had his own bathroom, and a TV in his bedroom with a built-in video player, where Jack and I watched the newest films with him because he got those, too. He was sent to Eton. The Drummonds went skiing every year. But Art never seemed different himself, spoiled or snobby. He was just my friend – until the day that he wasn't.

The train's tannoy system jolted me from the memories. 'Ladies and gentlemen, we will shortly be arriving in Morpeth. Please ensure you take all your belongings with you and…'

I shook my head at my reflection in the train's window, cross with myself for allowing these memories to break through. That was enough. No more wallowing, Eleanor Mason. You're going to the funeral, spending one night at home and returning tomorrow morning in a sensible, grown-up fashion.

★★★

Although he'd worked for him for nearly forty years, Dad didn't seem hugely affected by Lord Drummond's death. On the drive home from the station, he explained that the cause had been a heart attack, probably brought on because Lord Drummond had been in bed with his mistress, a lady who owned a dog-grooming parlour in Alnmouth.

'Not a bad way to go, eh?' Dad added with a loud laugh, thumping a huge hand on the steering wheel in approval.

To be fair, even to their employees, Lord and Lady Drummond had always been fairly remote characters in the village. They were the de facto rulers of Northcliffe who lived in the big house but were often away and rarely mingled with the rest of us. I'm pretty sure Lady Drummond thought we were peasants. She often gave that impression when Jack and I showed up at the hall as kids, looking for Art. Her nose would twitch with distaste as if we smelt of horse dung. Maybe we did.

I'd been scared of Art's parents as a child. Lady Drummond was tall and thin with a pointy face. She was a former model who'd been on the cover of *Vogue*, but I'd always thought she looked like a human stoat because her nose twitched at everything she disliked. It wasn't just me and Jack. The list also included mud, fat people, most types of food and anybody she deemed her social inferior. The locals called her Lady de Vil because she was only ever seen wearing some sort of animal – fox, rabbit, chinchilla, maybe even stoat itself. And when we were small she travelled constantly – to London, to Paris, to New York or to the latest spa in Switzerland – leaving Art with Nanny Gertrude since Lord Drummond was often away too, visiting racecourses in France, Dubai, even Australia.

If Lady Drummond was a stoat, then Lord Drummond had been a badger; shorter, rounder, with thick black eyebrows that almost met in the middle. He always wore tweed suits with bright yellow socks and some form of hat to hide his receding hairline – a trilby, a flat hat, a panama. Nanny Gertrude had been his nanny when small and he hired her to return to Drummond Hall when Art was born, the most sensible decision Lord Drummond ever made since she loved Art as if he was hers.

As Dad drove, I wondered whether I'd speak to Nanny Gertrude at the funeral. She still lived up here, in a cottage on the estate, and must be in her nineties now, although I hadn't seen her for years. She used to be the shape of a muffin with a huge bosom, always covered in a pastel cardigan, which she'd frequently clasped us to. Normal people have fears like heights and spiders but Nanny Gertrude's greatest fear had been that one of us would catch a cold, which was unfortunate given that we lived in a blustery village overlooking the North Sea.

Dad slowed the car as we approached the Northcliffe sign and I instinctively glanced to my right at the mile-long strip of sand and the cliffs overlooking it. From up there you could survey the whole beach: the dog walkers, the seagulls waddling in shallow puddles left by the retreating tide, even the odd kite surfer taking advantage of the winds that often battered this section of the coast.

It was also where Drummond Hall sat, on top of the cliffs, looking out over the waves below.

Dad pulled off the main road into a space outside the village pub.

'Hang on, we not going home?'

'No, lunch here, then straight to church. That all right, pet?'

'Oh right, yep, no problem, that's fine,' I replied, smoothing down my skirt. I'd been hoping to go home where I could more easily have touched up my make-up. What was the appropriate amount of make-up for a funeral where you'd also bump into your first love? Unsure, I'd bundled every brush, cream, palette and powder I owned into a Sainsbury's bag for life in the flat that morning since it wouldn't all fit into my usual cosmetic bag. I wasn't at all sure that I could make myself look like Nicole Kidman in the pub, but I'd have a go in the ladies' toilets.

The pub was called the Drunken Duck and it sat on the edge of the green. A squat, white stone house with a thatched roof, it was built by the first Lord Drummond when villagers must have been hobbits. The ceiling was so low, and the wooden beams lower still, that tall people were normally brained the first time they visited.

Its small windows would have made it dark inside but Marjorie, Terence the landlord's wife, had strung fairy lights across the beams and there was always a fire going at one end, even on a relatively balmy day in March.

'Hiya, love,' said Mum, waving at me from their table. I say their; it was really Dad's table. He and his farmer mate Roy sat there every evening, in the corner beside the fire, discussing the weather and Roy's cows. Mum normally stayed at home with one of her romance books.

'Hi, Mum. Nice hair!'

For as long as I could remember, every morning, before making her first cup of tea, or our breakfasts, or feeding the dogs or reaching into the metal bin in the shed for a scoop of corn for the chickens, Mum had tied her thick hair into a plait and thrown it over her shoulder, claiming it 'got it out the way'. But now the plait was gone and in its place a bob, a dramatic change which Mum had omitted to mention in any of her voice notes.

'D'you like it?' Her hands snapped back towards her face. 'It's a bit cold on the neck.'

'I love it. Looks amazing. Dad, what do you reckon?'

But he'd already taken a seat at the table and was glancing towards the bar. 'A pint, I think,' he muttered.

Mum rolled her eyes and we hugged while I was struck by a familiar pang of guilt that I didn't come home more often. It was only as I'd got older, and worked with other people's failing marriages, that I'd realized my parents' relationship consisted mostly of discussing the weather and talking about Wilma, their shaggy Irish wolfhound. It was a vicious circle of guilt: their relationship depressed me, so I came home less and less often, but this made me feel guiltier still.

I'd tried to pluck up the courage to say something to one of them, to put my professional hat on and offer advice. But I always wimped out in the end, deciding that Dad would only crack a joke and Mum would ignore me. Serious topics were not discussed in our family where 'emotion' was a dirty word. That's why, when I cried for so long after the Art debacle, it was easier for Mum to suggest I'd developed a new allergy than accept the more alarming idea that I was hurting.

We sat and Dad shouted a drinks order at Terence. Gus and I normally had a no-drinking rule during the week but I thought a glass of white wine, even Terence's white wine, which tastes like apple juice that has sat in the sun for too long, might calm the bats that had taken up residence in my stomach.

'How are you, love?' said Mum, lifting her gin.

'I'm all r—'

I was interrupted by a cry of welcome from Dad as Roy came through the door, followed by his two sons, Douglas and Jamie, who I'd grown up with and who now worked on the family farm. I hadn't ever seen them in suits before. It was like seeing a trio of monkeys dressed for the opera.

'Over here, lads!' called Dad, gesturing.

They trooped over and took up position beside us at the next table.

'Jamie, three pints of Tyneside,' instructed Roy. He glanced at our drinks. 'You lot all OK?'

'Grand for now,' said Dad.

Roy pulled out a wooden chair and sat. 'Nice to see you up, Nell. Been a while. No Jack then?'

'No, no,' Mum jumped in, 'he's too busy in London.'

This was Jack's usual excuse and Mum always swallowed it. 'The thing is, sis, it's the spring market at the moment so every Tom, Dick and Harry in London's trying to move house,' he'd said when I'd called him about the funeral a couple of days ago.

I would have believed this were it not for the fact that Jack was London's worst estate agent, constantly moving jobs, from an office in Fulham, to another in Hackney, then one in Clapham

South for a mercifully brief period because it was close to the flat and he'd taken to coming over and watching football on the sofa because we had Sky Sports. For the past year or so, he'd been based at a different office in Kennington. I never knew quite what had happened whenever he moved agencies; he just presented it as a fait accompli.

'How's your important job, Nell?' Roy asked, a smile lifting his ruddy cheeks.

'All right, thanks.'

'Any celebrities recently?'

I laughed to mask my discomfort. I tried to avoid talking about work up here because the gulf between Northcliffe and my existence in London was so wide that I felt almost ashamed, as if I'd betrayed my roots by becoming a spoiled professional who had strong opinions about London postcodes and knew what a nocellara olive was. In Spinks, the air smelt of money and furniture wax; in the pub, it smelt of old beer mats and scampi. 'No, no celebrities,' I fibbed, before changing the subject. 'What time's the service?'

'Three,' said Mum, 'so we should order. What do you all want and I'll go up.'

After we'd decided, the conversation moved on to Lord Drummond.

'May he rest in peace,' said Roy, lifting his second pint in the air as a toast.

'Unlike the poor woman who owns that dog parlour,' added Dad, raising his glass.

'Bruce, must you?' said Mum.

'I'm only saying I shouldn't think she'll ever sleep sound again, what with Lord D conking out on top of her,' Dad elaborated, winking at me as I tried to hide my smile. He loved an audience.

Mum sighed and we moved on to more serious ground. What was going to happen to the house? To the estate? Would Art move back from New York?

Whenever his name was mentioned I kept my eyes on the table, trying not to betray an unusual level of interest. Dad wasn't even sure if he and Mum would be allowed to stay at home, since, although he'd retired and been promised a pension for life, our house still belonged to the Drummonds.

The same applied to half the village, mostly living in estate cottages, farming or working in some other guise for the family. Having inherited the family fortune, Lord Drummond had done his best to spend it. Rumours began flying a few years earlier that the cash was running out and he'd started to flog land, much of his car collection, horses and pieces of art. The hall closed to annual visitors around the same time, which prompted a fresh wave of speculation in the village about the Drummonds' marriage. I had such happy memories of it, but in recent years everyone agreed the hall had slipped into decline.

'Surely he won't kick you out?'

Dad shrugged. 'Not sure, pet. I hope not but heaven knows what Art'll want to do with the place.'

'Probably flog it,' Roy muttered into his ale, which earned a reproachful glare from Terence as he appeared from the kitchen carrying several plates.

'Don't look at me like that. What's a fancy New Yorker

need a place like this for? He'll flog it to some developer, mark my words.'

I'd heard similar grumbling about Art in the pub before on my sporadic trips home. Since he'd married and moved to New York, the village had turned against him. The general view was that he'd married a millionaire's daughter and now thought himself too good for Northcliffe, living a swanky life in a big Manhattan townhouse, having forgotten where he came from.

'Let's bury 'im first before you start rumouring about what might or mightn't happen,' Terence told Roy as he passed me a baked potato. It was the safest choice in here where the beer was good, the wine terrible and the food varied depending on whether or not Terence was employing a decent chef.

The conversation moved on and Mum brought up Northcliffe's other big news – the opening of a coffee shop called Thanks A Latte next to the post office.

'Been there for a few months now, he's called Luigi, down from Edinburgh, and he makes a lovely flat white,' she explained for my benefit, while peeling a lone leaf of parsley off her cheese sandwich.

Dad and Roy glowered suspiciously, as if flat whites were weapons of mass destruction.

Terrible name aside, the opening of a place in Northcliffe where you could get a coffee that actually tasted like coffee seemed a positive development to me. Terence served coffee in the Duck but you might as well drink from a puddle.

'So long as he doesn't start taking my regulars,' growled Terence, returning with a bottle of ketchup.

'For goodness' sake, Terence, he makes his own panettone,' snapped Mum. 'I think your ploughmans' are probably safe.'

***

When I was small, we were always late to the parish church on Christmas Day because Dad made a big fuss about putting on an ironed shirt and a tie, and we usually snuck into a back row. (The Drummonds always sat in the front pew since the church had been built by their ancestor and so was, technically, their own private chapel.)

Today we were late because Dad and Roy insisted on a final pint before walking up from the pub, so we crammed into the final pew alongside three people I didn't recognize. Mum went first, then me, then Dad. Roy and his sons took the pew across the aisle.

I bent forward to put my bag on the stone floor and slide it underneath me. Had these pews got smaller? I could feel the warmth of both parents against my hips and smell beer on Dad's breath. I didn't remember feeling so squashed as a child.

Nudging the prayer cushion back towards my bag with my foot to free up more leg room, I looked down at the order of service in my hand. If I kept looking down, then I wouldn't see him, or accidentally catch his eye before I was ready. I needed more time to compose myself, more time to allow my heart to stop knocking so loudly I wondered whether those in the surrounding pews could hear it.

Thump, thump, thump.

For God's sake, Nell. This is a church service, not a bungee jump. Well, a funeral. But still, just sit and be calm. What did that lady on Calm instruct? Occasionally, if Gideon had been particularly rabid, I listened to meditations on the Northern line home after work. Box breathing, that was it. In for four, hold for four, out for four.

Beside me, Dad burped under his hand.

'Bruce!' hissed Mum. 'Not in church.'

'Pardon me for being rude,' Dad started, before I joined in and whispered along, a ritual he and I had performed at the kitchen table ever since I could speak and which used to make me squeal with pleasure. 'It was not me, it was my food. It just popped up to say hello and now it's gone back down below.'

'Honestly, you two,' Mum murmured, as I pinched my lips together to prevent a laugh. Poor Mum. She'd often remarked that she had three children, not two, but since jokes remained the main form of communication in our family, Dad always ignored this and continued with his clown act.

To try and make myself more sombre, I frowned down at the black-and-white photograph of Lord Drummond in a suit and tie. According to the dates underneath it, he must have been seventy-three. Impressive to still have enough energy for rolling around in bed with a mistress. But I knew from my own clients that some people didn't slow down in that department. In fact, some of them – mostly the male clients – seemed to get worse as they got older, pepped up by pills from a friendly chemist, as if they sensed that time was running out. It was John Betjeman who'd said, on his death bed, that he wished he'd had more sex. It must be exhausting, having a penis. Did they think of nothing else?

Why was I thinking about poets and penises in church? I chided myself and, slowly, dared to look to the front. It was packed, far fuller than it ever had been on Christmas Day, and since everyone was wearing black it made picking out individuals harder. Up ahead, daffodil-yellow sunshine glowed through the stained glass. Whenever I'd come home for Christmas or Easter as an adult, I'd avoided church in case I bumped into him, which meant I hadn't seen that image of Mary clutching her baby and looking mournful for over fifteen years. I could have drawn it with closed eyes.

Then I saw him because he stood above everyone else. I could have drawn that head, too. And even though I'd spent the past few days steeling myself, my breath caught at the back of my throat. He was the same: the same, slightly dishevelled mass of dark hair, the same broad shoulders, the same shape and mannerisms. As the vicar talked, Art nodded, then lowered his chin and swept one hand across his forehead, as if under strain.

Oh no. No no no. No thank you. It had been the work of fifteen years to bury the feelings I could sense uncoiling within me. I was absolutely not to feel sorry for him. Well, a bit sorry. It was his father's funeral. But on no account was I to feel too sorry for him, because what he'd done was unforgivable. And I definitely wasn't to feel sorry enough that I ended up fantasizing about him like a lovesick teenager.

Nell! Why are you thinking about sex again? Jesus. I glanced at the baby in the window. Sorry, Jesus, I don't mean to be sitting here thinking about sex and taking your name in vain. But this was a confusing situation. Although death did make people think about sex, didn't it, I'm sure I'd read that death was an aphrodisiac for some. Maybe it was Freud. I sighed more loudly than I intended, and the lady in front of me turned round as my breath fanned her neck.

Perhaps having a glass of wine beforehand had been a bad idea.

Art took his seat in the front pew, and I inched my head a few millimetres to the right to see who he was sitting with. Her, I presumed, and his mother. Would their son be here? Was he old enough to go a funeral? At least it was a closed coffin, instead of an open casket like in America. I'd never understood why anyone would want to stare at the waxy face of a loved one, but then Americans also called yoghurt 'yo-ghurt' so there was no telling with them.

I sneaked a glance at my watch and contemplated whether I could catch the last train back to London later. I should stay because Mum would have made my room up, but emails would be ticking into my phone and Gideon and I were meeting another new client tomorrow. Perhaps I should have a quick look now, to check he hadn't sent anything vital that I needed to read. Except just as I lowered my hand to grope for my bag, the vicar asked us to stand.

He spoke and we sang, then there was more speaking and more singing, but I didn't pay much attention to the proceedings until Art stood to deliver the eulogy.

I realized then I was wrong about him seeming the same. He was thinner; his cheeks had caved in on themselves. And I wondered when he'd last slept properly, although I guessed the dark shadows under his eyes could be jet lag rather than chronic insomnia.

He talked without notes, occasionally looking down at the lectern in front of him, more often gazing out across the congregation. There must have been 200 or so of us rammed in here. 'I had... a chequered relationship with my father. He could be difficult, irascible, intolerant and God help – sorry, vicar – anyone who ever dared mention they were a vegetarian in his presence.' There was a ripple of polite laughter at this. 'But he was a good man.'

I wondered whether the woman who owned the dog-grooming parlour was among us.

'And although the last few years have been hard, he did care deeply for this place,' went on Art, 'for this estate, and for everyone who lived here. It's quite a legacy to take over.'

I thought back to our conversation in the pub. Could he come back when his life was in New York? Had he given up on this place?

In the months after Art had left for America, Mum had been careful with what she'd told me. Dad was updated about his life by Lord Drummond, and he'd pass it on to Mum, who would tentatively mention selected information on the phone to me as if it was helpful. Art and Nicole had moved into a 'very gaudy' townhouse in Manhattan, she scoffed once, and Art had gone to work for his father-in-law's bank on Wall Street. More gently still, she told me they'd had a son called Felix. It had seemed strange when the Art I'd known had been so different. That Art had been shy and obsessed with aeroplanes, more into dogs than parties and happiest in the hall's gardens with us and Nanny Gertrude. So I'd pretended not to be interested, and Mum, sensing that mentioning his name to me was like pressing a bruise, changed the subject to the chickens. Safer, less emotional territory. Then I'd met Gus, and everyone, myself included, was grateful that we could move on and forget about him.

As I watched Art talk at the lectern, my overriding emotion was curiosity at how very different our lives had become. Although wasn't that really always going to be the case? It was only when I was ten, when my childish crush had begun, that I'd imagined we were the same. And I'd allowed myself to believe that right up until I was seventeen.

It was only after that night that I realized how naive I'd been, how sheltered and sweet my fantasies were. Really, I should be grateful that he'd taught me this early; in life, sometimes the people you least expected to could hurt you the most.

I was far from grateful at the time because I was so young, still a teenager, when he broke my heart. But it had given me time to work out that we would always have gone separate ways, in the end. How could it have been otherwise? Back then I'd burned with fury at the idea that he'd so easily forgotten me. Now, I understood it: our childhoods had overlapped but that didn't mean our lives would. Even Art probably called it 'yo-ghurt' by now, and I could never be with a man who said that as he opened the fridge every morning.

He finished speaking and stepped down, then we stood to sing again and I felt a spasm of nervousness at the thought of tea, back at the hall, when I'd presumably have to speak to him. At least my hair was better since we'd last seen one another, and I'd stopped wearing orange foundation to cover my freckles.

When younger, I'd always been aware, or insecure, that Art was much better-looking than me. Nanny Gertrude used to pinch his cheeks and declare he'd work 'in the pictures'. When he turned seventeen, since Lady Drummond was a former catwalk star, she tried to make him model in a Calvin Klein campaign. Art was tall, already built like a man by then, but he swore he wasn't interested, more into planes and his pilot ambitions than following in his mother's footsteps. And yet he'd never seemed to realize his effect on women until Nicole came along.

I'd spent so long deliberating over what to wear last night that Gus had asked whether I was off 'to a funeral or Buckingham Palace?' In the end, I'd picked my most expensive, Theory suit, bought after my last promotion, and thrown in a silk vest with one of my best bras. It occurred to me that it was inappropriate to spend so long considering one's underwear when choosing a funeral outfit, but this wasn't just any old funeral. And anyway, I wasn't flashing much, hardly even a whisper of cleavage. I just wanted to feel my perkiest.

Nell, stop thinking about your breasts in church.

The vicar droned through the final blessing and we watched Art and various other pallbearers shuffle Lord Drummond's coffin down the aisle and outside, to a plot on the side of the church overlooking the sea. That's when I spotted Nanny Gertrude, standing just in front of Art, leaning on a stick. Her gigantic bosom had shrunk and she'd become as crooked as a question mark but here she was, still going, still devoted to the family. She caught my eye and scrunched her face in a smile which made me beam back before remembering that I should look sad. Howard, the whiskery old Drummond Hall gardener, was standing just behind in a suit and the same tweed flat cap which I'd never seen leave his head, as if permanently attached to his scalp with superglue.

My eyes slid along the line to Lady Drummond, who was draped in a black fur stole and didn't look very mournful either. And beside her stood Nicole, wearing the sort of dress that would be useful if you had a funeral to attend, followed by the Oscars: a wraparound number which clung to her chest and hips and was slashed high up one leg. She was also wearing a veil, as if this was a Sicilian graveyard and she was the grieving widow of a mafia boss.

'He always did like a good hole,' Dad whispered as Lord Drummond's coffin was lowered into the ground.

Beside me, I felt Mum flinch. 'Bruce!'

I bit my lower lip again to stop a smile.

The sun had dropped behind the hall by the time we walked down the east drive, rays making laser beams between the turrets and chimneys. I relinquished any hope of making the last train back to London and shook my head as we crunched along the gravel, amused at the idea I could ever have lived anywhere so grand.

It was a Gothic, red-brick palace, with so many windows I was never quite sure, from the outside, which room was behind each one. Art's great-great-grandfather, a Geordie merchant who made his fortune from importing cocoa and became a Victorian chocolate baron, commissioned it in the nineteenth century. He wanted a country seat overlooking the North Sea within travelling distance of his office at the Newcastle docks, and his vision became one of the biggest private houses built in England during that era, which is saying something when all around the country, newly minted cotton and sugar magnates were competing to create the grandest pile of all.

From the imposing front door, surrounded by stone pillars, you entered into a hall with a vaulted ceiling, and from there into state rooms designed to impress Queen Victoria when she stayed with the chocolate baron on her way up to Balmoral, breaking her journey for the night. The rooms were wallpapered with silk, filled with antiques and hung with oil paintings by famous portraitists, including a Michelangelo etching of a cherub. But the most magnificent sight of all was the staircase with solid silver banisters, as Lord Drummond (RIP) had always been fond of boasting. It curled from the entrance hall to the first floor, the only such one in the country, and a team of specialist cleaners used to visit every spring to polish it with toothbrushes.

Outside, perfectly landscaped gardens fell behind the house like carpet but it was the front aspect that took everyone's breath away: the stone steps of the main entrance were angled towards the cliffs, and the wide, sandy beach and rolling waves below, just as Art's ancestor had wanted.

'Try harder and you might spy Denmark,' Howard the gardener told us on clear, sunny days when we were small. We believed him and spent a long time squinting over the waves. Other days, we'd comb the beach for gold coins from a pirate ship that, supposedly, had sunk in the bay in the seventeen hundreds. Needless to say, we never found one. Jack claimed he had once but it turned out to be a rusty bottle top.

A queue grew around the steps as everyone waited patiently to make their way into the vaulted hall.

'Will it be a free bar, do you think?' Roy asked, glancing hopefully at the huge front door.

'I reckon,' said Dad, loosening his tie. 'A big drink is exactly what he would have wanted.'

Roy nodded solemnly.

'It's barely tea time, and you had a couple earlier,' Mum murmured as we filed in.

Inside was a trestle table laden with silver tea urns and cups and saucers. Around the rest of the hall were circular tables, covered in white linen and plates of sandwiches and cake. The bar was set up at the back, beside the unlit fireplace. Dad and Roy immediately pushed their way towards it while Mum and I waited for a cup of tea. It even smelt the same in here, of furniture wax and old wood smoke, although the silver staircase looked dull and unloved. No toothbrushes had polished it very recently.

'Shall we sit?' I suggested, nodding at a table in the far corner once we'd been handed our teas by a waitress behind the trestle table. I wanted to face the room so I could see everyone, so there were no surprises. I wanted to see him but, also, I didn't want to see him.

We weaved our way through others and sat. Mum pulled a plate of sandwiches towards her while I looked around me. The last time I'd been in here, I'd been running through it, desperate to get back home.

Glancing across at the door which obscured the back route up to Art's room, I saw a young boy standing near it. Felix, I presumed, since he had Art's dark, tousled hair and Nicole's slanted blue eyes. I hadn't seen him at the funeral but he was in a suit that was too big and seemed lost in a room full of adults ignoring him. He must be almost a teenager, I realized, around the same age that I'd become attached to his father like a limpet.

'You're still staying the night?' Mum checked, from my other side, with an underlying note of anxiety.

I looked away from Felix. 'Yeah, course.'

The longest spell I'd spent at home here since leaving for university was, what, three nights? I came up for every other Christmas with Gus, and I tried to come up for Mum and Dad's birthdays but it wasn't always possible with work. Ever since moving to London, it was as if Northcliffe had become too small. Plus, Gus wasn't much of a countryman.

The first time I brought him home to meet my parents, while we were at law school, Gus had shaken me awake at 3 a.m. and turned the bedside light on, insisting there was a woman being murdered in our garden. I'd laughed this off and told him that it was January, which meant it was fox-mating season in the country, and those screams were the sounds of a vixen having sex. Gus had looked unconvinced by this but went back to sleep, only to step outside in the morning and inspect our overgrown lawn for signs of a struggle.

'Lovely,' Mum replied. 'And how's Gus?' she added, as if reading my mind.

'Working hard, got a complicated Google case which is dragging on and on. But, yeah, he's good. Sends his love.'

Sweetly, despite his case, Gus had offered to come with me

to the funeral while I packed the night before, but I'd decided that was one complication too many. I'd always thought that our differences made us compatible – I knew about fox-mating season; Gus knew the difference between a Cabernet Sauvignon and Merlot – but my parents were warier of him.

What did they have in common with a corporate lawyer who liked fancy restaurants and Homer? Also, Gus was allergic to dogs which my parents considered fairly close to a crime. I'm not sure Dad even believed it was possible. On the rare occasions Gus did come north, he'd spend much of his time sneezing and I'd often catch Dad squinting at him, as if he thought Gus was faking it.

I'd fallen in love with him precisely because he was so different from home, and anybody I'd met in Northumberland. We met in our first week at law school and, pretty quickly, spent all our time together – studying, going to pubs that served the cheapest pints we could find, having sex.

At uni, I'd slept with a handful of men and they'd all been fine. Perfectly fine. I'd felt a bit like a boiler being serviced and I didn't totally get what all the fuss was about – that was *it*? Why did the average person think about *that* every three seconds? – but it was nice to lie there afterwards, close to someone.

With Gus, it was different, more familiar, warmer. Less like a visit from the plumber. He was the first man who made me come, which seemed miraculous. Lying on my narrow mattress afterwards, Gus's head still between my legs, I felt a sort of grateful astonishment. I'd never even managed that myself. I read once that women always fall in love with whoever first does this to us, whoever makes our thighs wobble and fall in on themselves, but there were various other reasons, too.

Because Gus was brilliantly clever, because we could talk about law together, because he could cook and introduced me to strange food I'd never come across. On one of our first dates, he presented me with a flower on a plate and announced it was an artichoke. On another, he made me spaghetti stirred with shiny orange lumps which I presumed were tomato but tasted like fish. Sea urchin, Gus said triumphantly, which he'd bought that morning from Borough Market. It was disgusting but I was touched by his effort.

It wasn't the fairy tale kind of rescue where a prince plucks a princess from a tower or the clutches of a fire-breathing dragon. It was slower than that. Plus, Gus didn't look much like a prince. He had a large forehead and neat brown hair which he always combed into a side parting. He was dorky and liked Italian opera music and history. His idea of the perfect Saturday afternoon was strolling around a new exhibition about the Ming dynasty or Emperor Hadrian at the British Museum. Alternatively, he'd take me to see an obscure French film at the BFI and, afterwards, rifle for second-hand books from the stalls underneath Waterloo Bridge. Since I'd grown up in Northcliffe where the closest cinema was forty minutes away, I was dazzled by his sophistication.

Gradually, as he showed me another life, another option, Art stopped being the first thing I thought about when I woke up. It was like coming out of a trance. Love felt different to how I imagined it as a teenager, but I realized that was no bad thing.

Not that I could have explained any of that to my parents. Like I said, we didn't discuss emotions.

I changed the subject. 'I'm seeing Jack tomorrow night; he's bringing his new girlfriend over for dinner.'

Mum's face transformed into a smile. 'Is he? That's nice. What's this one called again?'

I tried to remember. Emily? Esme? Emma? Jack got through girlfriends quicker than I got through hair ties (where do all the hair ties go?). Before now, there'd been blonde Annabelle, a primary school teacher; before her there'd been blonde Mimi, an interior designer; before her a rare brunette, can't remember what she did; and before that was Trixie, the blonde burlesque dancer. Before that they all became a blur.

Jack treated women like his job and estate agency as a hobby. But then he'd always had plenty of attention from them. Like Art, he grew tall and broad early. Unlike Art, he understood the effect he had. At school, Jack seemed to emit just the right amount of arrogance and disdain to make girls laugh and swoon in turn. If they'd asked me I would have told them he was mean, picked his nose and left the bathroom stinking in the mornings, but I was never very friendly with any of the girls he went out with. I never saw the point when they wouldn't be around long. The same applied now.

'Can't remember,' I told Mum. 'Begins with an E.'

'You'll ring me after and let me know what she's like?'

'Not sure there's much point, Mum. She'll probably be dumped the following day.'

She tutted. 'Eleanor, don't be so harsh on your brother. You know he's always found things harder than you.'

This made me want to scream at the ceiling. Jack hadn't changed since we were teenagers. He remained a good-looking chancer who drank and shagged his way through life and when this occasionally landed him in trouble – with work or women – he'd simply shrug it off and move on. Today was a classic example of his priorities: too busy and tight to pay for a train ticket north for a funeral, but more than happy to bring whatever-she-was-called over to mine for a free dinner the following night. Classic Jack.

To distract myself, I reached for an egg sandwich and bit into the middle of it, so egg mayonnaise bulged from the sides and chunks of it fell to my lap.

'Have a napkin,' said Mum, passing me a damp one from her saucer.

And obviously, that's when he appeared at the table, just as I was rubbing the smear into my skirt and my cheeks were bulging with sandwich, like a squirrel preparing for a long, cold winter.

Chapter 3

'SOMEONE WANTED TO SAY hi,' said Art, grinning at me. 'Actually, we both did.'

I tried to swallow and smile at the same time which I'm afraid made me look like one of the stone gargoyles carved into the stone pillars outside.

'Nanny Gertrude!' I garbled, leaping up to give her a hug. She still smelt the same: Pears soap with a top note of talcum powder. 'I've missed you.'

'Oh, get on with you,' she said bashfully, smiling so hard that her eyes became coin slots.

'Good to see you, too,' I said, more stiffly, reaching up to give Art a less effusive hug, hoping he couldn't feel my heart hammering in my chest or smell egg mayonnaise on my breath.

'How are you?' I asked when I stood back, before realizing this wasn't the right question to ask someone at their father's funeral. 'I mean, I'm so sorry.' I swallowed again.

I'd practised this greeting on the train, over and over again in my head. I would be cool and calm, not remotely awkward or embarrassing. And yet here I was, being both awkward and embarrassing at the same time.

'Thanks,' he replied, with the same grin. 'I wasn't sure you'd come. Is Jack here too?' Up close, his green eyes met mine but betrayed no sense of awkwardness.

When we were younger, I'd felt as if his eyes could see behind mine, not just at me, but into me. It was the same now, and the closeness, the familiarity, made me feel fifteen again. Under his lip, I could still see the scar from where he fell on the beach as a kid, cutting it on a rock. Nanny Gertrude had become hysterical that day. She'd have kept him in a helmet for the rest of his childhood if she could.

'Jack couldn't make it. Too much work. But course I would. How's your mum doing?' There we go, that was more like it. Cool, calm, not embarrassing.

He glanced over his shoulder. 'Fine, I think, mostly in London these days anyway so...' He trailed off and looked back to me with the same expression, totally at ease. 'How's life with you? You look great. Tell me everything.'

'Have you got a nice man who looks after you? A nice husband?' added Nanny Gertrude, beaming up at me while clinging to Art's arm like a sparrow.

Before I could reply, the Sicilian widow appeared behind them. 'Art, honey, please don't leave me with locals I can't understand. I believe that man just propositioned me.'

'Which man?' asked Art, with a frown.

Nicole inclined her head towards the fireplace where Dad and Roy were puce with laughter. Dad was leaning against the mantelpiece, one arm resting across it; in his other hand he was holding a loaded glass of sherry.

'Don't worry about them,' he reassured his wife. 'You remember Nell?'

'No,' she said simply, before flicking her eyes up and down me as if I were a mannequin in a shop window. 'Hi there. You don't look like a local?'

'Er, no, I am. I grew up here, but I live in London now.'

'You escaped after all!' said Art. 'Whereabouts?'

'In London?'

He nodded.

'Clapham.' I cringed as I said this, as always. Must get over that. 'How long you back for?'

I was really asking Art but Nicole jumped in.

'Only until the day after tomorrow, thank the Lord. Listen, Art, sweetheart, I need the keys to the safe and Howard says he doesn't know where they are and I can hardly ask your mother bec—'

'All right, all right, I'll sort it,' said Art, and I saw a tiny muscle flex in his cheek before he looked at me again. 'Good to see you, sorry it hasn't been longer, but thank you for coming all this way. And, Mrs Mason,' he added, glancing around me at Mum, still sitting at the table, 'my apologies, I haven't even said hi, but thank you for coming too.'

'Good to see you too,' I said, but they'd already turned back into the throng of mourners.

I sat in a daze and stared at the tablecloth. That was it; after worrying for days, our whole interaction had lasted less than a minute and a half. It left me feeling a tangle of relief and deflation: the former that it was done, the latter because it had been so quick and inconsequential.

Mum pushed the plate towards me. 'Have another sandwich.'

'I'm OK, thanks.'

She picked up a cucumber sandwich and held it close to her face, inspecting it, before dropping a bombshell so strange I thought I'd misheard: 'Do you know, if I had my time again, I'm not sure I'd get married.'

I turned towards her. 'Mum, *what*? This is a new take. Since when have you decided that?'

Slowly, she chewed her sandwich and swallowed before answering. 'I was just thinking about what Gertrude asked you. And I've come to the conclusion that you and Gus are very brave not to do it if you don't want to.'

'Do you know what? I think I might have another one,' I said, reaching for the plate, suddenly feeling the need for a sugar hit.

When I told my parents about Gus's aversion to marriage some years ago, they'd boggled as if I'd told them he was a Morris dancer.

Then came all sorts of follow-up questions: what about children? Was it a religious thing? Did I not realize I was denying them a celebration since, clearly, my brother was never going to get his act together? And so on and so on until Dad tentatively asked whether I thought Gus might be gay. At this point, I refused to discuss it any further. It was our decision – well, Gus's more than mine, but, still, I'd agreed. Ever since then, whenever the topic was broached, I defended it, and had learned several answers by heart, as if a script, which I could trot out when required.

It was different for their generation; marriage was entered almost unthinkingly. Mum met Dad at a farmers' dance not far from Northcliffe in the 1980s. Back then she was Kath Wesley, the daughter of an accountant from Surrey, who came north to visit a university friend. She joked that she'd never been to the countryside before, like an evacuee child who'd never seen a cow. All the photos of her from this time show a proper Eighties fashion slave – she loved Bryan Ferry and Duran Duran, and wore frilly shirts and leather jackets with extremely bright eyeshadow. Dad, more used to local girls who wore rugby shirts, was charmed by her novelty. The local girls had ruddy cheeks and mud under their fingernails; Mum had pale skin and long strawberry-blonde hair that she wore in her loose plait.

She, in turn, was swept up by the wildness of the country and Dad, who seemed very unlike the boring accountancy students her parents were trying to marry her off with at home in Godalming. Dad was big, brash, didn't even own a suit and went after Mum with the same unrefined directness that he went after everything else. He promised her a romantic, rural life, quite different from her parents' three-bed semi, and that was that. They married and moved to our house in Northcliffe where Dad had recently landed a junior job at the Drummond Hall stables and rose from there, being almost as horse- and racing-obsessed as his employer.

I think Mum envisaged *Little House on the Prairie*, a life wearing pinafores and making jam like in one of her Mills & Boons, but the reality was very different. The house was cold and draughty; she didn't see her husband all day and when she did see him, realized that they didn't have much in common. They had Jack and me in quick succession, which gave her something to focus on, and she took on the dogs, chickens, the odd guinea pig when we were small, and Barry the tortoise who came from a dodgy market seller in Newcastle, although he didn't survive many Northumberland winters.

That was why she read those books, I understood now. Mum buried herself in stories about handsome, seductive men and pillow-lipped heroines because the great excitements in her life were whether Wilma did her business on her morning walk and the opening of a new coffee shop.

'Wait a minute, do you mean you wish you'd never had me and Jack?' I checked with her, before biting into my sandwich.

'No, no, no. Don't be daft. I wouldn't take anything back, it's just…' Mum paused and looked towards the mantelpiece where Dad and Roy were accepting sherry top-ups from a waiter. 'Marriage isn't the be-all and end-all, love. Now come on, eat up, and then we need to get your father home before there's some sort of accident.'

★★★

We walked back, the same route that Jack and I ran when little. Mum and I walked, anyway; Dad weaved his way down the drive while humming. I glanced over my shoulder, wondering how long it would be before I saw the hall again. Another fifteen years? More? I guess it depended what happened to the place.

'That's that then,' said Mum. 'All put to bed.'

'Mmmm,' I murmured back. I think she meant the service, the

day as a whole, but I did sometimes wonder if she had clairvoyant skills.

We crunched down the gravel and under the avenue of lime trees that led to the main gates, then across the main road and along the verge to the dirt track leading to Mum and Dad's house.

It was an old farmhouse made from grey stone with a wild, overgrown garden of brambles and long grass because neither Mum nor Dad bothered to cut it back. The same applied inside: it was chaotic, with piles of Dad's old *Racing Post*s on the kitchen counters, and clutter pushed to one end of the kitchen table: unopened post, pens, dog biscuits, loose batteries, recipes which Mum had ripped from magazines and would never make, odd gloves, odd socks, an empty box of tissues. We'd always had wolfhounds in the house: Molly first, then her daughter Luna, then Minnie (one of Dad's jokes, since wolfhounds were the size of small ponies), and now her daughter Wilma. They were shaggy, silver dogs with kind faces but their presence also meant a fine layer of dog hair covered every surface.

Upstairs was little better. My bedroom was decorated with flowery wallpaper from the 1970s and it was always cold since there was no heating. In the winters as a kid, after a bath, I'd wrap myself in a towel and run down the corridor to get under my duvet as quickly as I could. In the mornings, I'd wake and see my breath hanging in the air.

Mum unlocked the door and I was hit by the competing smell of fried food and laundry, which hung on a pulley over the cooker. Dad opened the fridge, pulled out a bottle of beer and went to flick on the racing highlights in the living room. Mum declared that she was going to have a bath. That left me and Wilma in the kitchen. She got up to greet me by pushing her nose into my hand, then I collapsed at the table with a sigh and she rested her head on my legs with a whine. Poor thing was desperate for a walk but I didn't have time for the beach.

I let her into the garden instead, pinching one of her grubby, mauled toys between my forefinger and thumb – I think it started out life as a badger – and flinging it deep into the grass so Wilma bounded after it, scattering the birds on the bird table. Then, with a sense of foreboding, I reached into my bag for my phone.

Sixty-three emails since lunch. No rest and all that. I suspect, even if it had been my own father's funeral, Gideon would continue to clog my inbox with very minor queries he could answer himself if he engaged his brain. I scrolled through to work out what I could ignore until tomorrow and what I had to answer now. Most were from him. One said that Linzi's letter of instruction had come back and that we had to 'press on' with petitioning Larry's lawyer before they filed first, plus a few about other, ongoing cases. I needed to reread a prenup we'd been working on for a client whose daughter was engaged to her personal trainer, and send Gideon my notes ahead of a meeting with another potential client the following afternoon.

This was with a character called Prince Rudolf III, a member of the Liechtenstein royal family, who lived in London and had recently separated from his wife. He'd emailed Gideon the previous week asking for a meeting and I'd spent the afternoon researching him. Previously, if you'd asked me to stick a pin into Liechtenstein on a map, I'm not sure I could have done.

Now I knew it was a tiny principality sandwiched between Austria and Switzerland. I'd also discovered that it was the world's biggest producer of false teeth and its royal family was the richest in Europe. Prince Rudolf was one of the younger members. At thirty-four he was only a year older than me, and had married his German wife – Wilhelmina, Countess von Holstein-Frankfurter-Schleswig, in a royal wedding a decade before. This had been splashed all over the papers and attended by every British royal, along with American presidents and Omani sultans. But now it was over because, according to a piece I'd read online, Countess Wilhelmina had discovered him shagging the nanny.

I'd relayed all this to Gideon who'd booked a meeting with Prince Rudolf for an initial discussion. He'd made it very clear that we needed to land such a high-profile case, that my potential promotion to partner relied on it.

A scratch at the kitchen door made me look up, so I let Wilma back in and we sat companionably until Mum appeared back downstairs.

She opened the fridge. 'How hungry are you?'

'Not very.'

'FAMISHED,' came a shout from the sitting room next door. Mum ignored this while pulling various packets and vegetables out, then started chopping on the side. Wilma moved to sit at her feet and gazed hopefully upwards. At the smell of fried onions, Dad wandered through.

'What you making, love?'

'Bolognese.'

'Great stuff, I might open a bottle. Nell?'

'No, I'm good thanks.'

Dad pulled a bottle from the rack and uncorked it and poured himself a glass.

'Do you know what I was thinking today, pet?'

'Mmm?'

'Are you sure you don't want to get married at the hall?'

At the cooker, Mum cleared her throat while I dropped my phone back into my bag. 'Dad, you joking?'

'No,' he replied, eyes wide. 'I know, you and Gus have all your beliefs and whatnot. But I was just thinking, today, in that church, it would be a smashing day, leading you down the aisle in there. Didn't you always dream of that when you were small? I'm sure Art wouldn't mind, if he doesn't sell it, that is.'

'Dad, come on, I've told you, we're not doing it.'

'I'll have a word with him if you like.'

'With Gus?'

'No, with Art.'

'Dad! Enough. No, thank you. How many times do we have to have this conversation?'

Plenty, apparently. And although I trotted out the lines from my well-rehearsed script, every now and then a little voice in my head queried whether it might actually be easier just to get married. Nice, even? Plenty of friends in London had got married and their lives hadn't spontaneously combusted as a result. But then I thought about attempting that conversation with Gus and dismissed it. At the last wedding we'd gone to, he'd squeezed my hand and whispered 'I love you more' to me as the couple at the top of the aisle – law school friends – said their vows, and

I'd been reassured all over again. He loved me, we'd made the right choice for us.

But still Dad persisted. 'All I'm saying is your poor old man wouldn't mind some grandchildren one day and if getting married means tha—'

'We've gone over this. You can have children without being married nowadays. It's even legal.'

'But what will they be called, pet?'

'I'm sure we'll work it out.'

'Because I've been thinking about this and you can't saddle a child with both your names. Poor little Mason-Bickerton will get the living daylights kicked out of him at school.'

I inhaled before replying. 'OK, thank you, I'll pass on these concerns to Gus.'

I called him from my old bedroom after dinner, so Mum and Dad couldn't overhear. Below me, the floor vibrated with the murmurings of the ten o'clock news which Dad always watched from his armchair. Mum had gone to bed with a book.

'Hello my little *sonnenblümchen*, how was it?'

Sunflower, that meant.

'Hi sweetheart, and all right,' I said, lying back on my bed, deciding I wouldn't mention Art. No point in raising the topic when he and I had only spoken for three seconds.

The previous night, in London while packing for the funeral, Gus had asked if I'd speak to him. Keeping my eyes on my suitcase, I'd replied 'maybe', and hoped that he wouldn't ask any follow-up questions. Fortunately, he didn't.

Gus knew about Art because I'd told him everything when we

met. I'd explained our childhood, the sweetness of our teenage relationship and what had happened because, at that point, I was still so hurt by it – a bird with a broken wing. But then Gus helped mend me and I'd stopped mentioning him because that period of my life seemed so distant. Art became one of those private topics which occasionally lurked in my head but I avoided talking about aloud. I had nothing to hide, it was just ancient history.

'You sound wiped.'

'I'm all right. Just a long day. But the service was fine, tea afterwards, then we came back here. How was your day?'

Sometimes I thought this is what all relationships came down to, each member of a couple asking the other how their day was.

Gus talked about Google while I blinked at the glow-in-the-dark stars Dad had stuck on my bedroom ceiling when I was eight.

'How are the folks?' Gus asked, having got work out the way.

'The same. Dad drank too much sherry. Interrogated me about getting married again.'

'What did you tell him?'

'What I always told him, that we're not doing it.'

'Good. I don't understand why your parents still can't get their head around it.'

I felt myself bridling in defence of Dad, my split loyalty going into reverse; I'd defended Gus in the kitchen, now it was Dad's turn. Did this happen in all families, and with all relationships, or was it just mine?

'I know but it's different for them. Everyone in their generation got married. And they only want us to be happy.'

'We are happy!'

'I know, course we are, it's just... yeah, a generational thing. Actually, talking of family, would you mind being in charge of dinner tomorrow night for Jack and his new girlfriend?'

'As it happens, I've already bought the lamb. Has he paid you back that money yet, by the way?'

Towards the end of last year, when Jack was between jobs, he'd asked me for a loan. 'Just a short-term loan, sis. I'll pay you back as soon as I can.'

I'd found it impossible to refuse. Although my brother still infuriated me, I'd started to feel guilt, over the years, that while I'd built myself a life – good job, my own place, stable relationship – he had none of those things, drifting from office to office and from one dingy Gumtree flat to the next. So I'd agreed, but he'd started his new job in January and hadn't mentioned the £10,000 again. I didn't mind so much; I'd remind him about the money at some point, but Gus had become increasingly wound-up about it.

'No, no he hasn't,' I replied as casually as I could.

Gus sighed. 'Nell, he can't drift through life like this. Honestly, it's not just your parents. You're too soft on him as well.'

'I know, I know, but can we not have this conversation now? I need to get some sleep before this Liechtenstein meeting tomorrow.'

It was such a subtle relationship irritation: I was allowed to grumble about my family but I'd still defend them against any criticism from Gus.

'Absolutely,' he replied. 'Has he officially instructed you?'

'Nope, Gideon's hoping he will after the meeting.'

'Course he will because my brilliant and dazzling girlfriend will convince him.'

'Something like that.' I smiled down the phone and then yawned. 'OK, I think that's my bedtime.'

'Go to sleep. Love you.'

'Love you too. See you tomorrow.'

We hung up and I remained motionless for a few moments, staring at the stars. Were they making me feel nostalgic for my childhood or was it the day as a whole? I could sense emotions I'd kept buried for years trying to surface like flotsam. Either that, or Mum had put too much Lea and Perrins in her Bolognese.

***

She was already in the kitchen the next morning when I came down. Dad had offered to drive me to the station the previous evening but Mum insisted it was her turn since he'd picked me up.

'Sorry,' I said, wincing when she turned round from the sink. 'Early, I know.'

'Don't be silly. I've made you some toast.' She peeled off her rubber gloves and reached for a tinfoil packet on the side. 'Marmite.'

I didn't want to say that I didn't eat breakfast, normally just inhaled Queenie's cafetière at my desk, so I took the packet and slid it into my bag, hoping that it wouldn't leak all over the documents I needed to read before my meeting. 'Thanks.'

Wilma got up from the dog bed and came towards me, but I jumped aside, having put a clean suit on. I imagined the scene when I reached Gideon's office later that day: 'Hello, Prince Rudolf, lovely to meet you, please forgive the dog dribble on my skirt and the stench of Marmite, I came from my parents' madhouse in Northumberland this morning.'

I couldn't wait to get back to London.

We climbed in the car and Mum reversed around Dad's old Jeep, dodging a chicken which clucked in outrage as it ran out of the way.

'Stupid thing,' muttered Mum. Then she reached out and turned Radio 2 off. 'Can't be doing with her in the mornings.'

'You all right?' I glanced sideways at her.

'Fine,' she said, as we bumped down the track to the main road. I glanced left as we reached the junction, an old habit. Left was the way to Art's drive.

'OK, just check—'

'Although since you mention it, there is something I want to talk to you about.'

Mum's tone was breezy but I recognized this tactic: it meant she was about to raise something serious. We only had serious conversations in our family when they were absolutely necessary – when Jack had been fired again, or when Mum thought Dad was drinking too much.

This morning, I suspected, would be why I really should think about children sooner rather than later. Or perhaps about being nice to Jack's new girlfriend, which would irritate me most of all. I was always nice to them. It was the way *he* treated them that was the problem.

'Mum?' I said, when she didn't continue.

'I've decided to leave your dad,' she announced breezily, as if she'd just announced she was off to the Spar for more milk.

'WHAT?'

'Yes, I've thought about it for months now, and I've had enough. That's it.'

'That's IT?'

She nodded and kept her eyes on the road. 'Yes, that's it.'

'Mum, what… how come… I don't get why all of a sudden? What are you going to do? Where are you going to go?'

'I'll be all right, and so will he, after he's worked out how to use the washing machine. I've spent all my life looking after him, and you and your brother, and now I want to do something for me.'

'Like what?'

'I don't know! Travelling, ballroom dancing, learning Italian.'

'Ballroom dancing? Leaning Italian? Mum, are you having an affair with Bruno Tonioli?'

'Don't be silly. He plays for the other team, anyway. I just fancy doing something different. I've had enough of cooking dinner for your dad every night, of every night being the same, every day being the same, the boredom, the lack of passion! Do you know what that man got me for my birthday?'

'No,' I said, with a pang of guilt. Her birthday was last month, in February, but I'd failed to make it home because work was taking up too much time. I'd sent a bunch of lilies with an apologetic note.

'A leaf blower,' said Mum, smacking her hand on the steering wheel. 'A leaf blower! What sort of present is that? It's not even autumn.'

'Perhaps he thought you wanted to get into gardening?' I ventured, although this didn't even convince me. Dad always forgot our birthdays when Jack and I were kids, leaving all the organizing to Mum, but even by his standards a leaf blower was a truly pathetic present.

'No. I'm sorry, Nell, but I need more than this. I'm not spending the next twenty years of my life lying in that bed listening to the racing predictions every morning!'

I glanced through my window at the pink sunrise while digesting her announcement. 'Is this why you were so insistent that I come home for the funeral? So you could tell me?'

She sniffed. 'No. I thought you should come to the funeral anyway.'

'Have you mentioned anything to Dad?'

'I'm not sure it'll come as a huge surprise. Do you know when your father and I last made love?'

'No, and shall we leave that as a rhetorical question?' I glanced at my watch: 7.03 a.m., too early to be discussing my parents' sex life.

'It was Christmas Eve four years ago, after we got back from the Drummonds' party and he'd had too much mulled wine. And it wasn't exactly memorable bec—'

'No thank you! I take your point. But marriages aren't just about sex, Mum. You've been married for, what, nearly forty years. Why give that all up now? I don't get it.'

This wasn't wholly true. The rational part of me understood completely why Mum wanted to go, was almost relieved that she was going to do something about the listless, loveless atmosphere at home, so she and Dad didn't simply coexist in silence, a war of attrition that dragged on for years until one of them conked it. But my emotions were cloudier than they would have been at work where I told clients they didn't have to stay trapped in the same relationship for ever. Because my parents being apart, leading separate lives: what would that even look like? The idea of Mum breaking it to Dad, his face crumpling, made my chest constrict.

'There's got to be more than this,' said Mum, more quietly, which was an argument I also understood. She'd lived in Northcliffe for the past four decades, and apart from the odd holiday to Europe, her life had been Dad, us, horses and dogs. I'd wanted to leave. Why shouldn't she?

There was silence in the car for a few minutes as we drove through Morpeth, then sat at the lights before pulling into the station.

'You going to tell Jack?'

Mum found a parking space and swivelled in her seat, an optimistic look on her face. 'I thought if you were seeing him tonight, you could give him the news? I don't want to upset him. You're much better at this sort of thing than me.'

'At what?' I felt a flare of anger at the idea she couldn't even give this news to her own son.

'Divorce and that sort of caper.'

'It's divorce now?'

She flung her hands in the air. 'I don't know. I've just had enough.'

'Who'll get Wilma?' I said pathetically, feeling more like a child than a thirty-three-year-old.

'We'll work all that out. Now go on, you'll miss your train.' Mum leant over and kissed my cheek and, although I could have sat there and asked a million more questions (where would they both live? How was she going to support herself? What about the chickens?), I opened the door and climbed out.

***

The coffee they served on the train was so disgusting I ate my Marmite toast to disguise the taste. Then I tried to concentrate on my notes about Prince Rudolf but my thoughts kept stubbornly returning to Mum's surprise announcement. Honestly, a leaf blower. What was Dad thinking?

It was while looking up the article about Prince Rudolf's affair with the nanny (important research), that another headline in the sidebar of shame jumped out at me: 'LORD SPENDTHRIFT!' it shouted, beside a little photo of a familiar face.

It was Lord Drummond, an old picture, but definitely him. I clicked on the link and the picture grew big on my phone screen, above a long obituary which detailed Lord Drummond's runaway spending on horses and cars, and included a source saying he'd been 'flogging the family silver' in the past few years to pay for repairs to Drummond Hall.

I scrolled further down, freezing at a picture of Art and Nicole at a charity party in New York. 'His only son, Arthur, is married to New York banking heiress, Nicole Cargill, whose father, Robert, is a scion of the Cargill banking family,' went on the story. 'Their family worth is an estimated $240m but it's unclear whether the new Lord Drummond will have access to these funds.'

It wasn't the only picture of them. There were several, all

very similar: Art in black tie, Nicole in a succession of dazzling floor-length dresses – a feathery dress, a sequin dress, a silver dress which shone like a mermaid's tail. There he was again with Nicole at something called the White Ball at the Rockefeller Center, the Young Fellows Ball at The Frick Collection, the Art Gala at The Met and so on and so on. They sounded like the sort of glamorous fundraisers I'd watched on *Sex and the City* and yet they were real parties, here was the evidence: Art and Nicole pressed together, the perfect all-American couple, both beaming at the camera with blinding white smiles. There was one with Felix too, at a charity baseball game, Art's hand resting protectively on his shoulder. According to a *Vanity Fair* article cited in the obituary, he and Nicole came in at number 41 on the magazine's list of 'Hottest Power Couples'.

All right, I'd googled Art before, once or twice. But not for years. And back then, all I'd found was a link to the Cargill bank website showing a smiling, professional Art in a suit, along with another link to an obscure website about the British aristocracy which detailed Art's family tree. Plus his LinkedIn profile, but I hadn't dared click on that because a colleague once told me that the person in question could tell if you'd been snooping on them. Then I'd deleted my search history, guilty as if I'd been watching porn, and sworn not to indulge in such online self-harm again. I'd never come across any of these society photos, which seemed to confirm the criticism about Art that I'd heard in the pub, that he led a tuxedo life of champagne and had quite forgotten about Northcliffe.

On the upside, the piece distracted me from thinking about the leaf blower.

Chapter 4

I ARRIVED IN LONDON a few hours later and caught the Tube straight down to Holborn. Outside the office, idling in the road, was an enormous blacked-out Bentley. This wasn't an unusual sight; clients often had cars that were worth more than my salary, only the number plate of this one gave its owner away: RUD0LF3.

Rosemary smiled over her desk as I hurried past and made for the lift. 'Morning, Eleanor, he's on the hunt for you.'

'Course he is, thank you,' I said, rolling my eyes.

'Good afternoon,' Gideon boomed, when I swept into our office, his attempt at a joke since it was 11.51 a.m.

I dropped my bag at my desk and replied coolly: 'Morning. You ready? His car's outside.'

Gideon sat up straighter and ruffled his hair with his sausage fingers. 'What? Yes, course. I've been ready for hours. Where have you been?'

'Up north, for that funeral. I got the first train this morning.' I slid the file I needed from my bag, picked up a pen and raised my eyebrows. 'Shall we go down?'

'Of course you did, of course,' he replied, his jowls shaking like jelly. 'Right, yes, will you call Rosemary?'

I leant over my desk and buzzed downstairs to say could she let Prince Rudolf up to the boardroom when he came in, then Gideon swept out and I followed.

Once there, he took his usual position at the top of the table while I stood behind a chair to his left. I always liked the board-room and its priceless wallpaper, where some of the biggest divorce cases in the world had been settled. Last year, I'd watched Gideon negotiate a £400m settlement for one of our clients, who'd been formerly married to Putin's second-in-command. She'd sent him a Rolex studded with sixty tiny diamonds as a thank you.

'Ask me what time it is,' Gideon now often demanded during quiet moments in our office.

I'd sigh but oblige, knowing what was coming.

'Three diamonds past the hour,' he'd reply, before barking with laughter at his own joke.

That same client sent me a jar of honey, which wasn't quite the same, although it did come from Harrods Food Hall.

'We should bow when he arrives,' Gideon instructed. 'Or, no, that's not right. I bow, you curtsy.'

'Gideon, it's the twenty-first century. I'm not sure we have to act the servile peasants. He's a client like anyone else.'

'Potential client,' he snapped, 'and I think we should. First impressions and all th—'

He was interrupted by the arrival of the prince, ushered into the boardroom by a trainee.

'Thank you, er…' blustered Gideon, scrabbling to his feet.

'Sarah,' squeaked the trainee.

'Yes, thank you, Sarah. And Prince Rudolf, how do you do? Gideon Fotheringham, at your service.' At this, Gideon cocked his arm at a right angle in front of his waistband and slowly bent over it. When he came back up, the exertion had turned his face pinker than usual. He looked like a boiled ham.

Prince Rudolf stood in the doorway with an amused smile. 'I'm very well, thank you,' he said, extending a hand towards him.

They shook and he turned to me. 'And you are?'

I refused to curtsy. This was a London boardroom not Versailles. 'Prince Rudolf, morning, I'm Eleanor Mason, senior associate in the family department. I work under Gideon.'

'Lucky Gideon,' he drawled. 'And it's Rudy, please.'

He was more attractive than he'd looked on the internet. Well over six foot, he had a tanned, broad face from which brown curls were lightly gelled back. These curls flicked up over the collar of a pale blue shirt which was undone a couple of buttons to reveal a triangle of similarly tanned chest. He looked like a cowboy who'd just pulled off his chaps and got dressed for a meeting.

I suddenly needed to sit down.

'Coffee, Prince Rudolf, I mean, Rudy?' asked Gideon.

'Please,' he replied, suavely undoing his suit jacket with one hand and draping it over the back of a chair.

'Eleanor, can you organize that? I'll have a cappuccino.'

'Sure,' I said, leaning on the table and picking up the phone to ring downstairs. 'Morning, Queenie, could you possibly send Carmelita up with a cappuccino, a black Americano and...' I glanced at Prince Rudolf.

'An Americano sounds good,' he said, smiling. He had a European accent with undertones of an American twang, which made sense: I knew from my research that, having grown up in Liechtenstein, he'd been sent to a Swiss boarding school aged eight and gone on to university in the States.

'Two black Americanos, please,' I said back into the phone, 'in the boardroom?'

Sarah the trainee left, closed the double doors behind her, and we sat.

'My wife tells me she's hired the best,' Prince Rudolf announced, suddenly more businesslike.

Gideon smiled. 'She can't have done because that would be us. But I presume you mean she's gone to Farrers?'

Prince Rudolf nodded.

'They're not a problem,' Gideon replied smoothly. 'You are in excellent hands here. I'm exceptionally good at divorce because I've been through it twice myself, ha ha!'

Prince Rudolf didn't laugh. Instead, he turned to me.

'And what about you?'

'Me? What do you mean?' I almost squinted when my eyes met his because of all the handsomeness. It was like trying to look directly at the sun.

'Are you married?'

'No, no, Eleanor doesn't believe in marriage,' interrupted Gideon. 'She's frightfully modern. Now, look, just as a preliminary chat, I think what we should do is run through your situation, clarify a few details.'

Prince Rudolf dragged his eyes from me to Gideon and leant forwards on the table. 'Of course.'

'So you and Countess Wilhelmina have been married for ten years, that is correct?'

He nodded.

'You have three children?'

'Yes. Prince Ludwig, Prince Karl and Princess Theodora – nine, seven and five.'

While they spoke, I wrote notes as usual.

'Who live and are educated in the UK?'

Another nod.

'You're resident in London, and have been for the duration of your marriage?'

'Yes.'

'And this separation has been prompted beca—'

'It isn't my fault!' said Prince Rudolf, a crinkle rippling his tanned forehead. 'My wife and I have been distant for years. The papers have made me out to be some sort of playboy!'

'Oh, the papers. Ignore them, we have people who can make them go quiet. But we do need to know if there's any truth to the reports? Any truth at all. It's very important that we know all there is to know. No secrets. But no judgement here, I myself have be—'

'Pffft! There has been the occasional dalliance. You know?'

Gideon nodded. He did know.

'But nothing serious. It is only because Willy is so cold. If she hadn't driven me to it, if she hadn't *made* me…'

'I quite understand,' said Gideon.

I noted this down while clenching my jaw at the idea that his wife had physically driven him into the arms of his children's nanny. This made him seem a bit less handsome.

After a knock at the door, Carmelita came in with a tray carrying the coffees.

'Thanks, Carm. Cappuccino for Gideon and the others for us,' I said, nodding at Prince Rudolf.

She handed them out and left a plate of shortbread on the table before closing the door behind her.

'The issue is,' went on Gideon, 'and you might already know this, but in British courts, one party has to admit fault, and there are grounds here for your wife to claim adultery. It shouldn't affect the financial decision, of course. By and large the court isn't interested in why a marriage ends, only that the assets are divided fairly.'

'Pffft!' Prince Rudolf repeated. 'She can claim adultery. I only want to resolve the financial situation quickly and discreetly.'

'Right, let's discuss that,' said Gideon. 'If you instruct us, we will send you a form that you need to fill in, a financial declaration form, divulging all assets. All assets, here and worldwide, you understand?'

Another nod.

The Mail had reported that he was worth £50m but newspapers usually got these figures wrong, underestimating our clients' actual worth since much of their money was hidden offshore, in trusts, tied up in complicated structures designed precisely to avoid it being easily discoverable. Every spring, the *Sunday Times* published the Rich List and, every spring, Spinks was inundated with calls and emails from clients asking what they could do to remove themselves from the list because they didn't want their financial details printed.

Prince Rudolf started listing his properties off on his fingers so quickly my scribbling could hardly keep up.

'There is our house in Kensington Gardens, an apartment in Chelsea, the house in Oxfordshire, in Scotland, an apartment in New York and Paris. Oh and the chalet in Zermatt. Plus a castle at home in Liechtenstein, but that technically belongs to my father.'

'Excellent, that doesn't have to be included, in that case. So long as your name isn't on the deeds. And as for trusts and liquid assets?'

Prince Rudolf fluttered his lips and looked as if he was trying to work out a sum in his head. 'Probably around two hundred million.'

'Pounds?' asked Gideon, hopefully.

'No no, only euros.'

'Right, well, you'll have to disclose all this in the form that Eleanor will send you, so long as you instruct us, of course, and then we'll go from there. Unless there's anything else you want to ask?'

'How long will all this take?'

Gideon leant back in his chair and opened his arms. 'That's almost impossible to tell right now. Some take eight or nine months. Some take eight or nine years.'

'*Years?*' Prince Rudolf's eyes became golf balls.

'It won't come to that. Let's hope this is all very easy and straightforward.'

'I will offer her the house in London and, say, ten million euros.' He paused. 'And the dog.'

'A very generous offer,' Gideon said soothingly. 'So if your secretary could look out for our formal letter of instruction and get it sent back, signed, later today, my colleague and I will get started. Important to maintain the upper hand in these situations.'

Prince Rudolf nodded and stood to put on his suit jacket.

Gideon did the same. 'Good to meet you. Eleanor will show you out.'

The boardroom was on the first floor, so I directed him downstairs and followed behind.

'You don't believe in marriage?' Prince Rudolf asked, pausing halfway and glancing back at me, his eyes dropping to my left hand.

'Er, no, not really. Occupational hazard,' I joked feebly, gesturing around me at the office.

He raised his eyes to mine and smiled. 'But you have a boyfriend?'

'Er, yes, yes, I do believe in those.'

'Then I do not understand why he doesn't want to pin down someone as beautiful as you?'

Clients occasionally flirted with me. Some men moved faster than a lion on his lunch break. Sure, they were going through a divorce, but they didn't let that stop them from asking me personal questions or if I was free for dinner 'to go over their case'. I'd politely decline their kind offer and that was that. But few had been quite as overt as Prince Rudolf.

'You should see me first thing in the morning,' I blurted, before realizing this was exactly not what to say to the flirty European standing on the stairs in front of me.

'If only,' he replied, before turning and carrying on down the stairs. 'But you have a boyfriend just as I become single again, Eleanor, that's too bad.'

I laughed this off, aware that Rosemary could hear us from her desk beneath the stairs.

When we reached the bottom, I held my hand out. 'Thank you very much for coming in. I'll be in touch later today.'

He took it and held it for a few seconds too many, skimming his thumb over the back of my palm, slowly and deliberately, while looking into my eyes. 'I hope so. A woman who's going to get me out of trouble instead of vice versa. That makes a pleasant change.'

Then he grinned and, without waiting for an answer, stepped outside to where his Bentley was waiting.

When I turned to make my way to the lift, Rosemary chuckled. The woman had the ears of a bat. 'What'll that one be then – Prince Charming?'

She was referring to my habit of nicknaming clients. Previously I'd dubbed a difficult Texan oil tycoon Forrest Grump because he never said please or thank you, and used to slam down the phone without saying goodbye. Before him there'd been Candy Man, the German Haribo heir who used to slide sugary packets of the stuff across the boardroom table at Gideon and me as if he thought they were bribes. I'd called the duke who was divorcing his second wife Colonel Mustard, since he only ever wore yellow socks, and the Russian woman who gave Gideon his Rolex was Ursula because she only wore black but with scarlet lipstick, like the *Little Mermaid* baddie. Some of our clients were pleasant enough but plenty were monstrous and I'd discovered some years before that nicknames helped make them less menacing, more human.

Gideon didn't know about this. Rosemary was the only colleague I let in on the secret since I wasn't sure anybody else would find it very funny.

I leant on Rosemary's desk and frowned over the top of it. 'Prince Charming seems too nice, somehow.'

'He's easy on the eye.'

I glanced down at my hand, at the spot that he'd rubbed with his thumb. 'I know but there's something a bit… creepy about him.'

'Hmmm. Prince Pervy?'

'Prince *Pervert*?'

She nodded. 'Works for me.'

Back upstairs, I wrote and emailed the letter of instruction to Prince Pervert's secretary and, after lunch, spent the entire afternoon redrafting the prenup.

***

By the time I got home that night, having wrestled my suitcase on and off the Northern line with eight billion others, Jack and his new girlfriend were already sitting on the sofa while Gus cooked.

I'd WhatsApped my brother earlier admitting that I couldn't remember what she was called, and telling him to come over any time from seven.

'Cool, sis. And it's Emma. She's a climatarian. Hope that's OK.'

'What is that?' I'd texted back.

'Only eats food that doesn't hurt the planet,' he replied. 'Like lentils and stuff. And no meat.'

I forwarded this information to Gus who immediately panicked about his Ottolenghi moussaka. He was obsessed with Ottolenghi. Five minutes later, he sent me an email saying he'd found a vegan moussaka recipe online which used mushrooms instead of lamb, 'so long as mushrooms don't hurt the planet?'

I replied that mushrooms were probably pretty blameless.

'Hi, darling, drink?' Gus asked, as I closed the door behind me.

I laughed when he turned round from the hob. Over his work shirt and suit trousers, he was wearing the apron I'd put in his stocking last Christmas: 'No bitchin' in my kitchen', it said on the front.

'You having one?' It was a week night but, if Gus and I agreed, we were allowed to break our rule. Dinner with Jack was often one of those occasions.

Gus nodded.

'Go on then, yes, please,' I said, snaking my arm around his waist and kissing his cheek. 'But I can do it. And Emma, hello, nice to meet you, so sorry you beat me here. Mad day.'

'That's all right,' she said, remaining in place on the sofa so I waved awkwardly from the fridge. Climatarians were obviously allowed to drink red wine since she was holding a large glass of it.

'Hey, bro, how's it going?' I asked my brother. His feet were on the coffee table which annoyed me, but I couldn't have a go yet. I'd been in the flat for under two minutes, that would be a record.

'All good. How was the funeral?'

I was about to put the cork back in the wine bottle but at the mention of this I sloshed another inch into my glass. 'Anyone need a top-up?'

They shook their heads.

I slid the bottle into the fridge. 'It was fine. All the old faces were there, had lunch in the Duck, tea at the hall afterwards. Not much to report.'

On the Tube home, I'd mulled over how to tell Jack about our parents. Was this really the moment, the evening he'd brought his new girlfriend over for supper? I glanced at Emma, who was exactly his type, which is to say almost indistinguishable from his last girlfriend. She was blonde and so thin that her head looked disproportionately large to her body, with big eyes and lashes like spiders' legs. Young, too. She had to be in her mid-twenties, tops, and Jack was thirty-five.

'Did you see Art?'

'Mmmhmm,' I said, before swallowing a large mouthful of wine.

Behind me, Gus made a pained yelp.

'You all right?' I asked, spinning around.

'Grated my finger,' he replied, holding it close to his face, 'but I'll live. Might even add a little something to the recipe, grated finger.' Then his eyes widened in alarm. 'Just joking, Emma. There's no meat in this.'

I smiled across the kitchen at him in a silent moment of reassurance, for his finger and for Jack raising the topic of Art.

'How was he?' my brother persevered.

It was typical of him to ask something he knew would needle me so soon. He did this every time we saw one another. Every time I'd thought to myself, 'Give your brother another shot. He's not a total dickhead, and he's your only brother, you love him really. Just have him over for dinner and have a nice evening, prove that you can go a whole evening without wanting to commit murder.'

But every time he ruined it. I glanced at the kitchen clock. Here we were, under five minutes in and I could sense the irritation that only a sibling can provoke surging inside me. 'Seemed fine, I didn't speak to him for very long.'

'What's he going to do with the place?'

'Not sure.'

'D'you think he'll sell it? Got to be worth a bit, that place, and all the land. I would if I were him.'

'Jack, I spoke to him for less than two minutes and said I was sorry about his dad. We didn't get into the intricacies of his inheritance.'

'Wonder if I should ring him,' mused Jack. 'Might be able to get some sort of deal. The commission on that sale would be epic. I could retire, probably.'

'Who's Art?' squeaked Emma.

'Old friend,' I replied, before turning back to the cooker and changing the subject. 'Gus, can I do anything? Can I lay the table? Oh no, it's laid already. Anything else?'

But Jack wasn't going to let the topic go so easily. 'He's the boy Nell was obsessed with when we were younger. He was my mate, really, at home where we grew up in Northumberland. But she always tagged after us because she worshipped him, like, was borderline weird about it. She used to keep photos of him under her pillow.'

'Aww, cute,' said Emma.

'Jack…' I warned.

'And then he broke her heart and she cried for about five years.'

'Aww, no, that's sad. How did he do that?'

'Never mind,' I said sharply, putting my wine glass down on the table. 'I have some news: Mum's leaving Dad.'

'WHAT?' shouted Jack.

'What?' said Gus.

'Aww, no!' added Emma.

'Mum told me this morning. Dad doesn't actually know yet. She's just decided she's had enough.'

Jack's face twisted with scorn. 'Of *what*?'

I shrugged. 'Home life with Dad, I think, the sameness of it all.'

'Why now? Is Dad having an affair? Oh Christ, he's not banging the old bat who runs the vet's, is he?'

'Is your mum all right?' asked Gus, turning round from the oven.

'Think so, and no, Dad isn't having an affair. Not that I know of, anyway. I think Mum just wants to do something different.'

'Then she should take up bridge or knitting!' exclaimed Jack. 'That's what old people do, isn't it? They don't need to get divorced.'

'My parents had their ruby anniversary last summer,' said Emma. 'Forty years.'

'Brilliant, well done them,' I said, slugging back more wine. Very grateful we decided to drink tonight.

'And where's she going to live?' added Jack. 'And why are *you* telling me this?'

'I don't know, I don't know!' I said, the surge of sibling irritation climbing higher. 'But you know what our parents are like about discussing things. Mum told me this morning in the car and I said I'd pass it on to you. But she hasn't told Dad yet, so can we just keep it between us? I'll ring her tomorrow and get the latest.'

'Blimey,' said Jack, leaning back on the sofa.

'Aww, you all right, sweetheart?' asked Emma, stroking his head.

'Yeah, it's just… weird. My parents are separating.'

'Aww, it'll be all right, baby,' she said, pressing his face to her chest. 'I'll look after you.'

I reached for the wine again. 'Baby' was an unacceptable pet name for someone you were having sex with.

'Dinner's ready!' announced Gus.

I quizzed Emma while we ate Gus's vegan moussaka (slightly watery, if I was being picky, but he was sensitive to any perceived lack of enthusiasm towards his cooking so we all made enthusiastic noises). She was young, just twenty-three, and a student studying Shoe Design at the London College of Fashion. She wanted to launch a vegan shoe line when she graduated, and lived in a Bermondsey flat that Jack had leased her via his estate agency. That's how they'd met.

'Your bosses know that you're offering client perks?' Gus teased.

'What they don't know won't hurt them,' Jack replied, with a grin. This was a theory he applied to all relationships in his life – personal and professional.

'How long have you two been together?' asked Emma, as I reached for the water jug.

'Eleven years,' I replied, grinning at Gus.

'Eleven! How come you're not married?'

I wondered whether eleven was also the number of brain cells that Emma was blessed with. Why do people think it's acceptable to ask such an intimate question about others' relationships having only just met? I didn't go around the place asking people about their sex lives.

'We don't believe in it,' went on Gus, before I could reply.

'What d'you mean?' she went on, with a tinkly laugh. 'You never want to get married, wear the big dress, have the party, all that?' She gazed at me with wide-eyed astonishment, so maybe not even eleven brain cells. Maybe more like six or seven. Perhaps being a climatarian wasn't *that* good for you after all.

'That's exactly what we don't want,' explained Gus, jumping in again. 'It's an artificial invention, marrying for romantic love, only made popular by the Victorians. And all those big weddings, honestly, they're a waste of money and effort.' He reached for my hand. 'We don't feel like we need it, do we?'

I shook my head and smiled at Emma.

'Goodness,' she said, as if this news had shattered everything she'd previously thought about the world. Then she turned to Jack. 'Do you not believe in marriage either?'

Jack laughed this off and kissed the top of her head, then slyly changed the topic back to me. 'I always thought you wanted to get married at Drummond Hall, sis?'

'What's that?' said Emma.

'Home, where we used to live, where Nell's crush lived, in this massive pile overlooking the sea. Come on, admit it, you did always dream of getting married there.'

'No I didn't! Why does everyone keep saying this? Can we just forget it?'

'All right, all right, touchy subject,' said Jack, which made me want to give him a dead arm, partly because it was true. My trip home, seeing the church and the hall again, had unlocked a wave of nostalgia which I was fighting to shut down. My thoughts kept replaying two moments: watching Art at the lectern, and speaking to him afterwards. I'd expected seeing him to be difficult, to make me angry, but it hadn't. Instead, I felt an old, familiar longing to have spent more time in his company, exactly as I'd wished as a teenager. But I just needed another couple of days in London to push these thoughts down. It always took time for the dust to settle, after a trip back to Northcliffe, to feel more like London me again. What I didn't need was Jack banging on about him.

'You wouldn't be able to anyway, if he sells the place,' he went on. 'I'm definitely going to give him a bell about that. You still got his number?'

'No, obviously not. Why would I have his number?' I felt for Gus's knee under the table and squeezed it.

'Chill out, just asking. I'll get it some other way. And on that note, we'd better be heading home.' Jack pushed his chair back and stood up. 'Thanks for dinner, Gus.'

'Lovely to meet you,' I said to Emma as she pulled on a pink coat that made her look like a stick of candy floss.

'You too,' she squeaked. It was like communicating with a mouse.

I turned to Jack and gave him a brief hug. 'I'll keep you posted on the parents.'

'Yeah, could you? I'll try and ring Mum tomorrow. Work's so mad at the moment.'

He always claimed this, that he was 'too hectic' to do anything like ring his parents or go to a family funeral, even though he worked from 10 a.m. until 5 p.m. in an estate agency where he also managed to fit in time to seduce the prospective tenants. No mention of my loan, either, which I suspected Gus would bring up later. Still, at least we'd ticked off the sibling catch-up for another month or so.

Gus let them out while I cleared the table of smeary wine glasses and loaded the dishwasher. I was often weary after an evening spent in Jack's company, but tonight I was so tired I could hardly stand.

'Why don't I run you a bath?' Gus said, coming back upstairs and kissing the top of my head.

I leant into him. 'Thank you for everything.' This was my way of apologizing for the subject of Art coming up. Sometimes I found it oddly difficult to talk about my emotions with Gus; if he'd done something to annoy me, I could have whole conversations with him in my head but find it impossible to get the words out of my mouth. I'd lie there in bed, willing myself to say them. How hard could it be? They were just words. But it often felt like I'd gone mute. At work I could talk to clients about the most intimate details of their marriages; at home, when it related to me, I found it much harder. I suppose it was an inherited trait; Mum and Dad avoided sensitive topics and I'd learned to do the same.

He kissed my head again. 'Don't be silly, you're mine to look after. No mention of the loan, I noticed.'

I sighed and stepped back. 'I know, it just wasn't the moment.'

Gus pulled a face.

'What?'

'He'll have to pay it back at some point.'

'What's the big deal? Course he will.'

'I just don't want you being taken advantage of, that's all.'

'I'm not! He'll pay it back.'

'OK, OK. Let me go run that bath.'

I lay in the hot water and felt emotions bounce around inside me like lottery balls. I couldn't tell if it was seeing Art, my mother's declaration of independence, dinner with Jack, or Gus carping on about the loan, but I knew that sleep, back in my own bed, would help restore things to a more normal equilibrium.

I climbed under the duvet in my damp dressing gown and turned on my side to see Gus undressing and carefully laying his trousers in his beloved trouser press. Oh no. He was getting into bed without his briefs on. This was a clue.

'I missed you,' he said, sliding towards me, under the duvet.

'Me too,' I said, using the sleepiest voice I could. If I could demonstrate that I was too tired rather than actually saying I was too tired, that would be a more diplomatic way out.

One of Gus's hands slipped underneath my dressing gown and around my back, pulling my body towards his.

I yawned and smiled through half-lidded eyes. Maybe that would work. I felt guilty but I couldn't see that there was anything very seductive about this situation, our stomachs sloshing with wine and moussaka. I felt like a water balloon that would pop if an erect penis came anywhere near it.

To be fair we'd only done it once this week and we were usually a two-to-three-times-a-week couple – Friday mornings, Saturday evenings, the odd Tuesday evening depending on how tired we both were from work. Apart from when we went away for the weekend to nice hotels, when we'd do it a bit more, sometimes even in the afternoons.

Once, we went away to a place in the New Forest where they had treehouses, and Gus had insisted on having sex in the hot tub on the balcony outside. The novelty had been amusing, although I'd worried about verrucas, but as soon as we'd finished Gus had said we should get out and put the cover back on, because too long in a hot tub is apparently bad for the blood pressure. There's very little that's erotic about the sight of your boyfriend, naked, tugging a cover over a hot tub as if he's tucking up his car.

My yawn didn't work: Gus's fingers continued to run up and down my bare back.

There should be a law against having sex after a big dinner.

Then his hand slid over my shoulder and tweaked a nipple, which turned hard and made me reassess the situation.

Maybe I could do this. If it was relatively quick and I was asleep in twenty minutes, then I'd still get over six hours before my alarm went off at six. Also, I still felt a lurking weirdness over Jack's mentions of Art, so perhaps now I could reassure Gus that he was the one, he was who I definitely wanted to have sex with even though it was 11.33 p.m. on a Thursday and I felt so tired I was almost a corpse.

I slid my face towards his and kissed him. His tongue tasted of Colgate.

At this encouragement, one of his hands pushed my dressing gown off my shoulder so I wriggled free from the other arm. There, both of us naked. Then he started kissing down my body, between my breasts, shifting himself southwards. His mouth reached my belly button as his hands held my hips and I know I should have felt electrified by this but what I was actually thinking was: If Gus goes down on me, I will be asleep on my back within three minutes, maybe two, and that's not a very titillating situation for anyone.

'Sweetheart, I have such a hectic day in the office tomorrow.' I mumbled this with my eyes screwed tight at the ceiling, wincing, wishing I could cut out my own tongue.

From between my legs, Gus lifted his head like Wilma looking up from her dog bowl. 'Oh, OK. Do you want to use your toy?'

This was a small, purple bullet vibrator we'd bought together on a shopping trip to Ann Summers a year earlier. I'd told Gus I would only go round the new exhibition of Ancient Roman coins at the British Museum if we could go to Ann Summers afterwards. Gus had reluctantly agreed and spent most of the twenty minutes in the shop goggling at the dildos. 'Have you seen the size of this one? Nell, look! Look at the size of this! And it's got veins!' He wouldn't admit it but I think he enjoyed the dildos even more than the coins, although we'd ended up with something tactfully small: the purple 'mini bullet' which Gus initially thought was a lipstick.

'No, no, it's OK, just come here,' I said, opening my arms for him to pull himself up into them. I felt his erection poke at my thigh and then push into me.

He kissed my neck before lifting his head to look at me. 'Wasn't bad, that moussaka, was it?'

'Uh-uh,' I replied, wrapping my arms around his back and wondering whether I should wash my hair when I got to the office the next day.

'Although I'm not sure about vegan cheese.'

I could probably make it last until Saturday. Just had to remember my dry shampoo in the morning.

'And I overcooked the aubergines.'

'It was good,' I assured him while rocking under his body.

'I might make some koftas with that lamb this weekend,' he puffed. 'Think… there's… a… recipe… for… it… in… that… Nigella… book.'

'Mmm, delicious.'

Gus stopped and looked down at me. 'You sound bored. Is this not nice?'

'No no, it's lovely, carry on,' I said, tightening my grip around his back.

He resumed his pace. 'OK, won't be long, getting closer.'

I raised my mouth to his shoulder and kissed it by way of encouragement.

'Much closer,' he puffed.

I widened my legs so he could push deeper.

'Ooooh,' he panted, speeding up. 'Much closer, much closer, so close! So close! I'm so close!'

Then the old favourite, I dropped my hands to his bottom and pulled him towards me.

'Oooooooooh!' There was a high-pitched shriek before Gus

shuddered and relaxed his body on top of me. 'That was lovely,' he mumbled into my left ear, before raising his head and frowning. 'Do you really think dinner was all right? It didn't need more salt?'

'Promise,' I replied, with a reassuring smile.

Chapter 5

'AH, NELL, GOOD MORNING, have you see th—'

'Emails, yes I have,' I replied the following day, already on my third coffee, when Gideon walked in.

While Rudolf's signed letter of instruction had come back overnight, Countess Wilhelmina's legal team had been quicker than us. They'd already petitioned for divorce and lodged her demands with the court: she was going after half of his fortune and full custody of the children.

'Which means we have a fight on our hands,' said Gideon, collapsing into his desk chair and rubbing his hands together. A long drawn-out battle was terrible for those most closely affected by the divorce in question: the couple, any children, bewildered pets. But it was excellent for the paid professionals involved. Not just lawyers, but barristers, therapists and, in certain cases, private investigators. This was the sort of high-profile case Gideon loved. No doubt he'd already picked out his suit for the High Court.

'Can you get all the relevant paperwork sent to him immediately and we'll get cracking,' he ordered.

For the rest of the day, I barely moved from my desk. I sent

Rudolf's secretary the financial declaration forms, checked in with Linzi, who sobbed down the phone saying that Larry had called her, also in tears, the night before. I advised that she stay strong and conduct all communication through us and his lawyers, which sounds heartless but was only to try and make the situation easier for both of them – less emotional, more professional.

'I'm so sorry, mmm, I know, yes, I know, mmmm, I'm so sorry, poor you, but try and imagine this is a business deal,' I suggested down the phone while Gideon rolled his eyes at his desk.

After lunch, I spoke to Mr Jalal, the father of the woman who was marrying her personal trainer. I'd drafted one agreement but Mr Jalal wanted it to be firmer, offering literally nothing in the event they divorced. I duly advised Mr Jalal that no prenuptial agreement was legally watertight in Britain, that judges only had to take them 'into account' in the event of a divorce. But he shouted down the phone that he didn't care, that he wanted a signed document in which his future son-in-law got nothing. Poor guy, although I did slightly see Mr Jalal's point. Darren was a personal trainer his daughter had met in a Knightsbridge gym, and having explained the concept of a prenup to him over the phone, I suspected his biceps were bigger than his brain.

Sometimes, my job probably didn't differ much from that of a primary school teacher; I spent all day trying to sort out intense squabbles, only in my case the squabbles were over money instead of whose turn it was to play in the sandpit.

★★★

That evening, I beat Gus home. This was how I preferred it on Friday nights since I had a ritual: get back, peel off suit, remove bra and put on elasticated clothing. After that, I'd pour a glass of wine and take it back upstairs to our single bedroom, where I'd open the drawer beneath the bed.

This drawer was quite full now, so I had to put my glass on the bedside table, sit on the carpet and lever it open while pressing the bed with my foot.

That done, I peeled off the scarves and reached for one of the dozens of bridal magazines underneath them.

Although Gus had suggested we never get married eleven years ago and I'd agreed, and he scoffed at other people's wedding lists and their 'predictable' choice of first dance, and he claimed that if he had to go on another stag do to Prague he'd feign an infectious disease which meant he couldn't travel, around a year ago I'd developed a curious habit.

It started by accident in the Clapham High Street Sainsbury's. There I'd been one Friday after work, loitering in the magazine aisle, looking for a copy of *History Today* for Gus, when I'd spotted a copy of *Brides*. I wasn't sure whether it was the cover model's radiant expression, her vintage lace dress or one of the magazine headlines: 'HOW TO GET KATE MIDDLETON'S HAIR!', but I grabbed it.

I smuggled *Brides* to the till like a fugitive, keeping the cover pressed against my chest so nobody could see what I was buying, and, when I got it safely home, ripped through the pages like an addict, totally absorbed by that season's dresses and cakes, and the pros and cons of a summer versus a winter wedding. When I heard

Gus's key in the lock, I'd chucked it under the sofa, flicked on the TV and pretended to be watching *Songs of Praise*.

That was it. I was hooked. I bought bridal magazine after bridal magazine: not just *Brides*, but any magazine I could find: *Perfect Wedding*, *Complete Wedding*, *What Cake?*, *Cosmopolitan Bride*, *Wedding Belles*, *Getting Married*, even *Martha Stewart Weddings* when I found a copy in an unfamiliar Waitrose. I bought so many magazines that I had to find a hiding place, which was where the spare room came in. Gus hardly went in there so it was perfect. I stashed them away, covered them with old scarves and only snuck in for my fix on evenings when I knew Gus would be back late.

There I'd sit and read articles headlined things like '27 ways to incorporate pampas grass into your wedding!', 'The correct wedding cake for your zodiac sign!' and 'What to put in your wedding bathroom basket'. It was mad, I knew, but I felt like if I could indulge my fantasies in here, every now and then, nobody else need know.

I liked reading about big dresses and tiny canapés. I liked look-ing at pictures of cakes and honeymoon locations and overjoyed couples, beaming into each other's eyes. I even liked reading about real-life proposals. Did you know the most popular place in the world to propose is Disneyland Paris? Me neither. People are weird.

Part of me loved the romance, and, after a long week of work, dealing with clients who only wanted their marriages over, I found leafing through the pages therapeutic. Love was still out there. Plus, the beauty pages really did include some very good hair tips.

But I was embarrassed about my fascination for two reasons: first, because it didn't seem very empowered or feminist, and second, because I knew Gus would go mad, so I kept it quiet and only indulged in my fantasies when I knew it was safe.

Tonight, I lay on the single bed and leafed through the latest copy of *Brides* ('Can I arrive on a horse to my country wedding?') undisturbed until my phone vibrated beside me. It was Mum.

'Hiya, love. You home?'

'Yep, I'm just, er, reading a magazine. You told Dad yet?'

'I will, I will. There just hasn't been the right moment. He's in the pub and I had to go to Morpeth for Hoover bags today.'

'Mum! Come on, this isn't fair on Dad, especially since I've told Jack.'

'Have you?' she snapped quickly. 'What did he say?'

'Was Dad having an affair.'

'Him! Who'd he be having an affair with?'

I reached for my wine. 'Jack suggested whatshecalled from the vet's.'

'Her! Your dad could do much better than that.'

'Mum, I think we're getting off the point—'

'Jack must be going mad. She's about to be seventy. And she has that terrible complexion. I'm quite offended that your bro—'

'Mum! Let's not get sidetracked. You've got to tell him, tonight.'

'I can't do it tonight because he'll roll back from the pub in a couple of hours, steaming, and that's never the moment to talk to him. I might as well try to have a conversation with Wilma.'

I took a deep breath. 'OK, fine, but tomorrow. You have to tell him this weekend, Mum.'

We chatted for a few more minutes and I gave Mum my verdict on Emma (sweet, slightly peculiar eating habits, probably only around for a few months) before hanging up. I tried to distract myself from thoughts about my parents by reading about a woman who rode a horse side-saddle to her wedding. But poor Dad, he had so little idea of what was barrelling his way.

Not long afterwards, I heard Gus's keys, so quickly stashed the magazine back in the drawer, threw my scarves on top – I'd got pretty efficient at this – and went downstairs to discuss what we felt like for dinner.

On Saturday morning, we woke, dropped our bundle off at the dry cleaners and decided to sit-in for croissants and coffee in the little French patisserie overlooking the Common. Gus leafed through *The Times*, tutting at several pages, while I read a piece about the rise of teenage botox in its magazine which was both bleak and interesting but also had the dispiriting effect of making me worry that I should have botox. If the teenagers were doing it, then what about us thirty-three-year-olds? Nicole definitely had had botox, I reflected, remembering her smooth, shiny forehead at the funeral.

'What *are* you doing?' asked Gus, as I scrunched my face up and down, inspecting it using my phone's camera.

'Do you think I should have botox?'

Gus lowered his paper and looked aghast. 'What? No! I love you just as you are, wrinkles and all.'

'Oh, thanks very much.'

'I didn't mean it like that. I just don't think you should tamper with your face because it's perfect.'

'Mmm,' I mused, glancing back to my phone. I'd noticed the little lines radiating out from my eyes in photos a year or so ago, just as I'd observed the hair above Gus's ears starting to grey. It wasn't that I minded too much, I'd never been that vain. It just felt a bit early. We were too young for all that, weren't we? What next, a Stannah stairlift to get us into the flat? I stared through the café window, imagining life stretching before me. I felt, suddenly, like I was standing on one of those flat airport escalators, unable to get off: work, partnership, buy a bigger place, kids, back to work, retirement, death.

'Although if you frown like that you'll only make the wrinkles worse,' said Gus. 'Come on, cheer up, we've got lunch with Jeremy and Tots to look forward to.'

It was sweetly optimistic of Gus to believe that lunch with his Cambridge friends would put any sort of spring in my step. Jeremy was a civil servant who name-dropped his meetings with the prime minister and cabinet ministers but, just as he was about to give you a piece of interesting political gossip, would say pompously, 'I'm so sorry, I've said too much already, I really shouldn't talk shop like this.'

Tots, or Totty (short for Charlotte), worked for an interior designer and, for the past two years, had always made sure that her gel manicure was perfect in case Jeremy proposed and she needed to photograph her left hand. She'd always made it clear she only wanted to work until they were engaged and could start having children. I found them both a tiny bit dull but we'd missed Jeremy's birthday dinner party because of work, so Gus had arranged this instead.

We met them at a new Italian restaurant on the Portobello Road, booked by Totty. She was very keen on going to the latest hot restaurant, irrespective of the food, so that she could Instagram it afterwards and prove she'd been. This was just her sort of place, I realized, as we pushed through Notting Hill tourists towards it. The brick exterior was painted with a multicoloured mural, and inside were waiters that looked like models, leather banquettes, low-lighting and palm trees.

'Are palm trees Italian?' I muttered to Gus as we walked towards their table. Then I told myself to stop being so mean. Jeremy and Totty were perfectly nice, they were just the sort of friends you only needed to see once, maybe twice a year.

'Hi,' I said, with a big smile, pushing a palm frond aside and waving as we approached.

Totty stood up and held out her left hand as if I was supposed to kiss it. Bubblegum pink nails, today.

I frowned, confused, and she waggled it close to my face. Oh right, course, there it was: a glinting, rectangular diamond – a baguette cut, as the magazines would have it – surrounded by smaller stones.

'You guys! Congratulations!' I clasped Totty in a hug while Gus shook Jeremy's hand and slapped his back.

Totty squealed so loudly into my ear I thought I might never hear again, then we sat.

'I've taken the liberty of ordering some Pol Rog,' said Jeremy. 'Hope you chaps don't mind.'

'Terrific,' said Gus.

'Can we tell them how it happened?' said Totty, looking imploringly at her fiancé.

'Darling, you've told everyone we've seen in the past week. She even told the Uber driver on the way here,' Jeremy said, looking from me to Gus with an indulgent chuckle.

Totty embarked on the story anyway, her pink nails windmilling around her face with enthusiasm as she talked. 'So, it was on our last day in Verbs, and we were queuing for the chairlift up to the pizza place for lunch and we got separated, so I had to go on the chair behind Jez, which I was furious about, but then halfway up, the excited Frenchman next to me starts pointing at the snow underneath us.'

She paused here and exchanged a knowing smile with Jeremy while I wondered how I'd become friends with someone who called Verbier 'Verbs'.

'So I look down,' Totty went on, 'and guess what was written in the snow?'

'The end is nigh?' Gus joked. He would grumble about this conversation to me later on, I knew. One of the first things he'd ever told me, on that early date where he revealed his scepticism about marriage, was that diamond engagement rings had been invented by an advertising campaign. I'd later looked this up, sceptical about Gus's claim, and realized he was right. In 1947, a copywriter for De Beers had coined the slogan 'a diamond is forever' to boost falling diamond sales and the modern concept of proposing with a diamond took off. I hoped that copywriter had been paid her weight in, well, diamonds.

'No, silly!' Totty told him. 'It said, "Totty, will you marry me?"' She squealed again.

'Congratulations, guys. That sure beats Disneyland Paris.'

She frowned at me.

'The most popular place in the world to propose.'

'What an extraordinary fact,' scoffed Gus, as a waiter appeared and filled our glasses with champagne.

'Just read it somewhere,' I said quickly, before holding my glass up. 'To you both. This is very exciting.'

After lunch, we meandered through an expensive antiques shop where Gus ummed and aahed over a leather armchair for half an hour before we decided it was too big for the spare bedroom. That night, we spooned on the sofa while watching an old Italian film; the next morning we went to the other café that overlooked the Common where we read the Sunday papers before collecting our dry cleaning on the way home.

All in all, it was exactly the sort of weekend which you'd expect from two thirty-something lawyers who lived in Clapham. I couldn't remember when I'd stopped worrying about whether I could afford to go out for breakfast or lunch. When I first moved to London as a law student with a big loan, I used to look at women on the Tube wearing long coats and nice boots, with perfect hair and discreet flashes of gold jewellery around their necks, and wonder how they afforded it. Did they look like that every day?

Over the years, I'd become one of them. Now I could walk into Whistles or Reiss and buy a new dress or a jumper and not freak out that I wouldn't be able to buy lunch that week. Life looked very different to that which I'd imagined as a teenager, lying on my bed in Northcliffe, staring through my window at the rain.

Except the thread between then and now reasserted itself when Mum called on Sunday evening.

She was in Wansbeck hospital, she announced, because Dad was in surgery.

I was lying on the sofa watching *A Place in the Sun*, and sat bolt upright at this news, like I was acting in a slapstick film. 'WHAT? What's happened? Is he all right?'

Mum sounded oddly calm. 'He's perfectly all right.'

'He's in surgery, he can't be that perfect.'

Gus, who'd been working at the kitchen table, hurried over and sat on the sofa arm. 'What's happened?' he mouthed.

'He's had a fall,' went on Mum, 'and broken his leg in two places.'

'What? How?'

'I had the conversation you told me to have with him this morning, and then he stormed off and went to the Duck, and the next thing I knew Roy was banging on the door saying there'd been an accident. He fell over a bar stool, apparently. How you do that and break your leg in two places I don't know, but anyway, he has and now we're here.' She sighed wearily at the end of this, as if Dad had broken his leg to spite her.

'What do the doctors say? When will he be out? What are they actually doing to him?'

'They're putting everything back in its right place and popping a cast over it.'

'Oh God,' I said down the phone, with a wave of relief. 'And when can he go home?'

'That's what I wanted to discuss,' she went on. 'The nurse says he'll be in for one or two nights but he can go home after that.'

'OK, that's not too bad.'

'But I won't be there so he'll need someone else to look after him.'

'What? Where will you be?'

'I'm moving out in the next couple of days, love – I'm sorry, but I just can't take it anymore. You or your brother will have to come home for a bit.'

Chapter 6

I DIDN'T GET HOLD of Jack until the next day.

I'd called him three times to discuss our parents the night before, but no answer. I called him a further three times that morning, tapping my fingers on my desk, willing him to pick up before Gideon arrived and grumbled about me making personal calls.

'Hey,' Jack answered casually, on my fourth attempt.

'Don't "hey" me. Did you not see my missed calls last night?'

'Yeah.'

'So why didn't you answer?'

'Didn't think it would be important.'

'You didn't think my first, second or third calls last night were important? Or this morning? But by the fourth call you realized it might be?'

'Sort of, yeah.'

I held my breath to try and stop a scream from escaping. 'OK, here's the thing: Dad's in hospital.'

'What? What's happened?'

'This is exactly why I've been trying to ring you. He's all right, but he's broken his leg in two places.'

'How'd he do that?'

'Fell over in the pub. But hang on, there's more. Mum has also chosen this moment to announce that she's moving out.'

'What? Where's she going?'

'No idea.'

'But who's going to look after Dad?'

Don't scream, Nell. Do not scream. Try very hard not to lose your patience. He is your brother, your only sibling. If you have him murdered, you'll have to deal with your parents by yourself, and that would be worse.

'This is why I've called you seven times since last night. We're going to have to work out a plan. So what I was thinking is I go up for this week, and maybe the next. Then you come up and take over?'

'Sis,' he said, 'the thing is I'm crazy busy for the next few weeks.'

'Actually?'

'Yeah, really, *really* busy. Like I said last week, the spring market, so we've got loads going on in the office. I didn't even get my lunch break until three yesterday. Too busy with viewings.'

'Oh no, that's sad,' I replied, deadpan, trying to remember the last time I took a lunch break. Maybe in 2016?

'And the sandwich shop had run out of ham.'

'That is a tragedy. But look, if I go up for the next two weeks, two whole weeks, Jack, then can you perhaps consider doing a stint?'

He sighed. 'Maybe. Emma and I were thinking about going to Spain for a week but we hadn't booked anything.'

'Well if you could not book a holiday for the time being, while our dad recovers from breaking his leg in two places, and perhaps pick up your phone the next time I ring so we can continue this conversation, that would be great.'

'How long do they say he'll be laid up?'

'Not sure.' After Mum had dropped her bombshell about leaving the previous evening, she'd gone on to say that the cast would probably need to be on for 'several weeks', so they'd send him home in a wheelchair, along with a pair of crutches, and that an occupational therapist would inspect the house in the next week or so, to make sure he could easily manoeuvre himself around it. All of this, I knew, Dad would hate.

'Also,' I told Jack, 'apparently his blood pressure's sky high, no wonder, so they're prescribing something for that, and he's been told to drink less.'

He laughed down the phone. 'Fat chance.'

In the end, I got Jack to agree to 'think' about coming up to Northcliffe in two weeks' time. 'But I won't have to wipe Dad's arse or anything, will I?'

I'd said I didn't know and hung up.

The next hurdle was clearing my absence with Gideon. In theory, this shouldn't have been a problem. I couldn't remember ever having taken a sick day and I very rarely took holiday, usually only one week in August, when Gus and I went to a nice hotel in Europe and did nothing but sleep, lie on sunbeds and eat, recharging from late nights and early starts in our offices. Spinks owed me literally hundreds of holiday days. Plus, I could do my job remotely, apart from the odd court appearance and client meeting, and I could come back to London for those if needed.

I had my speech all prepared when he blew into the office.

'Morning, Gideon, can I have a word about something?'

'Can it wait until I've had my breakfast?' he said, falling into his leather chair so forcefully that the cushion underneath him let out a fart. 'Heavy night.'

He looked as if he'd lost a boxing match: bloodshot eyes, red nose, hair sticking up in tufts.

'I've got to go home for a bit,' I pushed on, ignoring his plea about breakfast. A 'heavy night' simply meant he'd drunk too much red wine in a posh restaurant. 'North, I mean, back to my parents' house.'

He squinted at me across his desk. 'Again? Who's died this time?'

'My dad's broken his leg and needs someone to look after him.'

'Where's your mother?'

'It's complicated,' I said quickly, 'but what I was wondering was if I could take a couple of weeks off from tomorrow? Well, not off because I'll be on my phone and emails, but two weeks of working from up there.'

'Two weeks! Christ, I need my breakfast. Can you ring Queenie and get her to send it up?'

'In a minute,' I replied, trying to stay firm. 'But can we resolve this first? I very rarely ask for any kind of favour or flexibility, Gideon, but I have to go home for this, and I can work remotely all day, no problem. I can deal with all the Prince Rudolf paperwork from there, and Linzi's. And I've redrafted the Jalal prenup this morning. Everything's under control.'

He grunted and narrowed his piggy eyes at me again. 'I'll be honest, I don't think the timing's great, with decisions about partnerships coming up.'

I inhaled. In for four, out for four. 'I understand but sadly my father wasn't thinking of that when he fell over.'

'Fine, fine, fine, point taken, you can go,' he replied, waving his hands at me dismissively, 'but I expect you to be available at all times. At all times! Now, can you ring Queenie? And tell her I need my cappuccino extra hot. By the time Carmelita arrived yesterday it was tepid at *best*.'

★★★

Gus and I discussed the situation while I packed that night. He wasn't hugely supportive about the situation either. Men, honestly. I'd once read about a matriarchal society in southern China where women ruled, carried on the family name and were elected as the rulers of each village in the region. I bet they got more done there.

'I've told Gideon I'll be away for two weeks.'

'Your dad will be in plaster for longer than that,' Gus replied authoritatively, leaning back on our headboard.

'I know,' I replied, while burrowing through the top drawer for socks. 'Where are all my socks? What do I do with them? Do I eat them?'

'I've looked it up. Can be nine or ten weeks.'

'*What?*' I looked up. 'Mum just said a few weeks. Surely not that long?'

'It is, apparently. Or at least it can be.'

'I won't be away for that long. Jack's going to take over.'

'He's agreed?'

'Sort of. He said he doesn't want to wipe Dad's bum.'

'You won't have to do that, will you?' Gus sounded horrified.

'No! At least, I don't think so. I don't know!'

I hadn't thought much about my nursing duties until Jack mentioned it.

'I don't understand why your mum has to move out now. She's done nearly forty years, what's a few more weeks?'

'I don't know, do I? I think she's just had enough,' I muttered, back into my bag, increasingly annoyed at his unhelpful line of questioning.

He shook his head. 'Your family, honestly.'

'Oi, not cool,' I replied, swatting him with the only sock I could find.

'Sorry, I just don't like it when you're not here.'

'You could come up for the weekend?'

Gus wrinkled his nose. 'I'd love to but I've got the Google deal on, and I'll only spend the whole time sneezing.'

Because of the dog, he meant. 'You could go mad and buy a box of Piriton?'

'I wish I could, lambkin, but I simply can't escape with work like it is.' I'd complained about this term of endearment before, too, but Gus argued that it was Shakespearian, as if that made it all right.

'Fine, fine,' I replied, flinging the single sock into my bag. 'Don't worry. I'll go up and help Dad hobble to the bathroom myself for two weeks.'

★★★

The next morning, I caught an early train from King's Cross and a taxi from Morpeth station straight to Wansbeck hospital. Pulling up outside it reminded me of childhood scrapes – Nanny Gertrude once drove us here in a panic after Art fell over on the beach and cut his chin on a piece of flint, and another time when Jack claimed he'd been bitten by a python, although it turned out to be sunburn.

I heard Dad before I saw him since his voice carried the whole way down the ward.

'At least the vocal chords aren't broken,' I said, sticking my head around the curtain to see him glowering at a nurse.

His skin looked grey, almost translucent. It was Dad lying in that hospital bed with his cast stretched out in front of him, but it was also an old man.

I bent to kiss his head. 'Hiya.'

'Hi, pet, what a bloody mess this all is. Thanks for coming up.'

'That all looks fine to me,' said the nurse, sliding a pen back into her breast pocket. 'You'll just need to pick up your prescription from the pharmacy, Mr Mason, but otherwise you're discharged. And remember there'll be an occupational therapist coming to visit you in the next couple of days.'

Then she bent over and spoke more loudly, as if his hearing had gone too. 'Do you want hospital transport to get you home?' She inclined her head at an empty wheelchair on the other side of his bed.

He glared at her in reply so I stepped in. 'Yes, probably, if you wouldn't mind, thanks so much.'

The nurse gave me a nod and left. I sat in a bright purple arm-chair beside him and looked sympathetically at his cast. It ran from his toes to a couple of inches above his knee. 'How you feeling?'

'Been better.' Dad jerked his head at the curtain. 'That one asked if I wanted incontinence pads. I said I've broken my leg, not my todger.'

'Right, good, OK,' I said, briefly reflecting on the fact that I had two weeks of this sort of conversation ahead of me. 'Are you in pain?'

'Nah. They got me on these big pink pills, so big I can hardly swallow 'em.'

'You going to be all right in that?' I nodded at the wheelchair.

'Suppose I've got to be, not much choice, is there? What a bloody, bloody mess.'

'It'll be fine,' I said, not very convincingly. 'Have you, er, spoken to Mum today?'

His mouth drooped further and he lay staring at his toes, poking out from the end of his cast like cocktail sausages, then shook his head.

I'd called her on the train and discovered that she'd packed a bag and was moving in with Elsbeth. Elsbeth was a friend Mum went dog walking with (she had a very disobedient terrier called Bingo), who lived ten minutes inland of Northcliffe. But I wasn't sure how long that would last since I also knew that, on these walks, Elsbeth grumbled almost continually about her husband, Graham. When I'd asked how long Mum planned to stay with them, she'd been vague so I'd had one more go at persuading her otherwise. 'Mum, do you *really* need to leave when this has just happened to Dad?'

'I do. I've made my mind up. I'll only be down the road.' She added that Terence had helped her carry the single bed from Jack's room downstairs to the living room, so Dad could sleep there while his leg mended.

'Do you want to talk about it?' I asked Dad.

'Nell, my pet, if she wants to go then that's her decision. I'm not going to stop her.'

'Why not? You've been married a long time. That counts for something; for a lot, actually.'

'Does it? Is that what you tell 'em in your office?'

I pulled my mouth into a straight line before answering. 'It depends.'

'On what?'

I didn't want to get into this conversation overheard by the rest of the ward so I suggested we start the process of getting home.

This took hours. It's quicker to leave a marriage than a hospital ward. A nurse helped me get Dad into his wheelchair, ignoring his shouts that he didn't want anyone to see his 'tackle'; we waited for over an hour for his blood pressure pills, antibiotics and painkillers the size of broad beans; then spent another hour loitering in the main entrance, waiting for the van that would take him home in the chair.

'Thank Christ for that,' said Dad, when the driver, a nice man called Ben, waved and set off down our drive again.

I opened the front door; Wilma crouched down on her front paws and growled at the wheelchair.

'She left me the dog then,' said Dad.

There was a note on the kitchen table.

PIE IN THE FRIDGE FOR DINNER. HAVE FED WILMA
SO DON'T LET HER TELL YOU OTHERWISE. NELL,
REMEMBER TO SHUT THE CHICKENS UP. PS. THE NEW
SERIES OF VERA STARTS TONIGHT AT 8.

I smiled grimly as I put the kettle on the stove. I'd never come across any client who left a note for their estranged spouse informing them that their favourite TV show was on that night. Maybe there was hope yet.

'Sod that,' said Dad, as the kettle hissed. 'Pour me a proper drink, Nell.'

'Do you remember what the chemist said about your blood pressure?'

'Was that the part where he said whisky would make my bones heal faster?'

'Weird, I only heard the bit where he said no drinking on those pills.'

'I don't give a stuff. Go on, doll, there should be a Newcastle in there.'

'Mum wouldn't allow this,' I said, opening the fridge.

'Good thing she's not here then.'

'Dad!'

'Just kidding. Come on, Nell, if we can't laugh when I'm in a wheelchair and your mum's left me then when can we?'

I held the bottle out. It was going to be a long two weeks.

***

In the living room, one of the sofas had been pushed back against a wall and Jack's single bed was in its place, facing the TV. I helped Dad in and passed him the remote before going back to the kitchen to investigate the pie situation.

We made a curious pair: Dad ate in bed; I balanced a plate on my knees in the small armchair as we watched *Vera*. Then he insisted he didn't need any bathroom help, so hobbled agonizingly slowly to the downstairs loo on his crutches.

I sat in my armchair and winced at various alarming noises – the clunk of a pipe, flushing, what sounded like water cascading all over the floor, Dad's muttering.

'You all right? Do you need a hand?'

He bellowed back: 'DON'T EVEN THINK ABOUT COMING IN HERE.'

'All right, all right.'

I laughed when he reappeared: he looked like he'd had a shower. 'Why's your hair all wet? You didn't get your cast wet, did you?'

'It's fine,' he said, wobbling back towards me on his crutches, although he sounded exhausted. 'Just help me up, pet. I think these things are going to take some getting used to.'

'Course,' I said, crouching beside him so he could put an arm around my neck.

'Let Wilma out for me?' he said, once he was under the covers.

I nodded, kissed the top of his head and held out the remote. 'Want this?'

'Nah, you're all right. Think I'm going to conk out.'

'You all right, Dad?' He seemed suddenly deflated, an old man again.

'I'll be fine. Night, pet.'

'Night, Dad. Come on, Wilma.' I patted my leg for her to follow me and let her out into the dusk. As she sniffed around the garden, a belt of swallows looped overhead and I sighed into the air after them at the strangeness of putting my own parent to bed. Then I called Wilma in, went upstairs to run a bath and go through the seventy-four emails Gideon had sent that afternoon, every one of them red-flagged. I very much regretted the day I taught Gideon how to flag an email.

★★★

When I got up in the morning, there'd been a murder. Nothing to do with Dad. He seemed back to his perky self, shouting for tea, then shouting that it wasn't strong enough before shouting about toast. It wasn't wholly dissimilar, I reflected, while hunting for the Marmite, to dealing with Gideon in the morning.

The murder had occurred in the hen house. Despite Mum's note, I'd forgotten to shut them up the night before and although all four chickens had taken themselves to bed, the door of their hut had remained open and a fox had evidently crept in, like a burglar, and savaged Sandra, the smallest one. She was lying on her side in the sawdust while the three others – Fiona, Jane and Violet – remained on their roosting perches, eyes wide, clucking in shock.

I felt sick with guilt. Poor things, roosting happily and thinking they were safe, only to face a serial killer in the early hours.

Leaving the carnage outside, I went back to the living room to inform Dad, who was eating off a dusty old tray I'd found in the kitchen.

He gave me a dark look over his toast.

'What?'

'Your mother won't be happy; she loved that chook.' He picked up his mug and waggled it. 'Can I have a top-up?'

'Wilma needs taking out,' he added, when I returned with a full mug. 'And, pet, is there any chance you can nip to Spar for the paper? It opens at seven thirty.'

I looked at my watch. It was 7.28 a.m. Normally I'd be in the office, having run and showered, waiting for my first coffee before writing that day's to-do list and blazing through my emails.

This morning, I hadn't yet put on a bra, I hadn't run, and Wilma had smeared her wet nose all over my pyjama bottoms while I made toast for Dad, who now wanted me to go to the shop to buy today's *Racing Post*. Plus, I had to deal with the crime scene outside.

'Right, I'm going to shower, get dressed, take Wilma for a walk via the Spar, and then I'll come back and deal with the chickens. Is that OK with everyone?'

I looked from Wilma to Dad. He nodded. 'Chuck us the remote, pet.'

I debated taking Wilma to the beach but decided we didn't have time. 'We'll go tomorrow, I promise,' I told her as we crossed the green half an hour later.

It was while inspecting the papers and magazines that I saw Lucy.

'JIMBO, COME BACK HERE RIGHT NOW OR NO *PAW PATROL*,' she shouted as a small boy in a yellow coat ran away from her.

'Hey,' I said, waving awkwardly down the aisle.

'Nell!' she replied, before she glanced at what I'd been flicking through. 'Goodness, are congratulations in order?'

'Er, nope, definitely not,' I said, quickly putting *Bridalicious* back on the shelf. 'I was looking for this.' I reached for a copy of *Racing Post*.

Lucy was my oldest friend. Had been my oldest friend. We were the same age and had grown up 300 metres from one another since her parents ran the Northcliffe post office. Although our friendship hadn't solely been based on proximity; we'd also stuck together because, at school, nobody else wanted to hang out with us.

Little and Large, they'd called us, since Lucy was short and round, like an Asterix cartoon, and beside her I looked tall and lanky.

We were never part of 'the cool group', the gaggle of girls in our year who knew what to say to the boys, rolled their skirts up to impress them and had nice hair.

We did not have nice hair; mine was ginger so they nicknamed me 'Annie'. Lucy, whose parents moved to Northcliffe from a remote village in the Highlands, had pale, Gaelic skin and dark hair, cut with an unfashionable fringe that ran as straight as a ruler across her forehead.

As a pair of badly shorn outcasts, she and I clung to one another. Almost every afternoon, after school, we sat in her bedroom over the post office, and I thought about Art while she obsessed about Take That and whether she'd ever marry Mark Owen.

'JIMBO, COME BACK RIGHT THIS MINUTE,' she shouted again, before turning to face me. 'Sorry, Nell, always chaos.'

'That's all right,' I replied with a smile, but I felt stiff and formal, as if I was talking to a stranger, not somebody who I used to discuss kissing techniques with. As teenagers, we watched teen films like *Clueless*, *10 Things I Hate About You*, *American Pie* and *She's All That*, studying the snogging scenes again and again and again like little anthropologists. Then we'd practise on our hands, pressing our mouths against our thumb and forefingers, waggling our tongues through them. It never felt quite as exciting as it looked onscreen.

'Is this...?' I stepped forward to peer down at a papoose strapped to Lucy's chest. Mum had told me she'd had a second baby but I couldn't remember what it was called.

'This is Bonnie,' she replied, turning so I could see her tiny sleeping face, resting against Lucy's chest.

'Sweeeet. And how are you? How are nights?' I tried to alleviate my awkwardness but asking the sort of question you were supposed to ask people with babies.

'Not so bad. She's easy, it's that one who's more of a handful. JIMBO OLIVER, PUT THAT BACK!' she shouted again, and I glanced behind me at a small boy with both his hands wrapped around a can. 'Come here.' Then she looked at me again and smiled. 'I wondered if you'd be back.'

After travelling around Asia with Lucy one summer, the summer that we left school, we'd drifted. I'd moved to York for uni and then moved to London for law school; Lucy stayed in Northcliffe and helped her parents run the post office before working as an assistant at the vet's.

We'd emailed at first but, after a few months, I seemed to run out of things to say. We'd been friends because we came from the same village and nobody else liked us. Once that stopped being the case, once I'd moved away, it didn't feel like we had much else in common.

As adults, although our hair had improved (Lucy's fringe had become softer, swept to each side of her face), our friendship had not. Our lives had barrelled in opposite directions and I felt guilty about this whenever I saw her. She'd always been kinder and more gener- ous to me than vice versa, I knew, given that I'd always dropped her at a moment's notice if Art was home from boarding school.

In the past decade, I'd seen her a handful of times while back in Northcliffe but we'd never deliberately organized to meet up. It was normally a chance sighting in the pub, and we'd have a brief conversation about work, and check one another's family members were well, before I excused myself and went back to Dad's table. She'd married a local guy called Mike, and they'd had Jimbo (technically James) a few years ago; now Bonnie.

I nodded. 'Yeah, just for a couple of weeks.'

'Is your dad all right? I heard about his leg.'

'He'll live. Shouting from his bed about cups of tea and getting the paper. How's Mike?'

'He's good. Still at the fishery. I saw Colin yesterday, he's doing the same as ever.'

Colin had tagged along with Lucy and me at Morpeth Primary, and then secondary, since he didn't have any friends either. He always smelt like boiled ham and was obsessed with computer games, but had been very devoted to us, giving us both Valentine's cards every year, signed: 'Love from Colin'.

'He's just moved and lives out Saltwick way. Still by himself, poor old Col.' She smiled and reached down for Jimbo's hand as he wrapped a small arm around her leg.

'Look, Jimbo, this is Auntie Nell. Say hello!'

I felt even more awkward at this description when I wasn't his aunt and he had no idea who I was.

'Hi, Jimbo,' I said, with another forced wave.

He scowled at me from between Lucy's legs.

'And are you doing all right, Nell?' she asked, tilting her head slightly. 'You look tired.'

From anyone else, I would have found this irritating, taken it as a dig and made a mental note to buy more expensive eye cream. But I'd never known Lucy to be malicious. I'm not sure she was capable of it. When we were twelve, and I was too nervous to ask Mum if she'd take me bra shopping because the boys, and, actually, some of the girls, had started making fun of me in PE lessons, Lucy gave me one of her training bras instead. When our childhood dog died, Lucy made a collage of Molly photos on a big poster for my bedroom wall. She once spent three hours combing the Northcliffe beach for white feathers with me because I was feeling insecure that Art didn't like me as much as I liked him, and I wanted to try a 'love spell' I'd read about in some teenage magazine which required white feathers, a candle and a ribbon. When Lucy was sixteen and started going out with Andrew Lewis, and I was worried that I knew nothing about sex and would embarrass myself when Art came home for the holidays, she gave me blow job lessons by demonstrating on a can of vanilla Impulse. For years, she put up with me talking about little other than him.

I sighed at her question, not sure where to start, not sure when anyone had last asked me that, but the answer felt too complicated, so I decided to make a joke about it. 'Luce, I can't believe you're the one with the baby and you're asking me that. I'm all right, thanks. Just a lot going on with work and family stuff... I guess you've heard about Mum moving out?'

She nodded. 'I'm sorry, yeah.'

'It's fine,' I replied with a shrug. 'Feels a bit juvenile to be upset about your parents separating as an adult. I'm not sure it's even allowed given my job but, yeah, it'll be fine.'

'Course it will, and I'm pretty sure it's allowed.' She rolled her eyes at me as if I was an idiot for thinking otherwise. 'Hey, if you're up for a while, come to the pub one night? Mum comes over on Thursdays so Mike and I can go out for a drink. That's what counts for date night up here, an evening eating Scampi Fries in the Duck.'

'Yeah, I'd love that. So long as I can get a night off Dad-sitting.'

'I can't imagine he'll be away from his usual table for long.'

I laughed again. 'Fair. But listen, I should get back with his newsp—'

And then, before I could finish, she blurted another question. 'Is it true about your mum moving in with Luigi?'

I blinked at her. 'Who's Lui—'

'He runs the new coffee shop,' she replied quickly, her pale face reddening. 'Sorry, it's probably gossip, you know what this place is like.'

'Mum moving in with Luigi,' I repeated, as if in a daze. 'Mum and Luigi? Luigi from the coffee shop? As in, they're a thing? An item?' I reached out and put a hand on the magazine stand. 'I thought she was living with Elsbeth. But people are saying she's moved in with Luigi?'

'Um, not people, necessarily,' replied Lucy, now the colour of a post box. 'I just heard someone mention it. Can't remember who. I didn't mean *everyone*. I meant hardly anyone. Maybe it wasn't even your mum they were talking about? Could have been another Kath, and another Luigi. There are probably loads of Kaths and Luigis living round here.'

'In rural Northumberland?'

Lucy wrinkled her nose. 'Maybe?'

Then Jimbo tugged at her hand. 'Yes, all right, let's go home, shall we? Sorry, Nell, better get this one home. But lovely to see you, let me know about the pub. Come on, trouble.' She turned and hurried out of the Spar, pulling her small son behind her.

I remained frozen by the magazines for a few moments before trudging slowly towards the till. Mum and Luigi? Mum and an Italian coffee shop owner? She mentioned learning Italian that morning when she'd driven me to the station, I remembered, but she'd also mentioned ballroom dancing, so I'd assumed she wasn't being serious.

I handed the newspaper to the cashier and sighed, then untied Wilma outside and headed home across the green, determined to avoid even looking at Thanks A Latte on the corner.

Should I tell Dad?

Should I not tell Dad?

Arguments in favour of telling Dad: he deserved to know; someone in the village would only tell him otherwise.

Arguments against: we didn't talk about things like this in my family; Mum should be the one to tell him if it really was true; he'd already had his wife walk out on him and broken his leg in the past week so he hardly needed any more bad news; he would immediately demand a drink even though it was only 7.53 in the morning.

★★★

'Saw Lucy in the Spar,' I said, slinging the paper on Dad's bed.

He picked it up and started reading the front page: 'That's nice, pet, how was she?'

'Seemed good but she mentioned something about Mum.'

'Oh yeah, what about her?' he replied, without taking his eyes off the paper.

My voice went squeaky. 'Something about Mum and, er, the coffee shop.'

'Did she now? Was it about Casanova and his fancy cappuccinos?' He lowered the paper to his lap, turned the page, and picked it up again. 'I thought that would be out before long.'

'*What?* So it's true? And you know?'

'Seems to be true, pet.'

I stared at him as he inspected a photograph of a jockey taking a fall. 'Is that it?'

Dad glanced up, eyebrows raised in innocence. 'Is what it?'

'Is that all you're going to say about the fact that Mum's gone off with some Italian stranger?'

'What else can I say, pet?' He grunted and turned his head

back to his paper. 'Probably should have bought her one of them posh coffee machines for her birthday.'

'Instead of the leaf blower? Might have helped.'

'There's eff all I can do now, is there? If your mother wants to move out, that's her business.'

I tried to think of something consoling: 'Maybe it's a phase?'

Dad grunted again which meant no more discussion.

I exhaled and nodded at his mug. 'Another tea?'

'Go on then,' he said, lifting it towards me. 'I never understood all that fuss about posh coffees in the first place – caramel this and vanilla that. What's wrong with a tea? It's more honest, tea, it's not pretendin' to be anything else.'

'I'm with you, Dad,' I said, extending my hand for his mug.

He held it out but, as my fingers clasped the handle, he held on to it for a beat. 'I'm glad you're here, pet. I've missed you.'

For Dad, this was such a radically emotional statement that my eyes welled up. 'Me too,' I said, but then the moment was ruined because I remembered poor Sandra, still lying on her side in the garden.

'What do I do with her?' I asked Dad.

'There's a shovel in the shed. Why don't you put her in that flower bed at the front of the house?'

'What flower bed? We haven't got any flowers.'

'You know, round the front where the brambles are.'

'Oh, the brambles. I didn't know brambles were flowers. Thanks, Monty Don. Will do.'

So, after making another round of tea, and watched by a curious Wilma, I pulled on an old pair of wellingtons, used a pair of kitchen scissors to snip back the brambles underneath the living room window, and dug a small hole in which I could drop Sandra. It reminded me of the year we'd buried Michelangelo the fish at the hall.

I shook my head as I pressed down on the shovel with my boot. The fishponds had been where it all started, the year that I turned eleven and Art thirteen. There were two of them behind the Drummond Hall kitchen, huge stone ponds that rose from the raked gravel like giant soup bowls: mossy on the outside; murky and green, lurking with fish, on the inside. Scrubbing them every March had been an annual tradition for Jack, Art and me.

They had to be brushed clean with broomsticks, all algae and scum removed, before the hall opened every March for visitors who wanted to poke around the antiques and oil portraits before eating a cream scone in the tea room. Howard the gardener always left supplies for us: metal buckets, fish nets on bamboo sticks, assorted brooms, an old copper bathtub. It makes it sound an Edwardian practice but the year that Michelangelo died was the spring of 1996.

Unselfconscious children, we always stripped off – the boys down to their briefs, me to my knickers and vest – before starting work. First, we used the buckets to fill the copper bathtub with pond water, then we'd step up to the rim of each pond, our bare feet slapping the stone, and tried to catch the fish in our nets. It wasn't far off the fairground game where you have to hook a duck; we dragged the bamboo sticks through the water, looking for a flash of orange or white.

Jack and Art behaved like small gladiators, each trying to outdo the other by shouting how many fish they'd caught, although they fibbed about their numbers. Jack had been a good liar; it seemed to come naturally to him. Art not so much. I always knew when he was lying. Or at least, I'd thought I did.

Once caught, the fish were temporarily deposited in the copper bathtub and we'd shout for Howard to lift the ponds' heavy stoppers – like gigantic stone bath-plugs – to let the old water drain out. Then we jumped down into the empty ponds and scrubbed away the green sludge with the brooms, sluicing it with a hose which normally turned into a water fight, whereupon Nanny Gertrude would appear at the French windows and shout stern warnings about catching colds.

Howard reappeared to put the stoppers back in when they were clean, filled the ponds with a hose and tipped the fish back into them.

For us, the fish catching was the best bit and the biggest prize was Michelangelo, the fattest, oldest carp. We hadn't called him that in deference to the artist, despite the Michelangelo sketch in the hall's drawing room. Instead, the fish had earned that nickname in honour of our favourite Teenage Mutant Ninja Turtle. Michelangelo was the orange turtle, which seemed appropriate for a carp with orange scales.

That sunny morning in 1996, Art caught him and had shouted my name. 'Nell, look, I've got Michelangelo!'

I remembered this moment like a photo, Art standing over me, outlined against the spring sunshine. Attention from him was a novelty; usually, he and Jack chatted to one another and although I tried to keep up, they were two years older, which is a gap as big as a galaxy when you're ten. But as Jack was circling the other pond, I'd been the only alternative.

He'd jumped down to the gravel and slid Michelangelo from his net into the copper bathtub. I crouched beside him, my bare knee against his while we peered at the fish. He seemed stunned by his sudden, rough transportation.

'D'you think he's all right?' Art had squinted at me, a line of worry between his eyes.

'Yeah,' I replied, feeling even then that it was important I reassure him, although the truth was Michelangelo didn't look all right. Around him, the other fish swam after one another, tails swaying through the water. But Michelangelo was still, his mouth gaping open as if he'd got stuck on a yawn. 'I think he's just having a rest.'

I'd stood and Art grinned up at me. Behind us, Jack was shouting that he'd broken his net but for once he couldn't ruin things. Art held out his hand for mine so I could pull him to his feet and that was it, that was when Art became more to me than just Jack's friend or our neighbour.

When his hand touched mine that day, it gave me a wonky feeling in my chest and I came over all shy if I saw him looking at me from then on. I felt fairly confident that this was what being in love meant, because it was around the same time that I'd started reading Mum's romance novels. I'd marry him, I decided that spring, and live in his big house, just like all the Dianas and Arabellas in her books.

This conviction lasted much longer than poor old Michelangelo who, it turns out, did die that day beside the pond. Howard presided over a burial ceremony the next morning, saying the Lord's Prayer while Art, Jack and I stood solemnly in front of the rose bush, but I didn't even cry because I was so fixated by the concept of being in love with Art.

Having wrapped Sandra in an old tea towel, I lowered her into the hole and gently filled it in with dirt.

'Shall we say a prayer, Wilma?'

She looked up and made a small whine.

'OK, a quick one. God bless Sandra,' I said, patting down the soil with the back of the shovel. That would have to do; I needed to get to work.

I returned the shovel to the shed, full of cobwebs, and shut myself in my bedroom. I never started this late.

But just as I opened my laptop, balanced on a pillow in front of me, my phone rang: Gus.

'Morning, my little *igelschnäuzchen*, how's living beyond the wall?'

'That's a new one.'

'Do you want to know what it means?'

'Do I have a choice?'

'*Igel* is German for hedgehog, and *schnäuzchen* means, well, snout, really. Or nose.'

'So I'm a little hedgehog nose?'

'Exactly.'

'Good to know. And it's fine, although I've just buried a chicken and discovered that Mum's having an affair with the Italian man who runs the new coffee shop.'

'I beg your pardon?'

'Mmmm.'

'How long's that been going on?'

'Don't know.'

'What's your dad said about it?'

'Making jokes, the usual.'

'Christ. You spoken to your mother?'

'No, not yet,' I said, looking at a poster of Gary Barlow on my bedroom wall, ripped from *Mizz* when I was about fourteen. I'd put it up to placate Lucy when she'd said I needed to pick my favourite member of Take That, but I couldn't choose Mark because he was hers. 'I'll ring her later.'

Gus sighed down the phone. 'Sounds busy up there. And what do you mean about the chicken?'

'The fox got one last night. So it's been a pretty exciting twenty-four hours up here. You all right?'

'Fine, only sorry you're dealing with this all on your own. I wish I could do something more useful.'

'It's OK. A couple of weeks, then home.'

'Did the doctor say anything about how long your dad would need help?'

'Not really, but the occupational therapist's coming in a couple of days, so I'll speak to them about it.'

'OK, I miss you.'

'Miss you too.'

After we'd hung up I made a start on my emails. Top of my inbox was one from Prince Rudolf. And just to me; he hadn't included Gideon.

Good morning, Eleanor,

I trust you're well. I have a few questions about my written
statement that I'd like to go over with you, say, during dinner at
The Delaunay on Thursday. 8 p.m.?
R

I replied instantly that I was out of the office for two weeks and
working remotely, but was available to speak to him on the phone.

My mobile rang five seconds later.

'Hello, Eleanor Mason,' I said, in my most professional voice.

'That's a pity. I was looking forward to seeing you again. I trust
you're somewhere suitably romantic with that boyfriend of yours?'

I blushed. Had he been a less attractive client, had his head
shone like a light bulb and his gut hung over his trousers like many
of them, I'd have felt more capable of handling it. But Prince
Rudolf's directness, his cool confidence, made me stammer.

'Er, no, not really, at my parents' house in Northumberland.
But, like I said, very happy to answer any questions you have on
the phone.'

'That's a shame.'

'Do you, er, have any questions?'

'I have many questions.'

'That relate to your acknowledgement of service?'

He paused and I could only hear his breath down the phone.
'Yes,' he said, finally. 'In part seven, where it asks me to admit
fault, is this where I agree to the adultery?'

'You agree to accept their claim that adultery caused the breakdown of your marriage, yes.'

'And do I have to list all the times?'

I nearly snorted. 'No, you just have to sign where it says, which indicates that you accept it.'

'OK,' he said softly, 'I will do it. When are you back, Eleanor?'

'Um, maybe in a couple of weeks?' Why had I said it like that? Like a question, and so high-pitched?

'We will have lunch then,' he said, and hung up. I leant back against the wall, underneath Gary Barlow, and exhaled. What a morning: Sandra massacred, a runaway mother and Prince Pervert heavy breathing down the phone at me.

For the rest of the day, I juggled running up and downstairs – making Dad's lunch, letting Wilma out, making more tea, letting Wilma out again, plumping Dad's pillows, making another cup of tea, fetching him a plate of biscuits – with speaking to Gideon, who called me every other minute to ask me questions he could quite easily have worked out himself. He also wanted me to organize a paternity test for one of our oldest clients.

Lord Bedfordshire was a fifty-six-year-old British playboy who'd inherited a mining fortune in South Africa and been married and divorced four times, each wife younger than the former (nickname: Lord Bedhopper). We'd got him the official piece of paper for his last divorce just three months ago and yet, according to Gideon, apparently his latest fling had just announced that she was pregnant with his baby. Lord Bedhopper was contesting this so I had to liaise with her lawyer to arrange the test. Again, I felt like a kindergarten teacher. Fortunately, Spinks had an account with a Harley Street laboratory for such occasions.

When I slid downstairs at around five for my sixty-third cup of tea, Dad summoned me through to the living room yet again.

'Let's go to the pub, pet.'

'Dad, seriously? You can hardly move.'

'I can move, come on. A couple of pints is just the ticket.'

I glanced at my watch. I hadn't thought coming home was going to be a picnic, but after just one day, my patience was running low. If I was a mobile phone battery, I'd be hovering around 4 per cent. Gideon clearly didn't trust that I was working up here and Dad needed more attention than a two-year-old. I had a stack of financial declarations from Prince Rudolf's secretary to sift through, I needed to call Gus, take Wilma for a walk around the green and tidy up the kitchen. There were now so many mugs on top of the dishwasher it looked like they were mating. Half of me felt a renewed wave of sympathy for Mum, for managing home life here for so long; another part of me wanted to commit matricide for abandoning me to it.

'All right,' I told Dad, 'if I can work for another hour, then I'll take you.'

'Another *hour*?'

He sounded like a small child who'd just been told it had to finish its homework before going outside to play. 'Yes,' I said firmly, 'I've got a job, Dad! And it's a really crucial couple of months for me. So another hour and we'll go. Watch telly or something.'

Chapter 7

DAD WAS GREETED LIKE a returning war hero in the Duck.

'It's only been three days since he left!' I said, above the loud cheers from Terence, Roy and his sons.

'Bloody long three days,' said Terence, reaching for a pint glass. 'This one's on the house, Bruce. Nell, what you having?'

'Lime and soda, please.' It was a Wednesday evening, and I was determined to stick to the no-drinking rule during the week. I hadn't had time to run today, and I hadn't finished the reading I needed to do, but this felt like one small way that I could maintain a sense of control.

'Ah, go on, have a proper drink, it's a celebration.'

'It's a celebration every day in here.'

Terence grinned. 'Exactly.'

'Nah, I'm good thanks, just the lime and soda.'

We took our drinks to sit with the others in the corner. Dad waved from his chair at the other regulars like the Queen as I pushed him over, leg sticking out in front of him. He'd moaned and grumbled about having to use a wheelchair on the way home from hospital, but a day later seemed to have settled into it nicely.

'You're all right then, Bruce?' Roy asked, as if Dad had stubbed his toe.

'Yeah, yeah, not so bad,' said Dad, smacking his lips and lifting his glass.

Men are extraordinary. I sat quietly while the four of them discussed that afternoon's racing at Catterick, whether Douglas and Jamie could sign Dad's cast (a gruff 'no'), and the bout of foot rot that had afflicted a local farmer's herd of cows.

In the past few days, Dad had broken his leg and been in hospital for two nights during which time his wife had left him for another man. Was there any indication that they were going to address any of this? No.

The conversation only turned serious when the subject of Drummond Hall came up.

'You heard?' said Roy, looking at Dad and me over his pint.

We shook our heads.

'Sold,' said Roy, with all the satisfaction of a man delivering major news to two people who had no idea of it.

'What?' I snapped.

'All of it?' said Dad. 'The house and the land?'

Douglas jumped in. 'We dunno. But some posh twat from Glasgow's been down in his Range Rover and he's going to turn the whole lot into flats.'

'Douglas, Douglas,' said Roy, pumping his hands up and down in front of him, 'calm down.' He looked back to Dad and me. 'A developer's been down and apparently he's buying it, but we don't know for sure.'

'He's called Cameron Stewart,' added Douglas, 'I've googled

him. He builds these massive blocks, all glass and balconies. Did the Glasgow harbour apparently, made a mint.'

'But Art's not even here,' I blurted. 'How's he done a deal if he's not here? What about probate?'

'He doesn't have to be here to sign anything, does he?' said Dad, before sighing. 'Christ, that is bad news.'

'I told you,' went on Roy. 'That boy was never going to take this place on. Not in a million years. He's not interested. Get rid of it now and he carries on living the high life in New York.' He tutted and lifted his pint again.

'To be fair I'd stay over there if my wife looked like that. Did you see them legs at the funeral?' said Douglas.

'Could hardly miss 'em,' added Jamie.

'Boys…' warned Roy.

'I wouldn't mind her taking a bite out of my hot dog,' Douglas went on, with a sly grin at his brother.

'Boys! Pipe down. Otherwise Nell'll be on the first train back to London, won't you?'

I smiled and shook my head but I had to admit, at that moment, the idea of being back in my flat, on my own sofa, listening to Gus hum along to Puccini or whatever he had on, gave me a pang of homesickness.

'Sorry, Nell,' Douglas mumbled into his pint glass.

'How many times d'you reckon he's been back since leaving?' asked Dad.

'Since moving to America?' Roy looked thoughtful. 'Dunno. Maybe a couple?'

Dad nodded slowly.

'He didn't come back when they closed the place to visitors. And before Lord Drummond died he hadn't been back in the past, what would it be, couple of years? At least. Had he even brought that son of his here before? What's he called?'

'Felix,' I said quietly.

'That's 'im. But had he brought Felix here? I don't think so. No interest in it, I'm tellin' you.'

'Which is why this Cameron fella's been sniffing around,' said Douglas.

A silence fell over the table while my head rang with questions. Of course Art didn't have to be here to sign the papers. Big deals, just like divorces, were simple enough to organize even halfway round the world. We had clients all over the globe. But sold already? To a Glaswegian property developer? Shrugging off his inheritance and living in America for ever? I hated the idea of the hall gutted like a mackerel, its innards ripped out and replaced with soulless kitchens and bathrooms.

'How much d'you reckon?' asked Dad.

Roy puffed out his cheeks. 'All that land along with the house? Gotta be… fifteen mil?'

Dad nodded slowly again.

'But what's the developer going to do with the land?' I asked. 'He can develop the house but what use are the fields?'

'Build on 'em,' said Roy. 'That's what I'm thinking. He'll try and put up new housing developments, I reckon. It's gonna ruin this place.'

'Think about it,' chipped in Jamie. 'Build new housing for commuters since the train's not that long to Newcastle, is it?'

'Twenty minutes,' added Douglas. 'Doddle. And you've got a nice new house right by the seaside.'

'Exactly,' growled Roy.

I imagined the fields surrounding the village covered with dozens of identikit red-brick houses with the same doors and the same windows, and the same tarmac drive curling in front of them. It was unbearable. The wildness of Northcliffe was the whole point of the place, the unspoiled view of the coastline. And the otters and the hares! What would happen to them? Art had moved away, fine, but I couldn't believe he wanted the wildlife to be trampled over. This wasn't Watership Down.

'What about planning?' I said, with a touch of desperation. 'Surely he won't be allowed to build all over it?'

'I think you'll find a good deal can be built dependin' on the amount of money that changes hands,' said Roy. 'Such a rotten *waste*. All that land, all that history. Sold in a matter of weeks.'

'Lady de Vil still about?' asked Dad.

'Nah, she went back to London straight after the funeral. It's all shuttered up again now.' Then he drained his glass. 'Right, lads, and sorry, lady, who's for another?'

They murmured their assent. I shook my head.

'I'm good, thanks. Dad, remember your pills.' But it was a feeble warning. I didn't have the energy for a fight given the news about the hall.

I let him stay for three pints before wheeling him back. He held my phone out and used the torch like a headlight as we bumped down the track.

★★★

It was nostalgia that made me pull out the crate under my bed that night. The talk in the pub made me hanker for a time when the village was happier, when the hall was open to visitors, when there was no grumbling about Art, and when mothers didn't run off with Italian baristas.

I'd avoided this crate for fifteen years, having stashed it as far back as I could the summer after Art's party. For a long time, it was too painful to consider even looking at. But having helped Dad into his bed, I locked up and flicked off the downstairs lights before retreating to my room and deciding it was the night to go through it, to remind myself of more cheerful memories.

The carpet under my bed was disgusting. Dog hair, ancient bottles of body moisturizer, dust bunnies, long-forgotten books and dead spiders, I imagined, as I groped beneath the bed slats.

I heaved the plastic crate out and waved the clouds of dust away from my face.

It wasn't wedding magazines. Instead, on the top of the pile was the first letter Art ever sent me from boarding school when he was thirteen, still folded in its original envelope. I'd preserved it as carefully as an archivist charged with the sepia-tinted scrolls of ancient kings. Carefully, I pulled the letter out and smiled at his small, boyish handwriting. I remembered it exactly, line by line. It was dated October 1996 and Art talked about his hopes of making the rugby team, about being in a dormitory with an African prince, and asked after our new puppy, Luna.

She'd been born in our kitchen one night earlier that summer.

Jack, Art and I had been waiting for the puppies for days ('Is it time yet? Is it time yet?' we'd pestered Mum), but when the night finally arrived and Jack realized there wasn't going to be as much blood and drama as he hoped, he'd lost interest and gone to bed. That was the first time Art ever stayed over.

Once he'd called Nanny Gertrude for permission, Mum had let him and me camp out in the kitchen on makeshift beds made from sleeping bags and pillows, the floor hard under our stomachs, heads propped up on our hands so we could see into the dog bed where Minnie lay, panting in labour. Neither of us wanted to miss the fascinating miracle of birth and that event, combined with a whole night lying next to Art, was the most exciting thing that had ever happened to me.

Except we fell asleep and missed the entire process, only waking when it was getting light, to see what looked like six large, furry maggots sucking at Minnie's stomach. Art wanted to keep one but Lady Drummond forbade it, so five puppies were sold in the end, and we kept one at home who we called Luna. Art had been devoted to her, always coming over to ours in the holidays because he wasn't allowed to play with his mother's dogs at Drummond Hall. Cleo and Julius, they were called, and they looked like big pompoms but Lady Drummond always reminded us that they were a very expensive, very ancient breed which came from Japan and used to protect royal emperors. She lavished more love on them than she did on Art, and Howard had to hand-feed them beef from the estate farm.

I pressed his letter to my chest, smiling at the memory of eleven-year-old me. It pinched my heart to think I'd believed that a letter in which Art detailed his new dormitory arrangements signified we were destined to be together, but that's the awesome, imaginative power of a girl with her first crush for you. Get a whole room of them together, harness that energy, and you could probably power the planet with it.

I slid the letter back into its yellowing envelope and carried on through the crate.

Next, the CD case. This was the mixed Coldplay CD Art had burned me for Christmas when I was eighteen. I'd played it roughly forty-three million times in the months afterwards while Art was away in Anglesey, pilot training at the RAF base.

Flying had been Art's ambition for ever because of his grandfather, a pilot in World War Two who'd been awarded a medal for bravery after a battle over Malta. His bedroom wallpaper had been painted with little planes, and he'd Blu-tacked pictures of planes ripped from magazines over that. His favourite plane was called the Cody 1 (I'd committed this important fact to memory as a teenager) because it was the first British plane that ever flew. And every time a jet flew over us in Northcliffe, which happened often because there was an RAF base twenty miles away, Art would shout its name into the sky. 'Typhoon!' or 'Lightning!'

But his dream of flying was something else he seemed to have given up pretty easily, I mused, before reading the back of the CD case. The sleeve was written in the same, small, neat handwriting as his letter, listing tracks I hadn't heard for years: 'Clocks', 'A Rush Of Blood To The Head', 'Fix You'. Whispers of lines came back to me: 'Tell me you love me, come back and haunt me,' I'd sung under my breath for months, as drunk on teenage love as a pirate on rum. Even the dog was sick of Coldplay by the following summer.

I couldn't listen to them anymore. Gus once suggested getting tickets for a Coldplay gig at Wembley because he knew I'd liked them as a teenager, but I'd instantly said no, that I was 'allergic' to Chris Martin's voice. Poor Chris. It was a melodramatic reaction but I didn't want to see them live while Gus swayed beside me.

Under the Coldplay CD was a stack of folded A4 pages: all the emails Art had ever sent me, printed off, so I could read them again and again in my bedroom, since, back then, I'd had to fight Jack for my turn on our computer. It had been a constant loop of teenage yearning and excitement, and seeing a bold, unopened email in my inbox from Art used to make my heart burn like the sun. I flicked through them, smiling. How was it that I couldn't recall a single fact from my university dissertation on the legal system in Tudor Britain, but I *could* remember every word from an email Art had sent me in the spring of 2004? They weren't even that fascinating. He mostly wrote about flying, this plane or that plane, and the pub in Anglesey where he went on nights off and they served cockles by the ladle as a bar snack. But sentences came back to me like Coldplay lyrics: 'I miss you, June can't come soon enough,' he'd typed at the end of one, and I vividly remembered the lift those eight words had given me, not just for a day, but several days.

Rattling around the bottom of the crate was a heart-shaped stone he once found on the beach and gave to me, plus all his snow globes and postcards. He started sending these after a trip he and his parents took to New York one Christmas. They were always going on exotic holidays: America, the Seychelles, Kenya. But Art knew I was desperate to visit New York back then, mostly because of *Friends*, so I'd come home from school one afternoon to find a small package for me, containing a snow globe of New York with a postcard of the Empire State Building. 'Let's both come here one day!' it said.

After that, Art sent me postcards and snow globes from all his holidays, and my collection spread across my desk: from Rome, Melbourne, Cape Town, Singapore, San Francisco, Vienna and St Petersburg. But I loved the New York snow globe most of all because it had been the first one. Inside it was a miniature Statue of Liberty surrounded by skyscrapers and, at the bottom, tiny yellow taxis. I'd lie in bed and imagine Art and me there together while shaking it again and again.

Finally, there was the card and his twenty-first birthday present.

Seeing these made my face freeze. Neither were opened. The card came back with me the night of his party, carried in the small velvet clutch I'd borrowed from Mum, and the photo collage was still wrapped in the paper that I'd been so excited to find in the Morpeth Woolworths: yellow and decorated with little cartoon planes.

My hand hovered over both. Did I want to open them? Was this a bad idea?

Nell, it's an old teenage present, not the unsealed tomb of a cursed pharaoh. Get on with it.

I ripped the paper away and held up the frame. The pictures made me simultaneously happier and sadder than all the other treasures I'd stored away. After seeing Art so briefly at his dad's funeral, I almost felt as if I'd made our whole relationship up. Could we ever have been close, given he was such a stranger now?

And yet here was real evidence: on the beach one summer, mouths wide open with laughs revealing our milk teeth; on the lawn at the hall with a picnic; standing underneath the entrance to the maze.

There we both were the year Jack and I went to the annual Christmas party at Drummond Hall, me gazing at Art with wide-eyed devotion, like a hungry spaniel.

Here we were one spring, standing on the side of the fishponds, nets in hand, eyes squinting down at the glare on the water as we looked for Michelangelo.

I was right: it had been sweet, perfect, all-encompassing first love. For me, anyway. And the photos proved he'd loved this place, too, no matter what Roy said in the pub. He wasn't the Art in those glossy New York photographs, or at least he hadn't *always* been like that.

Then I opened the card and covered my mouth with my palm. I'd forgotten.

When I made the bus trip to Morpeth the week of Art's twenty-first birthday party, I'd bought two identical birthday cards and written them both with exactly the same message – apart from the sign-off.

In one, I wrote 'With love from Nell xxx', and in the other, I wrote 'I love you, Nell xxx'.

I'd spent days before his party agonizing over this, wondering whether I was brave enough to say I loved him. Dare I? Could I? Was it too much? But I'd assumed that we might sleep together for

the first time that night, the night of his party, so it had seemed
an appropriate declaration, the sort of dramatic confession that
would have happened in one of Mum's Mills & Boons. In the
end, I'd put the card that told Art I loved him in my clutch bag,
and threw away the other one.

Except Art never got the card and here it was. I screwed my
eyes closed, aching for my eighteen-year-old self, wishing I could
go back and tell her it would all be fine, that I'd cry for a couple
of years but eventually get over him, and move to London where
I'd live with somebody else and have Aesop handwash in the
bathroom. Also, to buy Amazon shares.

Too late for any wisdom, I thought, as I glanced down to my
phone, vibrating on the carpet beside my knee. It was a goodnight
WhatsApp from Gus: Sleep tight, lambkin, I love you.

I flicked my eyes from my phone screen to the card and felt
as if I'd been caught out. What was I doing, sitting here on my
childhood bedroom carpet, raking through memories like embers?
It was disloyal. If Gus had been sitting at home leafing through
old artefacts from past girlfriends I'd be furious.

Fortunately Gus didn't have any old girlfriends because he'd
been such a dork at school, but still, enough.

In the morning, I'd take the crate downstairs, slide it into a bin bag
and be done with it. There's no point in keeping these things, is there?

★★★

I woke early the following morning and decided on a long run
to try and feel more like me again. I needed to be sensible,

thirty-three-year-old lawyer Nell, not mopey teenage Nell wallowing over old romantic artefacts. Quietly, so I didn't wake Dad in the room beneath me, I pulled on my leggings and old running fleece, and picked up my trainers.

I'd always been aggrieved that running kit was so ugly given that it was also so expensive. My current pair of trainers made my feet look like crocodile heads – they were enormous, green and black monsters recommended by the specialist running shop near the office. Not long after I'd taken up running a sharp ache started radiating from my right hip to my knee. Off I went to an osteopath who, for a hundred quid, told me I had 'the flattest feet' he'd ever seen and duly dispatched me to the running shop where they made me run barefoot on a treadmill to inspect my 'gait'. For another couple of hundred quid, they then fitted me with corrective orthotic insoles and a pair of 'stabilising' trainers, which would apparently prevent my feet from slapping the pavement like Pingu.

My hip pain vanished and I could run again, but every pair I'd had since were brutally ugly. That was another reason I got up at 6.10 a.m. and ran into work; if I reached the office before seven, I could get into the shower and be changed before anybody saw me dressed like the member of a grunge band, with a sweaty upper lip and strands of hair plastered to my forehead.

I tiptoed downstairs and laced my shoes while Wilma pranced around me with excitement. 'Shhhhhh. Come on, let's go,' I said, opening the kitchen door before there was a cry of 'Make me a tea, pet!' from next door.

Sometimes I ran with music or podcasts; sometimes without. It depended on my mood but this morning was a no-music day. I wanted to clear the emotional debris in my head without anyone warbling in my ears.

I headed down the track and made for the narrow path that led to the beach. I'd always found running near water soothing, almost meditative. Whether the Thames or the sea, I'd run while staring at the ebbing tide and remember that whatever I was obsessing over didn't matter.

This applied to my parents' separation, I told myself, as Wilma and I trotted down towards the path. It would all work out. As would the sale of the hall, and my underlying anxiety that being away from the office would set me back from any promotion. The waves would come in and go out again; life goes on.

Be more Wilma, I told myself, watching her bound along in front of me, clearly delighted with the direction this outing was taking. There she was, simply happy to be outside, her only concern whether or not she'd catch a seagull. She wouldn't and she never had but she didn't let that stop her trying. Be more dog, I thought again, as I pounded along the hard, dark sand and she bounced in and out of the shallows.

On today's to-do list was call Darren the personal trainer's lawyer yet again about whether or not he'd managed to read, understand and sign the Jalal prenup; check in with both Linzi and Prince Rudolf's secretary and make sure his form of acknowledgement was coming along (easier to go via the secretary than Prince Pervert himself); confirm that Lord Bedhopper had been to the Harley Street clinic.

I stopped running to take a picture of the sunrise. The yellow and orange light looked like a nuclear explosion on the horizon and I already had roughly five million sunrise pictures in my phone's gallery but what was one more? I'd send it to Gus when I got home to make myself feel less guilty about picking through my crate of Art memorabilia the previous night. Lovely, sweet Gus, who I would go home to soon and then normal life would be resumed. Normal life with my normal bed and normal weekdays, apart from Gideon who was pretty abnormal, obviously, but everything else would revert to how it should be.

Reassured by my own pep talk, I pushed on, revelling in the familiar sensation of tired legs and beating chest. I reached the end of the beach, called Wilma and turned back before deciding to loop up the path that led to the hall. It was the steep way back but the exertion was helping my anxiety melt and part of me couldn't resist taking a look at the place, seeing it with my own eyes, given the previous night's discussion in the pub.

My lungs were screaming by the time I reached the top, but here the path flattened out and twisted around the rhododendrons towards the main drive and the hall itself.

Wilma ran ahead while I paused to take in the sight. As Roy said, the hall's windows were shuttered and perhaps the façade looked a little duller, the brickwork less bright, than when I was small. But other than that it was the same house I'd always known, the house I knew almost as well as my own, the house that I'd spent so many hours – thousands? An embarrassing number, anyway – dreaming about being mine. And now it was someone else's entirely, or it would be very shortly.

I started running again, hoping the developer would keep the fishponds and the maze as I circled the bushes. Maybe it was better that the place was sold and turned into apartments so it could be loved again. If Art didn't care about it, better that it be flogged and be lived in by others than not. This spot was too unique to be abandoned. Windy, true, but it beat living in a residential street of terraced houses in South London.

Oh Christ, Wilma, seriously?

Up ahead, right in the middle of a patch of lawn, she paused and lowered her bottom towards the grass. I slowed again and reached into my fleece pockets to see if I had anything that could feasibly be used for a poo bag. Nothing, not even a crumpled old tissue.

I glanced around me as if anybody was watching. I could leave it, right? This was the countryside, not Clapham Common. Nobody was here. But when she'd finished I stepped closer. My God, the pile was enormous.

'Jesus, Wilma, a dinosaur could have done that,' I muttered, as she happily bounded off again.

I'd kick it, I decided. Kick it with my enormous shoes into the bushes and then at least I could tell myself I'd tried to clear up after her. I wrinkled my nose as I drew my foot back and went for it like a footballer taking a penalty.

No! No no no! While half the steaming pile sailed into the flower bed, the rest of it stuck to the toe of my shoe.

I angled my foot and dragged it along the grass as a whiff hit my nostrils. Bleurgh, Gus was right, dogs could be revolting. I loved Wilma but this wasn't nice. If you had a baby and it did something like this, did you still love it?

'Urgh, urgh, urgh,' I muttered while I carried on dragging my shoe along the grass. I'd have to disinfect them when I got home. As if my trainers weren't repulsive enough already, now they smelt illegal too.

'Nell?'

I froze on the spot, my leg angled to the grass. Then, very slowly, I turned round to see Art frowning at my foot.

Chapter 8

'HI!' I SQUEAKED, GIVING my trainer one more wipe.

'What are you doing?'

'I'm… nothing. Literally nothing, just walking the dog.'

'I can see that.'

He grinned while I fought a wave of embarrassment at being caught in my running kit, red-faced, shiny, panting, and smelling of dog shit.

God, if you're up there, I thought, raising my eyes to the sky, we will have words about this later.

'How come you're still here? I thought you'd gone home? I thought you went home on Friday?' I regretted gabbling this as soon as the words escaped my mouth, giving away that I'd been aware of the day that he was leaving. That was amateur level psychopathy and I should be better than that by now.

Art shook his head. 'I was going to but then, er, something came up so I decided to stay.'

'With—'

'No,' he interrupted, anticipating my question, 'they went home. Home to America, I mean.'

'Oh. So you're here for how long?'

He shrugged. 'Not sure, probably a week or so. There's just quite a lot to sort out. I should have known really. Dad... didn't exactly leave things shipshape.'

'Yeah, I heard.'

'Heard what?' he asked, a frown creasing his forehead.

I'd said it without thinking because I was more conscious of the fact I was standing in front of Art sweating like a sumo wrestler and smelling like Wilma's bottom. 'Oh, not much. Just talk in the pub really... about the house and the estate and...' I tailed off because he sounded so defensive, but I couldn't help myself. 'Art, is it true that you've sold it?'

He dropped his chin to his chest as I stood there, the smell wafting from my feet.

'Art?' I ventured, after a few moments.

He lifted his head and I realized how tired he must be; his green eyes were hooded, his jaw covered with several days of stubble. I was struck by a sudden craving to reach forward and hug him but stopped myself. It would have been inappropriate on roughly eighty-six levels and, also, there was my shoe issue.

He exhaled and stared over my shoulder at the sea. 'This place never changes.'

'No. No, it does not.'

An awkward silence fell.

'You heard about my mum?' I said after a few moments, as if to prove that Art wasn't the only topic of conversation in the pub.

He frowned again. 'No, what?'

'She's left Dad and taken up with the man who's running the new coffee shop.'

'Serious? That place with the terrible name?'

I burst out laughing. 'Yes! Exactly, yes.'

'Is that why you're here?'

I fluttered my lips. 'Kind of, long story.'

Art opened his mouth as if he was about to say something, then stopped himself.

'What?'

He tilted his head and squinted. 'Want to tell me over a cup of tea? If you're not in a hurry, there's something I'd like to show you.'

I listened to a woodpecker in a tree above us while I thought of Dad at home. And my emails. And Gus. And my trainer.

'Sure,' I replied, before shouting for Wilma who'd disappeared in the bushes.

We turned towards the hall. My head was full of questions but I wasn't sure what to ask first, and most of the questions were too big. I wanted to ask how he was, but I didn't really mean how he was now, on this sunny morning. I meant how he was in a wider sense, with his dad gone and his responsibilities here, how he'd been for the past fifteen years, how he was generally in life. It felt intense before he'd put the kettle on, but I'd always been able to talk to Art more freely than anyone else.

When we were teenagers, in the holidays when Art was home from boarding school, he'd come over to mine, sometimes quite late, and stand outside my window, cupping his hands together to make the noise of an owl. At least, he said it was an owl. I thought it sounded more like a confused cow mooing for assistance. Still, it was our code and if I heard it, I'd sneak down to let him through the sitting-room window and upstairs as quietly as I could.

We'd sit in my room and talk about everything, from our parents to Van Morrison (Art's favourite singer), to which kind of food we'd eat if we were only allowed one sort of cuisine for the rest of our life (Art: American, which I disputed was really a *cuisine* but allowed after a long debate. Me: Italian, because you could have pasta and pizza but people also forgot you could eat things like meatballs), to how much we loved Nanny Gertrude, and Art's obsession with flying. We skipped from the high to the low with almost comic speed, from whether we believed in ghosts (supposedly, there was a ghost of a Victorian housemaid that drifted through the Drummond Hall corridors but Art had never seen her), to Tony Blair and the war in Iraq which had just begun; from whether I wanted to be a lawyer, which I'd started considering by then, to whether crisps or chips were better.

The only topic we never discussed, we never even got near, was our romantic lives. For some reason it was a no-go zone, but I was fine with that. It wasn't like I had anything to tell.

I always suspected that Art came over to forget that Lord and Lady Drummond were more interested in their horses and cars than him. But it was more than that for me. If Art was in my room, there wasn't another place on the planet that I'd rather be. That was my whole world, right there. I was unsure about so many things as a teenager but not when I was with Art. With him, I'd always felt the truest version of me.

I tried to think of a suitable opening question as we crunched along the drive. 'How's being the new Lord Drummond then?'

'Don't you start,' he warned, as we reached the side door and he stood aside to let me through.

'What d'you mean?' I kicked my shoes off and, with Wilma at my heels, followed him down the stone corridor. A spiral staircase at the end of this led upstairs to his wing, but Art ducked through a door to the left, into the old kitchen, where Frank, the Drummond's French chef, used to make us picnics in the long summer holidays, when Art, Jack and I would spend all day running around the hall's grounds. Every morning, he left a basket on the back steps, full of cheese and salami sandwiches, or small quiches, along with hunks of sponge cake and cartons of apple juice. Like swallows to a bird table, we'd come and collect it when hungry.

Art reached for the kettle and held it under the tap. 'Only that everyone else seems to be much more delighted by the title than I am. Nicole's ecstatic. Already ordered her new headed notepaper.'

He gave me a weary grin and dropped the kettle on the old stove. 'But it just makes me feel old. Lord Drummond was my father, not me. And it's the twenty-first century. Why are people still inheriting titles? It's one of the only things I like about America.'

'What?'

'No titles. None of the obsession with class and where you went to school and whether you say loo or toilet. It's just the *bathroom*,' he said, with a nasal American accent.

I smiled and looked around me with a dizzy sense of nostalgia. I'd always felt most comfortable in here. The rest of the hall was decorated with gilt furniture, marble busts and wood panelling, but the kitchen had been a cocoon. The cream kitchen cupboards were the same, the old pine kitchen table was the same, there were the same faded posters of aubergines and pineapples on the walls, although it had seemed warmer and cosier when I was small, and usually smelt of Frank's vanilla Madeleines or honey cake. Now there was a mustiness to the air which suggested nothing had been cooked in here for years.

'Coffee or tea?' asked Art, opening a cupboard door.

'Tea's fine, thanks.'

'A decent teabag is one of the things I miss most. The tea in New York is frankly undrinkable.'

I didn't reply because I'd moved to the kitchen's French windows, transfixed by the sight: empty fishponds, the stone entirely covered with lichen, and the paving around them strewn with weeds.

'Sad, huh?' Art said behind me. 'Remember the good old days of fishing them out? And Michelangelo?'

I turned to look at him. 'Yeah. What happened?'

He reached for two mugs from the shelf above the stove. I remembered those mugs too, a china set decorated with various types of flower. 'Dad burned through the cash,' he said, eventually.

'That's why you've got to sell it?'

'It's not the only reason.'

'So it is sold?'

Art tilted his head and smiled at me from across the kitchen.

'What?'

He opened his mouth and paused again.

'What is it?'

'I imagine you're a good lawyer.'

I frowned. 'How d'you know that?'

'Might have googled you,' he admitted, with a sheepish grin.

'Did you now?' I smiled back, feeling a spike of pleasure before horror: my mugshot on the Spinks website was horribly unflattering. I had multiple chins and a gummy smile.

'From time to time, just to check what you were up to. And it's probably sold,' he went on, 'there are just a few things to iron out.'

I turned to look out of the window again.

'I'm not sure what else I can do,' Art added. 'I feel guilty, as if I'm letting my family down, and the village down, and I feel like I'm giving away something incredibly precious. I get that, I know I am. But I've gone over the numbers endlessly.'

I turned around, too depressed by the ruined fishponds to keep staring at them. 'There's no way you can keep it? It's your home, Art.'

'Was my home. Look, take this, this is what I want to show you.' He handed me a mug of tea and inclined his head towards the kitchen door.

I followed him, back down the stone corridor to the baize door that led into the state dining room. Art pushed through it but I couldn't see anything at first since the shutters barred all natural light.

It was only when he pulled a shutter open that I saw the room was empty; no mahogany table, no chairs. The oil portraits had gone too, leaving faded rectangles in their place. It smelt of dust and mildew but looked worse. It looked like the setting for a horror film. If the hall *was* haunted by a Victorian housemaid, she wouldn't seem out of place.

He led me through the rest of the state rooms, opening the shutters to billowing clouds of dust and dead flies as we walked. Through the silk tapestry room, where there were no more silk tapestries; into the drawing room where the sofas and armchairs were gone and the carpets had been rolled back leaving bare floorboards. In the picture gallery, there were no pictures and the crystal chandeliers had been stripped from the ceilings.

Each room felt emptier than the last, with the marble side tables vanished, and the vases, the gold clocks, the gilt mirrors all removed.

Art and I walked while Wilma sniffed noisily into the corners. 'Mice,' he explained.

We reached the main hall, the only room with its shutters open. Beside the fireplace sat a single tea urn, a reminder of the funeral tea only a week earlier.

'He'd have sold this if he could have worked out how,' said Art, sliding a hand up the silver banister. He crouched and sat on one of the stairs. 'I wish I didn't have to sell but maybe it's better this way.'

'To a developer?'

He sighed. 'Nell, I don't know what else I can do.'

I lowered myself to the stair underneath him, cradling my tea. 'What about, I don't know, renting it to a Russian oligarch, or, no, I know! Making it a posh spa? Or launching a festival? Or patching it up for a TV series? You could get Howard involved. The comedy gardener. And Nanny Gertrude. They'd be great on TV. People are always doing that on the telly.'

'What people?'

'People who move to France and buy a chateau and spend the next few months doing it up with the help of amusingly French locals.'

He grinned over his mug. 'Sadly I think this place might be beyond that. The roof's collapsing and the electrics are ancient. And it needs new plumbing and a complete redecoration. And furniture. I just...'

I waited for him to go on but he stayed silent, staring into the depths of his tea.

'What?'

'I haven't got the money.'

'What about your mum?' I asked, remembering Lady de Vil at the funeral, smothered in black fur.

'What do you mean?'

'If there's no money...' I started, glancing at the worn patch of stair carpet between my feet, 'how'll she manage?'

Art made an amused grunt. 'There's a trust with a lump sum still in it. Enough to keep her in clothes, and in London, but not enough for this place, sadly.'

My mind flitted back to the newspaper piece about Nicole's family. 'Is there no way that you could borrow fr—'

'Don't even say it.'

I pressed my lips together and another silence fell while Wilma carried on sniffing the skirting boards.

'How is...' I started, wanting to ask about his life in New York. But as I started to form the question, my courage deserted me. It felt too personal.

'How is…?'

'New York. How is it? Living there, I mean,' I gabbled. 'I don't mean, like, crime rates or, I don't know, the economy. Just, yeah, how is it as a home?'

Art leant further forwards on his step and hunched over his knees. 'It's like another life, Nell.'

'To here?'

'Yeah. It's so different.'

'How d'you mean?'

'To what I assumed life would look like when we were running around out there.' He nodded through the entrance hall's window at the lawn and the North Sea beyond it. 'Though it's not all bad,' he added, looking back to me with a grin. 'The tea may be disgusting but they make up for it with their truly outstanding sandwiches.'

'What's so good about them?'

'What's not good about them, you mean. Nell, there's a place near my office which does a turkey, ham *and* bacon club this big, with Swiss cheese and mayonnaise and…' Art paused and groaned. 'I love that sandwich.'

'Do you say yo-ghurt now?'

He laughed and leant back against the silver banister. 'No, it's still yoghurt to me. Felix does though. And he says tomay-to, and trash. And vacation. Can you believe I have a son who talks about going on vacation?'

'You have a son,' I murmured.

'I have a son,' he echoed.

'How old is he?'

'Thirteen.'

'Thirteen, wow,' I said, stupidly, as if I'd never heard of anyone reaching the age of thirteen before. 'He looked sweet the other day, at your dad's wake. He looks like you.'

Art's smile became huge. 'You think? I'm glad. He's, well, he's everything to me. He makes it all worthw— Oh, shoot, hang on…' He glanced at his watch. 'No, it's OK, have to Skype him later. Little League game today. Baseball,' he added, at my puzzled expression.

There was a gap of about three feet between us but sitting there, discussing Art's son, it felt like the air was full of invisible questions. Or was that just me, reading the situation wrong? It wouldn't be the first time I'd misinterpreted an interaction between us.

'So what's the deal with your mum?' he asked.

I grimaced at my feet. 'I don't really know. I need to see her. To talk to her. All I know is that she decided to suddenly leave Dad, and the next thing I'm told is that she's moved in with this Italian guy who runs the new coffee shop.'

'Jeeeeez,' Art said, with a long sigh. 'Is it just me, or are things around here more complicated than when we were younger? It's like living in a Greek play.'

I laughed softly. 'Or maybe it's because we're not eight years old anymore.'

'Maybe. So you're not married?' he asked, eyes jumping from my hand to my face.

Talk of sandwiches and baseball had helped me relax but his directness made me tense again. 'Married? Er, no, no. I'm with someone, er, yeah, we haven't done that.'

'Who is he?'

'A guy called Gus, another lawyer.'

'Power couple?' he teased.

'Hardly. Not like you and Nicole,' I replied, thinking back to the photos I'd seen online of him and Nicole dressed up for society parties. Then I clapped a hand over my mouth, realizing I'd given myself away.

'Oh I see. Someone else has done a bit of googling, have they?'

My cheeks went hot. 'Er, well, not googling exactly. But, yeah, I... saw a few pictures online.' I dared to look up with a small smile. 'So you guys made *Vanity Fair*'s Top 100 list?'

Now it was Art's turn to look embarrassed. He screwed his eyes closed and pulled his shoulders towards his ears, as if bracing himself for a collision. 'Christ, you've seen that.' Then he made a mock shudder. 'Come on, you know me. That's all Nicole's stuff, she... well... it's more her territory, that stuff, put it that way.'

'OK, OK, I believe you,' I teased, meeting his eyes with a grin.

Over the years, despite the distance that had grown between us, I'd occasionally indulge in a fantasy that Art and I were still connected. It happened whenever I saw something that reminded me of him – a jet flying overhead, say, or a snow globe in a gift shop – and felt as if there was an invisible cord of energy that stretched from me in London to him in New York. I'd always wonder if he felt it too, as if we were telepathic. If I pulled on this invisible cord hard enough, would he feel it too? Would he think of me?

There was an element of both pain and drama to this fantasy which I enjoyed from time to time, before reminding myself that I was a grown-up lawyer with a mortgage who didn't need to indulge in romantic self-harm. Plus, I was with Gus, and I loved Gus, even though I still thought about Art at least once every day. Maybe several times. Or it wasn't even that I consciously thought about him; more that he was always with me, an illegal squatter in my head who I'd never quite managed to evict.

Obviously I'd googled this fantasy. Not at work in case Liam from the IT department could see the mad word combinations that I'd searched: 'psychic connection first love' or 'signs that you still love someone real???' But I'd look it up at home, every now and then, when I felt the tug of this invisible cord.

Mostly, people online said this was normal, that such feelings could last for years, or even decades, and I'd feel reassured until the next time that it happened, when I heard a Coldplay song on the radio or heard about something dramatic happening in New York on the news. Then, unsettled all over again, I'd wonder how Art still retained this place in my brain when we hadn't seen one another for years.

Once, during a particularly paranoid moment, I'd clicked on the website of a psychic called Gwendolyn Glossop who operated from a Harley Street office and claimed that this sort of connection existed when two people's souls remained 'romantically entwined'. For a fee of £200, Gwendolyn would perform a 'cord cutting' ceremony to sever the bond and allow both people involved to move forward.

It seemed far-fetched to me. And expensive. And, if I was really honest, I didn't want to lose the connection. Something about it comforted me, even after everything that Art had done. But could that really be normal? And did he ever feel it too?

The way he was looking at me on the stairs, as if he was seeing beyond my face, reading my thoughts, made me think he might have done.

Then I felt absurd, and scrambled to my feet. 'I'd better go,' I said, pulling myself up by the banister. 'Work and Dad and... stuff.'

He nodded slowly before looking up at me from his step. 'Good for you, Nell. Sounds like you've got life sorted.'

'OK, let's not go mad. I'm not sure anyone ever feels like life is totally sorted, do they?'

Art's mouth lifted in a lopsided smile. 'Maybe not. Hey, how long you here for?'

'Not sure, another week or so probably.'

'Yeah, I reckon it'll take me a week to tie stuff up. Want to hang at some point, for old times' sake?'

'Yeah, let's do it.'

Art took my number, then reached his arm towards me and, although I suspected that I smelt of dried sweat, that faint tang of frankfurter, I leant into him.

'I was after your mug, but sure, we can hug,' he said, sliding his arms around my back.

I pulled away and drained my tea. 'Right, sorry, here you go.'

Art led me to the kitchen door and I bent to lace my trainers as far away as possible.

Then Wilma and I ran back down the drive while I went over our conversation again and again in my head, just as I used to when we were small, trying to recollect every line. There was a small piece of me that felt the extreme glee, like a shot of ecstasy, that one gets from any interaction with someone you have a crush on.

But you don't have a crush on him anymore, I reminded myself, because of what he did.

As I ran, I decided that a day sifting through extremely boring legal documents would straighten me out again.

Chapter 9

BACK HOME, I MADE Dad's breakfast, gave Wilma her bowl of biscuits and took a pot of coffee upstairs to my bedroom where I opened my laptop and started the ticker on my dashboard that clocked up the time I spent on individual clients. Every time I drafted an email or picked up my phone I clicked on it, and the software automatically worked out each client's bill. Using Spinks to resolve your divorce worked out at something like £950 an hour, and the final bill for our clients usually ran into the high six-figures. I'd been shocked by this at first, shocked by clients demanding that I spend a day negotiating with their other half's lawyer about who was getting the set of Wedgwood dinner plates they'd put on their wedding list. Often, the bill for my time sorting out their squabbles would be higher than the cost of the plates in the first place.

Not anymore. That morning, it didn't seem unusual to ring Lord Bedfordshire's office to confirm he'd made his appointment with the Harley Street laboratory. Or to email Prince Rudolf's office and check he'd managed to fill out the form of acknowledgement correctly and had no further questions about his various infidelities.

Again, my phone rang seconds after I'd clicked send.

'Good morning, Eleanor, I trust you slept well?'

He had a very intimate phone manner, speaking so softly and smoothly it was as if his head was on a pillow beside mine. If he wasn't a prince, he could have made decent money from sexy chatlines.

'Morning, Rudolf,' I replied in my sternest, most professional voice. 'Yes, thank you. Can I help with anythi—'

'How is the north?'

'It's fine,' I replied curtly. 'Can I help with the form? Are you having any trouble?'

He chuckled into the phone. 'You sound very tense today, Eleanor. What's happened? Is everything all right?'

'Nothing's happened. Everything's fine,' I insisted. 'Have you finished filling out the fo—'

'And how is that boyfriend of yours? So cruel to abandon him in London; he must be heartbroken.'

'He's perfectly all right.'

'I am going to send you something to help you relax. What is your address?'

'What? No!'

'It will be my pleasure, Eleanor.'

I sat up straighter on my bed and tried to sound stern. 'Prince Rudolf, we have a company policy about gifts and I cannot accept anything, but thank you.'

'What is your address?'

'Like I said, we have a policy, and I cannot give you my address, but I'm very grateful. And if you don't have any questions about the form then I thin—'

'I do have one question.'

'Go on.' I almost sighed with gratitude that we were back on a work footing.

'Where it asks whether I agree to the statement of arrangements, what is this?'

'That's regarding your children. So say no there, because we're contesting your wife's claim. I'm preparing a written statement regarding joint residency which should be with you to read later today.'

'You are my angel, Eleanor.'

'Not at all, this is what I'm here for.'

He laughed again before announcing that he had to go.

I dropped my phone on my bed with a loud exhale. I was paid well for my job but some days, the days when I was at the whim of lunatic millionaires, I wondered whether it was quite worth it.

The same thought occurred to me an hour or so later when I called Gideon to update him and he asked if I was enjoying my 'holiday'. I had to have a restorative digestive biscuit after that. But the minutiae of the various cases I had to sift through that morning – Linzi's bank statements, along with the statement about Prince Rudolf's three children – required so much concentration that I *did* manage to expel all thoughts of Art.

I paused for a lunchtime sandwich break, and carried one through to Dad, along with that morning's post.

'How you doing, pet, managing with your emails and all that caper?'

My eyes boggled like he'd just sprouted another head.

'What?'

'You've just never asked me anything about work before.'

'Can't a father show a bit of interest?'

'Yes, absolutely you can, and it's all right thanks.' I stopped and sighed. 'I mean my boss is driving me ma—'

'Chuffing hell,' interrupted Dad, looking down at the letter he'd opened.

'What is it?'

'Lease renewal for this place, from the estate office. I need your mum to sign it, or not sign it.' He sighed while staring at the letter. 'I dunno. I dunno what we're going to do, or if I can even stay here.'

He glanced around the living room at the sagging blue sofa; the faded, floral curtains and the old TV, in the corner, which we'd had for about twenty years and only offered the terrestrial channels. I'd always gone over to Lucy's to watch more exciting channels like MTV as a teenager.

Against his pillows, Dad looked deflated.

'I'll go and see her,' I volunteered. 'Hand it over, I'll go and talk to her.'

There'd been a notable lack of communication from Mum in the past couple of days. She must know I'd find out about Luigi because, as Dad had implied, you can't change your underpants in Northcliffe without the rest of the village discussing it, but I hadn't heard a squeak. I hadn't even texted her about Sandra the chicken because I'd been too furious. But I knew I'd have to see her eventually, and it might as well be for practical reasons. I resolved housing squabbles for my clients so I could do the same for my parents.

His face brightened. 'Would you, pet?'

'Yes, as usual, I will sort out this family's communication problems,' I muttered.

Dad frowned up at me. 'Eh?'

'Never mind, chuck us the letter. Come on.'

★★★

The café's sign was unbearably twee, I thought, standing under it. Thanks A Latte was written in brown, swirling letters, designed to look like the steam coming off a cartoon coffee cup.

'Sorry, there is a notice outside, no dogs in here please,' said a short man with an Italian accent behind the counter, when I pushed the door open and ventured in with Wilma on her lead behind me.

'Luigi?'

He continued fiddling with the silver coffee machine. 'Yes, but like I say, no dogs please. There is a hook outside for the lead.'

'Is my mother here?' I felt ridiculous, like an abandoned kid waiting in the school playground.

He turned to look at me with a wide smile. 'Ah, you must be Elly-anor?'

I was momentarily taken aback by his friendliness before I remembered to be fierce. 'Yes, but where's my mum?'

He waggled a finger at me. 'Just you wait, I will call for her and then I will make you the best coffee you ever taste in your life.'

What was wrong with him? I didn't want a coffee. I wanted to speak to my mother.

Luigi disappeared through a door behind the till and I glanced around me. When I was little this place had been a chemist, run by a nice man called Brian and his wife, Mary. It was where Mum bought Calpol and worming pills for me and Jack; pots of Pond's night cream for her. But then the Spar opened and the chemist's business had dwindled and finally closed. Brian and Mary retired to a bungalow near Alnwick and the space lay empty for years, a fading 'To Let' poster stuck in the window.

Now, the counter had been transformed. The packets of cough sweets and tissues were gone and in their place was a vast glass cabinet displaying biscotti, fruit tarts, Florentines, little round doughnuts covered in icing sugar, biscuits dipped in chocolate and long tubes with custard squirting from each end, sprinkled with chopped pistachios.

Around me, the wooden floorboards had been covered with rugs, and floral sofas and armchairs, arranged around several mismatched tables, most occupied by punters. A man in a flat cap; two women around my age bouncing gurgling babies on their knees – and Terence.

'Terence! What are you doing here? I thought you didn't approve of this place?'

He looked at me sheepishly over his coffee. 'I've become very partial to the cinnamon latte. You should try one. It's not bad. How's your dad?'

'Fine, although I'm more concerned about my mother right now,' I said, as I saw Luigi sidle back through the door.

'I tell her and she's just coming. Now I make you the coffee.'

'I don't want a coffee.' That was a lie. I would actually quite like a coffee but I didn't want to accept one from this mother-stealer. If I was going to imagine Mum's type, this was not it. But then I'd never tried to imagine Mum's type. Mum's type, I'd assumed, was a man who wore jeans that bagged at the knees and an old Puffa waistcoat that smelt of horse.

Instead, here was a man who looked so Italian he could have been a cartoon character on a bag of pasta: dumpy, with arms like a butcher and a stomach as round as a football that protruded from his white T-shirt and over his chequered black and white apron. Plus, a small moustache.

I looked from him to the door at the sounds of footsteps as Mum appeared through it. Wilma, delighted to see her, leapt forward.

'Wilma, come here.' I tugged at her lead. 'Hi, Mum, just thought I'd drop in to say hello to you and Luigi.'

Luigi, who didn't appear to notice my tone, carried on cheerfully. '*Bellisima*, I say to Elly-anor I am making her a coffee. For you too?'

'I'm not having any coffee.'

'Yes, please, Luigi,' said Mum, smiling at him like a lovesick teenager. '*Grazie*.'

I stared at my mother. She was speaking Italian? This had to be a dream. Must be a dream. In a minute, I'd wake up in my bed in London, and laugh at the idea that my mother had taken up with someone who looked like he should be in a Dolmio advert.

'Shall we sit, Nell?' Mum gestured her head at a free table beside the mothers and their squawking babies.

'Fine, but I'm not having any coffee.'

'Honestly you should. It's very good,' she said as we sat. 'It comes from a roastery in York.'

'Mum! Why are you talking about roasteries as if any of this is normal? I've just left Dad lying in bed in the sitting room, worrying about where he's going to live. Also, Sandra's dead. Sorry.'

A hand flew to her chest. 'What?'

'Fox got her a couple of nights ago.'

Mum winced. 'Oh, love, I said could you lock them up.'

'I know, I know, I'm sorry, I forgot. There's a lot going on.' I glanced at Wilma, who'd flopped down under Mum's chair. 'The others are all right, or at least they seem all right.'

'They probably won't lay for a while, a shock like that.'

Luigi appeared at our table with a tray and, wordlessly, laid down two mugs, a metal cafetière, and a plate of small biscuits dusted in icing sugar.

'*Grazie*,' Mum repeated, beaming. Under his moustache, Luigi's mouth widened to reveal a line of extremely white teeth at her before he hurried back to the counter.

'You must try these. They're Italian biscuits called *genovesi*. Luigi makes them himself.' She poured coffee into the mugs and pushed one towards me.

I ignored it. 'Mum! This is extraordinary. Why are you talking like a tourist in Venice when Dad's laid up at home?'

She had a sip of coffee. 'Nell, as I said in the car, your father and I haven't been happy for years.'

I opened my mouth to make some form of protest, even though I knew this was true, but she held a hand up. 'Can I explain?'

I nodded and she carried on. 'Your father and I haven't been happy. And as I said last week, I've had enough. But what I should have told you then is that it was Luigi who helped me realize this.' She turned and glanced at the counter where Luigi was explaining the pastries to a customer, windmilling his arms at the glass cabinet.

'In the past couple of months he's helped me feel happier than I have for decades,' she went on, turning back to me with the same soppy smile.

'Months? That's how long this has been going on for?' I leant back in my seat and tried to banish the image of my mother rolling around in bed with her new Italian boyfriend.

A shadow crossed her face. 'Weeks, months. I'm not sure. I wasn't counting.'

'When did you tell Dad?'

'That night, Sunday night like you told me. Then he stormed off to the Duck and fell over. How's he feeling?'

'Better than Sandra. But I think just a bit… lost. Not sure what to do.'

Mum sighed. 'He's a wonderful man, your dad. We're just very different.'

Clients often used this word at Spinks. They'd realized, during the course of their marriage, how 'different' they were from their wife or husband.

Of course people changed over time but I'd come to believe that, in more cases, these differences were there from the start: one half of a couple liked tiddlywinks, the other was into thrash metal; one was more outgoing and always the last to leave a party, the other was shy and preferred evenings in.

Perhaps the differences weren't always as obvious as this, but whatever they were, they probably existed on the first date. It was just that, at the start of a relationship, we overlooked them. Or if we did see them, we pretended not to and told ourselves that all the other bits, the bits that made that person feel more like us, were what mattered.

Except, over the course of a relationship, as it aged and frayed, some of these differences did start to matter. In some cases it might be months, in others years, and some relationships could get around them. But I knew from my job that many relationships couldn't. And however long it took, when it came to separating from that person, it was less heartbreaking to tell yourself that the other person had become 'different', and that this was the cause for the sad end of something that had once seemed so perfect.

'He's very different,' repeated Mum. 'And Luigi is...' She paused and glanced back to the till where Luigi was hopping around in front of the coffee machine. 'He's very attentive. It's certainly true what they say about Italian men. Do you know, the other evening, I was just putting on my night cream when I felt hi—'

Like a traffic policeman, I held a hand up. 'Mum, I've got to stop you there.' I paused again. 'I can't believe you told me you were staying with Elsbeth.'

She shifted in her seat as if she had trapped wind. 'I'm sorry, and I'm sorry about your dad's leg, and you having to come up here.' Then she paused and sighed. 'I'm not very good at all this.'

'What?'

'Talking about things.'

'Communicating, no, I know. But it's not just you, it's this whole family.'

We blinked at one another until Mum broke the silence.

'I just couldn't do another day, love. It felt as if I was living the wrong life, just existing, eking the days out. And none of us have forever.'

'I know,' I mumbled, looking down and picking at my thumbnail.

'If you find something good,' she went on, 'you've got to jump, duck. It's called falling in love for a reason.'

I narrowed my eyes at her. 'That sounds suspiciously like something from one of your books.'

'I mean it, Nell. You can't resign yourself to a relationship just because it's there, just because it's safe. I should know, I did that for nearly forty years. And like I said, I'm very fond of your dad but there's more to life than getting through it, love. You have to jump. Who knows, things might not work out with Luigi but at least I'm living again.'

I felt the heat of tears spring up, although I wasn't sure if this was due to my parents' split, my mother living with a Nintendo character, because this was the most honest conversation I'd ever had with her, or something else entirely.

'I'd better get back to him,' I said, standing up. 'Oh but look, I forgot, this is the lease for the house. You and Dad both need to sign it so it's renewed for another year. But I don't know if you want to do that. I don't know if Dad can afford to keep the house, if you're not there? I don't know...' I trailed off. This was much easier in the office, when I was talking about other people's houses.

Mum took the envelope. 'Thanks, love, leave it with me. I'm not sure we need to do anything in a great hurry.'

'Right. And can you ring Jack and explain all this? He needs to hear it from you.'

'I'll call him this week.'

'Today, Mum, seriously. Please can you just give communication a go?'

'I promise,' she said, before biting into a biscuit which left her with a white, sugary moustache to match her boyfriend's.

I leant down for a quick hug, pointedly ignored Luigi's cheerful wave – 'Goodbye, Elly-anor!' – and stepped outside. Then I took Wilma down to the beach for a lungful of North Sea air. Art's comment about this place being like a Greek play came back to me as we headed towards the dunes. If Northcliffe had been as eventful when I was a teenager, I might have liked it more.

Chapter 10

OVER THE NEXT COUPLE of days, Dad and I fell into a rhythm. I'd wake and take Wilma for a run on the beach (avoiding the path up to the hall), come back and make breakfast before sitting on my bed behind my laptop for several hours. Lunch. More work. I didn't have to spend that weekend sifting through legal contracts but there wasn't much else to do and, mindful of my promotion, I knew it looked good if I was emailing Gideon on a Sunday.

At six o'clock every evening, I shut my computer and wheeled Dad to the pub, where he and Roy would discuss the weather, the racing, and continue to grumble about the sale of the hall. Roy had heard that Cameron, the Glaswegian developer, wanted not only to turn Drummond Hall into fancy modern apartments but also develop a golf course. Roy sounded so disgusted at this it was as if he'd have preferred the place to become a dogging spot.

I'd eventually managed to get a word in and told him that Art was still here, not in America, that I'd bumped into him and seen the state of the hall.

'Did he mention the golf course?' Roy demanded, slapping his palm on the table.

No, I replied, but this only provoked a fierce debate about what else they suspected Cameron was planning. Wind turbines in the sea? Solar panels across the fields to make the developer rich from government subsidies? Jamie even suggested a tower block to glum nods from everyone else.

'Art doesn't care what they do, does he?' Jamie added. 'He'll be back in his million-dollar pad in America.'

I didn't tell them that Art seemed reluctant to sell, that he'd said it was his only choice. I wasn't sure that defending him would help the situation.

Then Roy went to the bar to order another round and the matter was dropped in favour of whether or not he should get a new Land Rover.

One evening, I left Dad and Roy discussing this important matter and went to the bar where I'd seen my old school friend Colin sitting with a book.

'Hiya, Col.'

He turned on his stool and beamed from behind his glasses. 'Nell! I heard you were back. How are things? Another one?'

'I'm all right, thanks,' I said, holding up my drink and pulling myself up on the stool beside him. 'And they're good. Well, my parents aren't brilliant but I'm fine. How are you?'

'Me? I'm very well, thank you, yes, very well,' he replied, as if surprised that I'd asked him. 'Not much news, except I've recently moved.'

'Mmm, Luce said. Towards Saltwick?'

'She mentioned she'd seen you. Yes, that way. More space, bigger garden. I planted this year's tomatoes over the weekend.'

'That's exciting.' Colin, I knew from Mum, had become a keen competitor in Northcliffe's Giant Vegetable Competition. Held every summer, at the annual fête, this was ostensibly a civilized event where locals entered enormous cucumbers, leeks, cabbages and so on. Roy usually won with one of his marrows, although there'd been muttering in the pub that he injected them with a growth hormone. 'How's work?' I added.

When Colin wasn't tagging behind me and Lucy as kids, he'd absorbed himself with computer games. He'd been particularly obsessed with one called Civilization, I vaguely remembered, which always sounded like a historical version of Sims, and he'd talked endlessly about building roads and aqueducts. But Colin had the last laugh since, although he wasn't exactly running Amazon, he did now have his own company building websites for local businesses.

'Not so bad. Got a few jobs on, working on the site for that new coffee shop at the mom—'

He paused and blinked slowly, like an owl. 'Sorry, Nell, I shouldn't have mentioned it.'

I narrowed my eyes at him and said, in jest, 'Why? Are you having an affair with him too?'

Colin turned pink so I flicked a hand in the air. 'Oh, don't worry, Col, it's all right. I'm a big girl.'

We moved on to my job, then he updated me on a few other people from our year, before we reminisced about Lucy, him and me travelling together the summer before I left for uni. I'd spent much of that trip crying about Art on overnight bus journeys, listening to pirate CDs I'd bought from dodgy Bangkok markets, while Lucy and Col did all they could to distract me. We went hiking in the north of Thailand, boated along the Mekong in southern Vietnam, visited the war sites, got drunk at a Full Moon Party on a Thai island and tried a magic mushroom shake which made Luce and me laugh for five hours while Colin did impressions of a monkey. I knew I hadn't been the easiest, most carefree holiday companion that summer but they'd never begrudged it. Not openly, anyway.

'I've put some of those photos up in my new place,' he said proudly, which felt like a splinter to my heart. I knew I had pictures of our trip buried somewhere in the flat, but I definitely didn't have any on display. The only photos Gus and I had out were black-and-white shots of places we'd been on holiday. Snaps of Col, Luce and me, in neon face paint, sucking on straws dipped in buckets of Thai whisky would have looked out of place somehow.

'How about the love life, Col?' I asked, to change the subject. 'Any grand romances?'

He shifted on his stool and tittered nervously. 'No, no, nothing like that.'

'I suppose it's quite hard, up here, to meet new people.'

I almost added that my mother had managed it but decided that wouldn't do much for Colin's confidence.

'You know me,' he said, fiddling with the corner of his beermat. 'I'd marry my computer if I could.'

I laughed and he looked up gratefully, blinking at me from behind his glasses. Dear Col. I'd never known him to have a girlfriend, or boyfriend. Maybe he was asexual?

'You heard about the hall?' he asked, a sudden scowl twisting the lower half of his face.

I stuck my thumb over my shoulder at Dad and Roy. 'Yeah, it's all those two can talk about.'

'The council shouldn't allow it. I'm looking into the planning regulations.' He turned his book over so I could see the title: *Planning Obligations Demystified: A Practical Guide to Planning Obligations*.

'Oh right,' I replied, politely. 'Very, er, official.'

'You ever hear from him?'

'Art? Er, no, not really. I bumped into him last week but, no, I wouldn't say we're friends. Not really, not after everything…'

I tailed off and there was a beat of silence before I jumped down from the stool. 'I'd better get Dad home. But good to see you.'

'You too,' he said, pushing his glasses higher on his nose. 'Come back on Friday, if you're about. Quiz night.'

'Oh, cool, maybe.'

'I'm the quiz master.'

'What's the prize?'

'Nothing fancy, depends how generous Terence feels. A bottle of Prosecco normally.' He looked embarrassed. 'You don't have to or anything. You probably have much more exciting Friday nights in London, but we have a laugh.'

'No no, I'd love to. Count me in,' I said, feeling a stab of pity at Colin's enthusiasm for a village quiz night.

Every night, after his allotted two pints, I'd wheel Dad home again for supper and we'd watch a film. For someone so gruff, it had always tickled me that Dad had a soft spot for romantic films; old classics like *Casablanca* and *Gone With the Wind* as well as more contemporary weepies like *Notting Hill* and *The Notebook*.

Romantic films, especially films with weddings in them,

were right up my street but I never watched them with Gus. He preferred Italian epics from the 1970s which ran for hours and made me fall asleep on the sofa. Also, I always cried when the bride arrived and I wasn't sure Gus would appreciate this. I welled up just thinking about that bit when Maria glides down the aisle in *The Sound of Music*.

Watching them with Dad instead was bonding. He pretended not to be tearful when we watched *Three Men And A Little Lady* – 'it's the spice in the curry, pet' – although since he'd finished his curry an hour ago I found this hard to believe.

After chatting to Colin that night, as I wheeled Dad home underneath the pink Northumberland dusk, I spotted a couple of large boxes in front of the door.

'You expecting anything?'

'No, pet.'

I parked him next to them and squatted down.

'They're for me,' I said, confused. They were big brown boxes. Heavy, too. To lift them I had to inch my fingers underneath the bottom and hug each one with my arms.

I staggered into the kitchen and slid each box on the kitchen table, then pushed Dad over the doorstep.

Slicing a knife through the packing tape, I opened the nearest one and fought with several inches of polystyrene to discover six bottles of white wine underneath.

'It's wine. Must be from Gus.'

'Oooh, lovely,' said Dad, rubbing his hands, 'let's get it open.'

The second box was the same, except it was six bottles of red. And it was only when I pulled one of these out that I noticed the label. 'LIECHTENSTEIN,' it said, in gold letters, beneath what looked like a royal crest. 'Cabernet Sauvignon 2012.'

I ran my fingers around the red wine box to find a note taped beside the address label.

DEAR ELEANOR. PLEASE ENJOY THESE BOTTLES FROM MY WINERY. THEY SHOULD HELP YOU RELAX. R

'What's up?' asked Dad, as I stood staring at the note.

'It's wine from Liechtenstein, from a client.'

'Smashing. Corkscrew's in the drawer, pet.'

'We're not drinking any.'

Dad's face fell like a kid who'd just been ordered to bed. 'What? Why?'

'Because I'm not allowed to accept work presents, that's why. And you're not allowed another drink tonight anyway.'

Technically, the work excuse wasn't true. Spinks's policy was just that we had to *declare* any present worth more than £100, although Gideon ignored this. In addition to his diamond Rolex, in the past few months he'd also accepted and failed to declare a set of golf clubs and an enormous pair of Bose headphones from the Texan oil tycoon, which he thought made him look cool, but I thought made him look like a tool. Plus multiple bottles of vintage port and a marble chess set (even though I was pretty confident he didn't know how to play chess).

But Dad didn't need to know that since I didn't want to drink Prince Pervert's wine and be in any way indebted to him. At least, 300 miles away in Northumberland, I was safe from his strokey thumbs.

I pushed the boxes to the end of the kitchen table, up against piles of Dad's old newspapers, and opened the fridge.

'Right, what'll it be for supper? Spar pasta bake or Spar sweet and sour chicken?'

★★★

The next morning, I emailed the prince to thank him for the wine and he replied saying that he hoped I'd think of him while drinking it. Not likely. Then I called Rosemary at work to discover she'd given him my parents' address.

'Sorry, Nell. His secretary said he needed to FedEx some forms to you.'

I sighed. 'Don't worry, it's all right. Thanks.'

I debated calling Gideon to mention the situation but he would scoff and say I was making a big fuss over nothing, that Prince Rudolf was an important client, that if I wanted to be promoted I should grin and bear it, and so on and so on.

Instead, I called Jack, who answered on my third attempt.

'We've discussed this. What if there was an emergency? What if Dad had fallen over again?'

'Has he?'

'No.'

'There you go. What's up, sis? I'm in the middle of something at work.'

'What?'

'What d'you mean?'

'What are you in the middle of?'

'Having lunch.'

'I'm so sorry to interrupt your busy and important schedule but I was just ringing to check you'd asked for the time off? I've been here a week now and I need to work out when I'm coming back. What *are* you eating?'

He continued crunching down the phone, then swallowed and burped. 'Spicy Nik Naks. And yeah, sis, I'm working on it.'

'Jack, I can't be up here for ever. One more week and then it's your turn.'

'All right, all right.'

'Has Mum called you, by the way?'

'Mum?'

'Yep, you know the one. Strawberry-blonde hair, we used to live with her as kids, always sending us conspiracy theories on WhatsApp.'

'No, she hasn't, why? Any reason?'

'No,' I said, resignedly. 'Never mind.'

I hung up and texted her in big fat capital letters: 'RING YOUR SON.'

★★★

Art texted that evening, while I was lying in bed flicking through *Bridalicious* magazine. I'd finally bought a copy from the Spar that morning while buying milk and Dad's paper, smuggling it home in a plastic bag.

I didn't realize it was him at first, because it was a strange, foreign number.

Too weird to go to that new coffee place tomorrow? Quite fancy checking it out. Ax

I stared at my phone screen for a few moments. It would be a bit weird, but I wasn't sure where else to suggest. Going back to the hall, or suggesting here, seemed too friendly and too reminiscent of old times. And I absolutely didn't want to walk along the beach with him because that's what we always used to do. It had been my favourite thing to do with him as a teenager because there was a romance to it – whether the summer holidays and we lay out under the sun, or winter when we wrapped up with several coats and walked into the wind, laughing as we bent forward into it. The pub? No, alcohol was a terrible idea.

I guessed the café was our best bet.

Sure, 3 p.m.?

He replied instantly with a thumbs up emoji and I dropped my phone on my duvet, trying to ignore the guilt. It was just a coffee. Just a coffee with an old friend. The closure that I never had.

I returned to a piece in *Bridalicious* headlined '25 of the prettiest wedding canapés', but it was only a few seconds before my phone buzzed again.

It was Gus.

'Hello, my *liebling*, how was your day?'

'All right,' I replied, sliding the magazine to the floor and balancing my phone on my chest so I didn't have to clutch it to my ear. 'Yours?'

Gus embarked on a long story about a meeting where his colleague's laser pen didn't work. 'You all right?' he asked, after a few minutes.

'Mmm.'

'Seem quiet.'

'Sorry, just... not much to report.'

'Seen your mum again?'

'No, I'm, er, trying to avoid the café.'

I would go to Hell, but people in relationships fibbed about this sort of thing all the time. Also, a meeting over coffee wasn't cheating. A meeting over coffee was the sort of sterile social engagement you agreed to with colleagues you didn't even like.

'Very wise, your mother's probably making up for lost time, enjoying her Italian stallion.'

'OK, thank you, let's not.'

'Just saying.' Gus paused to yawn. 'It's another reason never to get married.'

'What do you mean?'

'So we don't end up stale and sexless like your parents.'

'Oi, careful. I imagine most relationships go a bit stale after nearly forty years, whether you're married or not.'

'We won't be,' Gus replied, indignantly. 'I can't imagine only wanting to make love to you twice a year.'

'Bleurgh, Gus, that phrase.' I'd told him before that it made me cringe so now he did it deliberately.

'Talking of which, where are you right now?'

'Lying in bed, why?'

'That's good, because I was thinking how much I missed my little lambkin earlier.'

Uh oh. I knew that tone. Gus had started talking in his special sexy voice.

We'd attempted phone sex a couple of times before when Gus had gone away on business. To be honest, I'd rather have used my purple vibrator alone but I do see that wasn't much of a participation sport, so I'd go along with it, cringing, finding the performance of phone sex embarrassing. I was a lawyer, not an actress, and I never felt like my gasps were convincing enough.

Also, one of Gus's trips had been to Hong Kong, so he'd been eight hours ahead of me, and he'd called from his hotel room one Saturday night, drunk, when it was only three in the afternoon in London and I'd been lying on the sofa leafing through recipes in the Saturday papers. It's extremely hard to feel erotic while reading a recipe for smoked haddock chowder and I'd tried, I really had, but I ended up faking it, making alarming noises and hoping that our neighbours were out.

'You in the mood? Go on, for me. Pretty please, lambkin?'

I wasn't really in the mood. I was lying on my childhood bed, in a room above my dad, watched by a dusty Furby on my bedside table and Gary Barlow smirking from the wall. But I knew Gus would be hurt if I said no, so it was easier, more straightforward, just to do it.

'Um, OK.' I picked up my phone and turned speaker mode off so Dad didn't overhear any of this below me.

'I'm unzipping my suit trousers,' he said.

'Remember to put them in your trouser press,' I teased.

'Nell, are you going to take this seriously?'

'Yes, yes, sorry. I promise I am. You're taking off your suit trousers and I'm, er...' I looked around my bedroom as if for inspiration. 'I'm, er, putting a hand under my T-shirt.'

'To do what?'

This was embarrassing. 'To, er, touch myself?' I said, like it was a quiz and I was guessing the right answer.

'Touch what?' Gus demanded.

Why was this so mortifying?

'Um, a nipple?'

'Just one of them?'

'I think I'm going to... touch both my nipples?'

'That's right. Until they're hard? Oh, lambkin, I wish my mouth was around them now.'

Oh no, not lambkin again.

'Me *too*,' I replied, trying to indicate enthusiasm, although as I peered under the neckline of my T-shirt, I realized I needed to pluck my nipple hairs.

Gus once made a disparaging remark about nipple hair, telling me he wasn't 'very keen' on feeling any hair with his tongue when we were having sex.

I'd felt like replying that I wasn't 'very keen' on picking pubic hair off my tongue after I gave him a blow job, but then I'd chickened out. I'd just started being more attentive with my tweezers.

'I wish you were here,' Gus said, panting more heavily into the phone.

'Do you? What would you want me to do?'

It was less mortifying, I'd learned, to ask questions rather than come up with seductive lines myself.

'I'd want you to strip naked and tell me about your special place.'

'What?' I squeaked.

'Your special place, your secret place,' said Gus, breathily. He could get quite carried away with the terminology during sex. Once, a few months after we'd started going out, he recited a Byron sonnet while we did it. '"She walks in beauty, like the night/Of cloudless climes and starry skies,"' he'd panted, between thrusts.

'Mmmm,' I murmured back. Please could Dad not hear any of this. The soundproofing in this house was non-existent because it was so old, and if Dad gave any sign that he'd overheard our conversation in the morning I'd have to leave this life and seek witness protection.

'What do you want to do to me?' Gus demanded.

What I most wanted him to do was stop talking like a bawdy Shakespearean so I could go back to reading my magazine.

'Er, I want you to throw me on the bed and then we can… do it?'

Gus huffed down the phone. 'Nell, are you actually into this?'

'No I am! I am!'

'Well you're jumping ahead,' he said crossly. 'We can't go from you getting naked to suddenly making love, that makes no sense at all. What do you want to do before then?'

'Oh, sorry. OK, I'm thinking, I'm really concentrating, and my hand's still on my nipple by the way.'

(This wasn't true but I thought it might mollify him.)

'Good.'

'Right, what I want to do to you before then is…' I glanced around my bedroom and looked at Gary, his thumbs hooked into his baggy white jeans. 'I want to, er, kneel in front of you and, um, suck you?'

Gus groaned louder while I prayed that Dad was asleep. Please, please GOD, could he be asleep?

'I wish you were here,' he went on. 'I'm not sure this is going to take me very long. I want you in front of me, like a French peasant girl, on your knees. Are you touching yourself for me?'

'Mmmhmmm,' I fibbed, while reaching for my water glass. I was too tired to masturbate and I hadn't packed the purple bullet for the trip because who packs a vibrator when they're going to stay with their parents?

'Can I throw you on the bed now? Let me do it, let me do it,' pleaded Gus.

'Do it,' I urged, having a sip of water. 'Throw me on the bed.'

'OK, OK, I'm doing it, I've thrown you on the bed and I'm pushing into your pleasure chest. Oh my god, Nell. Oh my god. Ohmygod, ohmygod, ohmygod. I'm coming, I'm coming, I'm coming!'

I lay still, frowning up at the plastic stars while Gus gasped down the phone. Then came the cough. He always did this after sex. A little cough to clear his chest after a bout of exertion. 'That was superb. Did you come?'

'Course,' I fibbed again, 'I just had to be quiet because of Dad.'

'OK, well, I'm going to get in the shower but I love you.'

'Love you too.'

We hung up and I went back to the canapés article in *Bridalicious*. The mini quail Scotch eggs looked delicious.

Chapter 11

THE NEXT MORNING, I woke to five missed calls from Jack. Nice change.

I called him back, mumbling when he picked up: 'Morning.'

'Morning?' he shouted. 'Morning! How come you're so chilled about all this?'

'Jack, it's just gone…' I held my phone away from my face and squinted at it, 'seven in the morning and I'm in bed. What's up? Why aren't you asleep, anyway?'

'Why am I not *asleep*?' he asked, as if he'd never heard of sleep.

I stretched under my duvet. 'Mmmm.'

'I'm not *asleep*, Nell, because Mum called me last night and announced that she's moved in with some barista.' He spat the word, as if being a barista was the same as being a burglar.

'She called you? That's progress.'

'What do you mean, progress? How can this be progress? How can our mum shacking up with another man be progress? I can't believe *she's* the one having an affair.'

'Jack, is that what you're so worked up about? That it's Mum who's been seeing someone else, not Dad? Those are some pretty incredible double standards. Anyway, it's not an affair if they've separated.'

I heard him draw a breath down the phone, like he was about to shout again, before he paused and replied more calmly, 'No, no, course not. I don't mean it like that. It's just, at her age? With this Luigi character? Disgusting.'

'She's fifty-nine! Presumably you want to still be having sex when you're fifty-nine? Or even ninety-nine, come to that.'

Jack made a noise of disgust down the phone. 'I don't want to think about it. Have you met him?'

'Who?'

'Who? This Luigi person.'

'Mmm. I went into the café a few days ago to give Mum the lease for this place.'

'What's he like?'

'Hardly talked to him. But he called me Elly-anor, so no doubt you'll be Giacomo.'

Jack groaned.

'You're like a teenager. What if he makes her happy?'

He groaned again. 'It's weird. It's easier for you.'

'What? Why?'

'Because of your job, you're used to it.'

'Jack, come on. My clients are different to our parents. And on the subject of work, have you discussed time off with your boss?'

'I can't come up, Nell. I can't watch our mum flutter her eyelashes at another man.'

I sat up in bed, anger uncoiling inside me. This was Peak Jack behaviour, to make our parents' separation and dramas about him.

'Jack, get a grip. You're a thirty-five-year-old man. I've been here for over a week.'

'Aw, sis…'

'Seriously, it's your turn.'

'All right, all right, keep your hair on. I will. It's just been busy.' Then his voice became deliberately casual. 'You, er, you found out what's happening to the hall yet?'

'Yep, bought by some developer.'

'What? Already? Did you put in a good word for me?'

'No! Funnily enough, I didn't, Jack, because I've been busy with our limping father and runaway mother and also not everything on this entire fucking planet revolves around you. Perhaps if you spoke to your boss and got some time off, then you could come up here and do it yourself.' I paused to breathe. 'Can't you claim it as compassionate leave?'

'Because our mum's boffing someone who isn't our dad? I don't think so.'

'Whatever. Just speak to him.'

'I will, I will. Stop going on about it,' he muttered, before I heard him whisper something.

'Huh?'

'Nothing, it's Emma. All right, got to go, bye.'

'OK, just, Jack, please can yo—' But he'd already cut me off.

I flopped back on my pillow and shook my head at the poster of Gary Barlow. 'Men, huh?'

Gary looked like he understood.

★★★

Later that morning, an email landed in my inbox confirming that love really could be blind: Linzi was dropping her case. She and Larry had 'decided to give it another go,' she wrote. 'He's not a bad man, and we owe it to the kids.'

It didn't wholly surprise me. She hadn't returned my last two emails and this often happened at least once with new clients. There was initial anger when one half of a couple found out the other had cheated or gambled or lied – in Linzi's case, it was the discovery of the cucumber – and they started divorce proceedings in fury. But after a few weeks, the other person had talked them down. Perhaps she'd be back in a few months, perhaps she wouldn't. Each to their own.

Gideon was predictably furious to lose a high-profile case and spent all morning sending me emails about Prince Rudolf's financials as a result. 'I need to know you're on top of him, Nell. We can't lose this one. It would look very bad to the board ahead of promotions.'

I almost replied that being 'on top' of Prince Pervert was the last place I wanted to be given his increasing creepiness. He'd started leaving a trail of kisses at the end of his emails to me which I was ignoring, firmly replying with my usual sign-off: 'best wishes, Eleanor'. But Gideon probably wouldn't get the joke or, worse, would tell me to go along with it. Anything for business, in his eyes. The bill sent to Linzi later that day, for our one meeting and a few hours of work, was £4,750.

I was immersed in his bank statements when the doorbell rang that afternoon: Dad's occupational therapist. When I'd reminded him about the appointment at lunch he'd simply grunted in acknowledgement.

Opening the kitchen door, I saw a large blonde lady squeezed into a nurse's tunic that was buckling at her chest.

'Hiya, I'm Bev.' She smiled, stretching her lipsticked mouth.

Wilma jumped up and rested her paws on Bev's tunic.

'Wilma, down! I'm so sorry,' I said, pulling her off. 'I'm Nell, Bruce's daughter. Oh, I'm so sorry,' I said again, noticing two paw prints on Bev's white tunic, like large brown nipples.

'No bother. I'm used to all sorts,' she said breezily. 'Dogs are the least of my worries, believe me.'

'That's lucky. Would you like a tea or a coffee?'

'I'd murder a tea.'

'Easy. Follow me and I'll show you through to the patient.'

I knocked on the sitting-room door in case Dad was picking his nose.

'Dad? The occupational therapist's here.'

I stuck my head around it to see him reaching for the TV remote. 'Now? The Chepstow race is about to start.'

'I don't mind that, darlin',' said Bev, bustling in. 'You just leave it on. I can work around it. Hiya, I'm Bev.'

She extended a hand towards him and I watched Dad stare at Bev in the way I'd only ever seen him size up horses.

She must have been in her late fifties, and was the shape of a ship's figurehead: tall, with enormous breasts you could rest a pint glass on and a doughnut of white-blonde hair piled on top of her head.

She seemed oblivious to Dad's gawping, bustling around his bed and moving the paper from the armchair beside it so she could sit.

'There we go,' she said, wiggling her bottom in the chair like a nesting bird. 'Ooh, it's nice to put my feet up.'

'Dad, do you want a cup of tea?' I asked, to try and snap him out of his trance. 'Dad?... DAD?'

He turned to me with a puzzled face. 'Tea?'

'Mmmm. You know, that hot brown drink you like so much?'

'Oh, TEA! Yes, tea. Tea would be grand, thanks, pet.'

I left them to it and went back to the kitchen from where I could hear peals of Bev's laughter.

Then I carried the tray back through and laid it on the side table. 'Here we go, tea and, Bev, I wasn't sure if you wanted milk or sugar, but it's here if you do.'

'No, ta, duck, I'm all right with just the milk.'

'Sweet enough already,' said Dad, with a chuckle which made me want to pour his tea into his crotch. On the one hand, Mum had left and he had every right to flirt with the occupational therapist. On the other, it made me want to cut my own ears off.

I announced that I was going back upstairs. 'Will you two be all right?'

'Yes, duck, don't you worry. We'll have a little chat and I'll have a quick poke around and see if you need anything in the way of handrails,' said Bev.

Then she leant forward to pour a splash of milk into her mug, straining the buttons of her tunic even further.

Dad's eyes bulged. Forget his leg, he could die of a heart attack before the afternoon was out.

'No problem,' I said, before retreating to my room. I had to get ready for my coffee with Art.

For the first time in a week, I peeled off my leggings and hoody in favour of jeans and a pink jumper from Maje, and I put a bit of make-up on. Not a lot. Just a dab of foundation and a lick of mascara. All right, and a bit of blusher. And highlighter. And eyebrow gel.

I'd do the same if I was meeting any old friend, I reasoned. Like Lucy. If I was meeting Luce I'd definitely make the same effort. Meeting Art was no different. He was just taller and had more stubble.

When I passed through the kitchen half an hour later, I could still hear Dad and Bev laughing through the door.

***

The first three minutes in the café were unbearable.

First, Mum greeted me with a 'Ciao!' from behind the counter. Then she asked why I was all 'dressed up'.

'I'm not dressed up, I'm just having coffee with Art. He wanted to check this place out.'

Seconds later, when Art appeared through the door in his old aviator coat, sheepskin collar turned up, Luigi mistook him for Gus and told me how 'bello' my boyfriend was.

I wanted to murder them both, although Art did look good. Better. Less tired. He'd worn that coat when he'd started RAF training and I'd always thought it made him seem heroic and dashing, as if he might be called up any moment to fly off and rescue a damsel from a burning building. And his hair, (which I'd been obsessed with as a teenager because he'd worn it quiffed, like a high-school movie star), remained thick and there was plenty of it. No longer quiffed, luckily, but he could definitely still make it as a shampoo model.

Nell, do not lose control.

I refused a coffee, determined to keep up my embargo, so Art ordered his, plus a sandwich, and I led him towards a spare table as far away from the counter as possible.

He glanced at the prints and the mismatched furniture as we sat. 'It's nice in here.'

I frowned at him.

'Sorry,' he said, shaking his head before leaning across the table. 'What I should have said is that it's terrible and after today I will never come here again. I just wanted to check it out.'

'Does it seem weird to you?' I asked quietly, my eyes sliding to the till where Mum was smiling at Luigi.

Art followed my gaze. 'No. Might have done a few years ago but now I just think, whatever makes you happy. Look at my parents. Miserable together, hated one another, and really were only happy again in the past few years, as far as I can gather, leading separate lives. You must see this sort of thing all the time in your job?'

'Yeah, but it's different when it's your own parents.'

'Your mum seems happy,' he said, glancing over his shoulder again. 'Happier than I remember as a kid.'

'You think she wasn't happy?'

He squinted. 'Not sure. But I look back now and realize my parents only stuck together because they didn't feel like there was another option, so perhaps the same was true for yours?'

Art and I had bonded over our parents as teenagers, sensing that the other was in a similar situation. There'd always been rumours about Lord and Lady Drummond's marriage, mostly about his affairs. Mum and Dad thought they were being subtle when they discussed them at home when we were younger, but Jack and I knew what they were talking about. The whole village had known. My parents' marriage hadn't been as obviously loveless but nor would it have made the cover of a bridal magazine.

'I'm not sure mine were miserable. Just… not ecstatic, either.'

Art nodded. 'Exactly. Drifting through life together simply because they'd made a choice they regretted decades before. I'm not sure it's a recipe for happiness, is it?'

'No, not necessarily,' I replied, while reflecting that Art sounded as if he was echoing Gus's thoughts on marriage, even though he was married himself.

'Do you remember much from back then?'

'When we were younger? Course,' I said, raising my eyes to his. 'I remember everything. The summers, your birthday parties, cleaning the fishponds, you leaving for school, swimming in the sea, Nanny Gertrude thinking we were going to die every time we came out of the sea.'

He laughed. 'Do you remember the year you got lost in the maze?'

That had been at Art's thirteenth birthday, a couple of months before he left for Eton. Lady Drummond had paid a fancy company from Edinburgh to devise a treasure hunt around the hall's gardens, but I'd become disorientated in the huge yew maze and panicked when I couldn't find my way out.

'When I cried and you came to rescue me?'

Art shrugged. 'What can I say? I wanted to save you.'

Whoa. Dangerous territory. Quick, change the subject, Nell. Anything, say anything. 'What happened to Frank?' I blurted.

'Not sure, back in Paris, probably. Jeez, I miss those picnics.'

'Me too. And do you remember the potato smileys?' Those were not made by Frank. Those were fried by Mum at home and deemed a treat by Art because he was never allowed anything like that at Drummond Hall, where it was all posh French stews and ratatouille.

'Sure do, they were the best.'

I smiled. 'They were. Actually, talking of all this, I found some old stuff the other night.'

'What kind of stuff?' Art asked, as Luigi approached us with a tray. 'This looks incredible, thank you.'

Luigi laid down not one but two coffees and a ham sandwich the size of a brick. '*Prego, prego,*' he said, before beaming and hurrying back to the till.

Art clamped his hands round both ends of the ciabatta and I narrowed my eyes at him. 'Traitor.'

'Sorry, I'm starving. Didn't have lunch because I had a meeting with the Glaswegian. Terrifying man, like a bouncer from a Guy Ritchie film.'

'How is all that?'

He frowned.

'The sale.'

'Oh, happening. Few details to sort out over the land but we're getting there.'

'What's he going to do to the place, Art? Because there are rumours that he's going to demolish it and build a golf course.'

He scowled while chewing, then swallowed. 'A golf course?'

'Mmm. It's been mentioned. And wind turbines.'

'Wind turbines?'

I nodded as he tore off another hunk of sandwich. 'It's all the talk in the pub. Is that what's going to happen?'

Art swallowed and tapped his plate. 'This is an excellent sandwich. Not quite up there with my turkey bacon club, but not far off.'

'Art?'

He laid down the ciabatta and leant back in his chair. 'There will be no wind turbines.'

'What about the golf course?'

'Neither will there be a golf course. I hate golf. Although not as much as I hate baseball.'

'I'm being serious.'

'So am I! You've never had to sit through a game. Goes on for hours; days, practically.'

'Art!'

'All right, OK.' He inhaled loudly and puffed up his chest before answering. 'It's not going to be demolished. No golf course, no wind turbines. According to Cameron, he's going to apply for planning permission to turn it into apartments.'

'Doesn't that make you sad?' I persisted.

'Yes, course. But like I've said, there isn't much else I can do. Anyway, let's not discuss this, it's too depressing. What's this stuff you found?'

He reached for his sandwich again and I gave him a deliberate shrug. 'Just stuff I kept. Like that Coldplay CD, and all my snow globes.'

Art dropped his head back and laughed towards the café's ceiling. 'Those snow globes! You kept them?'

'Course,' I said, stung by his surprise, as if they meant so little to him when they'd meant everything to me. 'And remember the stone you gave me on the beach?'

He shook his head, cheeks bulging.

'On the beach that day when you found me crying?' I said, ashamed that all of this seemed to have such significance for me and not him. 'The one shaped like a heart?'

I'd been sixteen, which would have made Art nineteen, and the crying-on-the-beach situation had come about after my school's post-GCSE party in the gym.

Mr Forbes, the caretaker, had made valiant attempts to jazz the gym up for this grand social occasion: a few clusters of balloons drooped in each corner, the lights dimmed, a trestle table with plastic cups of 'punch' on it, which Jennifer Taggart pretended to get drunk on but, actually, only contained a heady combination of Lilt and Um Bongo. If she got high on anything it was the sugar.

Luce and I hadn't wanted to go because we knew we wouldn't snog anyone, which was the sole point of the party for every other student. But both her mum and mine had told us we had to show up, 'just for a bit', so we sat on a bench at the side, along with Colin, and watched the snogging going on in front of us. Why would anyone want to get that close to Iain Duffy, I remember wondering, as Gemma Pritchard waved her arms around him like she was trying to put out a fire. My overriding memory of the gym that night was the smell of school disinfectant combined with teenage lust.

It was Gemma who made me do it. She wandered past us not long after and muttered 'lesbians' at me and Luce, before hissing with laughter. So, although Colin was still droning on about his new PlayStation, I reached for his hand and announced that we were dancing. He didn't have time to reply and we'd been on the dance floor, swaying to the music for less than thirty seconds when I lunged at him. His mouth felt stiff and robotic, not dissimilar to my hand, it turned out, and our tongues jabbed at one another like fighting snakes. Snogging didn't feel like I'd imagined and I decided, after another thirty seconds, that was probably enough. We sat down on the bench again and, after a stunned silence, Colin simply resumed talking about his computer game while the rest of our year stared in our direction.

I was all right until the following morning when Jack had found out about my romantic endeavours and laughed at me over breakfast. 'Colin Cruickshank! That's disgusting! His breath is disgusting! You're disgusting!'

As usual, Mum failed to tell him off so I'd run off towards the beach, angry at Jack, angry at Mum, angry at everyone in my year for laughing at me and angry at poor, blameless Colin because, actually, he did have pretty toxic breath.

That's where Art found me, a few minutes later, crying beside the giant boulder at the north end of it.

Although I thought about Art constantly, and my life felt like one long wait for him to return to Northcliffe, nothing physical had happened between us by this point. Occasionally, when he was home and came over to mine, our legs would fall against each other's or our forearms would brush, and it was as if we both knew we were touching but were incapable, or too nervous, to do anything about it. Once I thought he was about to kiss me because he leant in towards my face, but it was only to tell me I had something in my teeth – a flake of black pepper. I didn't put pepper on my food for weeks after that.

I'd fantasized about bumping into him on the beach too, when he'd throw me down on the sand and we'd actually do it, the waves lapping at our feet like Danny and Sandy in *Grease*. That the sand would be damp and hard and the sea cold didn't matter. This was my fantasy. In my head, I could do it with Art wherever and however I wanted.

None of my teenage fantasies involved him discovering me crying on the beach, wearing my school tracksuit.

Art's eyes widened and he nodded. 'Oh yeah. What were you crying about again?'

'Oh, nothing very important.'

I'd never told him the reason because I was too embarrassed. We'd simply sat by the boulder for half an hour or so while Art had tried to find out what was wrong, until I admitted it was 'school stuff'.

'Who cares?' Art had told me. I'd committed every line of this important moment to memory and replayed them afterwards for months.

'What do you mean?'

'They're idiots, Nell. Who cares what some moron from Morpeth High thinks? You're better than that.'

'Am I?'

'Yes, obviously.'

'What do you mean "obviously"? How do you know that?'

'I just know. You're different. You've always been different. In a good way.'

He'd blushed and my stomach had done a little skip. It was clumsy teenage flirting but this felt more like my beach fantasies, although I suspect my nose had been red and blotchy.

That's when he'd told me to plot my escape from Northcliffe, just as he had.

It was the summer he left school and was about to head to Cranwell, the base in Lincolnshire where all RAF trainees start. I'd looked it up on Dad's map and been dismayed to find it was so far from Morpeth.

'Fighter pilot, here I come,' he'd told me, holding his arms out to make wings.

I'd felt a strange combination of awe and pride that he was finally doing what we'd discussed for so long.

Then he'd found a stone in the sand and held it out towards me – grey and rubbed almost flat – and shaped like a heart. 'You have it.'

'For what?' I'd asked.

For right now, he told me, as a reminder of him.

In the café, across the table, Art smiled. 'And that was when I told you to work out what you wanted to do in life, right, to get outta here?'

'Mmmhmm,' I replied, before tilting my head at him. 'You've got an American twang, you know?'

'Yeah, fifteen years, I guess some things are inevitable.'

He grinned and chewed a final corner of sandwich while I remembered the vow I'd made to myself. After that conversation, I swore that I'd get out of Northcliffe and do something, find a purpose like Art. Two years later, I'd graduated from school with straight As and was accepted to study law at York, from there to law school in London, and then to Spinks. I certainly didn't attribute my whole career to him, but I had always remembered our conversation that day.

I nearly mentioned the photo collage and the card, but if I mentioned them I'd have to mention his party. And I didn't want to bring that up and reveal any soft part of me that could still be hurt by the memory. I'd spent too long getting over him, and it felt like we were tiptoeing over ghosts as it was.

'Do you fly anymore?'

His eyebrows drew together. 'No time really. Work's too full-on and I decided that, when I gave it up, that was that. Easier to stop completely.'

'Did you have to?'

'Give it up?'

He dusted flour off his hands and rested his forearms on the table. 'Yeah. Nicole was pregnant and Robert... you remember my godfather Robert?'

I nodded. Art talked often about his American godfather when we were small. Robert Cargill lived in New York, owned a bank and sent him expensive birthday and Christmas presents – a remote control aeroplane; a Nintendo 64; once even a miniature electric jeep. Art and his parents used to holiday with him. Robert had a private plane with beds in it, that was usually the element of the holiday which Art was most impressed by, and they'd fly from New York to one of his other American houses in it, where they'd ride horses, swim in lakes and eat burgers outside every night.

Having never been to America, Art's reports of these holidays were a fairy tale to me. America sounded like it looked on TV – apparently there were skyscrapers, and yellow taxis, and huge mountains and cowboys, and a different kind of chocolate called Reese's which tasted of peanut butter, which Art always brought back with him. But I'd become less impressed with Art's rich godfather when he became his rich father-in-law.

'Robert was pretty insistent about me getting what he called a "real" job,' went on Art. 'And my parents were only too happy for me to give up flying. Even then Dad was warning me about money, saying that I should get a proper job because the estate needed cash and I'd never make much as a pilot. So, yeah, I gave it up.' He sighed. 'I didn't have much choice.'

'Oh I see, so what you're saying is you *had* to go and work for a Wall Street bank on a huge salary?'

Art laughed. 'Yeah, all right, it's not much of a sob story. But I miss it.' Then his smile faded. 'I miss a lot of things.'

I glanced towards the door as it jingled and saw Colin appear through it.

He came straight up to our table with an air of purpose and a wave of Lynx, the same that he'd worn ever since we were teenagers. Lucy and I used to tease him about it, but this had only made him more devoted to the stuff.

'Hi, Col, how you doing?'

'I'm very well,' he replied, before turning to Art with the look of a headmaster about to deliver a lecture to a disappointing pupil. 'Art, hello.'

Art stood to shake his hand. 'Colin. How are you? Long time.'

'Is it true you're selling the hall to a property developer?' Colin replied, ignoring Art's question.

'Well, there's probate to sort first.'

'But you are selling it?'

'Probably, yes.'

Colin pushed his glasses up his nose before crossing his arms. 'I think that's very sad.'

'It is sad, but I don't have much alternative.'

'It'll ruin the village, a developer.'

'That's what I'm trying to sort out now. A plan before the sale, to make sure everyone's happy with it.'

'So there'll be some sort of consultation process for the village?' said Colin, pushing his glasses up again.

'Not sure, pal, but I assure you I'm not handing it over to just anyone, and there will be no golf course, if that's what you're worrying about. Good to see you.' Art deliberately caught my eye as he sat back down.

Colin didn't move. 'According to section 106 of the Town and Country Planning Act, there should be a consultation.'

'Like I said, I assure you the place isn't going to be pulled down and built over,' Art replied, glancing back at him. 'That's the last thing I want. Now, if you don't mind, I'm catching up with Nell.'

Col turned to me. 'You still coming on Friday evening?'

'The pub quiz?' I said, to make it clear to Art that I wasn't heading to Colin's for any sort of private event. 'Sure, Dad and I'll be there.'

'See you then,' he said, before leaving us, going straight out.

Art exhaled as the door jingled again and closed behind him. 'That guy's got weirder.'

'He's all right.'

'You would say that.'

I frowned. 'What d'you mean?'

'Nothing. How's your brother, by the by? What's he up to?'

We moved on to talk about Jack, about his many girlfriends and about our jobs. I made a joke about nightmare clients and mentioned Prince Rudolf.

'Hang on, the one from Liechtenstein? I've met him.'

'What? Where?'

'In New York. He's an old friend of Nicole's, think they went to college together.'

I winced. 'Eeeesh, will you not mention anything? Client confidentiality.'

'Scout's promise,' said Art, saluting across the table. 'But that guy's a creep. I've always felt sorry for his wife.'

'Yeah, me too.'

We discussed more imaginative ideas to save the hall – turn it into a theme park? Another outpost of Soho Farmhouse, where guests could bicycle around between their cabins and the outdoor swimming pool? One of those posh zoos where visitors drive through the monkey enclosure?

'I'm not sure the monkeys could handle the weather,' Art joked.

It felt like one of our teenage conversations, where we emptied our heads to one another and discussed everything, both serious and very unserious. It was only when I got home again, two hours later, that I realized, just as with our conversations back then, neither of us had talked about our relationships.

On the other hand, Dad seemed to be hurling himself right back into the game. 'I've told Bev to come to the pub on Friday. That's all right, isn't it?' he told me, as soon as I got home.

'Absolutely,' I replied, wondering whether it was awe or exhaustion that I felt at my parents' new romantic endeavours. 'The only question is, what are you going to wear?'

Dad's smile fell and he looked panicked. 'I don't know. I hadn't thought. Will you pick me out a shirt from upstairs?'

'Yeah, course, but not now. We've got three days to worry about shirts, Dad.'

I trudged upstairs feeling vaguely like the host of a dating show. I was more used to ending relationships, not encouraging new ones, and especially not those of my parents.

Chapter 12

IT DIDN'T HAPPEN INSTANTLY, but around day ten of nursing duties and tea making, I realized I'd settled into home life. As had Dad. He was niftier on his crutches and could get to the downstairs bathroom and back without shouting. At night, he settled into his chair like an emperor and off we went to the pub.

When Jack and I were kids, Dad took us with him on Saturday evenings for a pint of fizzy lime cordial and a packet of Skips. As a teenager, I worked there for a few months after leaving school to make some cash for my travels with Luce and Colin. But until now, I'd never fully appreciated the significance of the place for Dad, for Roy, and various others who staggered in every evening and nodded or waved at one another.

Since living in London, I'd become used to fancy pubs where they served wasabi peas that made my nose sting, but being back here for such a stretch made me appreciate the comforting familiarity of the Duck. It wasn't posh, the food remained inedible (potentially dangerous), and if you'd asked Terence for a ramekin of wasabi peas he would have thrown you out. But that didn't matter to the Northcliffe locals. For them, it was a kind of church.

I felt awkward about crashing Lucy and Mike's date night and making small talk since I didn't know him very well, but Luce summoned me with a hand, smiling across the tables of regulars.

'Left Mum at home, total bedlam. Both of them shouting the place down but too bad. Can't tell you how desperate I was for a night out,' she said as I sat at their table.

London Nell would have scoffed at the idea that an evening in the Duck was 'out'. Instead, I smiled and asked if Jimbo and Bonnie were all right.

Luce batted a hand in the air and took a swig of her wine. 'They're fine, alive. Let's not talk about them, let's talk about you. I never get the chance to see you properly. Mike, go to the bar and get a bottle. I think we'll need one.'

'I'm OK,' I said quickly, looking at my soda water. 'I don't drink during the week. Gus and I have this… rule.'

'What?' screeched Lucy. 'I never get to see you and I want to celebrate. A couple of glasses won't kill you, plus it's Friday tomorrow.'

I glanced over my shoulder at Dad, red-faced and roaring at a joke of Roy's. At least I hoped it was a joke and not his blood pressure. 'Go on then, yes please.'

'Great. Mike, the bar.'

Mike stood and saluted her. The size difference between them made me smile: Lucy was as short as a leprechaun while he was tall, with a barrel for a stomach and a wild, Hagrid beard. I'd been invited to their wedding a few years earlier but couldn't go. It was shortly before I'd been promoted to senior associate and I'd had to work through the weekend.

I regretted it now. Lucy and Mike were proper, unpretentious people. I'd gone to so many weddings of York friends I barely saw anymore, and law school friends, and Gus's Cambridge friends, but I should have made the effort to come back for theirs.

At a wedding the previous month for one of Gus's colleagues, I'd sat at a circular table in one of The Savoy's function rooms while those around me discussed where their children went to nursery, and would go on to school afterwards.

'State till eight,' one guest had proclaimed.

'What do you mean?' I'd asked, confused.

'State education until they're eight, and then private school,' he'd replied. 'You simply can't risk the system after that.'

I'd wanted to laugh but I knew nobody else at that table would laugh with me. Luce would have done if she'd been there. At school, she'd been one of those Marmite characters: most people had found her constant chattiness and enthusiasm for everything annoying, not cool. But I'd always wished I could be more like her, more relaxed about life, more optimistic, never taking herself, or much else, too seriously. What was so uncool about that?

'Tell me everything,' she instructed.

I took a breath. 'I don't know where to start, Luce. I'm good.'

'So you've still got your big amazing job, how's that?'

'It's all right. Quite full-on. And my boss is a maniac. And I work from seven in the morning until seven or eight at night. But that's what I've got to do, really.'

'For what?'

'For this promotion.'

'*Another* one?'

I pulled an embarrassed face. Luce always remembered whatever I'd told her on previous flits home when I couldn't even remember what her babies were called. 'Hopefully, but I won't know whether I've got it for a few months yet.'

'Nell, you're a superstar. And then what? Can you chill out a bit?'

'Er, no. Then I have to work harder. Longer hours, probably, but more money so, yeah, that's something…'

'Nice! And how's Gus?'

'He's good, working hard too.'

Lucy nodded encouragingly across the table at me, smiling, waiting for me to go on, but I couldn't think of anything else to add. 'How's your work going?'

She was the more creative one when we were teenagers and covered her bedroom walls with photo collages ripped from *Just Seventeen* and *More!*: pictures of her beloved Boyzone were mixed with fashion adverts starring a young Kate Moss. Luce had dreamt of going on to work for *Vogue* and we imagined sharing a flat when, one day, we moved to London. But then she went to college up here, met Mike and started working in the vet's. Then marriage, then one baby, then another. In the past few years, between pregnancies, she'd launched herself as a local photographer covering birthday parties and christenings, but I wasn't sure how successful this had been.

'Not doing much at the moment because of Bonnie, but hopefully I'll start again in a few months. Mike's taking over the fishery from Dan, so he's keeping us afloat at the moment, aren't you, love?' She beamed up at him as Mike placed a glass in front of me and poured a third of the bottle into it.

'Looking after the tribe,' he replied, with a grin.

'Congrats,' I said, holding up a glass. 'And cheers, guys, good to see you.'

We clinked them together before Luce asked her next question in a more deliberately casual way. 'You seen Art since you've been up here?'

I felt myself stiffen. She and I never discussed him after our travels. Whenever I'd seen her since, there seemed to be a mutual agreement between us that we wouldn't mention the subject. A no-go area. 'Mmhmm. Had coffee with him a couple of days ago.'

'He OK?'

'Think so.'

'How long's he back for?'

'Not sure, few days maybe. Just a lot to sort out, he says. Like, paperwork.'

I hadn't heard from him since our coffee two days ago but then I wasn't sure what I expected, if I expected anything. Another coffee? A walk? What would be the point? We'd seen one another. We'd caught up. That was it, closure.

And yet his presence in my head had become bigger again, the invisible cord between us strengthened. I imagined bumping into him when I went to get Dad's paper, or while walking Wilma on the beach, or in the pub.

Alternatively, I was being psychopathic and needed to stop over-thinking. I shouldn't be moping around Northcliffe like a teenager; I was a thirty-three-year-old woman in a long-term relationship with a man who, last night, spent ten minutes on the phone telling me about a new robotic vacuum he thought we should buy for the flat.

Gus loved a gadget because he was so impractical. A few months ago, we'd had a lengthy debate about whether we should get a boiling water tap. He wanted one; I'd argued that it was a waste of money when a kettle did the job just as well. He won in the end, and we agreed that it could be our joint Christmas present to one another. A thousand pounds for a very hot tap. Madness. Adult life involved much more time discussing home improvements than I'd imagined when younger.

Adult life was not worrying, or vaguely hoping, even, that you'd bump into your first love when you went shopping for more milk in the morning.

Mike wiped beer froth from his upper lip and looked at me. 'What was the beef between you and Art again?' He might have been asking how my afternoon was, or whether I preferred coffee or tea. 'Ow! What?'

Lucy had given him a very obvious dig in his stomach with her elbow. 'I've told you,' she muttered.

'It's all right,' I said, grinning at Mike's confusion. 'No beef, really. Well, extremely old beef. We just… fell out at his twenty-first.'

'I remember now,' he replied, nodding. 'Wasn't that when you went to fi—'

'No thank you, we don't need to go into it,' Lucy interrupted him as if she was talking to one of her children.

'Being in here with you reminds me of back then actually,' I went on, looking around at the beams, strung with Marjorie's fairy lights and knick-knacks that Terence had hung over the years: old horseshoes, Guinness signs, black-and-white photos of the village.

'When you worked here?'

I nodded. 'I was the world's worst barmaid,' I explained for Mike's benefit.

'You were,' she agreed.

'And Luce and Col used to come in, before we all went away together, armed with maps and Lonely Planet books.'

'Christ, Col and all his maps,' she sighed, running a hand through her hair.

'This before you lot went to Asia?'

'Mmm, Colin had very strong feelings about which bus routes we should take.'

'Fucking hell, those bus routes, and all the battlefields!' Luce shook her head before looking at Mike. 'You would not believe the number of battlefields he made us go to. I don't think there's a single battlefield in Vietnam that I didn't vomit on because we were usually *hanging* from something we'd drunk the night before. Nell, d'you remember that drink with the snake in it?'

I nodded. It had been in South Vietnam; a bottle of rice wine with a cobra curled in the bottom of it.

Luce shivered. 'Wasn't it supposed to be an aphrodisiac?'

'Yep.'

She opened her mouth to make a fake gag. 'Didn't do much for me. I just remember chucking up all over the Mekong Delta the next day.'

'I'm a lucky man,' joked Mike, raising his eyebrows over his pint glass.

'Poor old Col,' went on Luce. 'Such an oddball. Hey, do you remember that New Year's Eve when he sat at the bar reading his book all night?'

Mention of that evening was like a paper cut to the chest. It was the night that Art and I finally kissed. 'Yep,' I said again, smiling across the table to disguise my unease.

Luce turned to face Mike: 'Col had this huge book he was reading, all about the Vietnam War, which had a row of dead soldiers on the cover.'

'Festive.'

'Well that was the thing,' agreed Luce. 'It was New Year's Eve and… what year, Nell?'

'2003.'

'It was 2003,' she rattled on, 'and we all came here for the night. You were working behind the bar, right?'

I nodded as she carried on with the story while Mike grinned at his wife, listening loyally, laughing where it was required and sipping his pint.

I'd been working in the pub that night because Terence had promised overtime, but I was hoping that Art would drop in. He'd been home for a few months between RAF training deployments, and had taken to coming to the pub most evenings. Whenever he pulled up a stool at one end of the bar, I'd instantly abandon Colin, Luce and our Lonely Planet books, and slide down Art's end, where he'd talk to me about flying speeds and manoeuvres.

We never mixed as a four since Art wasn't really friends with anybody else in the village. It didn't seem strange to me. Jack and I had grown up with him, running around Drummond

Hall, because our dad worked for his. If Luce and Colin ever resented my friendship with the posh boy from the big house, or me dropping them in the pub as soon as he appeared, they never told me so. Terence didn't love my habit of leaning over the bar, all my focus on Art, but he couldn't say much because Art was Lord Drummond's son.

Colin came in early that New Year's Eve and took up a stool at the bar, clutching his depressing Vietnam book.

'It was mad that night, wasn't it?' said Luce, turning back to me. 'The whole village was in. And everyone was partying and getting pissed, but Col sat at the bar all night reading his book.'

'Until Art arrived.'

'Oh right, yeah, course.'

'What happened then?' asked Mike.

'Well, he was always a bit jealous of Art.'

'Why?'

Luce puffed out her cheeks and sighed. 'Because Col thought he had it easy. Like, all that money, massive pile. And he was gorgeous. Art, I mean. Just so…' She clawed her hands in front of her face and made a deep, growling noise, 'A real man, you know?'

'Like me, you mean?' said Mike, with mock solemnity.

'Almost exactly,' Luce replied, leaning sideways and joshing him with her shoulder. 'Col's wonderful in many ways but he's not exactly Clark Kent. Anyway,' she pushed on, 'that night, Col wouldn't move from the bar, where Art was trying to talk to Nell…'

'And Art was about to go away to Anglesey for RAF training, so I wasn't going to see him for ages,' I chipped in.

'That's right! So didn't you have to sneak outside with him?'

I nodded. In the end, Colin reached over the bar during the countdown, wrapped his arms around my neck and mumbled 'Happy New Year' into my ear, but I caught Art's eye behind him, and he'd gestured to the door with his head.

I found him in the dark and we'd stood in the freezing cold while the muffled noise of 'Auld Lang Syne' came through the pub wall. I'd anticipated this moment for so long it felt like the dramatic climax to a Christmas soap.

That was when he'd given me the Coldplay CD as a Christmas present. He'd burned it after hearing Jack rib me in the pub for not knowing any of the lyrics a few days earlier.

Then Art had folded his sheepskin aviator coat around me, pulled me into his chest and pressed his mouth to mine. This, I remember thinking, was *exactly* the sort of thing that would happen in one of Mum's books.

It seemed a miracle: Art, the boy who had occupied my brain, been my every other thought for so many years, was kissing me. And I was kissing him. We were kissing, real kissing like I'd seen in American high school films. Our mouths seemed to fit one another's and his tongue didn't writhe around mine like Colin's at my GCSE party. Even though we were standing outside the pub, freezing in the coldness of a Northumberland winter, it had been the most erotic moment of my life.

***

You should never wish to go back in life. Not really. I've long thought that was crazy. If you went back in time, you'd have to take all the bad, as well as the good, and I sure as hell didn't want to go through law school again, and all those exams. But as I sat there in the pub, taking turns with Luce to tell Mike this story like a comedy duo, I realized that kiss with Art was the moment I'd return to over and over again.

I'd go through all the subsequent events in my life a hundred times over for the sense of certainty I felt then, for the explosion of pure happiness and conviction that I had him, and he had me, and nothing else mattered. My young, unblemished heart had loved him so intensely. Maybe we all expected too much, to believe that we could ever reach those dizzy, delirious levels of devotion again after feeling them for the first time?

'But while you guys were getting busy, didn't you hear footsteps?' said Luce, interrupting my reverie.

'Mmm, behind us.'

'Enter, Colin!' she said, making jazz hands above the table.

Mike's mouth stretched wide and he belly-laughed at the pub's ceiling. 'Way to ruin the moment.'

'Kind of,' I agreed. 'I think he was going home but he said Terence was looking for me.'

'And then what?'

I shrugged. 'We all went home. No, that's not true, I went back into the pub to clear up eleventy billion party poppers.'

'And the next time you saw Art was at his party, wasn't it?' Luce checked.

'Yep, he went off flying again and only came back that July.

And that, as they say, was that.' I lifted my glass and drew in such a big mouthful of wine that it hurt my throat to swallow.

Luce exhaled loudly. 'Mad, seems decades ago.'

'It *was* decades ago, sort of.'

'Col's a funny one,' added Mike. 'He told you about his protest?'

I shook my head.

Lucy laughed. 'On Sunday. He's trying to get everyone in the village to stop the property developer coming in. Says he's designed a poster and everything.'

'What's your old man going to do if the hall's sold? Can he stay in that house?' Mike asked before Lucy dug him in his paunch again.

'Ow! What now?'

'Nell's got enough going on without you worrying her even more, that's what. Sorry, love.'

'All good,' I said, smiling into my wine glass. 'And not sure at the moment. It's a bit up in the air.'

'And is your mum all right?'

'Seems to be.'

'Is Jack coming up at any point to help?'

'Oh here she is, enquiring after her boyfriend again,' joked Mike, lowering one hand to his wife's knee.

When we were sixteen, Jack snogged Lucy on the beach and she spent a few months moping after him but it was a hopeless cause. There'd always been a string of girls after Jack, even then.

'He says he will, but you know he has a habit of wriggling out of things.'

'Would you ever move back up here, Nell?' asked Mike. 'Ow! Luce, can you stop it?'

'Can you stop asking such nosy questions? Now, Nell, have you heard about Tash Blackburn?'

I shook my head and she embarked on a long story about Tash, one of the coolest of the cool gang at school, and who'd been consistently mean to Lucy and me, being caught with a man who'd come into her beauty salon for a back wax.

'What, actually doing it?'

'Yes,' Lucy replied emphatically. 'On the massage bed.'

'Blimey, I wouldn't have thought those massage beds were strong enough for two.'

'See? This is why I miss you,' she replied, before continuing with her update about various people from Morpeth High.

While I sat there, listening to her rattle on, I felt the astonishment that occasionally overcame me that we were in our thirties when it felt like only yesterday I was sweating over my A-levels. Did ninety-year-olds feel this? Was that what life came down to, mounting surprise that you were thirty, then forty, fifty, sixty until one day you woke up with wrinkly hands and the same number of teeth that you had as a baby, and realized that was it?

I kept this morbid thought to myself, though, because I thought it might ruin the vibe. It was uplifting, laughing with Luce like we used to – reminiscing, gossiping, crying with laughter, doubled over at the table when I recounted the story of kissing Colin in the school gym for Mike's benefit, although I'm sure he'd heard that story ninety-five times before.

Roy wheeled Dad over to collect me in the end, as opposed to vice versa, and I pushed him home across the green, smiling to myself, puzzled by an unfamiliar emotion that was displacing my usual anxiety about emails and work and setting my alarm for early the next morning.

This warm buzz stayed with me while I heated up a Spar lasagne in the microwave, and remained with me as I sat beside Dad's bed and we ate while watching *Sleepless In Seattle*. Dad's choice.

I think it was contentment, maybe even a sense of relief at talking openly about Art after keeping my memories of him shut away for so long, although it could also have been Terence's house white.

***

'Good news!' Gus declared, when we spoke later that night.

'You've bought the robot hoover?'

'Two bits of good news. I've ordered the robot hoover, yes, but also I'm coming to see you this weekend.'

'What?'

'I've cleared the diary tomorrow afternoon and booked the 13:01 train.'

'No way!'

'Yes way. Why? That's not a problem, is it? You haven't got any plans?'

'That depends whether you count pushing my elderly father to the pub and back for a date in his wheelchair a plan, but otherwise no, I'm all yours.'

'Great. That's settled. I get in just after five.'

'I'll come and get you. But you sure? You hate it up here.'

'I don't hate it. I can manage it in small doses.'

'Thank you, that's very good of you.'

'I just miss you, that's all.'

'Miss you back.'

'Not sure we've ever done this long apart, have we?'

I thought. 'Not on any of your business trips?'

'They're normally a week, tops.'

'I guess. In which case I owe you an even bigger thank you for coming up.'

'You can make it up to me when I get there. Do you need anything from civilization? I thought I'd bring some wine but anything else?'

'Nope, we're all good. Just remember to pack some Piriton so you don't spend all weekend sneezing.'

'I've bought three packets from Boots because that's the kind of sex machine I am.'

'Mmm,' I murmured, as I lifted my T-shirt and looked underneath it to check my nipples. Must find my tweezers before his train got in.

Chapter 13

AS I DROVE TO the station to collect Gus the next evening, I realized I'd forgotten to tell him about quiz night.

'Hello,' he said, putting a large box down on the platform and reaching his arms wide for a hug. 'Did you miss me?'

'Yes,' I mumbled into his coat collar. 'Thanks for coming.'

'Not at all, and I've marched on the north armed with supplies like Emperor Hadrian.' He released me and waved at the box.

'What is it?' I asked, thinking how incongruous he looked, standing on the blustery Morpeth platform, still in his grey suit and tie.

'Goodies from Whole Foods. Fresh pasta, several cheeses, some salami, a bottle of truffle oil, a couple of ales I thought your dad might be interested in, some absurdly expensive steak which the butcher persuaded me to buy. And those olives you like.'

I was momentarily struck dumb at the realization that my boyfriend was someone who used the word 'goodies', but then came to my senses. 'Amazing, thank you.'

'It's mostly self-motivated because I didn't want some godawful ready-meal from the Co-op.'

'Spar,' I said, with instinctive loyalty. The Spar lasagne Dad and I ate the previous night had been so delicious I stood over the kitchen sink afterwards, scraping the crispy, dark curls of cheese from the side of the plastic container with my fork.

'Whatever it is,' went on Gus. 'I thought we could make the pasta tonight, with the oil and some parmesan. I've brought the parmesan too since I wasn't sure you could even get it this far north.'

'And yet astonishingly you can. We even have electricity now.'

'Odd-looking people though. There was a woman in my carriage who could only have been the product of inbreeding.'

'Gus…'

'I'm telling you, she had the most enormous nose and eyes that looked in opposite directions. By the way, what *are* you wearing? Have you gone native?'

I was in a pair of running leggings and one of Dad's jumpers because it was bigger and more comfortable than anything I'd brought north with me. Plus, I'd been running late to pick him up because I'd been finishing a draft contract for Gideon, so grabbed an old pair of wellington boots by the kitchen door on my way to the car.

I grimaced. 'Yeah, sorry, although it's liberating not having to put on a suit every day.'

'You'll be telling me you've started plaiting your underarm hair next.'

'Gus Bickerton, that's very unfeminist. Come on, let's go. I shouldn't leave Dad on his own for too long.'

He bent to pick up the box.

'I hope you don't mind,' I said, as we walked towards the car park, 'but I promised we'd go to the pub for the quiz tonight.'

'Promised who?' he replied with a note of indignation.

'My friend Colin.'

'Who's he?'

'Have you never met him? He and Lucy were my only two friends as a kid.'

'Who's Lucy?'

I sighed. 'Gus, you know this. You've met her.'

'Have I?'

'Yes, a couple of times. Short, dark hair, talks a lot.'

'Oh Christ, yes, doesn't stop talking, as far as I remember. Married to that fisherman?'

'Mike. Not an actual fisherman, but works in the fishery, yes.'

'I remember the smell,' Gus said with clear distaste. 'So who's this other one?'

'Other what?'

'Other friend.'

'Oh. Colin, the biggest nerd in the village but very sweet.'

'Careful about nerds, we're not all bad.'

'I didn't say you were. Obviously I'm a big fan of nerds. The car's over here.'

'And what about *him*,' said Gus, reaching for his seat belt once we'd climbed inside. 'You always say you had no friends up here but sounds like there were loads of you.'

'Him? Do you mean Art?' I replied, as lightly as I could.

Gus nodded.

'Er, he was my… friend. But away at boarding school quite a lot. Actually, he's up here at the moment too.'

'What? I thought he lived in America?'

I squinted through the windscreen, willing the lights from the car park exit to turn green. 'He does but since his dad died, and he inherited everything, he's here trying to sort out a sale and the paperwork and so on.'

'You've seen him?' Gus asked, his voice leaping in surprise. This was one of the downsides of dating a corporate lawyer; you couldn't get away with anything. No detail went unnoticed, whether a stray pair of knickers on the bathroom floor or an accidental meeting with your childhood sweetheart.

'Yep,' I replied breezily. 'I bumped into him a couple of times this week. On a run and in the coffee shop. Speaking of which, I need to talk to you about the coffee shop,' I said, keen to change topics. I started talking about Mum and Luigi, and Prince Pervert and his wine, and kept on talking about them until we reached home.

***

As I opened the kitchen door, Wilma jumped up and poked her nose into Gus's crotch.

'Get off, hound,' Gus said, swatting her away.

'Wilma, come here. Did you bring that Piriton?'

'Left them in the office,' he muttered, bending to inspect his crotch. 'There's a mark, look.' He pointed at a smudge the size of a stamp on his suit trousers.

I reached for a damp cloth from the sink and threw it across the room. Gus scrubbed at the damp patch but only succeeded in making it bigger and darker.

'Never mind, it'll dry. Come say hi to Dad.' I tilted my head towards the sitting-room door.

'Like this?'

'It's Dad not the Queen.'

With a scowl, Gus followed me through to where Dad was watching the racing highlights.

'Bruce, hello, how are you?' he said stiffly.

'Gus, lad, good to see you. Had a bit of an accident, have we?'

But Gus didn't have time to reply before Dad swung his gaze to me. 'Nell, pet, we off to the pub yet? I'm parched and I said to Bev we'd be there at six.'

'Yes, just need to give Wilma her tea and then we can go.'

'Do I have to change?' added Gus.

I took in his suit and shiny, lace-up brogues again. 'There won't be many suits in there, it's more a fleece and flat-cap kind of evening. But totally up to you.'

'I need a slash first,' said Dad.

'Fine. Gus, do you mind helping Dad into his chair?'

Gus looked horrified. 'And taking him to the bathroom?'

'Get away, you big pansy,' said Dad, with a chuckle. 'I can manage that part myself on my crutches. I'll just need a hand to get in there afterwards.' He nodded at the wheelchair and I retreated to the kitchen, leaving them to it.

Half an hour later, we were installed at the usual table, joined by Roy and Bev, who was sitting on the bench beside

Dad wearing a low-cut top which he was pretending not to look at.

Colin was on a stool at the bar wearing a floral shirt and a bow tie, sifting through a handful of notecards. Beside him lay a microphone and a clipboard, on which he had jotted down the various team names. Since Dad and Roy were regulars at this quiz night we were using their usual name, Laurel and Hardy, on the basis that Roy was short and thin, and Dad was neither of those things.

Around us most of the other tables were full. I only recognized a couple of them: Howard was on one with his wife; Colin's parents were on another; Mike was sitting with a group of colleagues but no Luce. The rest were strangers of varying ages, eyes darting around, sizing up the competition while they sank their first pints and opened up packets of crisps.

I felt optimistic about our chances given that Gus was the most competitive person I knew and already poised like an Olympic runner on the start line – answer sheet in front of him, pen in hand. His competitiveness was why we couldn't play Scrabble together anymore. Once, on a mini break in the Cotswolds, I'd put down 'quiz' on a triple-word score and Gus had pretended to 'accidentally' flip the board over with the bottom of his wine glass and declared the game over, when I know he'd done it deliberately. It was why he was good at his job; he refused to countenance losing any case.

'Ladies and gentlemen, are we ready?' Colin said into his microphone. 'Has everyone got a drink? You're going to need a drink because have I got some fiendish questions for you.' He grinned around the pub before bending his head to the microphone again. 'If you're new to us toni—'

The door opened and Mum and Luigi appeared. She'd put on lipstick for the occasion and Luigi had apparently come dressed as a Hell's Angel: leather jacket, jeans, black ankle boots.

'Roy, get a look at that, the man's come as a Goodfella.'

'Dad,' I warned, over the chesty rattle of Roy's laugh.

He held his hands in the air. 'All I'm saying is I didn't know it was fancy dress tonight, pet.'

Bev, fortunately, seemed oblivious.

'Mrs Mason!' Colin cried, having also spotted Mum. 'Come in, come in, find a seat, there's a table at the back there.' He pointed from his stool to a table, thankfully in the opposite corner from us.

'Him? Seriously?' Gus said, staring across the room. 'That cannot possibly be your mother's new boyfriend?'

'Mmmhmm, why?' I muttered, lifting my hand to wave at Mum. I was already exhausted by this evening and the quiz hadn't even started.

'How *extraordinary*. He looks like Tony, the man who wheels sandwiches round our office.'

'Oh shush,' I said, keen to keep Gus's snobbery under wraps.

'The more the merrier,' Colin said into his microphone, before embarking on a complicated explanation of the quiz which nobody listened to.

'Good heavens, it's a quiz, not the mystery of life,' Gus observed, too loudly, as Colin explained that the fifth and final round would cover history.

I shushed him again and put a hand on his knee. Admittedly, this was a scene which would require some people to have extensive therapy afterwards: I was sitting at one table with my father and his date while, across the pub, my mother was sitting with her Italian lover. But there was a cheerful camaraderie to the pub which made me pleased to be there. On a normal Friday evening in London, I'd be either lying on the sofa after an eighty-hour week, or Gus and I would be in some fancy new restaurant, drinking an oaky wine the colour of morning urine and eating a tiny piece of fish that came with foam. Tonight, I was happy with a glass of house red (Gus asked for the wine list when we arrived and Terence had actually laughed at him; the Duck had never had a wine list), and a bowl of chips.

'OK then,' said Colin, 'I'm going to ease you in gently with the general knowledge round.'

He paused as the door swung open again and Art stepped through it with Nanny Gertrude on his arm. Against the backdrop of whiskery, red-faced farmers, it was as if a Roman gladiator had arrived. He towered over them all, and smiled around the room as the pub's hubbub quietened. Art had been discussed most evenings in here as rumours about the sale of the hall swirled, but he hadn't come in until now.

Colin glowered from his stool. 'Oh look, latecomers. I'm not sure there's much room for you to join in anywhere,' he said, having apparently changed his mind about more being merrier.

'Art! Gertrude! Come and sit with us,' Mum shouted, waving them over. Art led Nanny Gertrude to their table before heading to the bar. Once there, he glanced around, caught my eye and grinned.

I waved lamely back and felt Gus stiffen beside me. 'And is that *him*?'

Reaching for my wine glass, I thought perhaps I would need therapy after all. 'Mmmhmm.'

'Question number one,' shouted Colin. 'What is the smallest planet in our solar system?'

'Uranus,' said Roy, to a snort from Dad. Bev followed, cleavage wobbling as she hooted like an owl.

'Very juvenile,' muttered Gus. 'It's quite obviously Mercury.'

'Next question: the average person does what thirteen times a day?'

Unfortunately, this also set Dad and Roy off, so Gus turned to me. 'Says sorry?'

I frowned. 'Not sure. Yawns? Laughs?'

'Laughs, that's a good guess,' said Gus. His pen scratched furiously across the answer sheet.

Colin continued through the first round and then into capital cities, at which point Gus and Roy had a terse debate about Australia.

'Sydney, I've been there,' said Roy.

'Ooh, lovely,' said Bev. 'I've always fancied going Down Under.'

Dad grinned and opened his mouth to reply but I immediately put my palm in the air to stop him. There were limits.

Gus muttered beside me: 'I assure you it's Canberra. People always think it's Sydney and they're wrong.' He lowered his head to write the answer down without consulting the rest of us.

Next came the 'guess the year' round before Colin announced a break. 'Get another drink, order some food, we'll carry on with the music round in…' he checked his watch, 'twenty minutes.'

'Another one?' asked Roy, standing up.

'Ta, guvnor,' said Dad.

Gus picked up the red wine bottle. 'I think we're all ri— Oh no, it's finished.' He looked at my glass. 'Nell, have you drunk all that?'

'Oi, it's the weekend, and you've had a couple of glasses.'

'Not as much as you.'

'Children, children, I'll get another one,' said Roy.

'And maybe some crisps?' I shouted after him.

'Should I go over and say hello to your mum?' asked Gus.

I followed his gaze to their table. Art had returned to the bar so it seemed the right moment. 'Yeah. You all right here for a tick, Dad?'

'Yes, yes, send my best to her and Freddy Mercury over there.'

'Dad, enough.'

'I'll keep him company,' added Bev.

Mum stood as we approached and held her arms out. She did a good job of pretending that she liked Gus more than she actually did. 'Come here, I didn't know you were coming up.'

'Last-minute trip.'

'Couldn't survive without her in London?'

'Want to make sure she's coming back, more like.'

'And this is Luigi,' said Mum, releasing Gus and stepping aside.

Luigi leant forward and clasped one of Gus's hands with both of his. 'Ah, so thees one is your boyfriend, Elly-anor. Now I see, he is very different.'

'To who?' asked Gus, frowning with confusion.

'Little mix-up in the coff—' I tried to reply before Luigi but unfortunately he interrupted.

'When I saw her with Arthur, I thought that 'e was you. But now I see. 'e was the old boyfriend and you are the new. Bravo!'

'And this is Nanny Gertrude,' I said quickly, keen to get away from this situation, aware that Art would shortly come back from the bar and my head might explode all over the ceiling with the effort of trying to control this evening. 'Colin's probably starting again soon so we should be getting back to our table.'

'How are you lot doing with the questions?' asked Gus, craning his neck over their table in an effort to peer at their answer sheet.

I elbowed him. 'Oi.'

Luigi waggled his head from side to side. 'We are OK. But music is not our strong point, is it, *belissima*?'

I didn't have time to be annoyed about this overt affection. 'Come on, Gus, let's head bac—'

'Love, who's that with your dad?' Mum asked, peering around me.

'That? That's Bev, the occupational therapist I told you about. Come on, Gus.'

'What on earth is she wearing? She might as well have come in a bikini.'

'Mum…'

'They must not have had that top in her size.'

'Mum! Don't worry about her, I think Colin's probably about to star—'

'Looks can be deceiving,' went on Gus. 'I'm hoping she knows her music.'

'Well I don't think she's going to be any good at the history round, from the looks of things.'

'Mum, stop it, you can't possibly tell that. Gus, come on, we should ge—'

'Evening, all,' said Art's voice.

Brilliant.

I turned round to see him holding a tray of drinks.

'Hiya, how you doing?' I asked, weakly.

'Good. Nanny Gertrude and I thought we'd come up and join the fun.'

'Cool, but on that note we really should be getting ba—'

'Hi there, I'm Art,' he added, sticking out his hand towards Gus.

'Gus,' he replied, taking it.

Before boxing matches, opponents shake hands in the ring. This looked similar, although it wouldn't have been a very fair fight. Art stood a head over Gus and had the shoulders of a former rugby captain who still looked like he smashed a quick 10k before breakfast every morning. Gus played the occasional game of squash with a colleague, or golf on a corporate awayday, but otherwise sat hunkered over his desk all week. In recent months, I'd noticed the beginnings of a kangaroo paunch bulging over his belt but didn't want to cause offence by making a joke about it. Plus, Gus hadn't changed out of his suit whereas Art was in jeans and a faded t-shirt that stretched across his chest. It would have looked like the school bully duffing up the swot.

'How long you up for?' asked Art.

Gus had never struck me as the fighting type. If you got into a fight with him, he might try and poke you in the eye or give you a wedgie but I didn't imagine he had much of a right hook, and yet he was glowering at Art as if he wanted to pulverize his nose. 'Until Sunday. You?'

'Another week or so probably. Just various issues to sort out up here.'

'Yes, I'm sorry to hear about your father. Nell mentioned that. And everything else, your childhood, growing up together, and your party.'

'Party?'

'Gus, come on,' I tried, desperation creeping into my voice, 'Looks like we're about to start again.'

He ignored me. 'Yes, your twenty-first, I think it was.'

'Oh right, yeah, that feels a hundred years ago now, doesn't it?' Art looked from Gus to me and grinned.

'Seriously, let's go,' I said, taking hold of Gus's elbow and pulling him away.

'May the best team win,' Gus said over his shoulder, as he followed me back to our spot.

'Everything all right?' asked Dad as we sat down. 'Elvis Presley sing you a song or anything?'

'Fine,' I replied, reaching urgently for my wine glass. 'And save it for the music round.'

Bev and I were no good at this, but luckily Dad and Roy could identify obscure Pink Floyd tracks from the 1970s in three chords.

Then we rattled through the history questions before Colin told everyone to swap sheets for marking.

The drama happened when we reached the answers for the history round.

'Question number six: when did George V become king?' asked Colin.

'1910,' Art shouted.

'What?' muttered Gus, frowning down at the piece of paper in front of him. 'That's not right. It was 1911.'

'Exactly, 1910,' Colin agreed into his microphone. 'Next question: in 1872, British engineer James Starley invented the what?'

'It's wrong, 1910 is wrong,' Gus went on, stabbing his pen at the sheet. 'His coronation was in 1911. I do know these things.'

'Never mind, we'll sort it out in a minute. What have they put for that one?' I pointed to the question we'd moved on to.

'But it's wrong.' He looked up and shouted towards the bar. 'Sorry, excuse me, Colin, is it? The answer you gave to the last question is wrong.'

Colin blinked at the notecard in his hand. 'What year did George V become king?'

'Yes, you said 1910 but he was coronated in 1911.'

'I'm not sure that matters,' Col replied.

'I think you'll find it does,' Gus said loudly. 'You only officially become a monarch once you've been coronated.'

'Gus, leave it,' I whispered, aware that everyone in the pub had stopped talking and turned to look at us.

'I will not,' he hissed, 'because it's wrong.'

'Tell you what, I'll google it,' shouted Art, pulling his phone out of his jeans.

I reached for my glass, although I wasn't sure there was enough wine in the world for this scenario.

'It's wrong. I know it's wrong,' Gus muttered.

There was a moment of silence while Art scrolled and everyone watched him. It was like waiting for the scores on *Strictly*.

He shook his head. 'No, 'fraid not – according to this, a throne can never sit vacant, sovereignty passes on *accession* rather than coronation.' Art looked up from his phone. '1910 it is.'

Beside me, Gus turned rigid with anger.

'All right then, 1910. Glad that's settled. And on we go. Question number seven. In 1872, James Starley invented the penny-farthing bicycle,' Colin rattled through the remaining answers while Gus marked in silence.

'You're ever so clever,' said Bev, leaning towards him. 'I'm terrible with dates, can barely remember my own birthday.'

I smiled gratefully but her efforts didn't make any difference. Gus didn't even reply.

'Sorry,' Art mouthed when I dared to look at him.

'It's fine,' I mouthed back quickly.

But it wasn't fine. It was extremely childish of Gus and it's an uncomfortable sensation, being embarrassed by your other half. Once the marking was finished, Colin gathered in the sheets and Gus sat mute, fury still radiating from him, while the rest of us chatted about the weather that weekend. I joined in with the odd line while remaining extremely aware of Gus's rage. It was only a quiz, not a medieval duel, I wanted to say, resigning myself to a tense evening when we got home.

'Right, ladies and gents, the moment you've all been waiting for,' shouted Colin, after sifting through the sheets. 'As always, I'm going to read from the bottom up so here goes. In bottom place is Universally Challenged.'

Groans came from a table beside the bar.

'Then there's Agatha Quizteam,' went on Colin, 'and then the Northcliffe Village Idiots…' More groans. 'Then my parents, better luck next week, Mum and Dad. In third place is the Eggheads, so well done, Howard and Betty.'

Howard raised his glass in the air.

'And it was very close at the top with just two points between them but in second place is Laurel and Hardy, which means first place goes to…' Colin paused and squinted at the name, 'You Wanna Pisa Us.' He glanced up at Mum's table. 'Very inventive. So, congratulations and please come and collect your bottle of winners' fizz.'

Mum and Luigi threw their arms in the air and I saw Nanny Gertrude look briefly confused before Art leant over to explain, and her face creased with a wide smile.

'Second place, I'll take that,' said Roy, tipping the bottom of his glass towards the ceiling and draining his beer. 'But I should be off.'

'I'd best be going too,' said Bev, bending over to pick up her bag and exposing smooth slopes of chest, at which point I thought Dad's eyes might fall from their sockets.

'Us too, come on, old man,' I said, standing up and stretching.

'Less of that, please. You're only as old as the woman you feel, isn't that right, Bev?'

'Stop, you cheeky sod,' she replied, with a peal of laughter.

It was absolutely, *definitely* time to go home.

I waved at Colin and glanced at Mum's table where Art was pouring glasses of Prosecco.

Gus didn't say a word as we made our way back across the green, or once we were upstairs, lying in my parents' bed. I'd hoovered, dusted, removed Dad's rusting nail clippers from his side of the bed and moved in here for the weekend since my room had only a single.

'You all right?' I asked, for the nineteenth time since we'd returned from the pub, turning and sliding a hand across his chest.

'Yeah, just tired,' he replied, before rolling away from me to face the wall.

I almost told him that I'd tweezed my nipple hair specially, but I wasn't sure that would help. It could wait until the morning.

Chapter 14

LUCKILY, GUS'S BLACK MOOD at having come second in the Drunken Duck's weekly quiz had lifted the following day and I woke to him kissing my ear.

'Hi,' I said sleepily.

'Hello.' He ran a hand under my T-shirt. 'Do you want to take this off?'

I pulled it over my head, and wriggled out of my knickers. Then I remembered that I was in my parents' bed, lying on Mum's side, and there was a family photo of all of us, taken on the beach years ago, on the bedside table. I reached out and placed it face down.

He kissed around my neck while I ran my fingers through his hair and traced the back of my nails over his shoulder blades. Then he rolled onto his back and pulled me on top of him. I was forgiven, it seemed. Then he reached one hand towards me, to try and make me come with his fingers while I moved back and forth. Except it felt pretty uncomfortable to be on top of Gus while staring at my parents' headboard. It was pale blue, and covered in a floral pattern that was as familiar to me as the sound of the kitchen door closing or the sound of footsteps on our creaking staircase. I'd known it from childhood, and past Christmases when Jack and I would bounce in to open our stockings. There was a patch on Dad's side which had yellowed from his hair oil.

Gus was trying, to be fair. I angled my hips forward and arched my back so he could reach my clitoris, but I kept glancing at the faded patch and it's extremely hard to orgasm while eyeballing a stain on your parents' headboard.

In the end, I fell forward and rested my hand on his shoulder. 'It's all right, don't worry,' I panted, breathing away from his face.

Released from the pressure of trying to make me come, Gus sped up underneath me, bucking his hips up and down, up and down, up and down while I tried to look anywhere but the headboard. His groans became louder until I moved my palm over his mouth, worried that Dad would hear downstairs. This seemed to tip him over the edge; he roared into my hand and went still again.

I slid off him and lay back on the mattress, panting while staring at the ceiling.

'What are we having for breakfast?' he asked.

***

'Didn't hear a thing,' said Dad, when I went into the sitting room fifteen minutes later.

'I'm going to pretend you didn't say that. Toast?'

'Please, pet.'

'I'll do that first, and then go and get your paper.'

'Gus all right?'

'Mmm, he's just having a shower.'

'I should think he needs one.'

'Dad! Seriously!' I shouted, retreating to the kitchen and opening the door for Wilma to head out and terrorize the sparrows.

Gus came downstairs just as the kettle boiled.

'There was a spider the size of a rat in the bath,' he said, with a shudder.

Gus was no good with spiders. If he found one at home and I wasn't there, he'd either drop a thick legal book on it or trap it under a glass. Either way, he'd leave it there until I got back and could deal with it.

'Sorry.'

'It's all right, I hosed it down the drain.'

'My brave boyfriend, thank you,' I said, kissing his cheek before making tea, buttering Dad's toast and asking Gus to carry them through to him.

He came back into the kitchen with a face like a thundercloud.

'What?'

'Your dad's just asked when I'm going to "make an honest woman" out of you.'

'Ignore it, he's only joking, you know him.'

'He didn't sound like he was joking.'

'I promise he was – joking is very literally his only method of communicating. Now, do you fancy an egg? Sadly they're not our eggs because the chickens are still too traumatized from the incident with the fox to lay anything, but I believe we have some from the Spar.' I opened the fridge and peered into it. 'And then maybe a walk?'

'In this weather?' Gus squinted through the kitchen window. A sea fog had rolled in overnight covering the garden in a thick white cloak, obscuring everything beyond the car in the drive.

'It'll burn off. Scrambled?'

'I don't mind,' Gus said, with a shrug.

He started sneezing as I cracked the eggs into a mug. One sneeze, two sneezes, three, four, five explosions in a row. He was bent double and sneezing into his knees by the final one.

'You find the Piriton upstairs?'

'Yes!' he said, looking up at me with a scarlet face. 'Where's that dog?'

'Outside. Why don't you go out too, fresh air.'

'It looks freezing.'

'It's just misty, go on. It'll be better out than in.'

Gus opened the kitchen door but had another sneezing fit on the grass. Unfortunately, hearing this, Wilma galloped across the garden towards him.

'Get off! Get off, dog. Nell, get this creature off me.'

'All right, calm down. Wilma, come on, inside, bed.' She lowered her tail and slunk into it as if she'd been told off.

I ran a glass of water and took it out to Gus, who was now bent double on the lawn. 'You OK?'

'No! I've just been interrogated by your father and assaulted by your dog and I had to deal with a monster in the bath and I just… I just really do prefer London to the country.' He said this with a pitiful smile to indicate he was half-joking, but I knew that he half wasn't.

'I'm sorry. Let's eat and go for a walk, that'll help.'

Back inside, he slowly pulled a kitchen chair from out under the table as if a snake might leap from it. 'This was supposed to be a nice weekend.'

'It is, and it will be. Let's eat and then go for a lovely walk on the beach.'

'If you insist,' he replied.

★★★

I didn't want to go into Thanks A Latte but Gus was grumbling about missing his daily macchiato, so I said we could duck in on the way to the beach.

The eggs had momentarily lifted his mood, but then he'd fussed about which boots he could borrow for a walk and declared he couldn't wear his woollen Massimo Dutti coat because he didn't want it 'to get wet'.

'It's not going to rain.'

'But what if it does?'

'It's a coat! It's literally designed to get wet.'

'It's not that sort of coat,' he'd huffed.

Eventually, with Gus in an old Barbour and a pair of boots that were one size too big for him (this meant another trip upstairs to get an extra pair of Dad's socks), and Wilma on a very short lead, held by me, we'd set off.

First stop: Thanks A Latte. I tied Wilma up on the hook outside and we pushed through the door.

'Morning!'

Mum, leaning on the counter, held up a hand. 'Bit quieter, please, Nell.'

I looked from her to Luigi. Both had the sort of half-lidded expression and pale cheeks that suggested a hangover.

'Late one, was it?'

Mum shuddered.

'Art made us have shots, and Nanny Gertrude! One of us should check she's still alive this morning,' Mum said, tapping Luigi with her elbow.

I laughed. 'No way! Shots of what?'

It was Luigi's turn to shudder.

'Not sure,' Mum replied. 'What's the one that tastes like liquorice?'

'Sambuca,' I replied. Years ago, while at York, I'd overdone it on the sambuca at a fancy dress party and woken up on my bathroom floor dressed like Pocahontas, smelling faintly of kebab. I hadn't touched it since.

Gus gazed at Mum disapprovingly. He wasn't much of a spirit drinker. He had the odd whisky if we were somewhere posh for dinner but he mostly stuck to expensive Italian wines and disapproved of shots.

'We'll live but it'll be touch and go,' said Mum. 'How are you, Gus? You look like Bruce, all dressed up like that.'

I widened my eyes at her in warning.

'I'm all right,' he said glumly. 'Could I have a macchiato?'

'*Certo!*' said Luigi, turning to his silver machine.

'Nothing for me,' I added.

'Anyway, it was a lovely evening,' went on Mum. 'And nice

to spend time with Art. He hasn't changed a bit, has he? He was always such a nice boy until, well, never mind all that. But he seems just the same.'

'Mmm,' I said, pretending to be interested in the bars of granola in front of the till. 'Shall we get one of these for our walk?' I asked Gus. 'Do you fancy one? Cranberry and oat or honey and raisin?'

I didn't really want one. I just wanted Mum to stop talking about Art.

'I wish he wasn't selling the place,' she went on, oblivious. 'There was a bit of a to-do about that last night, after you lot had gone.'

I raised my head. 'Was there? Between who?'

'Just Terence and a couple of others having a go at Art about the hall, so eventually he said he had to get Gertrude home and left. Then Colin started bleating on about his protest and section blah-di-blah of some council act. Poor Art.'

Every time she mentioned his name, I felt Gus flinch beside me. Luigi seemed to be taking an awfully long time with the coffee.

'He says there isn't even going to be a golf course,' Mum rattled on. Apparently her hangover had caused her to forget entirely that this was a sensitive topic for at least one of us gathered around the counter.

'Mmm, I know.'

'So I don't really see why it's anybody else's business. It's a pity that he isn't coming home to take it over but his life is in America now and that's all there is to it. Why should he be beholden to a place just because he was born here?'

'Mmm, no, exactly.'

'Although I'm not sure his mar— Well, actually, perhaps we don't need to go into that all now,' she said, as if suddenly realizing that Gus and I didn't want to hear another word on the subject. 'Look, here we go, here's the macchiato. Gus, you're very quiet this morning. You still upset about coming second last night?'

'No! Why would you think that?'

'You look like a man who's just lost his winning lottery ticket, that's all. What are you two up to today then?'

'Walk on the beach,' I replied, 'and then, not sure. Make some lunch, maybe watch a film or something this afternoon. I've got a bit of work to do.'

'Have you?' said Gus, turning to me with a frown. 'I thought we were going to spend the afternoon together.'

'Yes, sorry, this Liechtenstein stuff, but won't take very long, promise.' Then I turned back to Mum. 'Have you spoken to Jack in the past couple of days?'

She grimaced. 'No, love, sorry. Not since I called him and told him, well, about being here. I think he's cross with me.'

'Can you ring him today, please? Just to make sure he knows he's coming up next week?'

'Yes, I promise,' she replied, like a small child swearing they'd wash their hands before lunch.

Gus tried to pay for his coffee but Luigi waved him away, and we made our way to the bay.

'There,' I said, when we reached the bottom and the expanse of sand stretched in front of us. Although the mist was still hanging over the sea, as thick as wood smoke, it had rolled back from the beach so we could see the dunes and banks of marram grass to our left, and low tide to our right. 'I think it's my favourite view in the world,' I said, in an effort to be cheery, while two seagulls waddled away from us.

Gus inhaled a big lungful of briny air and sighed. 'Yes, not bad,' he admitted, grudgingly, as we started walking along the high-water mark.

I tried to think of what to say, whether to say anything about Art or our conversation in the café, but I didn't want to make the situation worse.

'Sorry about having to work this afternoon,' I said, after a few minutes of trudging along to the rhythmic, muffled sound of our footsteps in the hard, damp sand. 'It's just with the decision about partnerships coming up and, you know, our life plan…' I paused and smiled sideways at him, hoping that mention of this would provoke a moment of solidarity between us.

'I understand,' Gus replied, although he kept his gaze lowered at his boots. 'Bought a new book on Caligula at the station yesterday so I can occupy myself with that.'

'Was he the one who married his horse?' I asked, keen to try and talk Gus out of his bad humour, even if it did mean discussing Roman emperors.

'He didn't marry him.'

'Oh.'

'He just made him a senator.'

'Right.'

We trudged on in silence for a further few minutes and then, unhelpfully, it started raining.

Gus glanced at me accusingly. 'Lucky I didn't wear my coat.'

'It's nice and bracing,' I insisted. 'Put your hood up.'

But after another minute or so he stopped dead in the sand.

'What?'

'How can you stand it, Nell?'

'Stand what?'

'All this,' he said, sweeping his arms around him. 'It's so... parochial!'

'Gus...'

'And this weather! And the animals. And the people!' He shuddered. 'Half those people in the pub last night looked like they *had* married their horses.'

'Gus...'

'And your mother cannot be serious about that man and his ludicrous little moustache!'

'Gus...'

'And that woman!'

'What woman?'

'That enormous blonde thing in the pub with your father last night,' Gus shrieked, waving his arms in the air. I'd never known Gus to have a tantrum. He'd always seemed too cerebral, too measured. But he was properly losing it. 'She looks like a Swiss barmaid!'

'Bev. And that's unkind, she's helping Dad with his leg.'

He snorted. 'Bev!'

'Gus! That's enough. You're being ridiculous. This is my home.'

'It's not your home,' he said, stamping in the sand. 'London's your home. Lovely London where there are exhibitions and decent restaurants and civilized people who can talk about things other than their dairy herd!'

'Gus, have you finished?'

The rain was coming down in fat, heavy drops now and he was glowering under his hood, chest heaving from the effort of shouting. 'Yes,' he said sulkily, between breaths. 'But when are you coming home, Nell?'

'I've told you, next week. As soon as Jack comes up. Look, I'm sorry that you don't like it up here. But I didn't have much choice, did I? And have you stopped to think about me in all this, or is it just about you?'

Gus frowned. 'I don't understand.'

Now it was my turn to shout. 'No, you wouldn't, because you're only thinking about yourself! But have you considered that I'm pretty exhausted by all this, by looking after Dad all day? And by trying to juggle working for a maniac while up here?'

'I ha—'

'And have you thought about the fact that I might be upset by my mother leaving Dad for someone else? And having a brother who's less intelligent than Wilma? Have you thought about any of this, Gus?'

He glanced at the sand and kicked at it with his toe. 'No, no, I suppose not.' Then he looked up. 'I'm sorry.'

I sighed. 'It's all right.'

'No, I'm sorry for shouting. And for being rude about your parents.'

'It's fine.'

'This coffee's quite good.' He held up his small paper cup. 'Although his moustache really is absurd.'

'I know.'

'How can your mother bear to kiss it? It's like a little slug, balancing there on his upper lip.'

'I know,' I said, and then I laughed, before Gus laughed, and we kept laughing until we were both shaking, arms clutching our stomachs, mouths open wide at the sand.

My jeans became sodden, but the dismal weather, the mist which was still hanging above us, only seemed to make the situation funnier. It was relief from the passive-aggression of the past twelve hours, and it seemed to reset us.

'The good thing,' said Gus, taking my hand once we'd regained control of ourselves, 'is that this weekend has been so abysmal thus far, it can only get better. Agreed?'

'Agreed,' I replied. 'Shall we head back? I'm drenched. Could do with a hot bath.'

'Hallelujah. Can we? And then I'll cook us something for lunch.'

'Perfect,' I said, before summoning Wilma, and we squelched home.

***

We were wrong. It could get worse.

The afternoon passed calmly enough. Gus made fresh pasta for lunch, although he grumbled about the state of all our pans. Then I retreated upstairs to take in Gideon's suggestions on Prince Rudolf's residency statement while Gus sat beside Dad in the sitting room and let him ramble on about the odds for each race that afternoon at Chepstow. Every now and then, I heard a sneeze through the floorboards and winced, but at least his mood had improved.

It was while we were in the kitchen making supper that things took a downward turn, while Gus was opening a bottle of wine and I was chopping spring onions.

My phone vibrated on the kitchen table.

Gus picked it up to pass it over, but I saw him glance at the screen as he did, and his jaw clenched.

'Thanks,' I said, wiping my hands on a tea towel and taking the phone.

I'd assumed it would be Jack since I'd called him earlier and left a voicemail. But it wasn't Jack. It was Art.

> Gather I missed you in the coffee shop earlier. Hope it was all all right after the quiz last night. Good to meet Russ. Walk this week before I go?

I put the phone down on the counter and returned to the spring onions.

'Nell?'

'Hmm?' I looked up at Gus, standing with the open wine bottle in his hand.

'Who was that?'

'Just Art saying we missed him in Thanks A Latte earlier. And also that it was good to meet you. Although he actually called you Russ.' I laughed and rolled my eyes to indicate that Art was an idiot. I only told Gus because I thought it would alleviate the tension, but he didn't answer, so I resumed my chopping.

The kitchen felt oddly quiet, the only noise my knife on the board and the sound of a game show floating through from the sitting room, along with the odd chuckle from Dad.

'What's the deal with him?' Gus asked.

'The deal?'

'Yes, the *deal*. Is he important to you?'

'Important?'

Gus slammed the bottle down on the kitchen table, causing a jet of red wine to shoot from its neck and rain down on Wilma's head. 'Stop repeating everything I say like that.'

'What do you mean, "like that"?' I asked, before putting the knife down and reaching for a damp cloth. 'Wilma, sweetheart, come here.'

She padded towards me as a drop trickled down her nose and I crouched to wipe it. A wolfhound covered in Malbec was a ludicrous sight.

'Like you don't know what I'm talking about. Nell, I saw how he was looking at you last night. He kept looking over from his table.'

'He's married!'

Gus snorted and shook his head. 'So? You know very well that doesn't mean anything.'

I finished dabbing Wilma's head and stood up. 'Gus, this is mad. You're being mad. He's an old friend wh—'

He interrupted with another snort. 'Oh, an old friend? Sorry, Nell, forgive me for being confused, I thought he was the villain who broke your heart years ago.'

I tutted. 'Villain. Gus, honestly, I've seen him a couple of times since I've been up here and the th—'

'A couple?'

'Yes, a couple. I told you! I bumped into him on the beach and then we had a coffee. And he's having a difficult time with his dad dying and the sale of the hall so…'

'So what?'

'So I'm trying to be supportive.'

'I don't like it,' said Gus, opening the glasses cupboard. 'I don't like him, I don't like that you're here and he's here, and OH FOR HEAVENS' SAKE.'

He sprang back from the cupboard and dropped a glass, which shattered on the floor and sent shards skittering across the lino like ball bearings.

'What?'

'There's a spider in that cupboard.'

'Everything all right?' came a shout from Dad.

'Fine, just making dinner!' I looked at Gus. 'OK, I think we both need a drink. Take these…' I reached into the cupboard, ignored the spider that was the size of my little fingernail, pulled out two glasses and handed them to him. 'I'm going to get the dustpan and brush. Wilma, stay in your bed. You don't want splinters in your paws.'

Gus sat at the table with his wine while I brushed around him. Neither of us spoke but yet again I could feel a combination of anger and frustration rolling off him in waves. And although part of me wanted to say something soothing and helpful, another part of me was fed up with his testiness.

And another part entirely was thinking about what he'd said: how exactly *was* Art looking at me the previous night?

★★★

We didn't really speak, not properly, anyway, for the rest of that night. It was all 'Please pass the salt' and 'Would you like a top-up?' as if we were colleagues while we sat on the sofa watching *As Good As It Gets* with Dad, who gurgled with laughter throughout.

Sex was definitely off the cards.

Nor had the black cloud shifted when we woke the next morning, so we got up and avoided looking at one another.

'I'm aiming for the 11:43,' Gus said in the kitchen, looking at his phone. 'Then it means I'm not back to London too late. If you can give me a lift to the station?'

'Course,' I said, and then, even though it felt impossible and I could feel my heart thumping in my chest, I forced the words out. 'Listen, I'm sorry you've come all this way and not had a good time.'

There, I'd said it, what was so difficult about that?

I leant against the kitchen table and winced at him.

Gus sighed. 'No, I'm sorry. I didn't mean to shout and break glasses and pour wine all over Wilma. I just miss you and I miss things being normal.'

'They will be normal,' I replied, stepping forward as he stretched his arms out. 'This week, or tomorrow, or tonight, even, I'll get hold of Jack and say he has to come up straight away so I can come home.'

'You know your brother. He won't come up today.'

'OK, but by next weekend. Deal?'

'Deal,' he said, kissing the top of my head before sneezing into my hair.

'Take some more Piriton, and I'll do the toast. Then we can go.'

***

I felt a strange melancholy as I waved him off on the platform. It was almost as if I were being split in two. Gus was going, sliding on the train back towards London, but I was still here, standing on a windy platform in my wellington boots. For a second, I wanted to beat on the train doors and jump on it. But it was only a second, and then I felt an unsettling wave of relief that he was off. I didn't have to make Wilma lie in her bed all the time, or feel embarrassed about our old, stained bath and peeling wallpaper. Dad could make his terrible jokes and I wouldn't flinch at what Gus would think of them.

As I looked at it from here, my life in London felt so unbending. I got up at precisely 6.10 a.m. to be at my desk for precisely 7.15 a.m. every day; no drinking until Friday; tightly constructed weekends of exhibitions and lunches before Monday loomed and another week began. There were fewer rules in Northcliffe; almost none, in fact. True, I couldn't continue to dress in clothing that was 90 per cent elasticated every day and eat Spar lasagne every night, but there was a freedom to my choices up here, and a lack of judgement, which I realized was entirely absent in London.

For so long, after I'd moved to York for university and then London for law school, I'd viewed Northcliffe as a cage that had held me back from a more exciting life. But now I was here again, somehow it seemed the reverse. London felt like the cage. Or was it just human nature to be permanently dissatisfied with the present moment, always willing the future to hurry up because it would be better there? It sounded like something my meditation app would say.

My head was a muddle as I walked back to the car, the heels of my boots dragging on the tarmac. Although my gloom could also be because it was a Sunday, and nobody in history had ever been cheerful on a grey Sunday afternoon. I think it was a scientific impossibility.

Chapter 15

IN THE END, THE question of how much longer I was staying up north was decided by Gideon, who called that week to say a face-to-face meeting between us and Countess Wilhelmina's legal team had been agreed for the following Monday, and he was expecting me back for it.

I rang Jack to tell him he'd have to come up that weekend and take over.

'I'll have been here nearly three weeks by then, Jack. Your turn.'

'Chill yourself,' he drawled. 'I'll book my ticket. What'll I have to do? I don't have to wash him or anything, right?'

'No, he's not bad on his crutches now, but you'll still need to wheel him to the pub in the evening. And make tea. And lunch. And dinner. But I'll leave a load of stuff in the fridge, so long as you think you can heat ready-meals in the microwave?'

'No sweat, sis, I basically have a degree in that.'

Next, I told Gus I'd be home by Sunday evening. '*Knuddelbär!* I'll open one of my best Italians. Maybe even the Sassicaia.'

I didn't know what this was but replied that it sounded lovely.

Dad was, typically, fairly relaxed about my departure. 'Good

for you, pet, probably about time you got back to London. And
Bev says she can pop in anyway. Here, what do these little pictures
she's sent me mean?' He held up his phone.

'You'll be back on your feet in no time,' said her message,
followed by a row of dancing girls emojis.

'It means she's going to do a striptease for you in a red dress
when you're better.'

Dad's mouth fell open like a hungry hippo's. 'You're kidding?'

'I am, bad luck. I think she just means you'll be out of your
cast and shimmying your way around Northcliffe again soon.'

Dad looked back to his phone, confused. 'But they're women
wearing dresses. I'm not a woman wearing a dress.'

'I know, it's like an expression.'

'But what do I send her back?'

I inhaled, imagining the emails ticking into my inbox upstairs
while I taught my sixty-eight-year-old father how to flirt with
emojis. 'What about the smiley face?'

'Not the one that's an aubergine? Because Roy says the aub—'

'Dad, on no account take dating advice from Roy. Definitely
not the aubergine. Send the smiley face. You all right for tea? I need
to work.'

'Yes yes, grand, thanks, pet.'

Back in my room, I tried to concentrate on Countess
Wilhelmina's list of demands. According to her lawyer at
Farrers, she wanted the Kensington house, the New York and
Paris apartments, the Verbier chalet, plus all her jewellery,
a monthly allowance of £100,000 for the children plus a personal
monthly allowance of £100,000 for 'entertainment, travel, clothes,

housekeeping, flowers and personal training,' as well as Alan, the miniature dachshund.

'It is absurd!' Prince Rudolf exploded on the phone, minutes after I'd emailed him her demands. 'She is mad, Eleanor. She cannot get all this, can she?'

'Ultimately, it could be down to a judge, but let's start with what you're willing to give her first.'

'Completely mad,' he went on. 'You wouldn't ask for all this, would you? The more I think about it, the more I think you are very right never to get married. Pfffft! Marriage. It is just a trap. A trap!'

We spent over an hour on the phone. 'Why does she need so much money for flowers? Is she becoming a florist? And if she refuses to discuss custody of my children, I will insist on keeping Alan. I was the one who bought him!'

Apart from the Kensington house, Prince Rudolf refused to offer anything else. Next week's face-to-face was ostensibly to try and keep negotiations out of court, and settle the residency question that hung over their children, but it would resolve precisely nothing, I suspected, when I finally hung up.

The mounting stress of it, the idea that my promotion to partner might come down to who got the sausage dog, made me crave a run and fresh air, so I changed into my trainers and called Wilma. She'd got used to our route by now: down the track and straight to the beach. It was one of those perfect spring days: sun high, no clouds, but the air still cool enough on my face to be refreshing. I hit play on one of my more embarrassing playlists and chugged along the sand listening to Little Mix at full volume, singing snatches of lyrics in between breaths watching the waves slide over one another.

'I've triiiiiiied to find someb— Jesus, WHAT the hell?'

A blur had appeared to my left, very close, making me leap in the air like a circus horse.

It was Art, running to catch up with me.

'Are you joking?' I said, taking out my EarPods. 'I thought you were a mugger.'

'You've been in London too long.'

I grinned in acknowledgement. 'Yeah, maybe.'

'Sorry, I saw you from up there and thought I'd say hi. Nice run?'

I nodded and bent to rest my hands on my knees, trying to regain my breath as Wilma bounded up to him.

'Hello, Wilma, how you doing?' Art crouched to run a hand along the grey fuzz of her back, then looked at me. 'You all right? You didn't reply to my message.'

'Yeah, sorry, just...' I trailed off.

The truth was, after putting Gus on the train on Sunday morning, I'd decided not to message him back. It was too confusing, this chameleon existence. I couldn't be one version of me with him and another with Gus. And I was going home in a few days so there didn't seem much point in stirring old feelings any further.

'When are you going back to America?' I asked, standing up.

Art frowned at me for a few seconds before replying, as if he was trying to work out the answer to a more serious question. 'Maybe next week. Depends. You heard about this protest on Sunday that your friend Colin's whipped up?'

'Mmm.'

'I've got to deal with that first, reassure everyone that the Glaswegians aren't going to bulldoze anything.'

'Aren't they?'

'No!' He pushed himself up from behind Wilma and flung his hands in the air. 'What is wrong with everyone? I've told you, I care too much about this place to let that happen. Want to walk?' He gestured towards the end of the bay, and I pushed away my guilt and fell into pace alongside him.

'This is hardly what I dreamt of, Nell,' he went on, 'having to flog everything my family built up because my parents managed to spend it on cars and facelifts.'

'What? Facelifts?'

'Mmm. Mum goes to Paris for all sorts of treatments these days. Did you not see her at Dad's funeral looking a bit...'

'Taut?'

'Exactly.'

'Maybe.'

Art sighed and glanced sideways. 'Anyway, how are you? Russ seemed nice.'

'Gus.'

'What?'

'It's Gus.'

'Sorry.'

'He saw your message and it landed me in hot water.'

'What was wrong with it?'

'Nothing, only that it was from you.'

'What's wrong with me?'

I tipped my head back and shouted into the cloudless sky, 'Nothing!'

Men could be so dim. Women were accused of being complicated but at least we weren't so thick when it came to matters of the heart.

Think back through great romantic heroes and it's always the man who screws things up.

Romeo: fails to realize Juliet's merely asleep (why not check her breathing?) and tops himself.

Willoughby: can't keep his pecker in his trousers, misses out on marrying Marianne Dashwood and is miserable with his rich wife ever after.

Laurie in *Little Women*: marries completely the wrong sister.

Edward Rochester: keeps his previous wife shut up in the attic. Disaster waiting to happen.

Jack from *Titanic*: fails to realize there's plenty of space on that floating wooden door beside Rose, gets hypothermia, dies.

'Nell? I don't get it, what's the problem?'

I sighed. 'Because we're old friends and I think he feels threatened.'

We trudged on in silence while Wilma had a tug of war with a piece of seaweed attached to a rock.

'Should he feel threatened by me?' Art asked eventually.

It was a question that I could either answer with a long, convoluted explanation or a very short one. 'No,' I replied, without looking at him.

'Can I ask you something? How come you guys aren't married? If you've been together for so long?'

The reply to this was easier; I could roll it out like an actor delivering lines. 'We decided not to. Gus thinks it's too commercialized, and says he'll commit murder if he has to go on another stag do, let alone his. And we're not religious. Plus his parents had a bad divorce when he was eight. So, yeah, we don't want to do it.'

'He doesn't or you don't?'

Art sounded so serious I glanced across at him in surprise. 'It was his idea but I agree with him. It's just an industry. Fun fact: did you know that the whole concept of diamond engagement rings was created by an advertising campaign?'

He shook his head at the sand.

'Well it was,' I rattled on, keen to keep the conversation off my own relationship because talking about it with Art felt so strange. 'It was a De Beers campaign after the war, when they wanted to sell more diamonds, so they came up with the "A diamond is forever" slogan and that was that. And now people are obsessed with diamond rings. Isn't that crazy?'

He glanced sideways and his eyes searched behind mine.

'What?'

'I remember a Nell who was more romantic.'

'Yeah, and look where that got her.'

'What d'you mean?'

'Never mind,' I said quickly, looking back to my feet. 'But it's also that I see the bad marriages every day at work, a parade of miserable people desperate to extricate themselves from someone they once pledged to spend their whole lives with.'

'They probably meant it at the time.'

'I know.'

'And by not marrying Russ—'

'Gus!'

'Sorry. But not marrying Gus doesn't mean you're never going to break up with him. You can't insulate yourself from that possibility entirely, Nell.'

'No, I know that too.'

'Seems a shame when you had it all mapped out, big wedding, the dress, the marquee, the flowers…'

'Hey, you don't know that!'

'I do!' Art replied, and his face lifted into the sort of smile that suggested he had a secret. 'I heard you telling Nanny Gertrude once.'

'WHAT? Stop, Art!' I froze and stared at him.

He laughed. 'According to you, we were going to get married on the lawn in front of the hall and Luna was going to carry the ring for us.'

'Oh my god,' I mumbled into my hands.

'And you wanted a dress like Princess Jasmine's in *Aladdin*, plus a cake with ten tiers, and we were going to ride off on one of Dad's horses. I remember it all.'

'Don't laugh!' I said, reaching to hit his arm. 'I'm so embarrassed, I can't believe you always knew.'

'I always knew,' he said, before his smile became smaller. 'I always knew,' he repeated, more quietly.

I cleared my throat and started walking again. 'Anyway, what about you and Nicole?'

'What about us?' he asked, resuming his pace beside me.

'If marriage is so great, are you recommending it?'

He didn't reply.

'Art?'

'I heard. I was just trying to work out what to tell you.' There was a short pause. 'It's so much more complicated than I assumed when we were teenagers, Nell. I love Felix to death and I miss him but… I don't know.' He kicked a pebble with his boot and looked up at the horizon. 'I'm probably not the best advert for marriage. Nor were my parents. Or your parents, for that matter. He's nice, by the way, Luciano.'

'Luigi. Art, honestly, you and names.'

He ignored me. 'Exactly. I liked him. But I imagine it could be pretty great, with the right person. Marriage, I mean.'

He turned and squinted at me like a doctor looking for symptoms. 'But I'm not sure he is the right person, is he?'

'What?'

'And that's why you're OK with it, because deep down you don't want to marry *him*. But it's not because you don't believe in marriage.'

'Stop! Art, stop, I mean it. Why are you telling me this?'

'Because you'll waste years of your life, Nell. What's that saying? This isn't a dress rehearsal. Gus seems nice enough and I'm sure he's very successful, and he clearly feels incredibly strongly about pub quizzes. But you don't seem head over heels.'

'You can tell that, can you, from a single interaction?'

'I could tell enough.'

'Stop it, Art,' I said, freezing again in the sand, unwilling to press on with the walk or the conversation.

A step ahead of me, he turned round. 'You know you can love someone, but not be in love with them?'

'You're the expert on this, are you?'

'I'm not having a go, all I'm saying is I'm not sure he's your person. Trust me, I should know.'

'Trust you? *Trust* you? That's a joke.'

'Why? What d'you mean?'

'Nothing,' I spat, 'it doesn't matter. None of it matters now, Art. But there's no way that I'm taking relationship advice from you, of all people.'

'Ouch, Nell.' Art clapped a hand to his chest. 'I just don't want to see you settle! Don't settle for less than you deserve.'

This riled me even further. 'Deserve! Art, how can you possibly talk about what I deserve after everything you did?'

'Everything I did? Nell, I d—'

'Stop it, just stop. I don't want to hear any of this from you, sorry. Actually, no, scrap that.' Rooted to the same spot in the sand, I shook my head slowly, eyes slit with anger. 'I'm not sorry, I love Gus and he's a good, kind man who looks after me, who makes me feel safe. And you know nothing, literally *nothing* about it. We have different lives now, Art, you can't… I won't… you can't come back and trample all over it.' My voice was strained by the end of this, by the force of my words, and I gulped for air as if I'd just finished a run.

'Did you ever think of me?'

I didn't reply because it was another question that felt too big to answer. I could only stare at him.

'In the past fifteen years, did you ever think of me?' he persisted. 'Did you miss me?'

'Art! Seriously, why are you asking me this now?'

He looked up at the sky. 'Because…' he said into it, before

dropping his face towards mine. 'Forget it. But you shouldn't be with him.'

'You married her, you married Nicole!' I shouted at him, snapping and forgetting our surroundings, forgetting that we were standing on the beach and there might well be other dog walkers out for their morning stroll who were discussing what they watched last night on telly and didn't want to witness the embarrassing spectacle of two adults bellowing at one another.

'I know,' Art shouted back, throwing his hands either side of his head, fingers wide. 'That's why I'm telling you all this.' He moved towards me so I reversed a couple of steps. 'Don't make the wrong decision, Nell, please don't. It's like I told you that day, down here, you're so much better than this.'

I looked for Wilma, who'd found a stick of driftwood and was galloping along in the shallows with it, delighted with her treasure. 'Wilma, come on,' I yelled, desperate to get home.

'Nell, wait, I'm not trying to be a dick.'

'Wilma! Come on, off we go.' I patted my thigh to indicate that she had to follow, and turned to run from him.

'Nell!'

I reached into my pocket for my EarPods. I was hardly in the mood for Little Mix now but it was better than hearing Art shout after me.

Chapter 16

WE ALL HAVE A place in our head where we store old pains. Each of us walks around every day with mental imprints of past grievances and traumas. The oldest pains are probably locked away in a much smaller container than the more recent pains, but they're still there. If you want to, you can find an old container and unlock it, take out the pain and examine it, rake over whatever caused that hurt in the first place. But mostly we don't because we have to get up in the morning, get dressed and go on with our lives. Why would anyone want to keep sticking their finger into a live socket?

But for some time, years, really, that's what I'd done with the pain that Art caused. I'd take it out every day and go over it again and again, rolling it around my brain, trying to make sense of it. If I could make sense of what happened, then maybe I could get over it.

In the end, it was only time, and meeting Gus, that made the pain small enough to lock away for longer stretches. I stopped getting it out so often, realized I didn't need it, that you can't rationalize every experience in life, so the container shrank and was pushed further back. But this one conversation ripped it open again and I felt it physically, a sudden sense that I was back there again, that I might be sick.

It had happened in July 2004. Art's twenty-first birthday. I'd always loved his birthdays because they were so much bigger than mine or Jack's. It was the one time when the Drummonds seemed to remember they had a son.

One year, Lady Drummond organized a bouncy castle designed exactly like a mini Drummond Hall; another year, an adventure company built an assault course in the woods, including a zip wire that ran between the lime trees. For his thirteenth birthday there'd been the treasure hunt. For his sixteenth, an outdoors cinema was set up in the grounds for a preview of *Men in Black II*. It was Art and a few school friends, plus Jack and me, and we lay on huge beanbags and ate as much as we liked from popcorn and candy-floss stalls erected beside the screen.

But the biggest party of all was his twenty-first.

The first indication that it would be special came a couple of months before when two thick cream envelopes landed on our doormat: one for Jack, one for me.

'Miss Eleanor Mason,' said mine, in looping black calligraphy.

I opened it to find an invitation so thick and stiff it could have sliced bread, and several inserts that fluttered to the kitchen floor.

'Lord and Lady Drummond, at Drummond Hall, for their son Arthur,' said the gold gilt letters.

I bent to peel up the inserts from the lino before they got dirty. These asked about dietary requirements, offered details of nearby hotels and taxi companies, and included a pretty watercolour map of the village.

'Bit poncy if you ask me,' Jack said, when he opened his. 'Why does it say "carriages" at 2 a.m.? Who has a carriage?'

Mum peered over his shoulder. 'That's when the party ends, and nobody's saying you have to go if it's too poncy, Jack Mason. I'd love to go to a big party like that.'

'Obviously I'm going,' Jack replied quickly, 'it's just quite a posh do, isn't it?'

I hadn't said anything because I was too busy staring at the bottom right-hand corner of the card: 'Dress code: we're off to the circus!'

'Mum, what does this mean?'

Jack answered before she could: 'That's the theme, you moron.'

'Yeah, but what do we wear for it?'

'Dunno. Lion tamer? You could be my lion.'

'Cos I'm ginger? Fuck off.'

'Eleanor Mason, really?' Mum remonstrated.

'What? Why do you never have a go at him?'

'That's not a nice word.'

'Mum, I'm seventeen.'

'I don't care.'

I flounced upstairs with my invitation where I lay on my bed, holding the card to my chest, and spent the next two months thinking about my costume. Having never been to a fancy dress party, I was determined to go as something brilliant, something which would dazzle Art, who I hadn't seen since we kissed outside the pub, just before he left for the RAF base in Anglesey. We'd emailed, spoken on our Nokia phones and sent endless, lengthy messages that were delivered in three parts, but nothing else. And as those months passed, I decided, in dramatic teenage fashion, that our entire relationship hinged on this one night.

I made my costume in the end. It took weeks of frowning behind Mum's sewing machine, and trailing bright lines of cotton around my bedroom, but eventually it was finished.

I went as a clown. If I *did* ever have the choice to go back in time to that first kiss with Art, my choice of costume for his party might be something else I'd rethink. But it's a bit late for that now.

From the British Heart Foundation shop in Morpeth I bought eight of the brightest, shiniest shirts I could find, an electric blue waistcoat made from extremely flammable material, a pair of red braces and the biggest pair of black brogues they had.

I cut up the shirts and, borrowing Mum's sewing machine, made a pair of patchwork trousers which ballooned around my legs and were held up by the braces. I painted the shoes red and yellow, and stuffed the ends with scraps of leftover material so my feet didn't slide around in them. The waistcoat went over a plain white T-shirt and, on the night itself, I back-brushed my curls so they fluffed around my head – and spent over an hour copying the face make-up of a clown picture I'd printed off the internet. Finally, I added a red nose I'd bought from the party shop.

That evening, I walked downstairs carefully, the ends of my shoes sticking out over the edge of each step. Mum and Dad applauded when I staggered into the kitchen; Luna jumped out of her bed and growled until I spoke, reassuring her that I wasn't an intruder.

Jack went as a ringmaster, having bought an old suit from a vintage shop in Newcastle, plus a top hat which was slightly too small but he squashed down on his head. A whip, borrowed from the Drummond Hall stables, was draped around his neck.

Before we left, Mum took a photo of us; in it, I'm smiling nervously while one of Jack's arms is draped around me, the other tilting his hat. It stayed on the fridge for years afterwards, although I could hardly bear to look at it.

Since I couldn't walk very easily in my giant shoes, Dad drove us to the hall's gates, then Jack and I shuffled up the drive so we arrived when the party had already kicked off.

This being July in Northumberland, the sun took hours to dip below the horizon. It didn't get dark much before midnight in those middle months, and it would be light again by the very early morning. Midsummer. It always seemed so romantic, the long evening light. I remember clutching the small velvet bag I'd borrowed from Mum, which contained the card telling Art that I loved him. Plus, a red lipstick and two plasters in case my shoes rubbed.

As we came around the bend, out from under the avenue of trees, I stopped at the sight. The first glimpse of the hall was always impressive but that night it looked like a film set.

Between the house and the cliffs, spread across the lawn, was a huge blue circus tent linked to two smaller tents either side of it. In front of them was a fairground wheel, lit up, already ferrying guests around it. Beside that was a set of dodgems, from which I could hear squeals as the little cars slid across its floor. These shouts mingled with the notes of a saxophone floating towards us from a band playing on another patch of the lawn. Multicoloured spotlights swung from the roof of the hall, across the tips of the tents. And underneath it all, the falling sun shone a white glare on the waves.

'Careful, ugly, the wind'll change,' Jack told me as I squinted at the sea.

'Shut up.' I hadn't meant to sound so defensive but the scene in front of us had made me nervous. Even more nervous.

'Look at that!' He nodded towards a helicopter in front of the rhododendrons, its blades drooped towards the grass.

Although not even a helicopter parked on the lawn could outdo the sight of a bright red hot-air balloon hovering over the hall. The words wrapped around its canvas were only partly visible but I understood the gist: 'Happy Birthday, Arthur!' they said. From the balloon's basket, a cluster of partygoers waved, and a rope trailed down from them to three men standing on a small platform underneath, and a queue of guests snaking back from them along a red carpet.

Big tops. Big wheels. Dodgems and hot-air balloon rides. It wasn't a party. It was a piece of theatre.

'Beats a bouncy castle, doesn't it?' said Jack, with an admiring whistle, before he raised a hand to adjust his white tie, even though he'd stood in front of the kitchen mirror, primping it over and over again before we left. 'C'mon, let's go.'

I remained still as Jack strode forwards, then looked back at me and urged me to hurry up, worrying that the drinks would run out.

That, at least, made me laugh. 'Jack, I don't think it's a running out scenario.' I swept my arm in front of me. 'Look at this place. It's just…'

'What?'

I couldn't answer. I'd been both excited and terrified about the party for weeks, but the fear was winning. I remember wishing I could stay there and watch the party, then see Art afterwards without all these people. That would have been enough.

But Jack urged me on and I followed him, knowing that I couldn't really go home. Dad would only have sent me straight back out again.

A few moments later, I spotted a line of waiters holding trays of champagne.

That was the first moment of the evening when my heart plunged, since they were dressed as clowns too, all of them. Their outfit wasn't quite the same – they were in red and white spotted rompers with multicoloured wigs, and they wore sponge red noses instead of face paint. But still, underneath my own face paint, my cheeks turned pink. I was the clowniest clown of them all.

Jack didn't even notice. He took a glass and announced he was going to find Art and I didn't have a chance to say that I'd come with him. He was gone, so I took a flute from one of the clowns with a grimace of solidarity, and moved to stand on the edge of the gathering, my back to the sea.

Around me, guests mingled in their fancy dress. None of it looked home-made. All of it looked expensive. A blonde in a sequinned corset and a pair of fishnet tights laughed with a man in a red frock coat as if they wore these clothes every day. A mime artist, so convincing he could actually have been a mime artist, threw back his head at a jester in a pointy hat that jingled with bells. To be fair, there were dozens of other clowns. It wasn't just me and the waiting staff. But somehow their trousers, their wigs, even their faces seemed more convincing.

Then I noticed the other girls my age. Most of them looked pretty, not silly. They'd made small efforts with the theme – glittery eye make-up, feathers sticking from jewelled headbands, sequinned top hats – but they were also in corsets that showed their tiny waists and pushed their chests towards their chins. Just as certain sorts now insist on sexing up Halloween (sexy cat, sexy witch, sexy broomstick), these girls had vamped up the circus theme, whereas I'd gone full pantomime.

A wave of stupidity washed through me as I glanced down at my white T-shirt. I'd put on my best padded bra since tonight might be the night that Art and I finally did it, but I definitely, in no way, looked attractive.

'Want one?' asked a familiar voice, as a tray appeared extremely close to my face.

At least this made me laugh; it was Colin, the saddest clown I'd ever seen.

'I don't know what's funny,' he said, crossly. 'Look at you!'

'I'm sorry,' I replied, when I caught my breath. 'But why didn't you say anything? Why didn't you tell me you guys were going to be clowns?'

He and Luce had been taken on by the local catering firm to help out for the night, along with anyone else around our age in the area. I'd felt uncomfortable whenever the topic of Art's party had come up in the pub, awkward that I was going as a guest and they were going as staff, so tried to keep off the subject.

She appeared behind him, holding a tray of mini burgers.

'We didn't know until today. They asked for our sizes and gave us these stupid wigs when we got here. Anyway, don't worry, you look great,' Luce promised me.

I pinched my trousers and held the material out from my legs as if it was a skirt. 'Do I actually?'

She nodded.

'I haven't seen Art yet,' I said, peering around them. 'You seen him?'

'Er, yeah, he's over there somewhere.'

'Nell, can you hold this?' said Colin, offering me his tray. 'My head feels like it's on fire.'

I held the tray of canapés while he reached underneath his wig and scratched like a dog with fleas.

'What are these, anyway?' I asked, wrinkling my nose at the small, brown balls. They looked like pickled onions but smelt of garlic.

Colin shook his head. 'Snail bonbons. Snails with wild garlic wrapped in onion.'

'Bleurgh, no thanks.'

'Yeah, they're grim, I tried a few earlier.'

'Are you guys allowed any champagne?'

Colin shook his head as Lucy glanced over her shoulder. 'No, and we'd better shift. The woman in charge is a monster. But see you later?'

'I'm sort of hoping I'll be with Art later, if I ever find him.'

Luce rolled her eyes. 'All right, all right. Come on, Col.' She started walking off but shouted back over her shoulder at me, 'Good luck with losing your virginity, Nell!'

'Shhhh,' I hissed at her, as Col took his tray and followed. It was all right for her. She'd done it nearly two years earlier with Andrew Lewis, precipitating a bus journey to a chemist we didn't know in Bedlington to buy the morning-after-pill because she thought she might be pregnant even though they'd used *two* condoms. Now she got to do it all the time since she and Andrew were still going out, and he lived in the next village.

Meanwhile, my virginity had started to feel embarrassing. I don't know why anybody thought it was so special. Lucy tried to set me up with Andrew's friend Ewan on the beach one weekend but I wanted to wait for Art, so I'd claimed a headache and walked home.

I watched Luce and Colin walk towards a guest dressed in a lion's costume and briefly wished that I'd been waiting with them rather than standing alone on the fringes. At least it would have given me something to do.

That was when I saw him.

He was standing in the middle of a throng of guests. I recognized one of his best school friends, Jasper, plus Jack, who'd already managed to wangle his way into their circle.

Like Jack, Art was wearing white tie but he also had a white silk scarf around his neck and a leather hat with goggles on top of them. Some sort of famous aviator, I guessed. I still hadn't seen him since he arrived home from Wales a couple of days earlier. The hall was full of family and friends, he'd texted apologetically, and been consistently evasive when I asked what he was going as. 'Wait and see...'

That was the first time I saw Nicole, too, in a silk gown the colour of pink sherbet that fell to the grass. She looked exquisite, as if the dress had been stitched around her. I wondered if it was actually a nightie since she didn't appear to be wearing any underwear beneath it. She was my age, I later discovered, but she was so much more developed than me. How could any girl our age have breasts like a Hollywood siren? It shouldn't be allowed, to be that tall and willowy yet have the chest of a Wonderbra model. And her hair! It fell in blonde waves down her back and over her smooth, tanned shoulders. I'd never seen any woman like it in Northumberland. I'm not sure there'd actually been any woman like it in Northumberland before. The sight would have caused a pile-up on Morpeth High Street. She was standing next to Art, laughing up at him, which made me want to go up and insert myself between them. How was a pink silk dress a circus outfit, anyway?

I glanced at my shoes, poking from the bottom of my patch-work trousers like bowling shoes, and decided that I would simply march up and give Art his card.

But just as I stepped forward, a large figure appeared in front of me, like a solar eclipse, blocking all sight of Art and Nicole.

'Nanny Gertrude, hello. Are you a… pirate?'

The pastels were gone and in their place was a dress made of shiny purple taffeta, plus a purple hankie knotted around her head. She looked extraordinary.

'No, duckie, I'm a fortune teller,' she replied, thrusting a pair of playing cards under my nose. 'And you look very lovely too. Did you make those trousers?'

'Mmm,' I replied, ashamed that this was so obvious.

'Are you having a nice time?'

I leant sideways to see around her. Art was still standing in the group, the blonde girl by his side.

'I haven't seen Art yet. Who's that he's with?'

Nanny Gertrude followed my gaze and her face spasmed like she'd sucked on a lemon.

'That's Nicole Cargill, the daughter of Arthur's godfather. The American one. They arrived in that contraption,' she said, glaring at the helicopter, 'and it's been a long three days. "Can you wash this, can you iron that?" You should see the state of her bedroom. She's in the east wing and I took her dress up earlier, pressed like she asked, and…' she leant forwards conspiratorially, 'her undergarments were all over the carpet. But they're going to London tomorrow so then we can all calm down and get back to normal. Now, do you know where you're sitting?'

'Sitting for what?'

I was half-listening while still staring at Nicole. She resembled the pin-ups Jack had on his bedroom wall – perfect hair, teeth whiter than chalk and a body I knew I'd never have, no matter how many days I tried not to eat breakfast. I both hated and was in awe of her from the start.

Nanny Gertrude took my arm and led me towards the tent's main entrance. 'Come on, I'll help you.'

There was a big poster on an easel in front of it: the table plan. Each one had been named after a different type of plane – Spitfire, Falcon, Cessna, Osprey and so on.

'There you are, the same one as me,' said Nanny Gertrude, pointing at a list of names on the Airbus table. I scanned the others to check that Art was with us. But he wasn't. Apart from Nanny Gertrude, I didn't recognize a single other name. And much as I adored Nanny Gertrude, sitting with her wasn't how I'd envisaged my night.

'Where's Art?'

'He's with his parents,' she said, sliding a wrinkled finger towards the first table on the list. I read down the names: The Honourable Arthur Drummond, Lord and Lady Drummond, Jasper, the Marquess of Milton, and a few I didn't recognize until, at the bottom of that column, I saw her name: Nicole Cargill. They were on the same table, and I wasn't. I tightened my grip around my bag at the sudden stab of inferiority. This was a familiar sensation from school where Luce and I had learned early that there was a rigid social hierarchy in place: prettiest, thinnest girls at the top, everyone else in descending order depending on whether or not boys fancied us. But I'd never been made to feel that by Art. Not until now.

I didn't have much time to dwell on this though, because a man dressed like a penguin stepped from inside the marquee and lifted a microphone to his mouth. 'My lords, ladies and gentlemen, dinner is served. Please can you all start heading inside.'

'Shall we go in?' Nanny Gertrude took my elbow without waiting for an answer, a small purple bulldozer pushing others out the way. 'Excuse me, excuse me, thank you so much.' I'd blushed as she pulled me towards the marquee's entrance and had a mean thought: this was embarrassing, I didn't want to be seen with a seventy-eight-year-old. I wanted to be in Art's gang, laughing and chatting with them, but instead I was hanging out with Widow Twankey.

I was briefly distracted from this meanness by the interior. The black lining above our heads was studded with small white lights replicating the night sky. Ivy and white roses burst from ornate stone vases taller than me, as if we'd fallen into a wild country garden. Dozens of round tables jostled for space between these vases, decorated with flickering candles in glass lanterns. But the most breathtaking sight of all was an old-fashioned plane suspended by cables from the marquee's ceiling, nose down, tail up, as if it was about to loop over us. And either side of the plane was an acrobat, two of them twisting up and down ropes that hung from the top of the tent.

My amazement was soon trumped by the realization that our table was several away from Art's, and I was made more miserable still by the two characters I sat next to, school friends of Art's who I'd never met. Mungo Ponsonby was a tall, dark-haired man who looked like a bloodhound: long face and sad, drooping eyes. Barnaby Baldwin was also tall (what did they feed posh men? Why were they the size of oak trees?), but better-looking. He had sandy stubble and I vaguely remember thinking he looked like Ryan Philippe, the second of my great loves back then thanks to his performance as Sebastian in *Cruel Intentions*.

'So how do you know Art?' Barnaby had asked.

'I, er...' I'd paused, hardly able to say I'd been in love with him since I was ten, that he was the person I thought about most often, roughly every few seconds. I couldn't say that to these posh friends of Art's because they might laugh, so I settled for an easier explanation: 'My dad works for his dad, he's the stud manager.'

'So you're staff,' the bloodhound replied, with a mocking smile.

Barnaby laughed this off and told me to ignore him, but actually, during dinner, they both ignored me, talking over my lap to one another about mutual friends with strange names like Bongo and Raisin while I became steadily more wretched. On they went, discussing Bongo's internship at Goldman Sachs and Raisin's new labrador directly over my head, while my eyes hopped from table to table, trying to find him.

I spotted Jack first, already paying close attention to the blonde girl he was sitting next to. And then, on the table behind him, I found Art. He was in the middle of the marquee, sitting next to Nicole, their elbows almost touching. Occasionally, she laid one of her hands on his shoulder which made me want to fling a pellet of bread roll at them. The plane was suspended directly above their table and, in my fury, I remember vaguely hoping that it might come loose and crush her but spare him.

My dejection was total. In my head, this party had been different. In my head, I'd arrived and Art had instantly sought me out, had introduced me to his friends, had seated me next to him. In my head, this party was going to be the most glamorous, most thrilling night of my life.

In reality, I felt even more pitiful than I had at school. It was as if now that Art's more glamorous friends had arrived in Northcliffe, I'd been relegated. Every now and then I caught a glimpse of Lucy and Colin, laying down plates of smoked salmon and venison in front of guests, and tried to smile at them to prove I was having a good time. But I wasn't. Also, I needed a wee and nobody else seemed to be getting up.

At the 'ting, ting, ting!' of a knife on a glass, there'd been speeches. First from Jasper, who'd thanked Lord and Lady Drummond for throwing the 'party of the century', which made everyone cheer and clap, before he embarked on a story about him and Art being caught by their housemaster trying to sneak out from school to London, having stuffed their beds with pillows. More laughter and I watched Nicole giggle and flick a hand through her hair, smiling at Art with her hateful American teeth.

Then Lord Drummond took over the microphone and embarked on a speech about his son's achievements — head of house, head of games, and now trainee fighter pilot. It didn't include many jokes, but as he droned on, Art watched his father with an astonished grin which squeezed my heart. I wanted to rush over and say 'See? Of course he's proud of you,' but instead we stood for yet another toast before Art took the microphone.

He thanked his parents first, and then swung his arm around the marquee at everyone else. Go on, I'd willed, spot me, Art. Just look at me once, reassure me. But he didn't. Instead, he thanked all the guests who'd come from abroad then made a joke about his godfather offering everyone lifts home in his helicopter – 'the one parked on the lawn outside' – before announcing that it was on with the party.

At this, a huge black curtain fell behind him and revealed a new area with a chequered floor, neon lights and a band which launched into a rendition of 'Happy Birthday'. Art shook his head with embarrassment as 300 guests bellowed their way through the song.

'Wasn't that marvellous?' Nanny Gertrude shrieked across our table afterwards. 'I don't think I've been this pickled since 1953.'

She picked up her wine glass and I wondered whether I'd be

able to carry her upstairs to her room if necessary. It was a dismaying thought; I'd been hoping to peel Art's clothes off that evening, not an old woman's.

That's when I decided to go for a pee.

I excused myself and headed towards the marquee entrance. Outside, the sun had dropped and left a pink tint on the horizon, but I didn't want to stop and gaze at the sky, I wanted the loo. Automatically, I headed for the hall's front door but was stopped by a security guard with a neck as thick as an elephant's leg.

'House guests only.'

'Can I just use the bathroom? I'm a friend, I live just down there…' As if directions would help, I turned and pointed in the direction of the trees. 'It's only a wee.'

He repeated himself – 'house guests only' – before pointing towards a block of Portaloos. 'Everyone else, over there.'

'All right, if I wet myself it's your fault, but all right,' I replied, almost hobbling by this point. They were fancy Portaloos, with baskets of tampons and cans of hairspray by the sinks. I pushed open a cubicle door to check it was empty and sat, grateful to be shut in a space where nobody could see me, where I didn't have to make fake smiles, where I could have a few moments alone to process the evening.

I hadn't been there for long when I heard the clack of heels coming up the metal steps and a posh English voice. I'd always remembered every line of this conversation because it left me so winded.

'How was your table?' asked the posh English voice.

'Terrific,' replied an American. 'I hadn't seen Eloise for years.

Although her husband is such a drag. I still don't understand why she married him.'

'I can think of at least one reason,' squeaked her English companion, before they both cackled like pantomime witches.

I glanced down at my knickers, stretched between my ankles, and wondered whether I should cough or make some sort of noise to indicate they weren't alone. But before I dared, the posh English one had spoken up.

'Your daughter looks very taken tonight.'

'Doesn't she just! Robert and I were hoping as much. They haven't seen one another for a couple of years because she's been at Princeton but, I have to say, it does look very promising.'

'How long are you here?'

'I'm going to London tomorrow because Robert's got Wimbledon tickets but I'm hoping Nicole can stay for a few more days.'

'I do hope that works out,' honked the other. 'Another excuse for a party at Drummond Hall. Or would you do it in the Hamptons?'

The click of a powder compact. 'Who knows. Don't get ahead of yourself, Cynthia. But I'll let you know when to buy a hat.'

They tinkled with laughter and I listened to their heels clack back down the steps.

As I exhaled, my eyes fell on my clutch bag, leaning up against the door, and I felt my self-pity shift.

That was it, I'd had enough of feeling like a lemon at this party. I would go and find Art and thrust my card at him. How dare he ignore me all night? How dare he spend all his time with the braless supermodel? How dare her mother be plotting his marriage when he was supposed to be marrying me?

I would find him, I would give him my card, he'd apologize and tell me he'd been a moron, I would finally lose my virginity.

It seemed a foolproof plan.

I hoiked up my knickers and yanked down the loo handle, which unfortunately caused electric blue drops of water to fly out and land all over the front of my trousers.

After a brief tussle with the door, I stepped out of the cubicle to inspect the damage under better light. Disaster. I didn't think I could look any worse and yet, here I was, in patchwork trousers spattered with blue drops.

Also, by this point, my clown make-up had started to fade and patches of skin were coming through the face paint which made me look like I had a flesh-eating disease. But there was no time to waste. I washed my hands, bared my teeth at myself in the mirror to check they were greenery-free and set off to find Art.

I headed for his table first. Art wasn't there but his parents were, sitting with a gaggle of others who fell silent when I approached. Lady Drummond had gazed at me, horrified, and asked what had happened to my face before explaining, with clear disdain, that I was the daughter of their racing manager. As we'd got older, turning from children into teenagers, and Art and I became closer, she'd become increasingly frosty towards me. She waved (reluctantly) in the direction of the dance floor.

I hurried towards the bodies swaying under flashing lights and hovered on the edge of it, squinting. I remember one man, wearing an enormous fake moustache, who kept pointing his finger into the air and back at the floor again as if he was John Travolta.

Art wasn't there either so I turned to the wooden bar, built around a real palm tree. Behind it, staff in Hawaiian shirts were passing out drinks as fast as they could make them: pink drinks, blue drinks, brown drinks in martini glasses.

Nor could I see him there. Jasper was though. I didn't know Art's best friend much, only from the odd visit to the hall for the summer holidays or Art's birthdays, but I was oddly intimidated by him. It wasn't the grandness of Jasper that made me feel shy around him (he was the son of some duke and owned a castle in Yorkshire), more his general demeanour. He'd always been so good-looking you could hardly look at him without blushing, which gave him a confidence bordering on arrogance.

That night, he called me 'Art's little friend' with an amused smile, and asked if I was working as a waitress.

'No, I just came as a clown, too. Have you seen Art? It's quite urgent.'

'The birthday boy?'

I nodded.

'Everyone's after him tonight, aren't they?' Jasper drawled. 'But no, afraid not, I've been rather occupied with my friend Candida here.' He smiled down at a small brunette beside him who'd come dressed as a unicorn.

'Fine, thank you so much,' I muttered, heading back outside to circle the marquees again.

It felt like a real-life game of Where's Wally. Guests were still going up in the hot-air balloon and squeals were coming from the dodgems. To my left, the Ferris wheel had turned bright against the dark sky, and I could see multiple feet dangling from the top as it turned slowly around. Was Art up there? My eyes scanned each seat as it rotated back to the lawn. No sign.

Next I went and hovered awkwardly outside the male Portaloos for several minutes, but no joy.

There was only one thing for it, I'd decided. I had to get inside. If I could find another way in, I could run upstairs, check his bedroom, and be back down again in five minutes. I had to find him, I had to see him. I'd been counting on tonight for so many months and the idea of going home this disappointed, this deflated, made me feel as if the rest of my life would be ruined.

This is the level of teenage drama I was operating at.

'Nell!' came a shout over the roar of the generators, which made my hopes briefly leap until I realized it was Colin.

'Hi, Col. Just going inside for a bit.'

'Why?' His eyebrows slid together in suspicion.

I fibbed. 'Because I need to pee, if you must know.'

'But the guest toilets are over there,' he said, pointing at the Portaloos.

'Er, there's a queue. And I know where they are inside so I just thought I'd go in quickly.'

This seemed to satisfy him. 'You having a good time?'

'Er, yeah, sort of. Listen, Col, I'm a bit desp—'

'Want to come on the Ferris wheel with me and Luce? We're allowed, apparently, after eleven. They've got bar staff so the rest of us can knock off.'

'Yeah, maybe, I just really nee—'

'You don't have to, if you're embarrassed to be seen with us.

We just thought, might be nice. I bet the view's amazing from up there, I reckon you could se—'

'Col, I'm so sorry but I've got to pee, but yes, definitely, let's do a ride. I'll come find you guys back here in a bit, OK?'

'OK,' he said cheerfully, 'see you in a bit.'

I started heading towards the hall's side entrance before I turned back to him, 'Oh, also, Col, you seen Art anywhere?'

'Art?'

'Yes, you know, Art, the one who this party's for.'

'Why d'you want him?'

'Because it's his birthday! And I haven't spoken to him yet. Please, Col, have you seen him anywhere?'

'Nah, sorry.'

I'd turned and hurried on towards the side door before anything else could stop me. Success: it was unlocked. I took off my enormous shoes and tiptoed along the stone corridor to the back stairs. It was a route I could have managed in a blindfold for I knew it as well as my own home, every step familiar and smooth under my feet: up three flights and then right along another corridor to the east wing where Art's bedroom dominated an entire corner, looking out across the sea.

I had no idea of what I would find, creeping along the corridor. All I wanted was to see him, deliver my card and explain that I had a present for him at home. I knew he'd have great piles of expensive presents from guests downstairs: watches, cufflinks and, I later found out from Dad, a Range Rover from Lord and Lady Drummond. I couldn't offer anything like that but I could give him my photo collage.

It was a few feet from his bedroom door that I heard the noise: panting and groaning.

When you see this sort of catastrophe in a film, you want the person who's about to stumble into it to run away. 'Leave, quick, don't open the door, you mad lunatic! You don't want to see that!' But of course they always do carry on, like me that night, drawn closer and closer to Art's room as if it were a magnet.

I stopped in the doorway at what I could see, which wasn't much, but it was enough. His door was ajar and a strip of yellow light from the corridor fell through it, into his darkened room and across the bed.

I noticed his bare bottom first. It seems comedic now that he was presumably in such a hurry that he managed to pull his trousers down but didn't have enough time to take his shirt off. Not very gentlemanly. His bottom was thrusting underneath it.

And although I couldn't see her face, the pink dress was cascading down the side of his mattress and pooling on the carpet, her legs entwined around his shirt.

I opened my mouth but no sound came out; it was like trying to shout in a nightmare. But what could I have said anyway? 'Excuse me, Art, I've got a card which explains the birthday present I've made you, but don't mind me, I'll just pop it on your bedside table. You guys crack on.'

Instead, I'd turned and fled, back down the corridor, back down the stone stairs, outside, and back home along the drive between the lime trees, the noise from the dance floor fading behind me.

I completely forgot about meeting Colin and Luce, although they forgave me as soon as I explained. I completely forgot to find

Jack and tell him I was going. The cramp I felt in my chest made me completely forget everything and everyone else.

Later, I'd wonder whether I made our whole relationship up, whether my years of fantasizing about Art had warped my interpretation and made whatever there was between us seem more momentous than reality. Perhaps he'd simply been bored whenever he came back to Northcliffe and knew that he could always rely on me to be around, to drop others for him.

Because in the end, despite the years we'd spent growing up together and the time snatched in one another's company when Art was home from school or RAF training, all it amounted to was one kiss outside the pub that New Year's Eve.

Perhaps it was just a kiss. He'd been a twenty-year-old boy and I was a teenage girl. Didn't twenty-year-old boys take opportunities where they found them? Didn't teenage girls sweetly interpret this interest in them as evidence that the boy wanted to marry them, only to realize when older that relationships were more complicated than that?

Then I'd think of his letters and emails, and his snow globes, and the days on the beach together when he was home, and the afternoons spent lying under the giant cedar on the hall's lawns, and the hours and hours we spent talking, and the thousand times when his eyes looked at mine and he really saw me, and I'd doubt my sanity. How could I have fabricated a world of such significance to me when it obviously meant so little to him? It seemed the definition of madness.

As I tried to run down the drive in my enormous shoes that night, all I knew was that I never wanted to see him again.

Chapter 17

I WAS STILL STINGING from my row with Art the next day. Angry at him for daring to broach the subject of Gus, stirred up by our shouting, stressed because I also had to handle the increasingly deranged demands of a minor European royal (Prince Rudolf had sent me an email at 2.21 a.m. saying he'd throw in their wedding silver if Countess Wilhelmina conceded the diamond tiara), but there was something else lingering too. I felt rattled, because what if Art was right and I was simply settling for a life that was safe and comfortable?

Mum's advice came back to me as I crossed the green that morning: from time to time in life, one had jump. I was heading for Thanks A Latte to tell her that Jack had finally booked his train ticket.

'Has he?' she said with an enormous smile, as if I'd told her the Dalai Lama would be visiting Northcliffe. 'That is good of him.'

'He's taken long enough,' I snapped. I wasn't sure whether it was the argument, the stress from working on Prince Rudolf's case and Gideon emailing me about it ninety-three times a day, or tiredness since I'd been looking after Dad and sleeping in my narrow childhood bed for nearly three weeks, but I felt like a bear who'd missed breakfast.

Mum tutted. 'Give your brother a break. He's very busy with his job. Hiya, Colin.'

I turned around to find him standing so close I could tell he'd recently eaten onions.

'Colin, didn't see you there, millimetres from my face,' I said, taking a step back.

'Afternoon, all.' He produced a yellow folder from under his arm. 'I've got those posters I mentioned, Kath. Can I put one up in the window? We've got them in the post office next door, and Terence has said I can put one up in the pub too, although the Spar said no because apparently they can't be political.'

'I'll have to check with Luigi.' Mum stuck her head through the door behind the counter and shouted. 'Luigi! Colin's here with those posters he was talking about. Let's have a look then,' she added, turning back to face us.

Colin laid the folder on the till and, in the manner of a magician brandishing a rabbit from a hat, pulled out a red piece of paper with thick black capital letters across it.

'STOP THE DEVELOPERS, SAVE DRUMMOND HALL,' it said. The 'O' in the 'STOP' had a little red line across it, over a picture of a bulldozer. Then, in smaller letters underneath that, 'Come to the protest this Sunday on the village green, 9 a.m. Placards welcome! Organizer: Colin Cruickshank.'

Luigi appeared in his Dolmio get-up – T-shirt, chequered apron – and shrugged. 'It ees fine by me.'

'Grand,' said Colin, patting his pockets and then reaching

inside one to retrieve a packet of Blu Tack. 'I'll stick it up now. You about on Sunday, Nell?'

'To come to your meeting?'

'Protest.'

'I think this has all got a bit silly, Col. And I'm going home on Sunday, back to London.'

'That's a pity. And it's not silly, it's extremely important. Art's trying to wreck the future of this village. I think he'd pay attention if you came, take it more seriously.'

'He's not trying to wreck the village,' I said wearily. I wasn't in the mood to stick up for Art but on this point, at least, I thought Colin was wrong. 'I don't think the developer even wants to pull the hall down.'

'That's what they say now, and before you know it there's a planning application in to demolish the lot and build two hundred new homes. Where will all the birds go?'

'What?'

'The seagulls, the teal and the curlews. And the otters! Do you want all the otters to be murdered, Nell?' From behind his glasses, Colin's eyes bulged.

'No, obviously I don't want the otters to be murdered. But nor does Art. He's just trying to stop the roof of his old family house falling in. He hasn't got much choice.'

Colin tore a piece of Blu Tack from the packet. 'Choice? Course he's got a choice! All I'm saying is that there should be due process and the residents consulted.'

He stuck little circles in each corner and pressed his poster to the window, then stood back and squinted. 'There! Is that straight?'

'I'm off,' I said, turning to the counter. 'See you, Mum. And Luigi,' I added, more quietly.

They waved and I left Colin standing by the window, smiling at his handiwork.

By the time I got home, I had a message from Lucy.

Col says you're off again on Sunday. Goodbye wine in the pub tomorrow? Xxx

'YES PLEASE,' I replied, suddenly desperate for her company, for someone sane and comforting to talk to. 'I'll be there from six with Dad.'

***

Lucy hadn't arrived by the time Dad and I rolled up the following night, so I sat with him, Roy and his sons for a while, listening to their talk of the protest.

'He's got someone coming from the *Echo* to cover it,' said Roy.

I pitied the journalist that was being dispatched to cover Colin's gathering on the village green. It was hardly the Fall of the Berlin Wall. So far, Terence and Roy had said they were going, along with Jamie and Douglas; Dad seemed less keen.

'Art's not a bad lad. He's been left a helluva mess to sort out.'

Roy scowled. 'You say that now, Bruce, and what happens a few months down the line when you're chucked out your house?'

I started to protest. 'I really don't think he's trying to kick anyone out of their hou—'

'I'm making a placard,' Douglas interrupted, lifting his hand in the air to write the invisible words. 'It's going to say… kiss my putt.'

Dad and I frowned at him.

'Because they want to build the golf course, see?'

'Nell's off tomorrow so she won't be here to admire your handiwork,' said Dad, as he raised his pint to his mouth.

'You back to London then?' asked Jamie.

'Mmm, time to get back to the office. Jack's coming up to take over OAP duties.'

'Careful,' Dad growled.

'Been nice having you up here,' went on Roy. 'How's Jack then?'

'Exasperating. You'll see for yourself.'

'Another one of my kids refusing to give their poor old man a grandkid,' said Dad, with a mournful glance my way.

'Dad, we've been over this.'

'I always assumed you'd end up with Art,' Douglas chipped in from across the table. 'Remember that New Year in this place? We must have all been about seventeen or eighteen.'

I frowned, pretending I didn't when I knew exactly which night he was referring to.

'You do know. That was the year you were working behind the bar and got it on with Art outside.'

'What? No we didn't!' Every cell in my body cringed, embarrassed at this being an open topic of discussion, ashamed that they somehow knew what I'd believed was a private memory.

Jamie and Douglas both laughed. 'Yeah you did,' said the latter. 'We saw you through the window!'

'That's when Jack told us you slept with his emails under your pillow!' added Jamie.

'Boys, leave the poor girl alone. Look at the colour of her.'

I smiled gratefully at Roy.

'Lucky you didn't end up with him,' he added. 'You're much too good for him, gallivanting off to America the first chance he got and now selling us all down the river. He's lost his marbles. His father would b—'

'Dad,' cautioned Douglas.

Roy ignored him and thumped his fist on the table, sending several pints of beer slopping over their rims. 'His father would be turning in his grave.'

'All right, Roy, we get the point,' said Dad. 'Let's talk about something else. Who do you fancy for the big one at Doncaster tomorrow?'

Luce arrived a few minutes later so I left them talking about horses and pulled up a stool beside her at the bar.

'Hiya, love, glass or bottle?'

I puffed out my cheeks while weighing it up. 'Bottle, but it's on me.'

'Sure? Cheers. And I was hoping you'd say a bottle.' She sighed. 'I wanted to murder Mike earlier.'

'Where is he?'

'Told him he was babysitting and I was having a night with you.'

I squinted at her. 'You OK?'

'Fine. But the one time I ask him to do Jimbo's tea and he acts like I'd asked him to strip naked and do a lap of the village. The fuss! And the kitchen's a tip, and Jimbo ended up with sausage in his ear. Honestly, it would have been easier to feed him myself while putting Bonnie down at the same time.'

I caught Terence's eye and asked for a bottle of white.

'Takes me back, you both sitting there,' he said, handing it over in an ice bucket. 'Like old times.'

'Thanks, and I wish,' I said, unscrewing the metal cap.

Luce frowned. 'Do you?'

My hand stopped on the top of the bottle. 'No, not sure why I said that. I mean, some things were easier, right? But I wouldn't want to be a teenager again.'

'Sorry I missed seeing Gus,' she went on. 'Mike said he was up.'

I swallowed a mouthful of wine. 'Mmm, just for the weekend.'

Lucy leant forward and lowered her voice. 'Was there some sort of… moment between him and Art?'

'Moment?'

'Ignore me,' she said, leaning back, 'just being nosy. Mike mentioned some row during the quiz.'

'Oh, right. Yeah, Gus takes competitions very seriously. It was a stupid thing about the coronation.'

'Had Gus met Art before?' she asked, her tone more cautious.

'No, but then I hadn't seen him again until the funeral the other day, had I?'

'Oh yeah, course, since…'

'The party.'

I twirled the stem of my wine glass between my finger and

thumb, not sure whether to go on. Then we both spoke at the same time.

'I saw him yesterday on the bea—' I started to say, at the same time as Lucy apologized. 'Sorry for what?' I asked, frowning.

'No no, you go. You saw him?'

I had another slug of wine. 'I bumped into him on the beach and he started lecturing me about relationships, about Gus and me.'

'What about you guys?'

I stared into my glass.

'We don't have to talk about it if you don't want to.'

'No, it's fine. Basically, he said he didn't think Gus was the one for me and I told him I didn't think he was the expert on all this and…' I sighed. 'And then I ran off.'

Luce nodded slowly.

'I just… What does he want from me?'

She tilted her head while considering this question, then shrugged.

'What can he expect after everything that happened? How can he possibly believe he can dictate my relationship now?'

'I'm sorry, love. I don't kn—'

'It's so irritating! And confusing!'

'Confusing?'

'Well, it just doesn't help. I love Gus and OK, he has his faults. He uses peculiar terms of endearment and he has very strong feelings about which sort of plastic goes in the recycling bin. And his dog allergy is pretty trying, sometimes,' I added, thinking back to the weekend. 'Also, I've never known any man to be so feeble about spiders. But, apart from that, we have a great life! And Art's trying to ruin it all over again.' I paused and made a noise of disgust. 'Why does he even care? Why is it that some men have a radar for this kind of stuff? "Oh look, she seems pretty happy and settled, why don't I dive right in and fuck it up a bit?"'

'Maybe he's not trying to ruin it,' Luce suggested. 'Maybe he's trying to...'

'What?'

'I dunno. Make amends? We all did stuff we'd rather forget back then, love.'

'I don't care! It's too late, it's too...' I exhaled. 'Do you ever think...'

'What?'

'Do you ever think about what your life would look like if you'd stayed with Andrew Lewis?'

Luce threw her head back and gurgled with laughter at the wooden beams. 'No! God, no. He's a ranger up in the Highlands now, Fort William way. Can't imagine anything worse than living up there in the dark. Did you know Fort William is the wettest place in Scotland?'

'Nope.'

Her face fell serious. 'Why do you ask? Because you still wonder what might have been with Art?'

What was the honest answer to this question? Yes, sometimes, because he lurks in my head like a squatter? No, I tried never to open that container because it feels like another life?

'Not really,' I told her. 'He has his life, and I have mine. And it was all fine until he stuck his big nose in.'

'I'm sorry,' Luce said with such solemnity it was as if she'd just heard I'd developed a terminal disease. 'I'm so sorry for how it all panned out between you guys.'

'What? No! Don't be silly.' I swayed sideways on my stool and nudged her shoulder with mine. 'Wasn't your fault.'

'It was such a bad time. For you, I mean. And I always wanted to do more to help when we were away. But I didn't really know how or—'

'Luce, you guys were amazing. Honestly. You were always a much better friend to me than I was to you.' It was an admission I'd thought a thousand times but never told her until now.

Her head spun from side to side. 'That's not true.'

'It is! Anyway, old news. Let's not worry about him. It's just good to see you, to hang out again. It's been one of the best things about being up here these past few weeks.'

'Yeah, true. Come home more often?'

I laughed. 'Maybe. I'm not sure I'll persuade Gus but I'll probably have to keep an eye on that one for a bit.' I gestured over my shoulder at Dad in the corner. 'Although he's already moving on too.'

Her eyes made pantomime circles of surprise. 'What? No!'

'Mmmhmm. You ever come across an occupational therapist called Bev, lives down the other end of the bay?'

Luce shook her head again and I filled her in. Then we talked about Jimbo, Lucy's photography business, whether or not we should pitch up at Colin's protest (I said I'd be packing; Luce said she'd push the buggy past), and the latest series of *Grey's Anatomy*. She ordered another bottle while Dad, Roy and the boys ploughed into their third or maybe fourth pints behind us. It *did* feel like old times.

'When are you and Gus going to have kids?' she asked, slurring slightly, as she dribbled the last of the second bottle into my glass.

From anyone else, the question would have annoyed me. But Luce was well intentioned, my oldest, most honest friend; not nosy or interfering like others. I knew she was asking because she believed children would add joy to my life, instead of interrogating me because she believed that everybody in their thirties should be on the same timeline, competing in a giant race to see who could marry and have babies first.

'At some point. Hopefully. Just need to get this promotion and then, well, we need to find a bigger place but eventually…'

'Babiesaretiny,' Luce slurred again. 'You don't need much space for them. And they'reverylovely.' She paused and hiccuped. 'I did want to kill Mike earlier but I lovehimreally.'

I drained my glass and grinned. 'He's a good one. So you should go home to him and I need to get Dad back.'

She pouted. 'All right. AndIloveyoutoo. Comehomeagainsoon.'

'Deal. Give us a hug.' I leant over and draped my arms over her shoulders, but instead of hugging me back, Luce swayed in front of me, her eyes trying to focus on mine. 'And I meant what I said earlier.'

'Huh?'

''Bout Art. Sorry.'

'Don't be daft,' I said, folding her into me. 'It's fine. Like I said, old news.'

While I rolled Dad home, as he sang a Waterboys track loud

enough for the whole green to join in, I wondered whether I should say goodbye to Art before heading back to London. Even though I was bruised from our run-in, leaving without saying anything felt like a deliberate snub. But if I was going to say goodbye, how would I do it? Send a WhatsApp with a few waving hands? Knock on the door of the hall?

Probably best to leave it, I decided, as I climbed into bed that night with a comfort read: the latest issue of *Brides*. I'd seen it in the Spar that morning. A bride in a strapless gown seemed to be calling out to me from behind her plastic cover, and it came with a free packet of eco confetti. Plus, I was intrigued by one of its coverlines: 'Dare you ELOPE?'

Come on, who wouldn't want to read that?

***

It was an hour or so later that I heard it. I'd just switched off my lamp, and was lying on my back, trying to work out whether Prince Rudolf would concede the Paris apartment to Countess Wilhelmina if he could keep his New York penthouse, when I sat up and frowned at my curtains: there was a strange noise which sounded as if a cow was mooing under my bedroom window.

I tiptoed over, peered out and couldn't help but laugh, my breath making a misty circle on the glass.

In the dark, behind the brambles, was Art with his hands cupped to his mouth, doing his owl impression.

I pointed at the floor to indicate that I'd go downstairs and let him in and then considered what I was wearing: an old gym

T-shirt and a pair of knickers. Whenever this happened as a teen-ager, I'd sprayed myself with vanilla Impulse and slapped a layer of orange foundation on before letting him in. For Art, it must have been like greeting an Oompa-Loompa.

This time, I didn't bother with make-up. I just slipped on a pair of grey leggings and headed for the kitchen door to see what my late-night visitor wanted.

Chapter 18

'ART?' I HISSED INTO the dark. 'Art?'

He stepped into the yellow rectangle of light cast through the open door. 'Evening.'

'You could have texted?'

'Right,' he said, grinning. 'But I also thought, why not pretend to be an owl, for old times' sake? Can I come in?'

I stood aside to let him pass, hoping this wasn't going to be another lecture. 'Want a drink? Cup of tea?'

'I'll have a drink if you will?'

After sinking two bottles with Lucy in the pub, I hardly needed another drink. But the appearance of Art on the doorstep had turned my mouth dry. One more wouldn't hurt.

'Go on then,' I said, reaching into the fridge for two bottles of beer. I opened them, passed him one, then leant back against the kitchen counter.

He slugged from his bottle. 'I'm sorry. I'm sorry for interfering. What I…'

I waited for him to continue while he hovered by the kitchen table, both hands wrapped around his beer.

'Art?'

'What I hate, no, that's too strong…' He sighed with frustration, then raised his head and smiled. 'Talking to you used to be the easiest thing in the world.'

'It's just me. What is it?'

'Can I sit?'

'Course.'

I assumed he meant on a chair but he slid to the floor beside Wilma's bed and leant back against the wall, like we had as kids when playing with the puppies.

I copied him, sliding down the wall to sit at the other end of her bed. 'OK, come on, big Wall Street trader, you've got this. Hit me with it.'

The look he gave me punctured my lungs. It was the saddest version of Art I'd ever seen.

'Hey,' I said, softening at the sight of his face, 'what is it?'

'What it is,' he replied, 'is that I can't bear the idea that you'd be with anyone else.'

'Art, *what*?'

'Sorry. This is monumentally selfish, I get it, but hearing you talk about him, the idea that you're with someone who doesn't want to marry you tomorrow, to pin you down and make you his for ever, I just… don't think he's good enough, Nell.'

The small flame of anger that I'd been carrying around since I saw him on the beach leapt higher. 'Can I get this straight? Even though you're married, you don't want me to be with anybody else?'

'Yes! No!' Art dragged on his bottle. 'It's not that simple.'

'I don't understand,' I said, leaning forward to rest my elbows on my knees. 'I thought you'd come over to apologize, but now you say I shouldn't be with Gus because you don't want me to be with *anyone*? Are you high?'

He ignored this and asked another question: 'Why did you go out with Colin?'

I laughed and clapped my palm over my mouth, mindful of Dad, although I hardly needed to worry. In the charged silences that fell between Art and me, it sounded like we were storing a prize-winning pig in the living room. Luckily, given that he'd sunk several pints earlier, I suspected he'd sleep through any raised voices from the kitchen. 'What? I never went out with Colin. Why would you think that?'

'Because you did.'

'No! Art, are you kidding?'

'What about when you went travelling together?'

I shook my head. 'No! Seriously, no. Luce and I shared a room with him that trip but that was enough. He used to wash his socks and underpants in the sink because he didn't want to pay for any laundry.' I shuddered, remembering the sight of Colin's briefs draped over the balconies of various Asian guesthouses. 'Why would you even think that?'

'Because Lucy told me you did.'

'What? When?'

'Years ago.'

'When? When exactly?' I asked, more forcefully.

'At my twenty-first birthday party. I was trying to find you but bumped into her instead.'

I squinted at him like I was reading from an eye chart. 'Huh?'

'I asked if she'd seen you, and she said no. I can remember her exact words.'

I couldn't compute what he was telling me. It didn't make sense. 'What d'you mean? What did she say?'

'Lucy said she didn't know where you were, but that I should probably know you'd started dating Colin and I should also leave you alone.'

'Oh my god,' I murmured, as the shock made my heart thud harder under my ribcage. I put my hands to my waist and leant forwards, inhaling a big breath as I did. 'Oh my god.'

'I'd been looking for you, but decided, when she told me that, that, well, I should give up.'

I closed my eyes as my brain tried to work out what this meant. It was baffling. Art had been looking for me, and I'd been looking for him, but why would Lucy have told him I was going out with Colin?

'She was lying,' I said, opening them after a few moments. 'We weren't going out. We never did. We went travelling with him but only as mates.'

'Then why did she tell me th—'

'I don't know,' I said, leaning back against the wall. 'I don't know. But... how can you have been looking for me when I saw you in your room that night?'

Forcing myself to utter those words made my voice change. It became quieter and more reluctant, so now it was Art's turn to look confused.

'In my room? Doing what?'

'I was looking for *you*. And then…' I stopped as my throat shrank. I hated talking openly about that night. While still trying to get over Art, in my first year at York, I'd read dozens of self-help books which said you should talk about dramas, talk and talk and talk until they didn't have the power to make you flinch, but I'd decided long ago that the self-help experts were wrong and it was easier to keep the pain hushed up.

I lifted my beer bottle to discover it was empty. 'Another one?'

'Sure.'

I stood and looked in the fridge but we were out. 'Or a glass of wine from Liechtenstein?' I asked, my eyes falling on the boxes beside the fridge. They'd remained untouched until now but this felt like an emergency.

Art shrugged. 'Sure, but stop doing that.'

I frowned over my shoulder. 'What?'

'Evading a subject you don't want to talk about. I know you.'

I uncorked a bottle of red in silence and poured two glasses while working out what to say. I handed one over, then slid back to the floor and sniffed my glass. 'Smells all right.'

'Nell! What about that night?'

I inhaled. 'That night, OK, that night. I went to find you too.'

'When?'

'After dinner. I looked everywhere. I had a card for you which… Actually, never mind the card. I looked everywhere, and, oh my god, yes! I even asked Colin if he'd seen you and he said no.'

I lifted my glass to give me more time, to pace what I needed to tell him. 'I tried the marquee, the dance floor, the Portaloos.

And I asked your parents but they didn't…' I stopped because my eyes had filled with tears and my sight turned blurry. It was pathetic, sitting on my kitchen floor, discussing something that had happened so many years before and yet still capable of being undone by it. 'And then I got inside, not helped by those security guards you had, by the way, and I went along to your room and…'

'Nell, what?'

'It was you,' I said, more quietly still. 'You and Nicole, together, in your room. And I couldn't… I wasn't… I didn't know what to do. So I ran. I just left, and came back here.' One tear fell to my knee and made a small dark circle on my leggings.

Art leant forward, frowning. 'Doing what?'

I tipped my head back against the kitchen wall and exhaled towards the ceiling. 'What do you think?'

'Huh? Nell, that wasn't me.'

I turned to look at him, squinting again.

'I swear.' He shook his head. 'That wasn't me, in my room. I didn't sle— Nothing happened with us that night.'

We sat staring at one another to the backdrop of Dad's snoring next door.

'I don't understand,' I said eventually. 'It had to be you. Who else would it be? And why would they be in your room?'

Art reached for my fingers. 'Nell, I promise you, it wasn't me. I didn't even go inside that night. Not until I had to get Gertrude up to bed, anyway. That was a job and a half.'

I smiled, remembering how tipsy she'd been, then pulled my hand away. I wasn't sure what to believe.

'It wasn't you?' I whispered through a shallow breath, stunned by the idea that I'd been wrong about this for so long. It was as if the furniture in my head was being rearranged.

'No, I don't know who it was. Nicole's never mentioned anything about it.'

'And you were looking for me?'

'Yeah. Though I stopped after I spoke to Lucy. There didn't seem much point, if you were with Colin.' He shrugged his shoulders against the wall. 'I've always thought it was pretty brutal, being cast aside for Colin Cruickshank. But Lucy was so convincing, so insistent that you were with Colin… and I figured I'd been away a lot and maybe I'd been wrong about you, about us.'

'Us? You think there was an us?' I'd spent so long telling myself otherwise, doubting myself, that hearing Art say this felt like confirmation that the Earth was indeed round.

'Course. I know I wasn't here much but I thought of you when I wasn't. I used to try and remember every time we hung out when I went back to school, or flying, and it would make me less homesick. It always made me feel better, knowing that you were here.' His head had dropped towards his lap, but his eyes looked up and he smiled sheepishly. 'Pretty goofy, as Felix would say.'

'Except you still married her?'

He nodded with a sad smile. 'Yes, we got married, but for all the wrong reasons. No, not all the wrong reasons, I shouldn't say that because of Felix, and I'd do anything for him even though…'

He stopped very suddenly and his mouth drooped at the corners.

'Even though what?'

'Forget it. But it was… I tried to speak to you, you know? I must have called you a hundred times after the party. More, even. And I came here to try and speak to you but your mum said you'd gone away with Colin and Lucy, so I gave up. And then I went to London that summer and, well, I didn't behave very well, I was drinking too much. I missed you, Nell, and I didn't understand what had happened but you'd gone away. So I started seeing Nicole since she was still in town and I knew our parents wanted us to be together.' He stopped and blew out his cheeks. 'And then she found out she was pregnant so, yeah, we got married. I'm not sure we meant to marry one another. It was more… an accident.'

'An *accident*? Because she was pregnant?'

'No, I don't mean it like that. I mean we married accidentally, like neither of us really meant to. It's like it was… almost out of politeness.'

'Politeness! Art, you can't marry someone to be polite.'

'I know that. But it felt the right thing then. I think if more people could be honest, they'd admit the same.'

'So you moved to New York.'

'So we moved to New York,' he repeated, 'because Nicole said she'd never live here and back then I didn't want to be here either so…'

'Oh God,' I said, sighing, 'this is so weird. Sorry to go over this, but I was looking for you, and you were looking for me, and then… that was it? We got this whole thing wrong? All this time?'

'Looks like it.'

I snorted first, and then Art's eyes widened at my snort before he laughed too, and we sat there, shoulders shaking with silent laughter.

Then Dad let out an even louder snore, as if he was trying to join in, which made Art fall to his side on the lino and shake even harder, before Wilma leapt out of her bed and started licking his face.

'You going?' I asked, when we finally stopped and he reached for the kitchen counter to pull himself to his feet.

'No, I don't want to go anywhere. I'm just topping us up. It's not bad, this wine. Glass?'

I raised it and had an idea. 'Hey, actually, I'm just going to get something.'

As quietly as I could, I ran upstairs and reached under my bed to pull out the photo collage. I could feel my heart beating hard underneath my T-shirt. Not from the stairs or the laughing, but the adrenalin of our revelations.

With my fingers hooked over the edge, I slid the frame out, wiped the dust from the corners with my T-shirt, and carried it back to the kitchen.

'Here, look, this is what I never gave you that night.'

'You made this?'

I nodded.

Art held it in front of him. 'Look at us. My birthday! I remember that one. And that's Luna as a puppy, right?'

I leant over him. 'Yep.'

'And the fishponds. Jeez, I used to love doing that.'

'Me too. Do you remember, that was the year Michelangelo died?'

'Yeah! And Howard buried him?'

'The next day.'

'How old were we?'

'I was ten, you were about to be thirteen and go away to school. That was when my crush kicked off.' Embarrassed by the admission, I slid back down the wall and crossed my legs again as Art lowered the frame.

'I think mine dated from when I heard you telling Gertrude all about our wedding.'

We smiled at one another until Art glanced towards his boots and sighed. 'I'm old, Nell.'

'You're thirty-five! Thirty-five isn't old. Come on, self-pity's a bad look on you.'

'I know. But do you ever wish you were back there again?'

I twisted my mouth into a knot. 'No. You can't go back, so what's the point?'

'You never look at old photos, like these' – he waved a hand over the collage – 'and think you were happier then?'

'You're not happy?'

Art stared at a patch of floor in front of him. 'I don't know. I don't know if it's Dad, or the house, or being back here. I just feel like there's not much to look forward to. I don't mean to sound self-pitying when… Jeez, I know how lucky I am, but it's as if I've made all my decisions, you know? I married Nicole, and we live in New York, and Felix is at school there and I'll work in a bank until I retire. And that's it, that's my life. Or maybe this is a weird, Liechtenstein truth drug,' he said, raising his glass.

'If you're unhappy you can change it, Art. I say this to clients all the time.'

'Maybe.' He flicked his eyes to mine. 'But this is what I came here to say originally, before everything else tonight. If Gus is the right person then do it, spend the rest of your life with him. But if he's not then just be careful. Don't… get trapped.'

It was like the mention of his name pulled me out of a spell. I'd been sitting on the kitchen floor in my pyjamas, drinking wine and going over old memories with Art, but if Gus knew that, he'd have every reason to feel threatened.

'I should go to bed,' I said suddenly, draining my glass. 'I'm heading back to London tomorrow.'

Art looked startled. 'For good?'

'Yep, Jack's coming up to take over.' I stood and stretched, wanting to get the next part over and done with.

'Oh, OK,' Art replied, before pulling himself up. 'But I'm sorry, for everything.'

'That's all right,' I said, with a small, tight smile. 'I'm not really sure who should be apologizing for what now. It was so long ago, let's just… forget it, I guess?'

He reached out his arms and wrapped me in a hug. 'Deal. And good to see you, Nell.'

'You too,' I mumbled into his shoulder.

He pulled back to look at me. 'Does work ever bring you to New York?'

'Not really. You come to London?'

'Occasionally, once or twice a year. I'll give you a ring. Bring you a new snow globe.'

'Sure,' I replied, smiling up at him, desperately wanting him to go and also not wanting him to go. This situation was too intense to be braless.

We were standing, our faces only inches from one another's,

and for a brief second I thought he'd pull me towards him and lower his mouth to mine. I wanted him to do it, too. It was like we had skipped back in time and I was seventeen all over again, standing in front of Art, outside the pub that New Year's Eve, believing that his next move would dictate the rest of my life.

'Safe trip back,' he said, breaking the silence, stepping backwards, not forwards, as he reached for the kitchen door.

'Thanks, and you too,' I replied, trying to keep my voice steady and not betray any emotion. I didn't dare look down, either, since I was fairly certain I had erect nipples.

★★★

After sitting up in the kitchen until past midnight, I woke late the following morning. Nearly nine! I needed to pack but I needed to speak to Luce and Colin more, the traitors.

As Wilma and I approached the green, I heard Colin before I saw him.

'STOP THE BULLDOZERS, SAVE DRUMMOND HALL,' he shouted through his megaphone.

He was standing in the middle of the green surrounded by a very small gaggle of protestors. Seven, in total, although I presumed one of these was the journalist from the *Northumberland Echo* because she was scribbling in a notepad. Another one of them was Colin's dad. I waved at Roy, Jamie and Douglas, standing proudly with his poster. No sign of Lucy. The two others – one, a middle-aged lady wearing an RSPB baseball hat; the other, a wiry seventy-something with a Yorkshire terrier on a lead

– didn't look very menacing. I wasn't sure that this gathering quite warranted a megaphone.

Presumably the weather hadn't helped: it was a grey day with mist hanging in the air, cloaking us all. In his other hand, Colin held a placard which read 'STOP THE SALE' but the damp had turned the letters wobbly.

'Colin, can I have a word?'

He lowered his megaphone. 'Morning, Nell, and ye— What's the matter?'

'It's about the night of Art's party.'

'What party?' He lifted the megaphone again. 'STOP THE BULLDOZERS, SAVE DRUMMOND HALL.'

'Colin, can you stop that for a second? His twenty-first birthday party. You know exactly what I'm talking about.'

Colin glanced nervously at the others, then leant towards me. 'Can we talk about it later?'

'No, we can talk about it now. Colin! Col—'

He carried on shouting. 'SAVE THE BULLDOZERS, STOP DRUMMOND HALL.' He paused and looked confused. 'I MEAN STOP THE BULLDOZERS, SAVE DRUMMOND HALL.'

'Excuse me, are you from the paper?' I said, turning to the woman with a notepad. She looked young and immensely bored by this gathering. I can't imagine that writing about six people gathered on a damp village green was why she dreamt of becoming a journalist. I'd been to rowdier smear tests.

'Yeah,' she replied, disinterestedly. 'Are you connected with it?'

'A bit. Can I provide the other side of this stor—'

'Stop that right now,' shrieked Colin, putting his arms between me and the journalist as if trying to break up a fight. 'Nell, we can talk over here.' He ushered me towards a tree on the edge of the green just as I saw Lucy pushing a buggy towards us, with Jimbo trudging along behind her, waving a stick.

'Morning, guys,' she shouted. 'How's it going? Sorry we're late, Col. Hasn't been a great start today. We woke up to find Jimbo had an accident in the night and absolutely plastered his bed with sh—'

'I don't want to know,' I said sharply. I'd lain awake most of the night myself, going over and over the sequence of events like Agatha Christie working out a murder. Was Art telling the truth? Why would Lucy lie? And if Art was telling the truth then who had I seen upstairs in his room?

Lucy carried on, oblivious to my tone. 'All right, but just you wait until you have kids because I'm telling you there's nothing worse tha—'

I turned to face her, my hands on my hips. 'What I do want to know is why you told Art, all those years ago, that Colin and I were going out?'

Wilma, who didn't care much for any of this drama, yawned and flopped down at my feet.

'Oh,' said Luce. She bit her bottom lip and looked as if *she* was the one who'd had an accident in her bed.

'Why did you do it? Why tell him that I was going out with Colin? Colin of all people!'

'None taken,' mumbled Colin.

Lucy looked from him to me and took a breath. 'I'm sorry, Nell, but you were *obsessed*.'

'It's true, you were obsessed,' Colin chipped in.

'It was all you could talk about,' went on Lucy. 'Art this and Art that. And we were about to go travelling, all three of us, on the biggest adventure to see the rest of the world, and I just couldn't handle listening to you talk on and on and on about him.'

She turned round at a squawk from Jimbo, who'd splashed in a puddle and was surprised to discover water in his boot. 'Come on, you, out you come.' She stretched her hand towards him and then looked back to me. 'I'm sorry, Nell, but I thought I was doing the right thing.'

'How? How was lying possibly the right thing? You saw what state I was in after that fucking party.'

Jimbo stopped grumbling about his boot and pointed his stick at me with a gurgle of pleasure. 'Fuck!'

'Sorry.'

Lucy sighed. 'It's fine, he hears worse at home. And I shouldn't have done it but at the time I didn't think Art wasn't good enough, Nell. He was never here! And when he was here, you'd ignore us and go after him. It just didn't seem like it was what a relationship should be. And you were so desperate to sleep with him that evening I was… trying to protect you.'

'Protect me?' I replied, more shrilly. From the middle of the green, I saw the journalist squint at us with interest.

'Yes. I thought if I told him that, and he left you alone, then you'd stop running after him and, OK, there might be a few tears, but then we could go away and, I dunno, you'd fall for an Australian backpacker and get over it. I'm so sorry, Nell, it seems stupid now. Beyond stupid, and I've felt bad for years. But I was trying to help.'

'Hang on. Is this why you were apologizing last night in the pub?' I asked, as pieces of this confusing chain of events started lining up in my head.

'Sort of. I've felt guilty ever since, Nell. It was like you were in mourning that whole trip.'

'I'm sorry too,' added Colin.

'*What?* You were in on it as well?'

'It was Luce's idea,' he replied, waving his megaphone towards her.

'Oh thanks, Col, throw me under the bus. Yes, it was my idea, but we both thought it was the solution, didn't we?' She glared at him before carrying on. 'And anyway, you were the one who saw him come downstairs.'

'Saw who come downstairs?' I demanded.

'Go on,' Lucy said, nodding at Colin, 'tell her.'

Colin's face rippled like he had a bad case of constipation. 'I thought it was Art coming downstairs with her. And it was only later, when we realized what you thought you'd seen, that we decided, that Lucy decid—'

'Col! That's not fair, we both decided.'

'Fuck!' Jimbo tried again.

We all ignored him.

Colin stared determinedly at the patchy grass before looking up. 'All right, we both decided, but like Lucy said, only because we thought it was for the best.'

'What? Col, can you get on with it before we all die of old age?'

'The thing is,' he went on, now looking so pained it was as if his bowels were about to explode, 'they were wearing the same outfit, those penguin suits. So they looked like the same person. But I didn't get it until you told Lucy what had happened, and she told me, and we thought...'

'What? WHAT did you guys think?'

'We thought it was better not to tell you, to let you think it was Art with Nicole coming downstairs.'

'When it was who? Guys, come on,' I said, my head swivelling between the two of them. 'Who?'

Col grimaced. 'It was Jack, Nell. It was your brother.'

★★★

Fuelled by a dizzying combination of adrenalin and shock, I ran from them, pulling Wilma behind me, heading for the drive to the hall. I needed to see Art, to say that I believed him; that this whole, sorry episode was a mistake which should have been resolved long before now.

Jack! I might have known. After the night of the party, he'd come back when it was daylight, his tie loose around his neck, stinking of whisky. Mum and Dad had laughed, and Mum made him breakfast before sending him upstairs for a bath and bed. I'd spent that whole day weeping in different rooms of the house: my bedroom, the kitchen, the sitting room, until Mum dosed me with Rescue Remedy that evening and told me to go to bed, that it would 'all seem better in the morning'. Colin, Luce and I flew to Bangkok two days later, and I was still crying because it hadn't been better in the morning, or for many mornings after that. Jack and I barely ever discussed the party.

'Come on, Wilma,' I said, as we jogged up the drive, along the avenue of lime trees and around the corner where the hall came into view. I wasn't wearing the right trainers for running, or a sports bra, so my chest was bouncing around like oranges in a shopping bag, and I had jeans on which had definitely tightened since I'd arrived in Northumberland three weeks ago (all those ready meals), and strands of my hair kept blowing into my mouth. If Art looked out of one of his many windows, he might think it was a mad woman steaming up his drive. Luckily, they remained shuttered.

I reached the side door, panting, and pushed it open.

'Art? Art?'

I shouted between breaths as I walked down the corridor towards the kitchen.

Its door swung open and Art frowned. 'What the he— Nell, you all right?'

Seeing him, I stopped and reached an arm out to lean on the wall, panting. I could feel a thin sheen of sweat on my upper lip. 'Yes, fine, just lost a bit of fitness in the past few weeks.'

'Glass of water? Look, come and sit down.' He stood back from the door to let me in, then reached into a cupboard. 'Is something on fire? What's the drama?'

'Thanks.' I took the glass from him and leant back on the sink.

'Shit, the protest! What's happened?'

I smiled at the idea that the bedraggled gathering on the green might be any sort of threat. 'Uh-uh, I don't think you have much to worry about. Colin's shouting through a megaphone at four people, plus his dad, Lucy, and the journalist who looks extremely bored by the whole thing.'

'That's a relief. So why are you sitting here having a cardiac arrest?'

'It was Jack.'

'What?'

'Who was with Nicole that night; Jack who I saw upstairs with her.'

My stomach rolled as I said it. Until now I hadn't considered the fact that it was my brother's bottom I'd seen going back and forth like a builder's drill. And I'd pictured that bottom maybe a thousand times since, as I'd gone over and over that night in my head. Revolting.

'How do you know?'

'Colin told me, he saw them come downstairs that night.' I had another sip of water while Art looked at the floor. 'Sorry,' I added. 'Should I not have told you?'

He glanced up. 'No, no, you definitely should have told me. In the grand scheme of things, given the state of my marriage, it doesn't make much difference anyway. And don't you say sorry. You're the most blameless person in this whole scenario.'

I wrinkled my nose.

'What?'

'I'm not that blameless. Lucy said I was a bad friend, that she only told you I was going out with Colin because…'

I stopped, embarrassed by what I'd been about to say. My chat had been loosened by multiple wines and a beer last night. Tap water didn't have the same effect.

'Because what?'

'Nothing, forget it, doesn't matter now.'

'Nell, what? Tell me.'

'Oh for God's sake, this is all too much drama for before...' I glanced at my phone, 'ten in the morning. Fine, because I'd talked about you so much, because I'd been so obsessed with you.'

He grinned. 'Obsessed, huh?'

'Stop it,' I mumbled. 'I barely slept last night, I've just shouted at my two oldest friends in the village, I've got to pack all my stuff and get the train and I've got a meeting tomorrow with Prince Pervert...'

'Nell, what are you talk—?'

'Never mind.'

'Do you remember what I asked you on the beach?' he asked, after a few moments when the only sound between us was the clock ticking above the oven.

'Which bit?' I replied, giving him a warning glance. 'You said quite a lot that day.'

'Did you ever think of me? In the past few years, I mean. Did you miss me?'

I made a circle with my mouth and exhaled through it like I was in pain. 'Sometimes,' I replied after a few more ticks of the clock, thinking about the invisible connection I'd long imagined.

'Me too.'

I turned to the sink, feeling the heat from my flushed cheeks spread down my throat and across my chest. 'Can I top myself up?'

'Sure.' Art stepped forward to turn the tap on just as I did, and his hand covered mine.

'Sorry.' I pulled back again, nearly dropping my glass in the sink.

'Nell, stop,' he said, his fingers reaching for mine.

'What?'

'Stop everything. Stop talking. Stop worrying. Stop analysing, going over it all. This brain,' he said, lifting his hands and cupping them either side of my face, 'this brain must be exhausted.'

The glass did slide between my fingers then, with a smash that echoed around the kitchen.

'Ignore it,' Art instructed.

He lowered his face and rested his forehead against mine, close enough to feel his breath on my lips and I offered a small prayer of thanks to the Toothpaste Gods that I'd remembered to brush my teeth before leaving the house. Then he dropped one hand from my jaw to the small of my back, pulling me into him so our bodies were clamped at several points – our chests, our torsos, my hips against his.

Still holding me, he dropped his other hand and ran it down my arm, drawing his fingers across the back of my wrist and my hand until they reached my own and became entwined.

Our eyes locked, I arched my back and pressed against him, desperate for the feel of his mouth on mine. The deliberate pace of this, the teasing, was making me feel like I was melting inside.

His lips flicked upwards in amusement and he lifted his forehead from mine to shake it, while tightening his arm around my back so I couldn't wriggle.

'Art...' I whispered. Or maybe it was more a groan. Not sure. By this point, I was already losing control of my speech. I might have sworn my name was Margaret or confessed to membership of the Communist Party without understanding what I was doing.

And then he kissed me, so I stopped thinking altogether, and I kissed him back.

I remembered his mouth, the feel of it against mine. As our tongues touched, I felt the melting heat spread further down my body and I gave into him. This was familiar. Except it was more than familiarity; it felt as if I was reuniting with a lost part of myself.

He released my fingers from his and cupped both hands around my bottom before lifting me to the kitchen counter (vague, small worry here about being too heavy, but I kept that to myself), then he pushed the glass that crunched on the floor to the side with one foot.

I made a small, snuffling laugh into his mouth at the noise.

'Shhhhh, please, Nell. Ignore it.'

I ran my hands through his hair as we carried on kissing, harder, and Art slid his hands under my jersey, his grip spanning my ribcage.

I gasped at the sensation of his fingers pressing my skin. For so long as a teenager, I'd fantasized about his mouth on other parts of me, of his fingers running over me, of our bodies being pressed against one another's, but my imagination had been limited because my sexual knowledge only extended to what I read about in *More!* and *Just Seventeen*.

The actual sensation of Art so close that I could see each

stubble hair across his jaw made me shiver, even though his touch burned. He tugged my jersey over my head, taking my T-shirt with it, and as he tossed them to the side, I glanced through the French doors, and my eyes fell on the fishponds. It had been early April that year too, the year that I'd fallen in love with him as we stood beside them with our nets, exactly twenty-three years earlier.

The memory made me suddenly bashful as I reached for the hem of his T-shirt. I was sober and about to have sex with someone for the first time. I wasn't sure that had ever happened before. And it wasn't just someone, either; it was Art.

'What?' he asked.

'It's you,' I replied, our noses almost touching.

He nodded. 'It's me. You OK?'

'Yes,' I whispered, before pulling his T-shirt off and fluttering my fingers down his chest, noting how different Art's body was under my hands.

It was so disloyal but there was a small part of *me* that felt cheated. This could have happened years ago but it hadn't because others had prevented it.

That didn't make what we were doing acceptable but I was too caught up to stop. I traced my nails up Art's chest, over his shoulders and down his back, which made him sigh and murmur my name into my neck while he unhooked my bra. That, too, was thrown to the side.

Next, he bent his head to my nipples and sucked each one in turn, which made me drop my head and gasp. When he shifted his mouth again, they stung with cold in the kitchen air, making them harder still, so I pressed myself to his chest: my skin against his as we kissed. The sensation made me want to howl with pleasure.

Fumbling for his belt buckle, I undid it, gripped by a sudden desperation to feel him inside me. It was as if, having waited for so long, my body understood what we were doing and needed this to happen now. Immediately.

I unbuttoned his jeans before he took over, pushing them down. Then he wrapped one arm around my back, lifting me so I could peel off my leggings and pants, and pulled me on to him.

Oh fuck. This was everything. My eyes welled up with sadness that we'd missed this, that we'd never done it before. We'd wasted all that time as teenagers, too shy to touch one another.

I lifted my arms over his shoulders so I could hold his head, and my legs wrapped around him as we rocked, his hands on my hips, pulling me on to him again and again.

The heat started to grow from the other end of my body then. It made my feet arch and my heels press into his back, before it rushed up my legs and to my groin and I exploded fast and hard, waves of the melting sensation washing up and down me at the same time as Art's groans became louder into my neck.

He roared for the final time and exhaled into my collarbone, and we remained quiet for a few moments, listening to the other breathe, my hands still holding his head.

Then he looked towards the window: 'Do you think she watched the whole thing?'

'What? Who?' I asked quickly, before turning to see Wilma standing at the French doors, her nose making white smears on the glass, tail wagging.

Chapter 19

THE GUILT CAME FOR me as we started dressing, picking our clothes up from the floor in silence. What had I done? What had we done? I felt like a cliché from a TV drama. Having sex in Art's kitchen, on the counter where Frank used to lay out sponge cake for tea, hadn't been on the agenda when I got up this morning. And witnessed by poor Wilma.

I reached for my phone and winced harder when I saw a message from Gus.

> Morning, lambkin, I've booked La Delizia for dinner. I know it's a Sunday so booked it early. Just thought we should celebrate you coming home properly. Can't wait to have you back X

La Delizia was the tiny Italian restaurant in Chelsea that we went to for our anniversary every October and the odd birthday. It was staffed by men who could have been Luigi's cousins and served bowls of fresh Italian pastas that kept on coming. You didn't order. They just gave you whatever they'd made that day until you had to undo your trousers and roll home sideways. The wine list came in its own folder and it would have been cheaper to fly to Rome and eat pasta there for a weekend. But it was also very special – and romantic – so now I'd have to eat bowls of ravioli that tasted like they were stuffed with guilt and shame instead of pecorino and truffle.

'You OK?' Art asked.

I looked up from my phone and nodded in silence.

What was there to say? We all have dreams that we fantasize about on the way into work or while lying in bed, unable to sleep. Art had been mine for so long, even though I'd tried to bury it, and it had been briefly intoxicating to enact it in real life but nobody could live in a fantasy for ever. It was done; I had to go back to real life in London.

'Sure?'

I nodded again.

'Look, I know this is complicated…' he started.

'It's not complicated, Art. It's actually kind of easy.'

He frowned. 'How come?'

'I've got to go home.'

'Sure, but what time's your train? Do you feel like a walk? We talk about this?'

'Nope, I've got to go. And you've got to go back to New York. So let's just do this now. Quickly. Come here, give me a hug.'

'Nell…'

'No, seriously, this is better. Come here, I've got to go.'

'Why do you do this?' he asked, stepping towards me. 'You ran before and you're doing it again.'

'I'm not running, Art! I'm not seventeen anymore, sadly. No, not sadly because I hated being seventeen and my hair was diabolical. But I have to go home. We both do.'

I opened my arms, reached them around his neck and closed my eyes.

What had we done?

Art squeezed me against his chest. I was torn between wanting to stay there for ever and wanting to hurry from the kitchen like it was a crime scene.

I pulled away. Enough.

'I love you,' he said quietly, as he ran his hands down my arms and caught my fingers.

'Oh Art, pick your timing.'

He laughed. 'Only fifteen years too late.'

It was like I'd been winded. 'Ooof, OK, seriously, got to go.' I couldn't say it back to him. It would be one betrayal too many.

'I've got to go,' I repeated, letting go of his hands and heading for the door. 'Bye,' I added, without looking back.

Outside, I called for Wilma, apparently unaffected by the pornographic display she'd seen through the kitchen windows, and we ran down the drive.

I was still running when I reached the green and noticed the protest had dwindled to Colin, his dad and the woman with the RSPB T-shirt. Even the journalist had gone. I looked at my watch. Not far off eleven o'clock. I presumed Roy and the boys had sloped off to the pub.

'Nearly home,' I panted to Wilma, as we turned into our track, but I stopped at the sight of a car I didn't recognize pulling up in front of the house.

The passenger door opened and a familiar figure climbed out of it.

'Hiya, sis,' said Jack, standing up and stretching. 'Thought I'd come up a day early to stop you moaning at me. You got twenty quid I can borrow? Forgot to get any cash out.'

'You!' I roared, stalking towards him.

Jack frowned. 'What? Chill out. I can ask Dad if you haven't got it.'

'You!' I shouted again.

'What's your problem?' he said, taking a step back.

'What's my problem? WHAT'S MY PROBLEM? You're a selfish, spoiled, lazy, lying WANKER, that's my problem!' I said, jabbing a finger at him. 'No, you can't borrow twenty quid because you already owe me TEN THOUSAND POUNDS. PAY FOR IT YOURSELF. Sorry,' I added, more quietly, for the benefit of the taxi driver who was quickly buckling his seatbelt.

Then I leant down to speak through his open window. 'Actually, is there any chance you could hang on for ten minutes and take me back to the station?'

He nodded. 'Meter's running, mind.'

'Fine, fine, I'll pay for it,' I said, over my shoulder, as I headed into the house to pack.

I had to get back home.

★★★

To be very precise, the train from Morpeth to London takes three hours and fifty-four minutes and, although I spent five of those minutes visiting the buffet car for a watery coffee and a packet of ginger snaps, I spent the remaining three hours and forty-nine minutes giving myself a stern lecture. I was returning to my home, to London, and my sensible life. I was going back to Gus, and our flat, and my job where I would soon be made a partner. We'd spent eleven years building a life together and I couldn't throw that all away. I wasn't sacrificing all that effort. What would I even be sacrificing it for? A teenage fantasy? OK, the fluttering and fizzy excitement of our relationship might have waned, but in its place was stability.

The past three weeks had proved that Art could still make me feel like I was flying, like I was a teenager who'd just discovered that love is indeed a drug, and there was nobody in the world I'd rather hang out with than him, even now. But if we were together, that would vanish after a few months too. In the end, all relationships come down to asking someone if they could pick up more loo roll on the way home. It was just a matter of who you picked up loo roll for.

Whatever this had been with Art would rock me for a while. But I also knew from my job that people got through these hiccups. True, it was a pretty major hiccup, I thought, remembering the sound and feel of his breath against my neck, and his hands gripping my skin. But it was over and it wouldn't happen again. I bit my lower lip as I panicked that this made me as unscrupulous as Gideon. Did it? No, please no. I couldn't be as bad as that.

Prickly, hot shame came in waves for the entire journey; one moment I felt sick; three seconds later I'd reassure myself that it was nothing, it meant nothing, it was simply an act that should have happened years ago. It was the end of a very long play, or perhaps more like one of Gus's extremely dramatic Italian operas. This morning had been the final act and, now it was all over, everyone could go home.

Seconds later, I'd feel sick again.

I ignored several WhatsApps from Jack.

Nell, you all right?

That was mad.

I was always going to pay you back.

You didn't need to shout like that.

Do you know if there are any more dog biscuits in this house?

I also read and ignored a long message from Luce, apologizing again and reiterating that she believed she'd been doing the kindest thing.

I didn't think he deserved you and I was wrong and I wish I could take it back, I'm so sorry.

I turned my phone face down on the table and bit into a ginger snap.

At King's Cross, I caught a taxi because it was a Sunday

afternoon and I didn't want to faff about on a Northern line full of tourists and families visiting the museums. In my hurry to pack, I'd initially forgotten to text Gus that I was coming back early, and then decided against it. It would be a surprise. On the train, I made a plan to burst through our door, shout that I was home and fall into his arms. This thought made me feel (a tiny bit) better about what I'd done with Art.

As my Uber pulled up outside our flat, I reiterated my decision not to mention anything about the kitchen escapade to Gus. No point. Plenty of couples went through this. Sometimes it even made them stronger.

Oh for God's sake. Nell, you are a human being, not a Hallmark card.

I dragged my suitcase upstairs and opened the door.

'Gus? I'm back!' I shouted, before letting my bag fall on its side to the sitting-room floor.

'Nell?' I heard footsteps overhead and he appeared at the top of the stairs.

I smiled. 'Hi! Surprise! Jack came up earlier, so I decided to come home early. Want me to cook tonight? Or we could get a takeaway and watch a film? One of your films? Or go out? Oh, no, course, you booked La Delizia. That'll be nice. I wonder if they'll have that burrata again?'

Why was I gabbling about Italian cheese? Nerves.

Gus didn't move to come downstairs. Instead, he stood on the landing, scowling.

'You OK?'

Then I saw what he was holding.

'What's this?' he asked, holding up a copy of *Be More Bride* magazine.

Ah.

'Just a magazine,' I replied brightly.

'I can see that, Nell, because I'm blessed with the magical power of sight, but why are there six hundred of them in the spare room?'

'What were you doing in there?' I asked, playing for time.

How could I explain this? Blame it on a recently married friend? Research for a client? Some sort of sexual fetish?

Gus's scowl remained in place. 'I thought I'd tidy that room up, ahead of you getting back, and finally turn it into a proper office, but when I opened that drawer it was so heavy I had to really yank it, and I found them. All of them, Nell.'

I shrugged. 'So? No big deal. I just like reading them.'

'No big deal? It's like a wedding boutique in there, Nell. And keeping it a secret from me? Jesus, what else have you got stashed away? Is there a wedding dress in the wardrobe? A tiara in your sock drawer?'

I snorted. 'Gus, come on, you're being ridiculous.'

'I'm being ridiculous? Nell, I'm not the one sitting in secret reading pieces like...' he paused and opened the magazine he was holding, '"Twenty ways to arrange the perfect cheeseboard for your wedding"!'

'It's actually more complicated than you think because you can't let the soft cheeses sit out for too long and you ha—'

'Nell, I don't care about wedding cheeseboards! And neither do you. Do you know what else I don't care about?' He carried on flicking through the magazine, reading aloud, 'Whether to have a cake made from doughnuts or macarons. Or the best places to rent a tuxedo. Or, oh look, here's a good one, "Thirty-seven pairs of stylish socks for every groom". Why the hell does he need thirty-seven pairs? He's getting married, not walking to the South Pole. And what on earth is a mini-moon?'

'It's a holiday that you take after your wedding but a short one, like a short honeym—'

'I don't care, Nell! I don't want to know about any of this stuff. It's exactly what I hate, the crazy circus of getting married and worrying about what colour the napkins are. It's deranged.'

In protest, he flung the magazine on the carpet. 'I love you, Nell, but, Christ, it's like finding out you've cheated on me. Seriously, why are you reading this crap?'

'Because I want to!' I shouted back, suddenly finding the strength to retaliate. 'Because I like it. Because I want to read about weddings, and dresses, and cheeseboards and, yes, even socks! What's wrong with that, Gus? It's not illegal to read about mini-moons.'

I stopped to inhale, needing a breath for what I'd just realized I had to tell him.

'Because I do want to get married,' I went on. 'I'm sorry, I know you don't. I know we agreed, but I do want that. I want someone to commit to me. I want a man who loves me to stand at the end of an aisle and smile as I walk up it with Dad. Not at the moment, he can't walk anywhere. But I do want that, so *so* much.' I paused for another lungful of air. 'I want someone who wants to pin me down for ever.'

He shook his head. 'Marriage isn't necessarily for ever. You know that, we've talked about this.'

I thought again about what Mum told me in the café that day, that sometimes you just have to jump.

'Nobody knows that at the start, Gus. You have to jump, and… and… and I want someone to jump with me!'

He gazed at me from the top of the stairs for a few moments. 'I don't know if I can jump.'

'No, I…' I wanted to say I didn't want to jump with him but it felt too cruel. 'No, I know that.'

I reached for the back of the sofa because the implication made me feel faint. I hadn't planned to say any of this, but releasing it, letting it out, made me want to scream with relief and cry at the same time; laugh at this admission after years of pretending otherwise; grief at what this meant for me and him.

'How did I not know about this?' he went on. 'Why didn't you tell me?'

'Because we don't talk about anything real anymore, Gus. We talk about restaurants and wine lists and whether we should get a boiling water tap!'

'It's very energy efficient, that tap.'

'I know. But I'm not sure I can spend the rest of my life talking about energy-efficient taps.'

Gus frowned. 'What if I said I could? Do the marriage thing. That I might be able to consider it?'

I smiled sadly up at him. 'I don't think that's the dream, someone saying they'll "consider" marrying you because you've forced them.'

We fell quiet and, even though it was only a few seconds, I could feel us travelling away from one another. The speed of it was dizzying. This hadn't been the plan on the train. This was the opposite of the plan.

'So what do we do?' he asked eventually.

'I'm not sure there's much we can do. I think this means… I think it means… I thin—' I couldn't get the words out because I'd started to cry, which made Gus come downstairs and wrap me in a hug.

What I was trying to say was: I think it means we're over. But he didn't need me to say it because he'd realized the same.

That's the thing about being with someone for eleven years: there's a lot that you should talk about, but some things you don't necessarily have to say to communicate.

My tears ran into his shoulder while he held me and we stood like that for minutes, saying nothing. We loved one another but not quite enough. Art had been right, I realized: I loved Gus but I wasn't *in* love with him.

Even as I stood there leaving snot marks on his shirt, overwhelmed by what this would mean, I could also sense something else inside me: a tiny spike of delight that I'd never have to hear the word 'lambkin' again.

Chapter 20

I SLEPT IN THE spare room that night, although 'slept' is a pretty generous term given that I lay awake between 2 a.m. and 5 a.m. wondering what I was going to do in both the long and short term. It was a bleakness that I remembered after Art's party. I wasn't as heartbroken this time round but I still felt a sense of loss. When the ground underneath you shifts so fast, how do you get through not only tomorrow, but also the rest of your life?

Part of me wanted to drag open the drawer underneath the single bed and reach for comfort reading about veils and wedding favours; part of me was too nervous that Gus would hear the rumbling from our bedroom next door and know what I was doing.

In the short term, I had to get up and run into the office, pretend everything was fine and deal with the meeting between Prince Pervert and Countess Wilhelmina.

In the long term, I had to sort out everything else: not just the flat and the furniture but what life would look like without Gus. The fear of this made me want to sneak next door and get under the duvet, drape my arm across his chest and pretend it was all fine again, like it had been before my time in Northcliffe.

And yet I knew I had to hold out, that this was the right call. I'd told myself on the train that I could spend for ever living in calm stability, choosing comfort and security over anything more exciting. But it wasn't true. Ironically, my weeks at home, which I'd once thought of as so parochial and boring, had revealed that I wanted more.

As soon as light appeared behind the curtain rail, I gave up trying to sleep and decided to head into the office early. It was my first run through London for three weeks, just me and the rubbish collectors on the streets.

I showered and settled at my desk with a cafetière of Carmelita's coffee. There. This was more like it. I started sifting through my emails. Lord Bedhopper's paternity test had come back as positive ('I've got to pay for another little blighter!' he'd written in an email to Gideon and me), and he wanted us to draft a financial offer for the mother. Mr Jalal's daughter wanted a pet-nup clause inserted into her prenup, stipulating that she got their Burmese cat, Clive, in the event of any separation. It was normality, of a kind, and a distraction from my own private life. But dealing with these demands suddenly felt depressing, as if I was merely adding to the misery of each situation, instead of resolving them.

Gideon arrived a couple of hours later when I was reading Prince Rudolf's offer for a final time.

'Good God, who are you?' he asked, pretending to shy when he saw me behind my desk. 'Help, police, there's a stranger in my office!'

'Morning,' I said, ignoring this feeble attempt at a joke. 'I'm just going over the agenda for the meeting.'

'Did you have good weather on your little holiday?' he continued. 'And how were the hotel breakfasts? I do hope the pool temperature was to madam's liking?'

'The weather was mostly terrible because it's Northumberland but thank you so much for asking,' I replied, resisting the temptation to add 'YOU ABSOLUTE BELL.' I'd spent dozens, no, hundreds of hours behind my laptop while I was away, so many hours sitting cross-legged in my bedroom that my lower back felt as wonky as Nanny Gertrude's. But I refused to let Gideon rile me this early in the day and returned to the subject of the meeting. 'I've been looking at Prince Rudolf's statement again and I thin—'

Gideon grunted and threw his briefcase on his desk. 'Knowing Veronica, she'll go in hard on the adultery, so let me handle everything.'

'I think if we can get Countess Wilhelmina to agree to the weekends then he'll be more pliable when it comes to the hou—'

Gideon held up a hand like a lollipop lady. 'Nell! Stop fussing. It's under control and I will do the talking.'

I looked back to my screen, reflecting on the amount of time that I'd spent prepping for this meeting, researching and doing the spade work, answering emails about chalets and sausage dogs, only to be silenced when it came to the day itself because my boss thought women were largely ornamental.

'Such a berk,' I mumbled under my breath.

'I beg your pardon?'

'Just so much work!' I said, snapping my head up and stretching my mouth in a fake smile.

We tapped at our computers in silence until my phone vibrated on my desk ten minutes later and I made a strange, bat-like squeak. It was Art.

> Hope you got home safely. Signing the final paperwork today so flying back tomorrow. I'll let you know when I'm next in London. So good seeing you.

'You all right?' asked Gideon, looking up from his desk.

'Yep, just, er, a message from Gus,' I fibbed.

He narrowed his piggy eyes at me. 'No problems in that department, I trust?'

'No, all fine.'

'And your father's health is restored?'

'His leg. And nearly. My brother's there now, who's mostly useless but even he should manage for the next couple of weeks.'

'Good,' said Gideon, solemnly, 'because after all your time off, I need you to show me that you're serious about this firm, Nell, if you're still interested in a partnership, that is?'

I nodded quickly. 'Yes, absolutely. I'm back and raring to go. Although, just for the record, Gideon, I'd like to clarify that I worked every day while away, and I don't *believe* there was anything I let slide, was there?'

He squinted while weighing this up. 'No, perhaps not,' he admitted, grudgingly. 'Now, could you ring down to Queenie and get her to send my breakfast up pronto. She seems to be getting slower and slower with them these days. I don't know what she's doing, laying the eggs herself?'

★★★

We'd asked Prince Rudolf to come in half an hour before the meeting officially started to go over the details.

'Good morning, Eleanor,' he said, his gaze running up and down my suit as we stood in the boardroom. 'I trust your father is better?'

'Yes, thank you,' I replied crisply.

Be careful, the man is a pervert, Nell. He may be extremely handsome and wearing a navy suit over a blue shirt and tie which makes him look like an advert from a men's fashion magazine. And he has a jawline that could cut marble and smells so delicious that you want to lick his neck. But you must ignore all those things and concentrate on the financial details.

I cleared my throat. 'Anyone for coffee?'

'No thank you, Eleanor, I am good.'

'Cappuccino for me please,' barked Gideon, before offering Prince Rudolf a seat and sitting. 'Now, we need to brace ourselves. Veronica Wallop will breeze in here and be extremely charming but don't be fooled. The woman is a sniper in a skirt. If we let her, she would go after everything you own. But we aren't going to let her. So if we could just go over a few items now, I think that would be beneficial.'

Gideon outlined the statement that I'd prepared, listing what Prince Rudolf had, finally, agreed to offer: chiefly, the London house and the flat in Paris, plus most of the jewellery, monthly maintenance of £30,000 and Alan the dachshund, so long as Countess Wilhelmina would accept shared custody.

'It's a very strong opening position,' said Gideon. 'I need to warn you that things may get personal since Veronica likes going for the jugular, but it won't help anyone if tempers flare. Think of this as a business meeting and leave the negotiations to me.'

Prince Rudolf shrugged. 'I am not worried. She can say what she likes. I just want to move on from all this.'

He looked across to me and smiled. 'And then I may never get married again, like your wise colleague. How is your boyfriend, Eleanor?'

'He's fine,' I squeaked. 'All fine. No problems there.'

Luckily, then, the phone rang; Rosemary announcing that Veronica and Countess Wilhelmina had arrived.

I asked her to send them up and the boardroom door flung open a few minutes later.

I knew Veronica professionally since plenty of our cases involved her representing the other side. She was tall, with a beaky nose, and dressed as if it was still the 1980s: power suits with shoulder pads and pearl earrings, plus Princess Diana hair which surrounded her head like a helmet, and diamond rings the size of quails' eggs. Rumour had it she bought a new ring from Bond Street every time she won a case.

Countess Wilhelmina came in after her. She was shorter and rounder but pretty, with smiling eyes and pink cheeks. As she gazed around the boardroom, I noticed her fiddling with her handbag strap like a child with its rucksack on the first day at school.

'Veronica, how lovely to see you,' said Gideon.

'Spare me the niceties,' snapped Veronica. 'Where shall we sit?'

'Why don't you both sit here?' I gestured to two seats towards the other end of the table, but not the head. Gideon insisted on sitting at the top of the table for these meetings because he thought it gave us the upper hand. It was a tip he'd read in a management book.

'Countess Wilhelmina, good to meet you,' went on Gideon, smoothly. 'I'm Gideon Fotheringham, senior partner here, and this is my colleague, Eleanor Mason.'

'Hello,' she replied, in a fluttery voice.

'Would anyone like a coffee?' I asked.

'Yes, black, no sugar,' said Veronica, 'Wilhelmina?'

The countess looked uncertainly at me. She had the long lashes of a dairy cow. 'Could I maybe have a tea? Would that be possible?'

'Course. What sort of tea?'

The question seemed to flummox her. 'Er, do you have any English breakfast?'

'I'm sure they do.'

She smiled gratefully and I picked up the phone to give the order to Queenie, plus another round of coffee for Gideon and me.

'No time to waste, let's get started,' said Veronica, who'd laid out several folders and a notepad in front of her. 'Your client's offer is completely unacceptable to us as it stands.'

'Oh dear, I am sorry, Veronica,' said Gideon, leaning forward at the table. 'Could you enlighten us as to what is so unacceptable?'

'All of it,' she replied, with a sniff. 'The property offered, the paltry maintenance sums but most of all the custody suggestion. I hardly think that your client can manage shared custody given the lifestyle he chooses to lead, that he has, in fact, chosen to lead throughout their marriage.'

Beside me, Prince Rudolf snorted.

'Rudy, please,' interjected Countess Wilhelmina, 'be fair. You've never even collected the children from school.'

He snorted again. 'Yes I have.'

'Sending Vlad doesn't count,' she replied softly, before looking from Gideon to me. 'Vlad is his driver.'

'Let's not get distracted by details,' ploughed on Veronica. 'My client and I have come up with an alternative custody arrangement of every other weekend and I suggest we discuss that before moving on to anything else. Agreed?'

'That's preposterous,' Gideon replied. 'Every other weekend amounts to 15 per cent of the time. That isn't going to be something we can agree on.'

As usual, my job was to listen and note this all down, but it was while I scribbled Veronica's new custody suggestion, that I felt a hand on my knee.

Prince Rudolf's hand was on my knee.

Not just a casual brushing either, as if he was trying to scratch his ankle and had accidentally caught hold of my leg on the way down. This was a proper grip.

It surprised me so much that I jerked my knee up and thumped the underside of the table.

Gideon frowned at me. 'Are you quite comfortable, Nell?'

'Sorry, just a twitch,' I answered, before crossing my left leg over the other, angling it away from Prince Rudolf.

Prince Pervert indeed. What was he thinking, trying to grope me while we discussed his children? This was a boardroom, not a nightclub. I know the man looked like the handsome lead from a romantic comedy but that didn't give him licence to go around the place stroking women's legs. This wasn't 1953.

His hand returned minutes later as the discussion about custody became increasingly heated between Gideon and Veronica. I tried to shift in my seat, while writing notes, but Prince Rudolf seemed to construe this as encouragement and slid the hand higher up my thigh.

I squeaked when his fingers reached the hem of my skirt.

'Nell,' snapped Gideon, his glare switching from Veronica to me, 'is everything all right? Do you need the bathroom?'

'No! No, sorry, carry on.' Keeping my legs crossed, I swivelled my chair away from him, towards Veronica and Countess Wilhelmina at the other end.

'I really don't believe, given your client's multiple accounts of adultery from the very start of their marriage and his continued behaviour towards my client, that he can expect shared custody,' went on Veronica.

She glanced at her notepad. 'I'm not sure a man who has an affair with the nanny *and* the personal trainer and…' she paused and glanced at her notes again, 'the florist, is the sort of man who can adequately care for his three children.'

Prince Rudolf tutted. 'It was only the one time with the florist.'

Veronica peered at him over her glasses like a headmistress. 'Yes, well, if you're unwilling to accept this then I'm afraid I really don't see that we have much else to discuss today.'

While noting this, I felt a foot wrap itself around my ankle.

Footsie? What was he, fifteen?

To my left, Gideon laughed and leant back in his chair.

'Veronica, honestly, I'd thought you were a more adept negotiator. Since it's a hefty chunk of my client's fortune that your client is after, and not vice versa, I suggest you take the offer of shared custody more seriously.'

Veronica matched him by letting out a little peal of laughter. 'Gideon, Gideon, Gideon, do you really want this to come down to a judge, given your client's record?'

As I felt the toe of Prince Rudolf's shoe slide up my calf, I glanced across the table at Countess Wilhelmina. She retrieved a tissue from her bag as her eyes welled up and I felt another wave of sympathy. She was only twenty-two when she'd married him, presumably seduced by his cowboy swagger, totally unaware that she was marrying a sex pest in disguise.

When his toe reached the underside of my knee, I raised my leg again and tried to stab his other foot with my heel.

Unfortunately, the only thing I impaled was the boardroom carpet.

'Nell!' bellowed Gideon. 'What *is* the matter with you? I'm beginning to think you must have brought fleas back from the north.'

'No fleas,' I said, 'just… too much coffee. Forgive me, Veronica, Countess Wilhelmina.'

The countess blinked away more tears and smiled across the table.

'I'm not going to sit here and listen to threats about court, Veronica,' Gideon said, returning to the discussion. 'If you're not willing to accept joint residency then we might as well call this meeting over now.'

'Fine,' Veronica said coolly, as she gathered up her folders. 'I don't think this is in anybody's best interest but then that's the Spinks way, isn't it? We'll be in touch.'

She stood and swept out, followed by Countess Wilhelmina, clutching a damp ball of tissue in her hand.

Gideon rocked back on his chair legs and gave Prince Rudolf a wide grin. 'I love it when they get angry, don't you?'

I pushed my chair back and stood.

'Excuse me,' I mumbled, before Prince Rudolf could reply.

Desperate to get away from them both, I made for the ladies' loo and growled with exasperation as I threw the door back.

Countess Wilhelmina look up from the sink.

'Oh, sorry.' Since the Spinks office was mostly men, I wasn't used to other women being in here. Apart from the occasional client, it was normally only me. As an exhausted trainee, I'd sometimes escape into a cubicle for a twenty-minute power nap, using a roll of loo paper under my ear as a pillow and curling up on the marble floor. Now it was where I escaped for a break from Gideon whenever I felt like I was about to drive a pen into one of his ears.

She didn't reply, and had very pink eyes, so I pretended I needed a wee by shutting myself in a cubicle. I didn't actually need a wee, I just wanted a few moments of peace. I felt like a layer of my skin had been peeled off.

While I sat there, elbows on my knees, head in my hands, I could still hear Countess Wilhelmina's small sniffs so I tried to wee because otherwise it was awkward. Come on, come on, come on.

But she kept sniffing and it kept putting me off. I managed a tiny trickle before I decided to give up, otherwise this whole scenario became even more embarrassing.

At the sink, I looked at my hands until she spoke.

'How can you do this job?'

I met her eyes in the mirror. 'Sorry?'

'This job. How can you do it?'

I grimaced. 'Some days are better than others.'

'It is all so cold, so clinical. He gets this and she gets that. Why would anyone get married, if they knew this is what it wou—' She dissolved into a sob and lifted a crumpled paper towel to her face.

'Countess Wilhelmina, I'm sorry about that meeting. But it will be sorted, I promise. This is the worst bit.'

'Is it?' she asked, lowering the towel and looking at me hopefully.

I nodded.

Another sniff. 'I'm sorry, I don't mean to be rude. But it would hurt me too much, trying to divide children between their parents.'

'We're just trying to work out what's best.'

'For who, my children or him?'

'For everyone,' I said, with another sympathetic smile.

She nodded and slid her bag onto her shoulder. 'I hope so.' Then she left, and I leant on the edge of the basin and sighed.

I stayed like that for a few minutes. I could handle Prince Rudolf, I told myself. True, I'd never been groped by a client before, but I couldn't mention it to Gideon, not after being away from the office for so long. He'd see it as a sign of weakness.

No, I wouldn't say anything. I'd go back to my desk and have another coffee, and perhaps a piece of Queenie's shortbread. That would sort me out. Nothing was going as planned today, but then the first day back after time away, settling into the routine again, was often tricky.

'Ah, Nell, there you are,' said Gideon when I walked into our office. 'What on earth was wrong with you in that meeting?'

'Nothing, I'm fine. Shall I draft a court application then?'

'Yes, I think that's probably a good idea. Let's call Veronica's bluff. Good God, imagine being married to a woman like that! Oh and, on his way out, Prince Rudolf mentioned a friend of his who's leaving her husband and needs our help. She's worth a small fortune and so is he, apparently.' He paused to rub his hands together over his desk. 'Money, money, money. I do like these sorts of clients. So look out for that email please.'

'Sure,' I said, sitting heavily in my chair. If I became a Spinks partner, it would become my responsibility to bring in new business like this, to encourage unhappily married rich people to come to us instead of a rival firm. It was the part I dreaded most, hustling potential clients over expensive lunches, trying to convert their misery into billable hours for us. Unsurprisingly, Gideon revelled in it.

I called downstairs and asked Carmelita if she'd mind bringing up a coffee and a piece of shortbread, then got to work on the application. This was an immensely long form asking multiple questions about the family situation and children which a judge would evaluate.

As I compiled notes, going back through all the information

we'd gathered on his family, I tried to think of what was best for little Ludwig, Karl and Theodora, and not their father. I tried to forget the image of a weeping Countess Wilhelmina. Her phone case, I'd noticed in the bathroom, was a smiling photo of the three children.

I bent my head to my desk, telling myself that I could only present the facts for a judge to decide upon.

It was a relief to have something to get lost in, which was why I didn't notice the email that dropped into my inbox until later that afternoon.

When I saw her name, it didn't immediately register. Nicole Cargill. Sounded familiar, but it was out of context, like seeing a polar bear on the beach. It was only when I opened the email and started reading that it dawned on me: it was Nicole, Art's Nicole. She was the one who'd been put in touch with us via Prince Rudolf, she explained at the start of the email.

'He's an old college friend who suggested I contact you regarding my marital situation,' she wrote. 'My husband and I currently reside in New York but my husband is a British citizen and I gather that the divorce courts in London are more sympathetic when it comes to certain judgments. There's also a question of paternity that I need to discuss, so I'd appreciate it if we could find time to discuss this in the next two days.'

I was still goggling at my screen when Gideon returned from lunch with one of the other partners.

The move made sense on one level, and it was clever of her. In America, inheritances were excluded from divorce settlements because they weren't deemed marital property. But the opposite was true in the UK, where all assets were considered jointly owned. So even though Nicole's family was already worth millions, it looked like she was going after her share of the sale of Drummond Hall.

But what did she mean by 'a question of paternity'?

'That referral from Prince Rudolf has come through,' I told Gideon.

'Has it? Let's have a look.' He flicked the vents of his jacket out behind him and collapsed into his chair.

'The one from Nicole Cargill,' I said robotically.

'Nicole Cargill, Nicole Cargill, Nic— Gotcha, here it is.' He muttered under his breath as he read.

'Sounds good to me,' Gideon went on. 'Hang on, Cargill, isn't that the American banking family?'

'Yes,' I said quietly, while he tapped at his keyboard.

'Christ almighty. They're worth over two hundred million! Who's the husband?'

'He's called Arthur, Arthur Drummond.'

Gideon carried on tapping and then squinted at his computer screen. 'I see, yes, Lord Drummond. I wonder why she wants to use the British courts.'

'Because he's selling the family estate. I believe, anyway,' I added quickly.

'Well this is excellent news, looks like we might have another big case on our hands. Thank you very much, Prince Rudolf. Can you go back to her immediately and arrange a time for a conference call tomorrow? And have you seen that email from him regarding shared residency?'

'What? No.' I'd been too dazed by Nicole's email to concentrate on anything else.

Gideon tutted from behind his computer. 'Dear God, Nell, it's as if you're still in holiday mode, dreaming about pina coladas. Please do *try* and get up to speed.'

I clicked back to Outlook and saw two emails from Prince Pervert at the top of my inbox. One to both Gideon and me reiterating that he wouldn't negotiate on custody; another only to me. As I opened the second email, I wondered – briefly – if it would be to apologize for his behaviour in the meeting. But of course it wasn't. Instead, it asked what night I was free that week for dinner.

'Yes, will do, I just need to, er, go to the bathroom,' I said, pushing my chair back and heading for the safety of the ladies' bathrooms for the second time that day.

I'd never cried in this office. I didn't want Gideon to see me weakened by the strain of the workload (or by clients with hands like Mr Tickle), but today had nearly finished me.

I locked myself in a cubicle, put the seat down, sat and leant against the marble tiles. I felt wrung out, a husk, sick of other people's demands. But there was one person that I needed to ring.

I brought Art's number up on my phone screen and stared at it for a few seconds. Alerting him would be a firing offence but, suddenly, I didn't care.

I'd had enough of rich clients and their spoiled demands.

I'd had enough of billionaires screaming about their chandeliers and earls who couldn't keep their pecker in their pants demanding paternity tests in order to protect their trust funds.

I was sick of drawing up prenups for people who believed their wealth was more important than their child's happiness.

I certainly didn't want to sit opposite a weeping mother again, trying to restrict access to her children while her husband tried to touch me up with his shoe.

And I'd finally, finally tired of sharing an office with a pig in a suit.

I'd had enough of it all.

I hit 'call' on my phone.

'Nell?'

'Art, it's me.'

'Nell? Where are you? It's not a very good line.'

'Art? Art? Fuck.' The women's bathrooms were a windowless box at the end of the corridor, and the phone reception in here was abysmal. I pressed myself up against the door and shouted. 'Art? Can you hear me? I'm in the loo.'

His reply was muffled. 'Good to know. Why are you calling me from in there?'

'Long story. Listen.'

'Can you speak up?'

'OK, CAN YOU HEAR ME?' I was now close to screaming at my phone.

'Yeah, you all right?'

'YES, FINE, LISTEN – I JUST GOT AN EMAIL.'

'OK.'

'FROM NICOLE.'

'Huh? As in my Nicole?'

'NO, NICOLE SCHERZINGER. YES, YOUR NICOLE.'

'What about?'

'ABOUT DIVORCING YOU.'

'What?'

'I'M SORRY, I WANTED TO WARN YOU. SHE'S TRYING TO DIVORCE YOU HERE, IN THE UK.'

'What? Why? Nell, what's going on?'

'IF SHE DIVORCES YOU HERE, SHE CAN TAKE HALF YOUR ESTATE.'

'My cake?'

'YOUR ESTATE!' My throat was starting to hurt. 'AND ALSO SHE MENTIONED SOMETHING ABOUT PATERNITY. ART? ART?'

Art didn't immediately reply.

'ART?'

'Yeah, I'm here. I just… Nell, I'm sorry, I've got to go. Forgive me. I'll call you back.'

He hung up just as there was a rap on the bathroom door.

I lowered my phone and looked in the mirror. My cheeks were flushed and my hairline had frizzed around my forehead where I'd pushed my fingers into it. 'Hang on, just coming.'

I re-tied my hair and opened the door, my face braced to smile politely at whoever it was.

It was Gideon, standing with his hands on his hips and an expression of such fury it was like I'd just snatched his last bit of bacon.

'Nell, would you like to explain why you're standing in the lavatory hollering like a football hooligan?'

'Er, well, the thing is th—'

'I could hear you from our office; I imagine the whole of Spinks could hear you. It's extremely concerning, this erratic behaviour, Nell. I'm sorry to say it's making me seriously consider whether you're ready to step up to partnership level.'

'Gideon, can I ju—'

'Now, can you please head back to your desk and continue with the court application? I want to go over it before the end of the day.'

'No.'

'I beg your pardon?' Gideon's eyes were straining so hard I thought he might burst a blood vessel.

'I said no, I won't. I won't go back to my desk and I won't finish the court application.'

'And might I ask why not?' His nostrils were flaring now too.

'Yes you may: because I quit. Do the court application yourself. I'm leaving.'

'Nell, have you gone mad? Did you have a drink at lunch? I would ask you to consider very seriously what you're saying.'

'I haven't gone mad. And I'm not the one who drinks like a dehydrated camel at lunch, Gideon. It's quite simple, I've had enough. I've had enough of our clients, and this firm, and I've had enough of you, actually. Now if you'll stand aside, I'll be off. Actually, no, hang on, one more thing.'

I lifted my phone and started writing an email.

'I'm afraid I'm not free this week or any week until the end of time,' I typed to Prince Rudolf, 'because I'd rather be felt up by Captain Hook.'

Click, send.

'There we go,' I said, looking up at Gideon, who'd remained in the corridor, his face and neck turning steadily more crimson as he bellowed a pathetic threat about this being my final warning. '*Now* I'm off.'

Chapter 21

I LOADED THE CONTENTS of my desk into three plastic bags (why, when someone leaves their job on TV, is it always boxes? Where do the boxes come from?), and caught the Tube home.

The flat was quiet and still. I felt like a skiver, unused to being here on a weekday afternoon.

'Staying with Hector and Harriet,' said a neat, handwritten note beside the cooker. 'Remember to put the plastics out on Thursday morning.'

Upstairs, Gus had taken his trouser press from our bedroom which at least made me laugh, breaking the silence. The idea of him wrestling his precious gadget downstairs and into an Uber before heading off to Hector and Harriet's house in Fulham was simultaneously tragic *and* darkly comic.

I stripped and dropped my suit and shirt on the bedroom floor, before pulling on leggings and an old hoody from the bag I still hadn't unpacked since coming home from Northcliffe. No time like the present, I told myself, as I squatted in front of it and threw the dirty laundry into a pile of darks and whites, then I put the first wash on, decided to strip the bed (too sad to sleep in sheets that smelled of Gus), hoovered, cleaned the bathroom, mopped the bathroom floor, wiped the bathroom mirror down, scrubbed the kitchen sink, hung up the first wash, put on the second wash, remade the bed and finally flopped on the sofa, oddly satisfied by the smell of bleach and fresh laundry that hung in the air.

It was strange, though, being back in the flat, as if I was home-sick even though I was in my home. I glanced at my watch. Right now, I would have been taking Dad to the pub and hearing about Roy's cows before wheeling him home again, debating what we'd have for dinner and settling on a film. I missed it. I found myself almost wishing it was this time three weeks ago, when I was packing to head up there. Not that I wished Dad to be back in hospital. But I'd go through it all again if I could. I'd sleep in my cold bedroom and shower in the Arctic bathroom; I'd rediscover the news about Mum and Luigi; I'd make ninety billion cups of tea and take Wilma on walks to the beach; I'd help Dad with his flirtation tactics; I'd sit through the pub quiz again and I'd relive every moment spent with Art.

Since he'd hung up that afternoon, I'd been phone watching. He said he'd call back, and I'd assumed that meant soon. Like, an hour. Maybe two hours. Three hours, max. I'd just delivered major news. He'd call back tonight at some point. He had to. Although I didn't know exactly what I wanted him to say. 'Thanks so much for alerting me to the end of my marriage and destruction of my life as I know it, Nell. How's being back in London?'

As time had ticked on that afternoon, I couldn't shift the lurking fear that I'd angered him. Nicole wanting a divorce was one shock but a question of paternity? That was an entirely different level of devastation. I'd dealt with a few such cases at Spinks, normally when there was a row over a will, and no matter how rich the client, how padded by wealth, the discovery that a child a man had assumed was his actually wasn't, cut so deep, at such a primordial level, that it had reduced clients to ghosts in our office. A Danish study had been published a few years earlier suggesting that up to 10 per cent of the developed world's population had assumed the wrong father. Did this apply to Felix? What had Nicole done? Did Art have any idea?

These thoughts continually circled my brain that afternoon. What if I'd been poking into his business and he was furious with me for interfering? What if he'd called Nicole and she'd cried and apologized and said it was a terrible misunderstanding and I should never have called him in the first place and…

Nell, you're being hysterical. You didn't eat lunch and your blood sugar level is dangerously low.

Fuck it, by 7 p.m. I decided I'd have a wine even though it was a Monday. No need for that rule, any more.

I crouched before Gus's wine rack and pulled out a bottle of something that didn't look too expensive. Didn't need to be expensive, just needed to get me drunk.

Then I reached for the corkscr— Oh for God's sake. Gus had taken his special corkscrew as well as the trouser press.

I opened the cutlery drawer, unable to remember if we had another. Come on, please. What kind of metropolitan wankers had a special, £250 aerating corkscrew but not a simple, metal curly-wurly? I rifled through the knives and forks like an intruder was coming up behind me and I needed a weapon to defend myself.

No corkscrew.

Fine. I slid the bottle back into its place in the rack and hunted for one with a screw top. Nope, nope, nope, nope. Not a single bottle had a screw top.

This was a sick joke. I'd have to go to Sainsbury's.

Once there, around me, commuters in bicycling Lycra and suits hurried along the aisles with slick efficiency, grabbing bags of salad and sweet potatoes.

I didn't want salad or a sweet potato. Instead, I picked up two packets of Quavers, a salami pizza, a can of Ambrosia rice pudding, a bag of Haribo Tangfastics and three bottles of screw-top Sauvignon Blanc, chosen for no other reason than the label had a penguin on it. My basket was a nutrition-free zone.

Back upstairs, I drank a bottle and ate everything while watching a reality show about the crews who work on super yachts. I spooned the rice pudding into my mouth directly from the can, scraped my tongue along each and every sugar-crusted sweet and left the pizza box lying by the recycling bin, instead of flattening and folding it inside like Gus would have done.

Then I passed out.

***

'CAN YOU RING ME IT'S URGENT,' said a message from Jack when I opened one eye to peer at my phone screen the next morning.

I hadn't replied to any of his messages since leaving Northcliffe. I knew I should, but it meant raising the subject of Nicole and Art's party, and the idea felt both exhausting and painful.

Still, I couldn't ignore this message. What if something was up with Dad?

'Fiiiiiiiinally,' Jack sighed into the phone.

'What's so urgent? Dad all right?'

'Dad? He's fine. I just wanted to ask what the best cycle was for towels.'

'*What?*'

'On the washing machine. Dad and I stayed up late last night, I woke up at 3 a.m. in the sitting room, the lights still on and everything. I'd fallen asleep in the chair! And I spilt some beer so I've mopped it up but need to put a wash on.'

'You sent me a message that you claimed to be urgent when it's actually about the washing machine?'

'You haven't replied to any of my other messages, so I thought this might work. And it did, see?'

I felt a familiar urge to smash my phone against the wall. 'You know Dad's not supposed to drink that much on his heart pills?'

'He mentioned that but what's the harm in a few cans?'

'He could have a heart attack.'

'You worry too much, sis. He'll be all right.'

'JACK!' I shouted, my last threads of patience with him snapping. 'You've got to grow up!'

'All ri—'

'I mean it! You can't carry on like this.'

'Like what?'

'Behaving like a teenager.'

'I don't beha—'

'You drift through life and jobs and girlfriends as if it's all one big joke.'

'No I don't.'

'You do! You always have done ever since we were children, as if there are no consequences. But there are consequences, Jack! You don't even know… there are consequences!' I was hoarse by the end of this sentence, my lungs emptied of air.

'Sis, are you all right? You sound like you're losing it.'

I inhaled to the count of three before replying. 'Jack, I'm not losing it.'

'You sound mad. Just saying. I know I haven't always bee—'

'Why did you never tell me that you slept with Nicole at Art's party?'

'Who's Nic— Oh.' Jack went quiet for a few seconds. 'Art's wife?'

'Yes, Art's wife.'

I could sense his brain working from 400 miles away. 'The thing is, sis, they weren't married at the time.'

'I know that. But that's not the point. The *point* is I thought I might die from heartbreak. This is what I mean about consequences.'

'I didn't know that's what you got all upset about!' he scrabbled, his voice high-pitched. 'Honest, I didn't realize that you thought it was Art with her until Mum said something that Christmas. And I thought it was too late to say anything by then.'

While clutching the phone to my ear, I dropped my head and

rotated it from shoulder to shoulder, stretching my neck: a boxer readying for a fight. 'Jack, you let me assume, for years, that I'd seen him and Nicole in that room instead of…'

Then I stopped. The vision of Jack's bare bottom pumping back and forth had returned and I didn't feel strong enough for it. Suddenly, the anger I'd been carrying around for fifteen years blew out. Jack hadn't been the only person who'd let me assume as much and the whole episode – who did what, and when – seemed absurd. Who was it who said that resentment was like drinking poison and hoping the other person would die? A pope? Nelson Mandela? Elvis? One of them, anyway. I didn't want to hang on to it any longer.

'I'm sorry, sis. I know I'm a crap brother. If I could make it up to you somehow I would, but I don't kn—'

'You can, you can pay me back.'

'Huh?'

'The loan. You can pay me back because I'm jobless.'

'What?'

'Long story, but I've handed my notice in, and Gus and I have broken up and he's moved out, so I need the cash.'

'Blimey, that is a lot of information. You all right?'

'Er, yeah, I think so… I think…' I stopped as I felt a wave of loneliness. Being asked if I was all right by Jack, of all people, seemed to undo a knot inside me and my words started wobbling. 'Um, actually I don't know. I thought I was but I'm just…' I stopped again and said, through a thick voice, 'I'm just a bit sad.'

'Ah, sis, you'll be all right. Don't worry, it'll all be fine. Break-ups aren't much fun, I should know. What you need to do is go to the nearest pub and get absolutely smashed. I'm telling you, so drunk you can hardly see, and that'll make everything better.'

I couldn't remember any of my self-help books saying this but I suppose it was Jack's way of trying to make an effort. 'No, it's all right,' I said, sniffing down the phone. 'I don't mean to cry on you.'

'Glad you have actually,' he said, cheerfully. 'Makes me feel useful. But yeah, course I can pay you back. Sorry, I've been meaning to but, er, just forgot. And I'm sorry, for everything else. I don't deliberately try to drift through life like, well, like what you said. I do try, it's just... I dunno... life's a bit harder than I thought it might be, you know, when we were kids.'

His earnestness nearly made me laugh but I thought it might ruin the moment. 'It is, yes.'

'So, um... do you know what the best kind of wash is?'

'Huh?'

'For the towels.'

Still in bed, I closed my eyes in resignation. 'Put them on a cotton wash at sixty degrees.'

'Cottons, sixty degrees. All right, thanks, sis, and I'd better go. But look after yourself. Go to the pub.'

'Jack, it's 8.37 a.m.'

'Exactly. The Wetherspoons at Clapham Junction should be open and they do a solid fry-up.'

'Right, OK.'

'What temperature again?'

'Sixty's fine.'

'Cheers, sis.'

He hung up and I swung my legs out of bed, then stared at the rug. What to do?

I went for a run around the Clapham Common bandstand.

I came back, made a coffee and a piece of toast.

I started writing an Excel document on my laptop called 'Nell's job options' which listed all the pros and cons of staying in law, plus a few other jobs that I might be able to do.

Some sort of legal teacher or professor? I'd have to go back to study.

Dog walker? Maybe, except I had a sneaking fear that dogs were a bit like other people's children. I loved Wilma because she was mine, but I might not like other people's dogs so much.

Entrepreneur? What could I invent? Sometimes I thought everything useful had already been invented, that there wasn't anything left for the rest of us to dream up. Then I'd read in the paper that someone had made a waterproof phone, the cronut or a suncream pill and wish I'd tried harder.

But that afternoon, loneliness crept up on me again. I wasn't used to doing nothing and I wasn't very good at it.

I scrolled through my phone and saw that Gus had already changed his WhatsApp profile picture from one of us in Tuscany to one of him on the squash court, making a thumbs up at the camera.

Afternoon telly? I flicked it on to see a woman discussing how to clean the loo with a Berocca tablet and turned it off again.

A book? It feels weird to lie on the sofa reading at three in the afternoon, like a consumptive invalid.

So I cried. Instead of holding my breath to try and prevent tears spilling down my cheeks, I let them. I cried until my face blew up and my nose felt like a concrete breeze block. I cried for the past eleven years and for the strangeness of now. If my neighbours had been in, they might have called the police but they were a young couple who both worked in the City and wouldn't be back for hours. I could wail until 6.30 p.m. and nobody would know. The thought made me cry harder.

Roughly twenty minutes into this afternoon activity, my phone vibrated on the carpet. It was Luce.

'Nell? I just saw Jack in the shop and he sai— Nell? Nell? Can you hear me?'

'Bibe ball right!'

'Nell? Are you OK, Nell?'

'Bibe ball right, borry.'

'Nell, I can't really understand you. Where are you?'

I got up and tugged off a piece of kitchen roll, then blew my nose into it. 'Sorry, Luce, I'm all right, and at home. It's just… all gone a bit wrong.'

'Oh, my love. Jack told me, I'm sorry. JIMBO, STOP DOING THAT TO YOUR SISTER PLEASE. Have you got anyone with you?'

'No, but it's OK, just nice to hear your voice.'

'You too. I've felt so bad since Sunday, Nell. It's all I've thought about. If I could go back and do things differently, I would. If I could spare you that hurt, I would.'

'I know.' I felt the same weariness that I had while speaking to Jack, the same ebb of anger. Aside from Art, she was my oldest friend, and she was here for me now. 'It's fine, honestly. Can we forget the whole thing?'

'Course, but do you want me to come down? I could come down for a few days and stay, and we could get pissed and watch films? I don't like the idea of you being on your own.'

'What about the kids?'

'Don't worry about them. Mum and Mike can take over. JIMBO OLIVER, I MEAN IT, BONNIE DOESN'T WANT THAT UP HER NOSE.'

'Nah, don't worry,' I said, hearing this. 'It's OK. I'm OK. I've written a to-do list.'

She laughed. 'Course you have. And all right, but come back up here for a bit instead?'

'And stay with both Jack and my dad? I don't think so, Luce.'

'Have you got enough wine?'

'I hav—'

'Oh my days, JIMBO, IS THAT BLOOD OR PEN? Sorry, Nell, might have to go, but ring me any time, OK? Any time, I'm up half the night with Bonnie.'

'I will.'

'Promise?'

'Promise.'

We hung up and I looked at the time: 3.44 p.m.

Time for more toast, I guess.

***

By the following afternoon, the flat looked like a property you might see on a TV show called *Hoarding: Buried Alive*.

Beside the recycling bin lay a second empty pizza box.

Milky cereal bowls, toast plates and knives, sticky with jam, were piling up on the kitchen counter.

The side table in front of the sofa was covered with mugs and wine glasses, smeared with greasy fingerprints.

To celebrate the repayment of Jack's loan, which landed in my account that morning, I'd returned to Sainsbury's to stock up on extra Quavers, plus more Haribo, a packet of Maryland cookies, more bread, more wine. Various half-eaten packets lay within arm's reach of the sofa. Every time I changed position, crumbs and sugar granules pricked my palms.

If possible, I looked even worse than the flat. On the hem of my grey T-shirt was a dark stain from a globule of tomato sauce that had escaped my pizza the previous night; my dressing gown sleeve was tinged brown on account of trailing it through my coffee that morning. I hadn't washed my face yet and it was nearly 2 p.m. If I could be bothered to get up and look in the mirror, I imagined my hair would look demented.

I'd also carried armfuls of wedding magazines from the spare room down to the sitting room and fanned them around the sofa so I could easily reach for another when required. Except it felt even more pitiful to be reading them than before; the toothy, grinning brides seemed to be cackling at me and the articles felt taunting. I'd definitely never need a vegan wedding cake now, or have to pick the right shape dress for my bridesmaids. Nobody would ever propose to me, not even at Disneyland Paris.

I'd decided to wallow in self-pity like a recently bereaved rhino until the end of the weekend. It was very me, very goal-orientated. It wasn't that I was heartbroken by the end of my relationship with

Gus. I was more heart-*bruised*, but I wanted to take a few days to treat the break-up like a Nashville country singer before resuming normal behavioural patterns. Actually, being able to wallow, to dress and eat what I wanted, and go to bed without having to leave the kitchen spotless, made me realise how much of my previous existence had been decided by Gus. It had been so regimented; weekdays were spent working towards our plan, which was really his plan; weekends were spent at museum exhibitions, inspecting old bits of stone.

OK, an exaggeration, but I'd definitely lost my sense of self along the way and I needed to find it again.

On Monday, I'd start emailing head hunters, I'd contact Gus about the flat, I'd restart running and some sort of personal hygiene routine. I'd think about moving, too. Until then, I had magazines to flick through, ITV on as constant background noise so the flat didn't feel too quiet and a steady supply of beige carbohydrates.

I was ignoring my phone since I still hadn't heard from Art and knew that, by now, he'd have flown home. Sort of ignoring it, anyway. I'd tucked it under the sofa where I couldn't see it, meaning I wouldn't pick it up every four and a half seconds. But, unable to resist, my fingers reached for the familiar shape every now and then. Luce had sent me a link to some piece about meditation; Jack had texted to say that Tinder was the best dating app and Dad sent me a string of dancing girl emojis. Mum's multiple voice notes were the sweetest of all:

'Hi, duck.'

'Only to say I saw Lucy. She came into the café this morning and—'

'I pressed the wrong button. But only to say I'm very proud of you. I might not always have been very clear about this—'

'But I *am* proud of you. Brave girl, that can't have been an easy thing to do.'

'Ring me when you feel like it.'

'Love you.'

'Oh it's Mum, by the way.'

This set me off again, weeping into a magazine piece about the most Instagrammable swimming pools for a honeymoon destination. An adults-only, rooftop pool on a skyscraper in Miami, apparently.

After a gourmet lunch of cookies and a large hunk of cheese, sliced from a packet I'd found at the back of the fridge, the doorbell went, which would be the expensive multivitamins I'd ordered on Amazon to counteract the effects of eating nothing of any nutritional value for several days.

I tied my dressing gown around my waist, wondering, as I did, whether the gown smelt of cheddar or that was just my breath. Then I wedged a trainer in the door and traipsed downstairs.

'Thank yo—' I started to say, as I stuck a hand through the door for the vitamins.

It wasn't Amazon.

'Er, hi,' I said, quickly wiping under my eyes with my fingers. 'How did you… what are you… why are you in London?'

Art grinned and held out a small box. 'I needed to give you something. Two things, actually.'

I gazed at him, standing on my doorstep in his aviator coat, his green eyes shining at mine; for a few seconds, it was as if we were standing outside the pub again, that New Year's Eve, and nobody else even existed.

'What's this?' I asked eventually, looking down at the box, noticing the coffee stain on my sleeve. Perhaps this was one of those dreams which I half-knew was a dream, and I should just go along with it, act normal? Any second now, a murderer would appear from behind the bins and I'd look down and realize I was pregnant, then all my teeth would fall out.

'Open it,' he replied.

But Art did seem pretty real, and I did still have all my teeth, although they felt furry under my tongue, and my stomach was bulging beneath my dressing gown cord which could be a dream pregnancy, but it could also be because I'd eaten a packet of biscuits and half a loaf of bread that morning.

'It's not a engagement ring,' he added, with a big smile. 'Don't worry, I know how you feel about those.'

I peeled a small sticker off the top of the box and lifted the flap.

It was a London snow globe.

'Thought you should have it for your collection,' Art said, as I held it up in front of me. Small white flakes fluttered over a miniature red bus, Big Ben, and a tiny soldier in a scarlet coat and a bearskin hat.

'Thanks,' I said shyly, as I lowered it into the box again. 'But I don't get it, what are you doing here?' Seeing Art standing on my doorstep, set against the city sounds of car horns and rumble of traffic from Clapham High Street, seemed like something that would have happened in one of my teenage fantasies.

'Lucy came to see me yesterday and mentioned that you were

having, er, a bad week, and I was about to head to the airport, but then realized I hadn't said goodbye to you.'

'Oh, right,' I said, feeling foolish. He was here to say goodbye, which was pretty mortifying since I was dressed like the bird lady from *Mary Poppins* but it was just a goodbye, no need for my heart to be beating like a war drum in my chest.

'But how did you get my address?' I asked, confused. 'And what about your flight? Have they let you push it back?'

Art shook his head, grinning. 'Nell, your brain…'

'And what's happening with Nicole?'

'It's all right, I'll explain everything, but can I come in?'

'Er, sure,' I said, still puzzled about why he'd travelled 420 miles to say goodbye. Was this definitely not a dream?

And then, just before I turned to show him the way upstairs, I remembered what he'd said when handing me the box. 'What was the other thing you were going to give me?'

Art smiled again and bent forward to kiss me, and as I felt his lips press against mine, my whole body responded by arching into him. I'll admit, my worries about my breath, and the coffee stain on my dressing gown, and the faint smell of cheddar that was wafting from my T-shirt, faded here.

'Can I come in now?' he asked, pulling back from my face after a few moments.

'Um…' I thought about the sitting room, about the mugs and the plates and the empty packets of Quavers that were decorating the floor. Also, all the bridal magazines.

'Sure,' I said, smiling and reaching for his hand to lead him up. Sometimes, you've just got to jump.

Six months later...

'ONE OF THE GENTS' is blocked,' announced Art, striding into the kitchen. 'Tissue paper swimming all over the floor.'

I turned from the French windows where I'd been looking out, wondering if anyone in history had ever married in such cataclysmic weather. The glass panes were running with water as if a fireman's hose had been turned on them.

'Rain on your wedding day is good luck,' Nanny Gertrude pronounced that morning over breakfast. 'A symbol of the last tears a woman will ever shed. Eat your porridge, Felix.'

I hadn't wanted to point out that since Nanny Gertrude had never married herself, she probably wasn't the person to be handing out such pearls of wisdom.

'Seriously?' I said, looking over my shoulder at Art. 'We've only just built them!'

'I suspect that's the trouble. New bathrooms, glitches with the plumbing. Have we got one of those...' Art held a fist in the air and circled it as if winding a clock.

'Huh?'

'You know, you use it for eggs.'

'A whisk?'

'Yes! A whisk. That's the one.'

'Art, you're not using a whisk in the loo.'

'Why?'

I threw my hands up. 'Because you're not beating eggs, that's why. If it's blocked and there's tissue paper all over the floor it's going to take more than a kitchen utensil. I'll call Nigel.'

'No, please, Nell, on no account call Nigel,' said Art, hurrying back out of the kitchen.

Nigel was the local plumber who, over the past few months, had become extremely fond of telling Art about his health problems. These included but were not limited to heartburn, indigestion troubles and a recent erectile problem; you name it, Nigel told Art about it. Fortunately, I was never privy to these conversations because Nigel considered it men's business.

'I think there's a plunger in the boot room,' I shouted after Art. 'In one of those boxes under the sink.' Then I thought: how come so much time in adult relationships is spent sorting out plumbing issues?

Drummond Hall Weddings had only been running for three weeks and, so far, I couldn't say it had been a *runaway* success. For our first wedding, each of the sixty guests was supposed to be served an individual quail for dinner. When they'd cut into them, the quails were pink and raw in the middle. The gas in the new catering ovens had gone out, so I'd had to make huge pan after huge pan of pasta on the oven in our kitchen and dole it out in the marquee with a ladle.

At our second wedding, there was a power cut during the

first dance so the couple were plunged into darkness during their choreographed performance of Savage Garden's 'Truly Madly Deeply' (Art had said this wasn't much of a shame, and that, actually, the guests should have been grateful).

At our third wedding, the father of the bride got so drunk he was incapable of making his speech and had to be put to bed in Nanny Gertrude's room. And now this, our fourth wedding, and someone had thoughtfully blocked the loo.

I turned back to stare through the French windows and slid a thumbnail between two of my teeth. I suppose it would be boring if it was too easy.

Ironically, the uncertainty about what would happen to the hall had been solved by Colin. After his protest on the green, the journalist from the *Northumberland Echo* did write a story. It was only a small paragraph at the bottom of page thirteen but unfortunately for Glaswegian property developer Cameron Stewart, it attracted the attention of the local council's senior planning officer. He started asking about Cameron's proposals and, after a few weeks of investigating, insisted that the hall was a Grade I-listed property with a silver staircase of 'inestimable value', meaning it couldn't be transformed into apartments without contravening multiple planning regulations. Cameron lost interest and pulled out of the sale.

Meanwhile, the idea had come to me one afternoon while I was still in London, lolling on the sofa, eating my third Wagon Wheel and watching a restoration show on Channel 4: the hall should become a wedding venue. It made perfect sense. It had its own church, and the reception could be outside, on the lawn overlooking the sea. Or inside using the state rooms, if guests preferred. They could even stay, if they liked, and Terence could sort out the catering. Or, no, maybe not Terence. But still, I was sure there'd be a decent events caterer nearby.

I'd opened my laptop and made a PowerPoint presentation. Into this nerdy document I poured all my wedding knowledge, my ideas for the hall and research about rival stately houses nearby. If you were the sort of slightly peculiar adult who talked of being in Gryffindor or Ravenclaw, you could get married twenty miles away at Alnwick Castle, where *Harry Potter* was filmed, but only if you had a spare £35,000 knocking about.

Drummond Hall could charge much less.

I investigated marquees, found a business that could put up bell tents for guests to stay in overnight and compiled a list of local musicians and DJs. I even made a fancy Excel spreadsheet of cost estimations for the hall's redecoration and the fee per head that could be charged per wedding.

It was partly a distraction technique. After Art appeared on my doorstep in Clapham, he'd come inside and talked to me while I tried to slide most of the wedding magazines under the sofa with my foot. Nothing that Nicole had said in her email came as a shock to him, he explained. He wasn't surprised that she wanted a separation, and he'd always known that Felix might not be his biological son.

He told me this calmly, matter-of-factly. Not long after their wedding, Nicole had a fling with her plastic surgeon (he'd given her more than a nose job, apparently). But she only confessed this during a screaming row she and Art had a few years after Felix was born. Perhaps he was Art's; perhaps he was Dr Kaminski's. Instantly terrified of losing the toddler he considered his own, Art had made Nicole promise they keep this secret between themselves for the time being. No paternity test, no question of telling anyone else. One day he'd have to have that conversation with Felix, he told me, but not yet.

It was a lot to take in that afternoon but you have to remember I'd previously worked in a family law office where one client cited irreconcilable differences because she could no longer bear to listen to her husband's jaw click every night while they ate. Very little surprised me.

When Nicole started divorce proceedings, Art was, mostly, relieved to be able to disentangle himself from an unhappy marriage. His only worry was what this might do to Felix. On my recommendation, he appointed Veronica Wallop to represent him against Gideon. Nicole did want half his estate, mostly out of spite, but once the sale fell through, gave up any claim to the hall and switched her focus to custody of Felix. Art spent weeks agonizing over whether to buy his own place in New York or return to Northcliffe for good.

If he stayed in New York, he could still pick Felix up from his Upper East Side school and go to baseball games.

If he returned to the hall, he could resurrect his family home, but at what cost to his relationship with his son? Giving up his marriage wasn't difficult, but he couldn't bear to abandon that.

I remained neutral during those discussions. Having seen clients reduced to husks by divorce negotiations that dragged on for years, I didn't want that for any of them, even Nicole. Nor did I want to sway Art. He had to make his own mind up. If he decided to stay in New York, we accepted this would make any relationship between us too difficult. If he moved back to Drummond Hall, well, that was another matter.

I had enough to worry about myself. Around the same time, a 'Sold' sign went up outside the flat in Clapham. Jack begged and pleaded to sell it off the market, insisting that he had 'loads' of private clients, but Gus put his foot down so we used a different estate agency and spent an entire Saturday circling the flat, going though our very detailed cohabitation agreement, which stipulated who got which lamp and allotted Gus all the cookery books (I also let him take the new robot hoover). He told me that day he had a new girlfriend, a management consultant called Charlotte who spoke four languages and had strong opinions about 1970s Italian cinema, which made me feel only relief (obviously I later looked her up on LinkedIn and was annoyed to see she was pretty, although she did have quite a large mole on her cheek).

I kept my wedding idea quiet until Art told me that he and Nicole had reached a settlement. She'd agreed to keep the paternity question a secret so long as Felix could live with her in New York during term time, and come to his father's in Northumberland during the holidays, plus Art would fly to New York from Newcastle every other weekend. He was moving back to Northcliffe.

'Actually?' I said down the phone when he rang with the news. 'You don't mind, not being in New York? And Felix is all right with it?'

'He thinks it's kind of cool, although he seems to have told all his class mates that his dad's inherited a castle in Scotland so I need to have words with his geography teacher. It's a lot of travelling but it'll be worth it, Nell.'

Art was less convinced by my PowerPoint presentation.

'What about the planning regulations?'

'It doesn't need any. All you'd have to do is spend a bit of money on redecorating.'

'A *lot* of money, Nell – you've seen the state of that place.'

'Yes, all right, a lot of money. But I still think there'd be demand. Did you look at the slide where I listed the other places in Northumberland you can get married? They're awful.'

'Was that slide number 382 or 383?'

In the end, I won and he agreed we could try it. I hadn't spent over a decade negotiating with lawyers for nothing.

I moved up to Northcliffe and we spent four manic months clearing out the hall, repainting, building the new block of loos, plus the new, professional kitchen for the cater-ers. I found a decent firm in Morpeth who could take care of the food, plus a Newcastle wine merchant, and, finally, after he waged a campaign that lasted several months and kept bringing us trial slices of lemon cake and Sicilian fruit cake and *torta Caprese*, I promised Luigi that he could do the cakes. Colin had been charged with building the new website – Drummond Hall Weddings. Finally, after I'd nearly killed the local health inspector during his tour of the hall (he had a fatal nut allergy, he explained, as he reached for one of Luigi's hazelnut biscotti), we were allowed to open for business.

At the sound of footsteps, I looked over my shoulder to

see Luce unhooking her camera strap from around her neck. 'Right, I need a drink. There's an old lady in the marquee who looks like she's died.'

'What?' I squeaked.

'She's fine. She's had too much champagne. I got a great photo of her.' As an impression, Luce dropped her head back and stuck her tongue at the ceiling.

'I'm not sure the bride will appreciate that.' They were a young couple from Newcastle – Danny and Jessica – and she'd told me at our first meeting that she wanted everything 'to look perfect for Instagram'. She wanted a pink doughnut-wall, pink rose petals strewn down the middle of each trestle table, bridesmaids in salmon-pink dresses which suited precisely none of them, pink cocktails and a pink cake which Luigi had made a good deal of fuss about. That morning, Jessica had asked whether there was any way we could 'make the rain pink', and I'd wondered whether she was even old enough to get married.

'Ah well,' Luce replied, unbothered. 'Fancy a glass of something?'

I glanced at the old clock and then at my clipboard. In a minute I'd tiptoe to the marquee entrance to check that speeches had started and alert the caterers that they had half an hour before the prawn cocktail starter (pink sauce!) had to be served.

'I might once they've sat down. You seen Felix anywhere?'

'Yeah, he's outside with your dad.'

'What? In this?' I turned to gesture at the windows.

'Yeah, last time I checked, your dad was teaching him to fart with his armpit.'

I screwed my eyes shut, instantly fearing this might prompt another threatening email from Nicole, citing 'bad influences'. Art had already been sent one, after Dad took Felix on a trip to the pub.

We had him for a few more days before he went back to America and school started again. I was dreading it. I hadn't appreciated that falling in love with Art all over again meant I'd come to love his son so much too. It had been one of the happiest outcomes of all this year's upheaval. Plus, over the summer, Felix had become Dad's small shadow, a longed-for kind-of-grandson. It was symbiotic since, at the same time, Dad became the English grandfather Felix had never known because he'd only met Lord Drummond a handful of times. Every time I saw the pair of them together, my heart clenched.

This was also fortunate since Dad's relationship with Bev had fizzled (turns out she was more of a cat person), although he and Roy were keeping an eye out in the pub for a replacement.

Luce threw back a glass of water and picked up her camera. 'Better get back, but wine in... half an hour?'

'When they've sat down,' I repeated, rolling my eyes.

'Slave driver,' she shouted as she disappeared.

I bent my head to the clipboard: speeches for half an hour, then the prawn cocktails, then the beef was coming out at 7.00, then another round of champagne for a toast at 7.35 which should be poured just before the waiters served slices of cake; the first dance was due to start at 7.55, after which the band was playing until 11.00, with a coffee break for them at 9.30 when a DJ would take over for half an hour. I looked up and squinted into the distance, trying to remember whether I'd told the caterers to put the band's coffee and sandwiches out in the utility room.

There was a weird, squelching noise in the corridor and Art reappeared in a pair of rubber waders, holding the plunger in the air like an Olympic torch. 'No need for Nigel, I've fixed it.'

I smiled before wrinkling my nose and nodding at the plunger. 'Thank you, my hero. But gross, can you take that thing away?'

'Can I check something first?'

'Mmm?'

'Will you marry me?'

I looked up from my spreadsheet, eyes round with shock. 'Art, what?'

He lunged one foot forward and, with his waders squeaking, knelt on the kitchen floor. 'I was just thinking…'

'While you were sorting out the floating loo paper?'

'Yes. No! I've been thinking for ages, years, really. Eleanor Mason, I know I haven't exactly set a shining example of marriage, and I know you have incredibly strong feelings about weddings, and diamond engagement rings, which is lucky since I don't actually have one yet, but will you do me the tremendous honour of marrying me?'

I pressed my lips together so I didn't laugh. As a teenager, I'd imagined this moment a thousand times, but it had been outside the hall, overlooking the sea, or on the beach, or in the maze, a deeply romantic scene with the sky tinged pink behind us, perhaps doves flying overhead and some sort of classical music playing in the background. I'd never seen any doves in Northumberland but that didn't matter.

In all my years of fantasies and undercover research, not once had a wedding proposal been carried out by Art dressed like a fisherman, clutching a plunger in one hand and my fingers with the other. But this time it was real and, even with the faint smell of urinal cake hanging in the air, all the better for it.

Acknowledgements

I didn't learn to make sourdough during the Covid pandemic. Nor did I learn a new language or lose weight. I tried to read *Middlemarch* (my third attempt) and failed. I drank too much wine, ate too much cake and spent too much time on Twitter.

Having said that, I did manage to write this book and I'm very grateful for the space lockdown gave me to do that. I'd been mulling over the theme – first love and 'what if?' – for a while. I believe many of us have done this. If we'd taken that route, stayed with our first great loves, what would our lives look like? Better? Worse? Certainly different. But what if we were given a second shot at it? I decided to write the story of Nell and Art (and poor Gus, although he's all right in the end. He has nice Charlotte who speaks four languages to look after him).

While writing, I was powered by cake and several other people. Chiefly my editor, Katie Seaman, who helped me via Zoom, sent me brilliantly incisive notes and corrected an embarrassing mistake about Mr Rochester that I'd included in an early draft. Katie, thank you for everything, particularly for saving me from literary disgrace.

As always, I owe everyone else at HQ huge thanks. A particularly big thank you to the best-dressed publicist in publishing, Joe Thomas. Thank you, Katrina Smedley, for working so tirelessly and for the very best social media assets around. Also to Mel Hayes for never minding when I sent her an email begging for 'one more day' to finish off something that she needed. To Charlotte Phillips, who designed the cover, thank you for putting up with my incredibly fussy demands about what Wilma the wolfhound should look like. She's perfect. A whopping thank you to HQ's sales and production teams who do all the behind-the-scenes work, and to Liz Hatherell for copy-editing duties, as well as picking up various other embarrassing errors. Finally, undying thanks to Lisa Milton, Queen of HQ, for running the show. I'm so proud to be part of the team and can't wait to visit the office with the best view in London again.

Continued, devoted thanks to my agent, Rebecca Ritchie, for her support and ongoing serenity, even when working from her kitchen table. I now no longer have to explain any concern or worry I have about writing and delivering a new book; Becky seems to pick my neuroses up by osmosis and solve them. Thank you barely covers it.

To my friends and family, although there have been odd moments where we've been allowed to hang out in the past year or so, it hasn't been enough. I miss you all and I can't wait until we can be merry in person. I normally look pretty wild when I finish a book, but this time, with the addition of yet another lockdown in the UK, I look like something you might find on the seabed. Please don't be surprised when we meet again in real life. Or, if you are surprised, try not to show it.

Special thanks to Jules Perowne for lending me The Mouse House, the most heavenly retreat in North Norfolk, where I spent a couple of weeks when I started writing this book. You are generous and kind and I wish my hair was as good as yours.

Finally, to Deliveroo and Majestic. You guys really helped me out while I was writing this. Cheers.

Don't miss the new feel-good romantic comedy from Sophia Money-Coutts

Looking Out For Love

Stella Shakespeare isn't having a good day, or month come to think of it. She's been unceremoniously dumped by her boyfriend, cut off from the Bank of Dad and at thirty-two years-old, she doesn't know what she's doing with her life.

What Stella really wants is to find love. She wants all-consuming, can't-think-about-anything-else, can't-even-manage-to-eat kind of love. What she found beside her in bed that morning wasn't love. But when a tall, handsome man in a well-fitting suit walks into her life, she thinks she's finally found The One.

Everything seems to be falling into place now Stella has met the man of her dreams and has an actual job working with a private investigator nicknamed The Affair Hunter. Although, seeing relationships in trouble shakes Stella's own trust and makes her question if she's been looking for love in the wrong places all along…

Coming January 2023

Keep reading for the first chapter …

Chapter 1

STELLA SHAKESPEARE LONGED FOR love. She longed for love so much that it felt like a dirty secret, something that she should hide lest her desperation put others off. She wanted all-consuming, can't-think-about-anything-else, can't-even-manage-to-eat kind of love.

What she found beside her in bed that morning was definitely not love.

She lifted her face from the pillow and frowned at the unfamiliar headboard. A studded leather headboard. She didn't remember that from last night.

Next, she glanced at a strange bedside table on which there was a glass of water – full – which might explain why her tongue felt like a boiled owl.

At the sensation of someone stirring under the cover beside her, she looked right at a head of dishevelled black hair she didn't recognise, and a pair of broad, male shoulders.

The stranger made a waking-up groan and Stella looked back to the leather headboard, uninterested in observing the intimate morning ritual of someone she already regretted. What sort of man had a leather headboard anyway? Or maybe even pleather. Stella reached her fingers towards it. Yes, pleather. This definitely wasn't love.

'Morning,' came a low drawl.

Seconds later, Stella felt a hand slide along the back of her thigh and over her bottom.

'What time is it?' she asked, ignoring the hand as it snaked up her back. The audacity! He hadn't even looked at her yet.

The hand retracted itself and he raised his head to squint at his watch. His hair was obscuring his face so Stella's eyes slid to the curve of his bicep as he pushed himself back from the mattress. Where had she found this guy? She'd been in the pub, having drinks with Billie, and then Jez had shown up and insisted on taking Billie home, but Stella wanted to stay. It was a Thursday night. It wasn't *illegal* to stay up past ten on a Thursday night. So she'd stayed, and chatted to Jack behind the bar for a bit, and then, well, Stella wasn't entirely sure.

'Nearly nine,' he replied.

'Nine! I need to go.' Stella turned her face away and noticed a black smear the size of a thumbprint on her pillow. 'I've got some mascara on this, sorry.'

She glanced at him and was met with an easy smile.

He was attractive, actually. Thick stubble lined his jaw and his eyes – green, alert, betraying no signs of a hangover – softened as they met hers. He looked as if he could advertise a new line of coffee pods. Stella mirrored his smile as she remembered flashes of the previous night; his body moving above hers, his mouth hot against her neck, his hands running down her arms, holding her, teasing her, the confident way he'd shifted her around, as if she was an instrument he was playing for the pleasure of them both. It had been good, Stella recalled, still smiling. Really good. Maybe she could stay in bed for a few more minutes. She couldn't possibly fall in love with this stranger, but lust was very different to love.

'Don't worry,' he replied, nodding towards the mascara, one side of his mouth curving higher. 'Probably not yours.'

There was a brief pause while Stella digested the implication before she kicked her legs free from the duvet and stood up. 'I need to go.'

She scrabbled around on his carpet, peeling up various items of clothes in the gloom. Jeans, t-shirt, sweater, one sock. Every time she bent over, she angled her bottom away from him, towards the shutters. Not her mascara indeed. He might be handsome but he was also an *asshole*. Another one. Stella would have a stern word with herself later. She was never going to find her great love if she continued to behave like this, drifting through London like some sort of asshole magnet.

Still grinning, he pushed himself up on one arm. 'I was joking! You're welcome to stay. My shift doesn't start for...' He paused and looked at his watch, '...four hours.'

'I don't think so. I think you've had quite enough.' Stella dragged her eyes away from his chest, as muscled as a museum statue, and spotted the missing sock. 'I bet you don't even know my name,' she said, reaching for it.

He laughed. 'You weren't very interested in names last night. What's mine, anyway?'

'I haven't got time to stand here talking about names! I've got an interview.' She scanned his bedroom floor for her knickers.

'It's Sam. And you are?'

'Hardly matters now, does it?' Stella mumbled while squinting at a small dark item on the foot of the bed. It was one of his socks.

'Here,' Sam said, retrieving a pair of pants from under the duvet and dangling them in the air.

'Thank you.' Stella snatched them and made for the bathroom only to discover she'd opened a wardrobe door and was facing his shoe rack.

'That way.' He nodded towards another door.

'Yes, ok, thank you,' she muttered again, hurrying for it before shutting herself in and reaching for a mirrored cabinet above the sink. Please could that man have some sort of painkiller. Paracetamol, Nurofen, morphine, even. Stella's head felt like it might burst.

She peered into the cabinet. There was a can of shaving cream, a tub of hair wax, a few razors, a yellow tube of athlete's foot cream and, beside them, a metallic strip of Nurofen. Only one pill left but one would have to do. Stella tossed it into her mouth and leant over the sink to palm tap water into her mouth. Then she squeezed a globule of Colgate onto her index finger and smeared it around her teeth. She rinsed and stood to inspect her face in the mirror. Not ideal: her eyelids were puffy and faintly purple; her skin dull and dry. And now she had to get to Holborn to convince a legal contact of her father's that she was a responsible, presentable employee who'd make an ideal assistant.

She sighed. What was the population of London? Stella wasn't sure of the exact number but she knew it was a lot. Millions. Millions of men in this city. Alright, a few less if she discounted the gay ones, and the ones who were too old for her (over forty-five) or too young (under twenty-five). Obviously she also had to ignore the men who sneezed without covering their mouths, and the ones who wore pointy shoes. Nor was Stella interested in any adult man who insisted on calling his mother 'Mummy', or the sort of man who gave his car a name. Or his penis, for that matter. But even if she took *all* those men away, there still had to be plenty of others. So how come every man Stella ever met was an asshole?

She sighed again. No time for philosophy; she had to go. Stella ran a finger under each eye to remove the sooty stains of eye-liner and peered back into the cabinet for a moisturiser to inject some colour back into her cheeks.

When she emerged from the bathroom, he was still in bed, leaning back against the pleather headboard. Grinning, he ran a hand through his hair, flexing one of his biceps. 'I definitely can't persuade you to stay?'

Stella glanced pointedly at the pillow with the mascara stain before picking up her bag and marching towards his kitchen. 'No thank you, I've got a very important interview.'

'Any chance of a number?' Sam shouted after her.

'If it's meant to be, you'll guess it,' she shouted back, slamming his door behind her. Which is how Stella Shakespeare, thirty-two, set off for her important job interview with Scholl's athlete's foot cream smeared all over her face.

Escape with laugh-out-loud and feel-good romantic comedies from Sophia Money-Coutts

Polly's not looking for 'the one' just the *plus one* . . .
Polly Spencer is turning thirty, still single and fine with it. Although she does need a plus one to her best friend's summer wedding. But is a simple arrangement of a wedding date about to get more complicated?

'Perfect summer reading for fans of Jilly Cooper and *Bridget Jones*.' *HELLO!*

One first date. One *not* so little mistake.
When Lil has a one-night stand with handsome mountaineer, Max, things go from bad to worse. First Max ghosts her, then she finds out she's pregnant. Will Max return her calls or will Lil have to be ready to do the baby thing on her own?

'Hilariously funny – I couldn't put it down' Beth O'Leary

He's perfect on paper . . .
When Florence Fairfax writes a wish list describing her perfect man, she's shocked when Rory, a handsome blond man, walks into her life. He seems to tick all of the boxes but is Florence about to discover there's more to love than being perfect on paper?

'Feel-good and enormous fun' Sophie Kinsella